Fiona had been so sidetracked by their debate that she'd paid scant attention to where they were going.

But when the door swung open and Edward's footman flipped forward the step, all breath escaped her. She scrambled from the carriage. Once both feet were on solid ground, she looked up, holding her bonnet to her head with one hand, to take it all in.

The Royal Society. It was the epicenter of the finest minds in Europe. For centuries, the birth of scientific discovery began in this building.

"It's beautiful," she whispered.

"It's not the only thing that's beautiful," Edward said.

Her pulse quickened at the compliment, but she didn't take her eyes off the building in front of her. "What are we doing here?" Because surely, surely, it couldn't be what she was thinking.

"I thought you might want to look inside." He put a hand on her lower back. Even through gloves and her velvet pelisse she could feel the warmth of his fingers. Inexplicably, the sensation flowed across her skin and a red heat crept up her neck.

She stepped away from him, fanning her face in an effort to quell the desire snaking through her. She could not entertain this want for him, no matter that she knew well what his touch could lead to, how he could make her toes curl and her skin shiver. "But I'm nae allowed in there," she said.

"I am the Duke of Wildeforde; I'm allowed anywhere, and I will bring whomever I please."

Praise for Samara Parish and the Rebels with a Cause series

ALSO BY SAMARA PARISH

How to Survive a Scandal

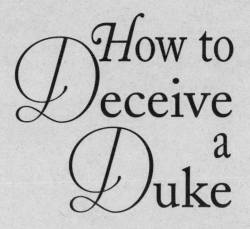

How to Deceive a Duke

SAMARA PARISH

FOREVER
New York Boston

Copyright © 2022 by Samara Thorn

Cover design by Daniela Medina
Cover art and photography by Sophia Sidoti
Cover copyright © 2022 by Hachette Book Group, Inc.

Forever
Hachette Book Group
1290 Avenue of the Americas, New York, NY 10104
read-forever.com
twitter.com/readforeverpub

First Edition: January 2022

Forever is an imprint of Grand Central Publishing. The Forever name and logo are trademarks of Hachette Book Group, Inc.

The publisher is not responsible for websites (or their content) that are not owned by the publisher.

The Hachette Speakers Bureau provides a wide range of authors for speaking events. To find out more, go to www.hachettespeakersbureau.com or call (866) 376-6591.

ISBN: 9781538704547 (mass market), 9781538704523 (ebook)

Printed in the United States of America

CW

10 9 8 7 6 5 4 3 2 1

*For my husband and the breath that I
draw when you're near*

For my sister, whose love is unyielding

Acknowledgments ───────

This book was written during the dumpster fire that was 2020 and the first few months of 2021. I could not have written it without the help and support of some very dear friends. Lauren Harbor, you are the best of writing buddies. You know when to cheerlead and when to get the whip out. Your support through the launch of *How to Survive a Scandal* meant so much.

Justine Lewis, our brainstorming lunch dates were responsible for some of my favorite moments in this book. Thank you for your willingness to drop everything and read any time I needed feedback. You are such a generous soul.

To my stable mates at Forever: Christina Britton, Kate Pembrooke, Emily Sullivan, and especially Bethany Bennett, it has been such a pleasure meeting you all and sharing this crazy journey.

To the best publishing team in existence, thank you. Madeleine, you have somehow managed to take an unwieldy—sometimes bonkers—first draft and help me craft it into something that makes actual sense and that I'm super proud of. Debbie, I am in awe of your brain and how you manage tiny details. Jodi, I am so appreciative of your work on *How to Survive a Scandal*. I didn't know you when I wrote the acknowledgments for that book, so I'm putting them here, because your incredible efforts are why it was such a success and I'm so grateful.

There are many other people on the team who do incredible work, from cover designers to production editors. To everyone who has touched this book and the last, thank you.

Susan Bischoff and the rest of the WBF team, thank you for teaching me so much about myself.

Finally, to my family, whose enthusiasm over the past year has kept me going, and to my husband, who does all the animal wrangling, cooking, and housekeeping whenever I'm on a deadline in the hopes that this book will allow us to retire. I love you.

P.S. Kit, you were born an hour before I turned this in. Welcome to the world.

Content Notes

Content notes are available on my website so readers can inform themselves if they want to. Some readers may consider them spoilers. You can find these notes at www.samaraparish.com/content-notes.

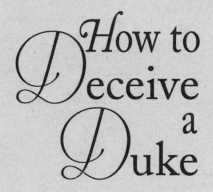

How to Deceive a Duke

Chapter 1

London, 1816

The rattle of carriage wheels on the drive outside alerted Edward to his mother's arrival home. From the window by his desk he could see her take the footman's hand as she stepped down. She would be walking through his door without bothering to knock in approximately ninety seconds.

Which gave him ninety seconds to steel himself for the job ahead of him. Most men, especially dukes, would be ashamed of fearing their mothers so. Once those men met Her Grace the Duchess of Wildeforde, they would understand.

A colder, more heartless woman had never lived. If she was, in fact, a living being and not one of the undead.

But he was determined. He'd come to London with the express purpose of informing the duchess that he had found the woman he wanted to spend the rest of his life with.

And that she wasn't going to like it.

Because it wasn't the young girl his mother had saddled him with in an arranged betrothal inked before he'd even left his teens. Nor was it any other young girl of the *ton*.

No, Fiona McTavish was an entirely unsuitable choice to be his duchess. Bold, forthright, smarter than most men of his acquaintance and totally unwilling to disguise the fact.

And common born. The daughter of a trouble-making farmer.

Were his mother like most women, she'd have an apoplexy when he broke the news. But his mother was more sharp and bitter than most women, so he was preparing himself for a stake through the bollocks.

He was determined. He'd been taught to avoid any hint of scandal, to repair the Wildeforde name after his father's infamous passing; for thirteen years, he'd done exactly that. He'd not set a foot wrong. He'd fashioned himself into the epitome of the perfect aristocratic gentleman. Marrying Fiona would undo all of it.

He didn't care. His brother and sister would forgive him. Once they'd met her, they'd understand. Fiona made him sing, quite literally. She challenged him to think and say radical things and indulge in pastimes that his peers would deem frivolous. The Duke of Wildeforde was never frivolous. She held him to a different standard, at once easier and more difficult to meet. He didn't need to be flawless, but neither would she accept polished opinions of messy issues.

For her, he would ruin his good name.

Precisely ninety seconds after he'd seen her exit the carriage, his mother opened his study door and marched in.

He stood. "Mother."

"Duke." She moved to the wide, wingback chair in front of his desk and sat. "I was expecting you back two weeks ago."

"I apologize for the delay." Curse it. He was already on the back foot. "Actually, I *don't* apologize for the delay. Mother, I have some news."

She sniffed. "I have some news myself."

He swallowed, opened his mouth fully ready to declare his intentions, yet all that came out was: "By all means, you go first." That was the coward in him, choosing to put off the skewering for another few seconds if he could.

"No, no. Get your news over with." It was the sum amount of enthusiasm she'd ever shown for his personal interests. He pushed aside his disappointment.

"I've met someone," he said quickly. "I know that complicates things because obviously I'm betrothed to Amelia. And Fiona, well, she's unique in a way that will no doubt infuriate you but makes me so happy, Mother. Happier than I think I've ever been. I want to marry her."

There, the words were said. It was like a tonne had been lifted from his shoulders. Whatever the consequences, the hard part was done.

So he waited.

Waited for his mother to rage, or to find some way to cut him. Instead, she regarded him for a long moment before shrugging. Just a little. That indifferent movement hurt more than anger or expletives ever could have.

"The Lady Dunburton died last night."

"Graham's wife? Curse it, what happened?" His cousin had been married less than a month. The last time Edward had seen the viscountess, she was blushing prettily on the way out of the church.

"A fish out of water dies gasping. You should remember that."

His heart dropped and a pit of nausea formed in his stomach. His cousin had gone against social expectations. Despite immense amounts of backlash from his family, he'd married a young woman who manned the counter of her father's bookstore.

Edward's mother had turned crimson when she'd found out. They'd needed to replace a rug, two vases, and the wallpaper in the green, now yellow, room.

Edward had tried to talk sense into his cousin at the time. Graham had been resolute. *To hell with society.* He was in love and that was all there was to it.

Now that Edward had found Fiona, that conversation left a bitter taste. "What, precisely, are you saying?" Edward asked.

"The girl took her own life. Here, Dunburton sent a letter." She tossed a parchment onto his desk, the seal broken.

"I don't understand." He'd had little chance to become acquainted with Eliza, but from their brief conversation she'd seemed perfectly happy.

"Have you not been getting the papers in the country?"

He had been getting *The Times*. He'd just been too preoccupied with Fiona to bother reading it.

"The upstart got what she had coming. What could she expect? That she would marry a viscount and be welcomed to society with open arms? I must say, the papers did their best to shred her to pieces, but they had nothing on the young ladies. A delirium of debutantes scorned and all that." His mother chuckled. *Chuckled.*

A young woman had just lost her life. His cousin, his mother's nephew, had just lost the woman he loved, and she laughed?

"Of course, you'll need to do something about the gossip. Call your man at the paper. Have it put out that she came down with a fever or something of that manner. Death by one's own hand is unseemly. We can't have *that* getting out."

He would handle it. That's what he did. But first he needed to get it straight in his head.

"Are you telling me that the men and women of our

acquaintance were so cruel to this girl that she chose to…"
He couldn't bring himself to finish the thought.

"A fish out of water dies gasping. Now, tell me more about
this…*Fiona*."

His heart stopped. A sudden cold chilled him. The look
in his mother's eyes was deadly. He should never have said
Fiona's name. He should never have breathed a word of her
to this woman. "There's nothing to tell," he said.

"Good, because I would hate to think that you'd forgotten
what mattered."

*The Wildeforde name, above all else. Above one's wants.
Above one's self.*

"I haven't forgotten, Mother." It was where his father had
failed. The previous duke's inability to put family before his
selfish desires had cost them all dearly. "If you'll excuse me,
I must send Graham my condolences."

His mother gave a cruel, satisfied smile. "I expect to see
you at dinner."

He nodded, unsure he could get further words out without
his voice breaking. Once his mother had closed the door
behind her, he collapsed into the chair. A maelstrom churned
within him. He loved Fiona with everything he had. He
wanted to wake up beside her every day, forever. The thought
of not doing so ached.

But she wouldn't be safe. If he married her, she would be
in his mother's sights for as long as the witch lived. He'd be
setting her up to be society's next victim. If he really, truly
loved her he would do what his father couldn't. He would
end things.

Chapter 2

London, 1821

Sitting on the cold stone, the hard metal bars of the prison cell pressing against her head, Fiona inhaled and exhaled with shallow breaths trying not to notice the smell of vomit or give any sign that she was not exactly who she was pretending to be—Finley McTavish, country lad.

She'd lost her cap in the chaos of the protest as well as her right shoe. But somehow, despite being roughly shoved into a wagon with fifteen men, her wig had remained in place and the binding around her breasts hadn't shifted. The thin layer of coal dust she'd put on her jaw that morning to give a hint of stubble was now covered in mud and a constable's spit. She supposed the dried blood that ran in a trail from her hairline across her brow and into her eyes probably helped with the disguise.

"Ye mongrels," a man standing next to her yelled, banging on the bars and causing reverberations to travel through her skull and into her teeth. They had been in the cell for three hours, and her headache, which had started with an elbow to the temple before the authorities had even shown up, was intensifying with every minute.

Three feet away from her, another cellmate turned to face the wall, reached into his trousers, and pulled out his cock, a steady stream of urine hitting the bricks and splashing. As disgusting as the sight of a wrinkled, limp member was, it was nothing compared to the sudden urge to pee let loose by the sound of the trickle.

Fiona pulled her knees into her chest, drawing herself in tightly. Even if she was inclined to piss in public, which she would never do, there was no way of doing it without revealing herself as a woman. That was neither smart nor safe.

Neither of the trusted friends whom she would normally turn to were in any position to help her.

Benedict was in Abingdale with his very pregnant wife.

John was in the Americas.

Talking to the jailers had accomplished nothing. All she could do was hope she was dragged in front of a magistrate soon, so she could convince him that while she had attended the protest against the current inequalities in the parliamentary system and the lack of fair representation, she'd had no involvement in the rotten fruit being thrown at Palace of Westminster guards. The tomato she'd thrown had been directed at someone else entirely. It was bad luck that her elbow had been knocked at just the wrong time.

And she had to hope she appeared credible enough to be released, because she had a meeting with the patent office in roughly eighteen hours. Years of work developing a tool that could change society was being held up by some clerk and his tangle of impenetrable paperwork.

It had taken two months to get this appointment and there was no guarantee she'd be able to get another soon.

She silently cursed herself for being fool enough to go

to New Palace Yard. But when she'd heard exactly who was leading today's protest, who would be speaking at it, she'd been unable to stop herself.

Charles Tucker had been responsible for inciting the riot in her village last year. He was responsible for that, and the boiler explosion, and the death of her friend. The bastard had cleared out before the watch arrived and avoided any form of consequence for the damage he'd done.

So she'd thrown a blasted vegetable, and here she was while he, presumably, was free. Yet another example of how iniquitous the world was.

She shook her head, trying to put aside the anger and concentrate on what mattered *now*—the single focus of her past five years. The plan that got her up each morning and kept the fire inside her burning late into the night as she worked. She was going to change the world—shift the scales of disparity just a smidgen—and in the process, earn enough money to buy herself some independence. To purchase a home that no man could take from her. To earn a living that relied on nothing but her own hard work.

She would never again find herself without fire, food, and shelter because a man had let her down.

It was the thought of her matches—an invention that would make fire accessible to all—that filled her with a stubborn determination that settled in her stomach and straightened her spine. She'd come to London with the express purpose of finding a distributor. She needed to be in her laboratory, not in a cell.

Andrew, the sixteen-year-old footman she'd brought with her from Abingdale, had tagged along to the protest. He'd seemed like the best choice when leaving their small country village. She needed an escort around London—as ridiculous as that societal expectation was—and the wide-eyed country boy would not protest her choices. She had all the semblance of an escort without any of the hassle an actual chaperone might pose.

But now her freedom hinged on the scrawny lad's ability to get out of the riot and send word to Ben that she'd been arrested. Surely, he'd manage that. He was innocent, not daft.

It would take three days to reach Abingdale to deliver the message and three days back. Worst case scenario, she'd be looking at seven days in prison.

She shivered. There was no way she was getting through seven days in here without revealing her sex to the rest of the inmates, and this was no place for a woman. It would be a gamble to even trust the guards.

Think, Fiona. Think.

The cold from the stone floor began to seep past the thick fabric of her coat and breeches. As the temperature dropped, her heartbeat quickened the way it always did when she got cold. She fell into deep steady breathing to ward off the shivers and began her usual mantra.

The warmth will return, like day follows night. It will return.

She was in Old Bailey, for goodness' sakes. They wouldn't let anyone freeze to death in here, would they? Next to her, her cellmate shifted. The sound of piss on bricks trickled off. The smell didn't.

Edward stared down his younger brother. William sat with his ankles crossed, slouched back in the chair, scratching at the wooden arm. He shifted every thirty seconds or so, as though the two-hundred-year-old, perfectly polished chair had splinters.

Good. Will should be uncomfortable, given the number of times this scene had played out in the eighteen years since their father's death.

Edward drummed the tips of his fingers against the mahogany wood of his desk. He already knew how the conversation would go. He would express his disappointment. William would make a sarcastic quip. He'd deliver the required lecture, and nothing would change.

Because nothing ever did.

But what are the alternatives?

"You're home early. School's not out for another week."

William shifted his gaze to the window before looking back. "They're changing tack. Shorter terms. Longer breaks. Cutting down on the rhetoric." He tugged on the cuff of his jacket.

"After six-hundred-and-fifty-odd years, Oxford has suddenly decided to change their approach? I assume your exam results should be arriving soon, then."

William rubbed at his jaw. "Well, about that—they decided not to do exams this term. Trialing different assessment methods."

"How progressive of them." One would think that given the never-ending string of predicaments William found himself in, he'd be better at lying.

The silence stretched. Edward had long ago made friends with stillness. It was one of the most effective weapons in his arsenal.

Finally, William sighed. "I got caught breaking into the dean's office. With a pig."

"Of course you did." It would almost have been preferable for Will to be tossed out for fighting or sneaking a woman into his rooms. Anything, really, other than these idiotic, childish pranks.

At twenty-one Will should be a man, not a boy still getting into scrape after scrape.

"I'll send word to the vice chancellor. He can send an examiner to London and you can take your exams here."

"That's not necessary," Will mumbled, staring into his lap.

Edward leaned over his desk, hand curled into a fist, eyes level with his brother's.

"It *is* necessary because you will take your exams. You will graduate, and you will take a career. I don't care if it's the clergy or the military. You *will* grow up, William."

His censure was met with sullen silence, his brother's typical response. "Start studying. Someone will be here to supervise your assessments next week."

Finally, Will looked him straight in the eye. "Because you say so? The university is just going to pack a professor onto the mail coach and send him to London to supervise one student?"

Edward raised a brow.

"Of course they will. You're the Duke of Wildeforde. People do what you say." Will shook his head. "Do you ever get bored of being so bloody perfect all the time? Always correct. Always doing the right thing."

Edward had long ago hardened himself against that particular blow. His heart had formed a necessary callus. It barely felt the hit.

"Perfection is our duty. Family must come first. What you do reflects on all of us. It's time to stop thinking about having a moment of fun and instead think about how your actions impact others. It's time to stop being so selfish."

William's face twisted at the insult. His eyes—such a bright blue when he was born; the most wonderful thing Edward had seen—darkened. "Has it ever occurred to you that the line our mother fed us our entire lives—family above all else—is wrong? That there's more to life than duty and honor?"

Any patience Edward had for this conversation vanished, driven out by the bitter cold of their past and the reminder of what he *had* given up. "You were too young to understand what she went through."

"Please, she's been shoving it down our throats our entire lives. I may not remember Father, but I know more about his faults than I would if he'd lived longer."

"Be glad you don't remember him. You'll never know the grave disappointment he was."

Because of everything that had happened, that was what hurt the most. Not the shock of his father's death or the relentless bullying he'd taken from his peers afterward. Not the way his mother, already cold, had become sharp and brittle as they left London to escape from the scandal.

No, it was discovering the good, kind man he'd thought he'd known had been willing to put the health and happiness of everyone he loved in jeopardy so he could indulge in his affair.

Their entire relationship had been a lie.

That was the disappointment that cut deepest—the wound that had never healed.

There was a discreet knock at the door. Simmons entered.

Taking the butler's interruption as a chance to escape, Will jumped up from his seat. "Well, I'm off then. You're clearly busy."

"Will, let's talk tonight." They'd never managed to have a proper conversation about the events of their childhood. It was a subject matter on which they couldn't see eye to eye, and the conversation quickly became an argument each time. But with Charlotte coming out this season, and the increased scrutiny their family would endure as a result, it was time for his brother to see reason. He had to toe the line, for his sister's sake, at least.

"I'm going to stay with Pulfrey for a few days," Will said, neatly avoiding the confrontation. Again.

That his brother found it so difficult for them to be under the same roof hurt. But it had always been that way. Nothing he did could change it. "Your sister will be home on Friday. I'd like you to be here."

"Of course I'll be here. You didn't need to ask."

And he probably didn't. Charlotte-Rose and William shared a bond that Edward didn't—couldn't. Being head of the family came with responsibilities they didn't understand. Those responsibilities had always held him slightly apart, never quite one of them.

Simmons's expression didn't change a whit as William passed him, even though Edward suspected the butler's opinion of his brother was even worse than his own. "I'm sorry to bother you, Your Grace, but there is a footman here to see you."

"A footman? One of our footmen?"

"No, my lord."

"What does he want?" Simmons was head of staff and had full authority to hire, fire, reward, and reprimand as he wished. There was no need for Edward to be involved in the day-to-day of the household. Off-loading that burden was why he paid his butler and housekeeper a king's ransom.

"He said he's here with information about a Fiona McTavish."

Fiona?

He hadn't seen or spoken to Fi in almost a year. Not since the night of the Abingdale riots when, in a moment of fear and weakness, he'd told her that she would always own his heart. Then he'd taken her hands in his and kissed them.

That moment had stirred up all the longing, passion, and love that he'd worked so hard to smother.

That moment had almost been enough for him to throw caution to the wind. To take what he wanted and damn the consequences. To put everyone he loved—including Fiona—at risk so he could have her near.

Which was why he'd left Abingdale the next day, as soon as the watch arrived, and he knew the village was safe. It was best. It was the only way to keep her safe.

A fish out of water dies gasping.

Every time he let his mind turn to Fiona, his mother's words slithered their way through his thoughts and down into his gut where they sat, their poison leaching into him, making him nauseous.

He wanted to tell Simmons to send this footman away—nothing good would come of entangling the two of them again—but his gut couldn't do it.

"Send him in."

The scrawny lad who entered was covered in mud, his hair wild, his eyes frantic. "Your Grace." His bow was hurried, as though he was running out of minutes. "It's Miss McTavish, Your Grace. She's in trouble."

Chapter 3 —————————————————

The day had stretched out and the fragment of light that crept through the window at the end of the hall had dimmed. A guard, completely deaf to the calls of the inmates, had lit the gasoline-soaked wall sconces with a torch. The curling stream of sooty, oily smoke now hung over her head, filling her nostrils with an acrid smell that she should be used to.

The need to urinate was becoming unbearable.

Fiona, sitting in the front corner of the cell, her back against the brick wall, and her shoulder against the bars so that no cellmate could creep up on her, tried to focus on her plan for the week—tomorrow's meeting with the patent office and then a list of distributors to approach—but the increasing pressure on her bladder stole her focus. She shifted, looking for a more comfortable position, but the sudden redistribution of weight made it worse.

To hell with this.

Wrapping her hand around a bar, she levered herself up.

"Excuse me," she called.

There was no answer. The one guard sitting down at the end of the corridor didn't even look up.

She banged on the bars with her fist, a pointless movement that did nothing but hurt her hand.

"Excuse me. Sir? I need the privy!"

Behind her the men in the cell snickered.

"Wot? You shy?"

"Embarrassed about the size of your cock?"

Heat crept up the back of her neck and beneath the edge of her wig, which felt heavier and less well-fitting with every minute.

Ignoring the comments of the group behind her, she pressed against the bars. "Mister! Kin ye hear me?" She leaned into the Scottish side of her heritage, hoping it would strengthen her disguise. The bloody guard didn't even look in her direction.

A man approached from behind, the hairs on the back of her neck rising as he leaned against the bars beside her. Close. Too close.

Her heart beat double time as he murmured in her ear. "Pr'haps you got a reason not to drop your drawers in front of us, eh lad?"

She swallowed. "I dunnae ken what ye'r talking about." The words felt tight and forced.

"Remembered to drop your voice, have you, lad? Coulda sworn it was higher a second ago."

She faced him, arms crossed in a way she hoped looked confident while hiding her chest. "Ye got a problem?" she asked, trying to ignore the smell of stale beer emanating from him and his hot, putrid breath that mingled with hers on her lips. She pushed back the urge to vomit and managed to cock one eyebrow.

He grinned down at her. "I got somethin'." He ran a finger across her temple, brushing against the edge of her wig. "Mebee I should explore that more."

Her racing heart abruptly stalled and she reflexively reached to her hairline—holding the wig to her head firmly. In her periphery she saw some of her other cellmates straighten, attention firmly on her. One dropped his gaze to her backside and began to run his hands together.

Her throat closed completely.

This is bad. This is very, very bad.

Her only possible savior was the guard determined not to hear her. "Sir?" She looked over her shoulder, praying to see him coming in her direction—and she saw something else entirely.

Edward, strolling down the cold, dark corridor as casually as though he were walking down a busy street. Edward, looking like the devil himself. He was taller than most men, six feet something of furious, tightly held violence. His pale blue eyes were ice cold, and they were fixated on the man whose breath she could still smell.

All the tension drained from her, and she sagged into the bars, forehead resting on the frigid metal.

She was safe.

At least, safer than she'd been a second ago.

But despite the relief, a pit of nausea formed in her stomach. Edward. Of all people to come to her rescue, it had to be Edward. Her throat tightened and hot tears pricked at her eyes as she looked up at him. He was harder than the man she'd known years ago. His lips, once soft to kiss and quick to smile, were pressed thin. There was a deep furrow between his brows, the groove accentuated by the severe, fluctuating flame from the torches.

He was mere feet away now, his arms crossed. When

his stare shifted to her, it lost none of its anger. It didn't soften a whit.

She swallowed.

"Finley," he said in a loud voice with a razor's edge to it. The cretin next to her dropped his hand and stepped backward. The other men in the cell found somewhere else to look. Edward had that effect. He expected to be respected, feared, obeyed, and he was.

The man next to her didn't need to know Edward was a duke. The royal power rolled off him.

How had she not noticed? How had she not picked him for what he was? It was so damn clear just looking at him that he was a man of actual influence. Clearly a lord with a title and estates and a whole damn society that yielded to him.

How had he fooled her for two entire weeks?

She prided herself on her intelligence. She might be an "odd" creature, completely incapable of behaving like a young lady should, but she was smart. Smarter than most men. Educated—if not traditionally. She should have spotted his ruse from a mile away. That she hadn't was humiliating, and she didn't really want to examine why she'd missed it, because then she might need to admit that it was because she'd wanted to. She'd been so taken with him, so utterly besotted by his attention and his confidence and the way he filled a room with his presence, that she'd willingly overlooked the clues that he was more than what he said.

And that deliberate obtuseness had been her undoing. Her broken heart was her own fault.

"Your sister sent me, *Finley*. You're a troublesome lad."

The arrogance in his voice rubbed raw. It was the oxygen needed to fuel her burning anger. What she wanted was to tell him to go jump into a pigs' wallow, but she'd keep her mouth shut until she was out of this mess.

She looked away, avoiding his gaze. Just behind him was the guard who had steadfastly ignored her. He held the best-looking ring of keys Fiona had ever seen.

With a rattle and heavy click, the guard unlocked the cell door. The squeal of non-lubricated metal on metal was as welcome as it was jarring. She brushed past Edward as she escaped and didn't turn around as the door clanged shut behind her, or as the men in the cell started to shout, or as Edward's steps sounded behind her. She held her head high and walked as quickly as she could down that corridor, and to her freedom.

Chapter 4 ——————————

Fiona stared out the window of the Wildeforde carriage. Grey cobblestones, grey buildings, grey sky. The people they passed were almost as colorless—clothes worn, faded until they almost blended into a muddy sea.

Every face turned as the ornate carriage with its gold-leaf crest passed—each face gaunt, expressionless. It was a look she was only too familiar with. She swallowed the lump that formed in her throat.

You haven't been starving in years.

Across from her, Edward—a man who'd never wanted for anything—stared at her, his expression grim. He was waiting for her to speak. It was a power game. The great Duke of Wildeforde flexing his might.

"What?" she snapped. The disguise she'd donned that morning to attend the rally itched. The wig, the breast bindings, the boot she'd stuffed with newspaper to give her extra height—it was all irritating. "What are you looking at?"

"Why are you in London?" He crossed his ankle over his knee, folding his hands on his thigh in a paternalistic manner, as if she were an errant child who needed scolding. But the aloof posture belied the anger in his voice.

"It's nae of your concern." Because it wasn't. He had no claim on her. He'd made that clear five years ago when he ended their betrothal in a *letter*.

He cocked his head—it was a minuscule movement that carried more censure than physics would warrant.

"It's business. You wouldn't want to sully your pretty gloves with it."

"Your business is my business, remember? I have a ten percent stake in whatever you're up to."

Aye. She remembered.

Last year, when Lord Karstark announced he was evicting all the tenants on his land to make way for better hunting grounds, she'd been forced to turn to the only other significant landholder in the area for help.

Edward—or rather—the Duke of Wildeforde.

Asking him to provide land and homes for the twenty-three families that had been displaced had been the single most humiliating moment of her life. While she may have been compelled to plead with him, she would not accept charity, so she'd made it a business deal, despite knowing he would have leased the land gladly.

He would provide land for new homes to house all those who had been booted from Karstark farms—including her and her father—for a ten percent share in her work. Ten percent that would come off the top of her earnings because she refused to tell her business partners, Benedict and John. They would do something good and noble like insist on the business covering it.

And she wasn't about to let anyone fight her battles.

"Then if you must know, I'm seeking a distributor for my matches."

"Why isn't Asterly doing it? Why is he risking your safety by sending you to London on your own? Curse it, Fi. Do you know what could have happened to you in there?" Edward's voice grew progressively louder.

"Nothing happened. I am perfectly well. I'm here because they're *my* matches. They're my idea, my work, and I'll be the one to sell them." That sounded boastful even to her. So she shot the arrow she hoped would land. "And because he's with his wife, who is expecting their bairn any day now."

"Amelia's with child?" For a fleeting second, the disapproval on his face morphed into surprise and then... thoughtfulness. As though he was picturing the life that might have been had Amelia not exposed his family to scandal. Had he not ended his engagement with her as a result.

That carelessly shot arrow rebounded and lodged in her chest.

Fiona had had no knowledge of Edward's title, or his long-standing engagement to Amelia. He'd simply been *Edward, just call me Edward.*

So when he'd talked of a life together, she'd believed him. She'd pictured growing old together in a small cottage not far from her current home. They would each go to work during the day and come home in the evenings where they would sit around the fire and read to each other.

Learning he was the Duke of Wildeforde had crushed that dream. Hearing that he was choosing to honor a commitment to a faceless young woman had been all the proof she needed that their love affair had been naught but a lie.

Her eyes burned hot.

"That must make Amelia happy," he murmured, though she couldn't tell if he realized he'd said it out loud.

"Aye. It does. They're very happy." And she was happy for them, even if their unexpected marriage sometimes made Fiona question her decision to forgo a relationship and focus on her work.

Edward shook his head, his eyes focusing. On her. "That doesn't explain what you're doing dressed like...that." He waved a hand in her direction.

"You didn't mind me wearing breeches five years ago. You couldn't keep your hands off them." Those brief weeks had been a frenzy of hot kisses, wandering tongues, and roaming touches that never crossed *the* line but explored every inch of it. Her blood had been on fire and her skin aflame with need.

"Wearing men's clothing in your factory is one thing, perhaps even sensible given the environment," he said grudgingly. "But such costumes in London is another thing entirely."

The comment burned. "I couldn't very well attend the protest in a dress. You may nae have noticed, shielded behind your title and money in Mayfair, but tensions are high. The people are angry. It isn't safe to be a woman in a mad crowd. I'm nae an idiot."

She rocked in her seat as the carriage hit a deep pothole, reaching to the window frame to steady herself.

He raised an eyebrow, the arrogance in that tiniest of gestures making her skin sizzle. "Not an idiot? That is very much up for debate." His tone remained measured, but his lips thinned a fraction and the hand he rested on his thigh curled slightly. "Attending that protest was incredibly foolish. You placed yourself at enormous risk for what? To listen to talk of overthrowing the crown? You should be more levelheaded."

Fiona bristled at his censure. He was so used to those

beneath him—practically everyone but the king—being eager to obey. Well, not her. Not today.

"I should do as you say, I take it? Your word is law. Except, you forget—I'm the only one who knows your word is useless." Fiona shifted in her seat, slouching a little, taking her legs wide. A direct mimicking of Edward's body language. "'Fi,'" she said in a slightly deepened, roughened voice. "'I want to marry you. I want it to be me and you for the rest of our lives. I have to go to London to sort out some business, but when I get back, we're going to have a life together.'"

Fiona swallowed the ball that had formed in her throat before continuing. "Do those words sound familiar?"

He frowned. A muscle along the line of his jaw ticked. He paused for a long moment. "That was...regrettable."

"Regrettable? Regrettable! You pursued *me*. You lied about who you were. Ye told me that I could trust ye, and then ye broke things off with a *letter*! You bloody coward."

"That was not...I wasn't...Granted, I should have..."

"Well, ye dunnae need to concern yourself. I can take care of myself. I don't need you or anyone else who thinks they can waltz in and out of my life with nae concern for what such fickleness does to people. You've left me twice now. Ye willnae get another chance."

Because his disappearance last year had almost broken her. He'd ended his engagement, he'd told her he loved her, and then he'd charged into the middle of a riot. And all those feelings she'd stuffed away came seeping through the cracks he'd created. Then he'd left again, this time without even a note.

Mercifully, the carriage pulled to a stop outside Benedict's town house, where she was staying during her time in

London. She didn't wait for Edward's footman to open the door; she shoved it wide and took satisfaction as it banged against the lacquered wood.

Her blood was boiling.

She was halfway to the door when she heard him call her name. She turned around. "What?"

"I'll send a carriage for you at half eleven to take you to my lawyer's office. We have a meeting with the magistrate at one."

"Just send me the address. I can make my own way there."

Edward took the stairs one at a time, because two at a time would reveal too much of what he was thinking.

Damned, stubborn woman.

Most people would be grateful to be bailed out of jail, saved from a crowded cell of ne'er-do-wells. Most people would be professing their never-ending appreciation.

Not Fi.

Only she would put herself in such a precarious position and then argue after being rescued.

He nodded to the footman who opened his study door, tossed his gloves onto the leather armchair, and settled into the seat behind his desk. He took a deep breath, hoping the familiar scent of leather, parchment, and ink would calm him down.

His heart had been racing a mile a minute since Fiona's footman had arrived. He'd almost killed Atlas, his most beloved horse, getting to the jailhouse in order to reach her before something happened.

And he'd been just in time.

He knew men well enough to recognize the look on that

cretin's face. The way he'd leaned over Fi, encroaching on her space with his body.

No, Edward had arrived with seconds to spare, and the thought of what might have happened if he hadn't made him want to cast up his accounts.

He couldn't remember the last time he'd been this angry. With her. With Asterly for allowing her to come to London with naught but a scrawny youth to look out for her. With the brute who'd made her turn white as a sheet.

That slimy bastard had better hope Edward never saw him again.

Edward flexed his hands, stretching the fingers out of the fist they'd formed. Mostly, he was angry that every word she spoke had been the truth.

He had pursued her. She had been a spark in his grey and heavy life. A moment of comfort in his grief that became two weeks of pure joy.

For a fortnight he had lived as though he wasn't the Duke of Wildeforde, as though he didn't have the weight of all his responsibilities pressing down on him, as though he wasn't tainted by his father's actions, forever trying to work his way out from that shadow.

For those weeks he'd experienced a different kind of life—free, kind, relaxed. He'd laughed more than he ever had. He'd slept through the night without nightmares, he'd done things the perfect Duke of Wildeforde would never even consider, and he'd foolishly hoped the change could be permanent.

A fish out of water dies gasping.

His mother's words rang through his head as did the malicious glint in her eye that made it clear she'd enjoy tearing his love down.

Society could be vicious to anyone who dared break their

rules. He'd experienced it before in the years of torment following his father's death. And yet he'd fallen in love and foolishly forgotten the strength of their venom.

Stupid. Thoughtless. Selfish. Just like his father.

He'd broken both their hearts to keep her safe, to keep her away from London and yet, here she was.

Fuck. Fuck. Fuck.

He dragged in a deep breath, wresting his thoughts under control. Fiona was at Asterly's town house. His mother was at one of their country estates. There was no good reason for them to come in contact. Edward would fix this blasted nuisance charge tomorrow and send her back to Abingdale. Asterly could come to town himself to sell these matches.

He needed a distraction, something to stop him from going to Fiona, bundling her into a carriage, and sending her out of London—or worse, going to her, bundling her into his arms, and kissing her senseless.

He reached for the package that sat square in the middle of his desk, neatly wrapped in oilcloth and tied with twine. His steward at Dunlochlan trusted no one and nothing, but particularly not the mail coach. His monthly report could have floated from the coast of Aberdeen to the River Thames and it still would have arrived secure and dry.

As he lifted the packet, he saw a delicate letter beneath with thin, spidery writing on the front.

His mother's handwriting. The reminder he needed that there was no escaping his life. His path had been laid out for him since birth, and trying to alter it would only hurt the people he loved most. Snarling internally, he slid the letter opener beneath the wax and unfolded the paper.

The briefest of salutations.

The usual reminder about his responsibilities as head of the family.

A terse notification that she was unwell and would be in the country for another few weeks.

And a list.

Six. Six women who would each make a suitable duchess, each of them without the slightest hint of scandal attached to her name. Because, as his mother was constantly reminding him, after the year they'd spent hosing down the scandal of his broken engagement to Amelia, he needed a lady who was above reproach.

That each of them was either dull as dishwater or as prickly as a thorn bush was not relevant. It was his duty to repair the Wildeforde name, and choosing an appropriate Duchess of Wildeforde was imperative, regardless of whether every mealtime moving forward was heavy with stilted conversation. His own feelings didn't matter. As long as she exceeded society's expectations, then she would do.

> Lady Luella Tarlington
> Lady Anne Livingston
> Lady Emma Clifford
> Lady Agatha Dormer
> Lady Henrietta Hastings
> Lady Catherine Kenworthy

Six women. Highborn, gently bred, well-spoken, mild in temperament, pliable, and completely above reproach. As unlike Fiona as it was possible to get.

He'd resigned himself to the need to marry this season. With any luck, his sister's coming out would attract enough attention that his hunt for a wife would go unnoticed.

But the appearance of Fiona...complicated things. It made it harder to focus on what he needed to achieve— marriage to a lady who would be beloved by his society.

Fi was a damned spitfire with more opinions than were useful in a woman. There was nothing mild about her. Everything she did, she did to the extreme—work, study, love. She was stubborn, immovable, and impassioned, and if he let himself spend too much time with her, there was every chance he'd weaken and toss decades' worth of reputation management to the wind.

That carriage ride had been hell. Those searing green eyes pinning him down, eviscerating him with their fury and intelligence. The licks of flame-colored hair escaping from under her wig. It had taken every inch of self-control he had not to reach across the space between them and pull her into his arms. He wanted to yell at her and devour her in equal measure.

Instead, he needed to do as the Duke of Wildeforde should. So he took a fresh sheet of parchment and began to write his own list, because like hell was he acquiescing to his mother's demands.

But no names came to him.

He put the sheet aside. He would get Fiona free from the debacle she'd put herself in and send her away. Once she was out of his mind, he could do what needed to be done: find a perfectly respectable woman to marry, one who didn't drive him crazy, so he could finally put an end to this whole marriage business.

Chapter 5 ——————

Fiona sat in the outer room of the patent office, waiting for Mr. Jones to call her in. She smoothed the fabric of her skirts. The dress was the best one she owned; the one she wore to church on a Sunday and the occasional dinner.

It was practically the only dress she owned. She was much more comfortable walking through the factory in soft breeches and a comfortable shirt. Dresses got in the way. They were cumbersome; they restricted her movement; and flowing skirts were more likely to catch alight as she walked past an open flame. Besides, in a dress she always felt constricted—tightly laced and buttoned up, lacking the freedom to even breathe deeply without the gentle reminder of the constraints the patriarchy put upon her sex.

The frustratingly restricting bonnet she wore—honestly, why did women consent to having their peripheral vision obscured?—itched more than the wig she'd donned for the protest yesterday. But it was proper, wearing a bonnet and gloves, and she needed to be proper if she was to have any success here in London. Asking businessmen to work with a woman was one thing. Asking them to work with a woman in pants was potentially a step too far.

"What should I do, miss?" Andrew asked. Her footman had recovered from yesterday's misadventure with a hot chocolate and a good meal—proof that young men were ruled by food—and had been waiting at the foot of the stairs, ready to chaperone her again.

"Nothing, Andrew. When he calls me in, you wait here."

"Is that proper?"

Fiona sighed. Perhaps yesterday had made him less pliable than she'd hoped. "I need to be taken seriously, and that won't happen if he's reminded that I can't be trusted without a sixteen-year-old boy there to supervise me."

Andrew nodded, but the way he rubbed his palms against his breeches showed his unease. She clasped her hands in her lap to stop from mimicking his body language. He was not the only one whose nerves were on high alert.

Against her skirts leaned her worn leather satchel with copies of all the patent office forms, the most relevant design sketches of her matches, and her most recent testing results.

What should've been a relatively simple process, able to be conducted from her home in Abingdale, had become a series of complicated back-and-forth letters that became more obscure with every response. Which was why she was here to see Mr. Jones in person.

Finally, the door to his office opened, and he appeared—short, round, and with a disapproving look on his face. "Miss McTavish?"

Fiona stood, smoothed out her dress once again, and picked up her satchel. "Yes. That's me."

In the office, she perched neatly on the edge of her chair

and laid out all the documents in neat piles in front of her. She had color coded each pile with a bookmark.

Mr. Jones didn't smile. He didn't talk.

Nervous, she attempted to take control of the conversation. "It's a pleasure to finally meet you, Mr. Jones," she said, careful to speak with her mother's perfect English accent rather than her usual mishmash of Scots and English. "We have been going back and forth on the papers for this application for a while now."

"Yes, well, we need to dot all the i's and cross all the t's. I take it you brought your latest round of test results with you as well as a working sample of your . . . invention."

"I have, though I can't see why the test results are necessary." She took the folder marked with a green bookmark and handed it over the desk.

Mr. Jones took the papers from her. He sifted through them quickly, giving a *hmph* and head nod as he looked at each page. "I believe these shall be sufficient," he said sliding them into the file in front of him. "And the sample?"

Fiona retrieved a small metal box from inside her bag. Lead-lined, this box weighed more than everything else in the bag combined. Gently, she placed it on the table, unlocked the latch, and opened the box, pulling out the matches. She looked up at him. "Would you like to see it work?" she asked.

"Very much so," he replied.

It had been eighteen months since the first iteration of her matches had nearly set her hair on fire. Since then, she'd lit thousands of them. But even after all those trials, she still felt a slight giddiness every time she created flame at her fingertips. She had mastered fire in a way no one else had. It was one of mankind's most basic needs, something she knew better than most, having near frozen to death night after night on the side of the Great North Road.

Striking the thin wooden match against a sheet of sand-paper, she smiled at the responding hiss.

Mr. Jones seemed equally awed, his eyes fixated on the flame. "Exceptional. Very exceptional," he said.

She breathed a sigh of relief. "So it's all settled then? You can sign off on the patent?"

He shrugged. "Well, there is the issue of having your documentation certified by a third party who can attest to the fact that it is your work. I believe there are several men as part of your business partnership, correct? A Mr. Asterly and a Mr. Barnesworth? Their signatures will do."

Her fingernails bit through her gloves into the palms of her hands. "The application said nothing about additional certification to prove the ownership of my work. Do you ask all applicants to do this?"

"Well, this is a singular situation."

"Singular how? Because I'm a woman?" It was all she could do to keep her voice measured.

"It is irregular to see a patent request being filed by a woman, given she clearly has no schooling or education that would give her the knowledge to create such a product. Surely you can understand the need for something like this to be verified."

Her jaw ached from clenching. She may not have had a man's schooling, but she'd spent six years working under the very intense private education of John Barnesworth, one of the country's preeminent philosophers. Her instruction had been of a higher quality than that which the men of Oxford received.

"Is it necessary? It will take at least a week for the papers to reach Benedict and return. I'm in London *now* specifically to seek a distributor. I must have that patent."

"I'm afraid I must insist."

She gathered up her papers from the desk, tapping the edges hard against the table. "Very well then. Once you have those signatures, the patent will be approved, correct?"

"Once we have those signatures, your application will be assessed. Now if I can just get you to go back into the waiting room and fill out page six of this application because it seems to be missing."

Fiona took a long, deep breath, using those few seconds to revise her words to ones more suitable to a professional environment. "I checked the application ten times before I sent it to you. Nothing is missing."

Mr. Jones shrugged. "I don't know what to tell you. I have your application, but I don't have page six. We can do this another time if you have somewhere more important to be. Shopping, perhaps?"

Fiona ground her teeth. Truthfully, she was supposed to be going to court. But she could hardly admit that. "Certainly. I'll copy that page out now and leave it with your man at the desk."

They both stood and she offered him her hand to shake. He looked at it as though her gloves smelled like sulfur and clasped his hands behind his back.

"Good day, Miss McTavish. When you provide page six, please try and use the same handwriting to avoid any awkward questions arising during your application assessment."

Edward stood, arms crossed, in the center of his lawyer's office at noon. The clock had chimed with each tap of his fingers against his coat. Rollins, the Wildeforde family barrister, was looking at his pocket watch with a disapproving stare that deepened with each bong.

Fiona was running late.

Another reason she'd make a terrible duchess.

Another five minutes passed. Edward stared at the bookshelf studying the dry legal titles. It was the only way to stop himself from staring out the small window that overlooked the street.

He would not wait for her like a mooning boy.

After twenty minutes, just as Edward had decided to take his carriage to Asterly's town house and physically drag Fiona here, there was a sharp rap at the door.

Rollins's man opened the door and Fiona entered, tugging the edges of the ridiculous wig she'd worn the day before. Her cheeks were flushed, and she moved with a flightiness that suggested her mind was not where it needed to be.

"I'm sorry. We're going to be late. I know. I had to go from Loffman Street to Ben's house and then here. And there was an overturned cart that was causing all sorts of delays." She looked at Rollins first, then turned to Edward, clearly apprehensive.

As she should be. "What are you wearing?" he ground out.

Fiona looked down. She held out the edges of her coat, revealing a pair of clean, buckskin breeches filled out with the absurd padding other men of the *ton* sported, a pressed linen shirt, and a waistcoat that was simple but elegantly made. They did a good job of hiding her figure. The costume displayed none of the curves he knew were beneath.

But surely no one was blind enough to mistake her for a man. Her eyelashes were too long, to start with, and her lips were too full. They were lush and pink and currently pursed in a way that made his hands itch to reach out to her.

"These are the nicest clothes I own," she said, oblivious to his thoughts. "I realize they aren't silks and jeweled buttons, but they cost eight pounds. Surely it's suitable for court?"

She turned to Rollins as though she expected him to support her. Fool woman.

Rollins swept his gaze from the tips of her boots to the cap she'd placed on top of her wig, before turning to Edward. "I was under the impression I was representing Miss Fiona, Your Grace."

"You are," Edward bit out. He took Fiona by the shoulder and towed her toward the window, feeling every bit as he did when talking to William. "You can't go dressed like that," he hissed.

"How else am I supposed to dress?"

Lord save him from quarrelsome women who were being deliberately obtuse. "Like a lady. In a dress. With your hair done and a bonnet and gloves."

She held up her hands, a satisfied smirk on her face. "I have gloves."

He exhaled, trying to find the calm that had abandoned him the moment her footman walked in the day before. "For heaven's sake, Fi. You've been arrested for disturbing the peace. They're not going to send a finely dressed lady to jail but they may well send a cocky lad too big for his britches."

Her expression shifted to something that was almost apologetic. "That's a risk I'm going to have to take. I cannae go to court as Fiona McTavish. No businessman will take me seriously if they read that I'm just out of Old Bailey."

"Then one would think you should have thought about that before you joined the frenzied throng of protesters outside Westminster Palace." Curse it, she was going to give him an apoplexy. Not even his brother was harebrained enough to turn up in front of a magistrate in disguise.

"It's not an option." Fiona shook her head. "Besides, no judge is going to put me in prison with the Duke of Wildeforde speaking for me."

Edward tugged at the cuff of his coat, avoiding her gaze. Her swift intake of air told him when she'd put the pieces together.

"You aren't going to speak for me!"

It took every ounce of his control not to run his hands through his hair in exasperation. "Fiona, be reasonable. At the moment, the only story the newspapers have is of another rally gotten out of control. If I enter the courtroom, tomorrow we'll both find ourselves on the front page of the gossip section."

"You...oh..." She clenched her fists. "I should have expected this." She whirled away from him and toward Rollins. "I assume we'll be taking your carriage then? Wouldn't want the illustrious Wildeforde crest to be seen in the wrong part of town."

"Yes, sir. I mean, miss." He looked at Edward with a confused expression.

Edward waved his hand. There was no reasoning with her, and showing up to court any later than she already was would certainly not help. "Finley it is, then. On your head be it, *sir*."

Fiona *hmph*ed and stalked out of the room. Rollins looked to Wildeforde for direction.

"Do not botch this," Edward said, trying to keep the anxiety from his voice.

Rollins frowned. "I've never given you a reason to doubt me, Your Grace."

"And I've never felt the need to suggest you might. But if you value your career, Fiona McTavish will not go to jail. Understood?"

Rollins swallowed. "Understood, Your Grace."

Chapter 6 ————————————

In the three hours Fiona was gone, Edward had paced every inch of the room. He'd counted the number of books on the bookshelf, all sturdy legal tomes. He'd studied the well-worn leather armchairs, counting the number of metal studs along the edging. And he spent more time than he'd care to admit staring out the window, waiting for his lawyer's serviceable carriage to pull up out front.

There was no need to worry. Disturbing the peace was a minor infraction. Merely attending a protest rally, even one that had gotten out of control, was not a legitimate cause to send a person to jail. Particularly not when that person was represented by one of the best barristers in London.

But knowing that he did not need to worry was not the same as not worrying. Every inch of him itched to walk into the courtroom, pull the magistrate aside, and have a quiet word to smooth the whole mess over. A quiet word from the Duke of Wildeforde could always put out a fire.

But he had to balance the dangers of Fiona's going to

jail with subjecting his family to ridicule. His family, their happiness, came first. Family always had to come first.

He needed to trust Rollins to manage the situation, even if trusting other people to manage things of importance had never come easily. Particularly not when it came to the people he—his fingers tightened around the window frame—people who mattered. Fiona mattered. They might not ever be able to have a life together, but she still mattered.

A fish out of water dies gasping.

He began to count the windows in the building opposite, alternating between French and German. It was a trick he'd learned from Amelia. A way of occupying the mind.

He couldn't get past "sechs" before his thoughts drifted back to Fi. Last night he'd been cursed by dreams of her. They'd started out benign—fleeting memories of her laughing, reading, lying on her back and pointing out stars. Images that tugged at his heart, an organ he'd spent years ignoring.

It was the memories that came next that caused his restless, broken sleep—of the crush of her lips, the press of her body against his, the scent of jasmine and honey in her hair as he trailed kisses down her neck. Those memories, which tugged at a place farther down than his chest, were the ones that kept pulling at him, dragging his attention.

Twelve windows on the top floor.

One, deux, drei...

Her hands wrapped into his lapels.

One, deux, drei...

His hands reaching beneath her shirt.

Three, vier, quatre...

By the time the carriage pulled up in front of the offices, the sun was starting to set. Stark shadows thrown by London's skyline were offset against the radiant oranges and pinks of the sky.

He moved away from the window before Fiona could see him brooding and sat in the armchair with its 284 metal studs, bringing with him a book to make it appear as though he hadn't been anxiously waiting for them to return.

About a minute later the door opened. Rollins entered first. Sweat beaded across his brow and he looked at Edward the way one might look at a rabid dog.

Blast. A dozen different ways things could have gone awry careened through his mind. "What's wrong? Where is she?" he demanded, standing abruptly.

"Your Grace—" Rollins shrank back as Edward crossed the room. Before the lawyer could finish, Fiona walked through the door.

Edward's relief at the sight of her was quickly replaced by a potent fury. Her face was pale, the fresh blood on her swollen lip standing out. Her morning coat was rumpled, stained by muck, and her eyes were rimmed with red.

He was going to kill someone. She just needed to point him in the right direction. "Curse it. What happened?" He cupped her face in both hands and was reminded of how delicate she was. She might be bold. Her presence might command the room, but she was also more fragile than she first appeared.

Her breathing hitched at his touch, from pain or relief, he wasn't sure. His gut twisted at the sound. "What happened?" he asked her in the gentlest tone he could muster.

She paused, as though debating what to share with him. "Nothing. I'm fine." She ducked out of his grasp and bee-lined straight for Rollins's liquor cabinet.

Frustrated that she wouldn't share it on her own, he turned to his lawyer. "Explain."

Rollins looked at Fiona, clearly wanting her to respond.

Fiona simply took the lid off the whiskey decanter and poured herself a drink, throwing it back in one hit.

This is not good. He should have gone to the courthouse, should have paid off whoever he needed to in order to resolve the matter himself, quietly. "Well?"

Rollins took papers from his bag, shuffling them around in his hands as though the key to diffusing Edward's wrath was somewhere in those sheets. "What Miss McTavish neglected to mention was that she wasn't arrested for *attending* the protest. She was arrested for throwing rotten vegetables at the authorities. A somewhat irate officer of the King's Guard attended the hearing to testify against her. He was very determined and... the charges were upgraded to assault. She faces trial in a month."

Throwing vegetables. Did she truly not have a shred of sense? She'd always been political; it was part of what attracted him to her. They'd spent long nights debating philosophy, religion, and matters of state and not once had she placated him. But *this*. It was idiotic.

"And the bloody lip?"

Rollins's Adam's apple bobbed. "Given your instructions not to mention your name, Your Grace, she was remanded into custody until the trial commenced. I believe the injury occurred after she reached the prison."

Fiona in prison. In a cell with criminals. Assaulted. A pounding thundered in his ears. "I told you she was not to go to jail."

The blood drained from Rollins's face. "Which is precisely why I asked for a private meeting with the magistrate following the hearing," he said, his voice shaking. "I explained to him that Mr. Finley McTavish was a personal acquaintance of yours and that you had interest in the case. He agreed to release her... him. With some conditions."

"Which are?"

"That you would pay a surety of a hundred pounds and that she, he, she would reside under your roof until the trial commenced."

Curse it. Obviously, he was relieved that she was not in any immediate danger, but to have her under his roof for a full month? The magistrate could not have known how unreasonable a suggestion that was—a single young woman residing with an unmarried man—because Fiona had chosen to hide her true identity, and now Edward was faced with a month of avoiding unnecessary rumors.

If word got out, it would not only put Fiona in the sights of the *ton* but also put Charlotte's chances of a decent marriage this season at risk, as well as his own. Then there was the danger to him: his reputation, his resolve, his heart.

He should have just gone to the blasted courthouse. He should not have trusted something this vital to another. And now, there was no escaping her.

Chapter 7 ─────────────────

All Fiona wanted to do was cry but she was too dumb-founded. Really, who went to jail for throwing a *tomato*? She hadn't even been throwing it *at* the authorities. It had been squarely aimed at Tucker as he riled up the crowd. Instead that bloody guard stepped right into the path of it.

Not that his story to the magistrate had even remotely resembled hers. No, to hear him tell it, she'd looked him dead in the eye, sworn at him, and then pelted the tomato at him directly. It was his word against hers, so she'd been bundled up into the back of a wagon for the second time in two days and taken to Old Bailey—not the upper-level holding cell where she'd been yesterday, but deep in the bowels of it.

She'd watched as inmate after inmate was stripped and doused with a bucket of lye before being tossed a bundle of prison rags.

As the line got shorter and shorter and her charade got closer and closer to being revealed, she'd done the only thing she could think of—she'd turned around and thrown a punch at the man behind her, clocking him in the jaw.

Whether that was a mistake or pure genius she still didn't know. She'd suffered a busted lip and a bruised hand in the all-out brawl that ensued, but instead of being processed with the rest of the criminals, she was dragged away into a cell on her own.

Barely six feet by six feet, it had held just a bucket and a moldy, threadbare blanket. That's when she should've cried. But the tears hadn't come.

According to Rollins, she'd only been in the cell for an hour, but damn that hour had stretched. It had felt as long as that first night after British troops had tossed her family out of their home during a cold Scottish autumn.

Except this time, she'd at least had a moldy, threadbare blanket.

Ha.

Haha.

Hahahahaha.

In the safety of Edward's carriage, her chuckles turned into maniacal cackling. Tears streamed down her face, and she bent double, wrapping her arms around her legs and smothering her face in the damp, smelly fabric of her breeches.

Hahahahahaha.

She took breath where she could get it, but the laughter wouldn't stop. Her midsection burned from it and her mouth and cheeks soon ached.

She sat up and wiped away her tears with the back of her coat sleeve, but as much as she tried, she couldn't stop them falling. Tears mixed with snot and the blood on her lip—a salty, ironish taste in her mouth.

"I'm sorry," she gasped, looking at Edward. He had an expression of utter horror and was holding out a clean, pressed handkerchief as though that expensive scrap of linen had any chance of righting the mess she'd become.

That thought sent her off into another fit of giggles as she took the handkerchief from his hand and wiped her nose.

"Are you quite well?" Edward asked with an apprehensive look that suggested he thought her completely mad. Which perhaps she was.

"I'm fine. Perfectly, absolutely, fine. Why wouldn't I be? I mean, what could possibly have occurred recently to make me nae fine?" She waved her hand over her wrinkled, blood-stained, reeking clothes.

He frowned—seriously, duke-ishly. His hands were folded neatly in his lap, the amethyst buttons on his gloves matching his amethyst cuff buttons, which played nicely with the purple and blue embroidery on his waistcoat. The perfect Duke of Wildeforde. And here she was, a teary, snotty, muck-covered mess.

Hahaha.

"I cannot see the humor in the situation."

She snorted back a laugh. "Truly? You cannae see the humor in my being arrested for vegetable throwing, of all things? Of you and I being forced to reside under the same roof? Ye dunnae find that straight from a farce?"

Because the judge's decree was Shakespearean in its twisted humor. She laughed again, her stomach aching from it. The more his countenance flattened, the more his hands gripped together, the harder it was to keep the giggling at bay.

"No. I cannot see the humor in that."

His expression! As if the day's events were being force-fed to him and tasted of sulfur and iron. Of all the ridiculous things that had happened in the past twenty-four hours, his expression was the most ridiculous. A fresh wave of tears ran down her face. She wiped them away with the back of her glove, wrinkling her nose at the smell.

"This is childish," he said.

She nodded. What else could she do? She couldn't argue. It's not like any of this was *actually* amusing.

Her business deal was at risk.

Her actual freedom was at risk.

And living under the same roof as the man she once thought she'd marry? Oh, her heart was at risk.

No, this really wasn't funny. She drew in a deep breath and let out a shaky exhale. Then she repeated until, finally, she was able to draw in her facial expressions and bring her voice under control. She also placed her hands primly in her lap. "You're right. I apologize."

Edward grunted. "It has been a remarkable day. It's no surprise that you are overset."

Overset.

"Overset?"

He held his hands up in defense. "I'm simply saying that most men would feel rather shaken having been thrown into prison, so it's not a surprise that your sensibilities have reached their limits."

If it weren't for the fact that her hand was already throbbing from the fight she'd started, she would have slapped him. She was tempted to open the carriage door and toss him out.

"I am nae overset."

"Then what would you call it?"

"I am..." She didn't know what she was, but she knew that it was nothing as weak and frivolous as that.

Exhausted? Frustrated? A smidge terrified of being thrown back into a cell?

What false energy her giggle fit had lent her fled, and she sank into the bench seat, leaning against the carriage door.

Four days ago she'd arrived in London with a plan and all the confidence she knew a man would have in her position. She was about to change the world.

Now she wasn't sure she had the energy to change out of her piss-covered boots.

Edward shifted in his seat. "I think we should devise a strategy," he said.

Good. Strategies were good. Sir Francis Bacon had developed the scientific method and following that had gotten her this far. "If ye take me back to Ben's house, I promise, ye willnae see hide nor hair of me for the duration of my time in London. Your problem will be solved."

He raised both eyebrows. "There's an agreement with the magistrate. You're residing at my house until the trial."

Oh, for heaven's sake. "Good God, Edward. They're nae going to have investigators watching yer front door. Leave me be and I promise I'll show up to the trial. By then, hopefully, some sense will have prevailed. It was a bloody tomato."

He shook his head. "I'm not going to break my word, and I'm definitely not going to risk people discovering that I'm ignoring the law because you find living under my roof inconvenient."

And in those words she saw the duke—the lord who valued rules above feeling, expectations above empathy. He was a cold night to Ed's affectionate day and the reminder of the loss stung.

"I find it hateful. You're the last man alive that I want to see on a daily basis." She didn't want to see him at all. Seeing him was painful. Seeing him was a reminder that if you made the mistake of loving someone, you were bound to be hurt. Seeing him stoked memories of why she'd fallen for him in the first place.

He was sinfully handsome—elegant and graceful with an aesthetic that might have been considered pretty if he hadn't been so tall, so broad shouldered, so hard. His eyes were framed with the kind of long lashes women dreamed of. His lips were soft and pink. But the strong planes of his face and iron set to his jaw were far from pretty. They were bold and handsome.

Looking at him stirred up a maelstrom of unwelcome feelings, all knotted up. He could never know what the sight of him did to her, even at this moment, when his frown deepened and his eyes went flat.

"Luckily for you, my house is large. I can't see that we'd need to interact more than a handful of times over the month."

"Splendid," she said. If he heard the sharp tone to her voice, he didn't grasp its meaning.

"You'll have everything at your disposal, of course. If you need anything, ask one of the maids and they'll pass the message on to my housekeeper."

"I'll nae need anything. I'll be out on business." She flicked aside the curtain that shielded them from view, as clear a dismissal as she could manage in the confined space.

"Of course," he said as he mimicked her movement, turning his focus to the building they passed, "for your little sticks of fire."

The sniffy tone with which he described years' worth of work made her vision turn red like the flames she worked with. She leaned forward, fingers grasping the carriage windowsill to keep her balance. "My little sticks of fire are going to change the world."

He turned his attention back to her, rubbing the spot between his eyebrows. "That was not intended as an insult."

Which made it worse. He was so high in the instep he

didn't even notice the way he looked down on her. The sharp incline of his perspective was simply second nature.

The carriage pulled to a stop outside Benedict's town house. Which was a good thing because had she been forced to spend another minute with him, she wasn't sure murder charges wouldn't be added to the assault ones.

She opened the carriage door without waiting for the footman, jumped down, and strode to the front door. "Good afternoon, Greaves."

"Good afternoon, Miss McTavish."

Behind her, Edward scoffed. "So the household knows what fraud you're running." He allowed Greaves to help him remove his coat, and handed the butler his gloves and hat.

"It's nae a fraud. Greaves, the esteemable Duke of Wilde-forde." She moved to storm upstairs but before she could get more than a handful of steps in that direction, Greaves called out.

"A caller, miss," he said.

As she turned to face him, she plastered on a smile because it wasn't his fault she'd been arguing with the duke.

"Your father is in the drawing room," he continued.

The words sapped what little energy she still had. The very thought of dealing with whatever mess Alastair was in exhausted her. Moving away from her father, finally, was half of the appeal of selling her matches. *What is he doing in London?*

"Your father is here?" asked Edward. "That's excellent. Perhaps he can set London alight too."

She whipped her head around to face the duke. "That's enough."

"I hear there were only a handful of arrests yesterday and that tomato throwing was among the worst of the charges. Why doesn't your father make an appearance at the next one and convince all in attendance to take up pitchforks and attack?"

"Sarcasm does not become ye, Your Grace." But other than delivery, there wasn't much she could disagree with. Her father, who'd spent his life drifting back and forth across the line of the law, had been completely taken by Tucker and his seductive visions of a world without the aristocracy. He'd been one of the instigators of last year's riots. If Edward hadn't stepped in, hadn't risked his own safety to convince half of the crowd to go home, more people could have been hurt than the one casualty: Jeremy, who'd died when he set off a boiler explosion.

Edward had every right to be furious with her father. Hell, she had yet to forgive Alastair herself.

She stalked to the drawing room. Her father sat there slumped on the settee, mud-covered boots making a mess of Amelia's damask-covered footstool.

"What are ye doing here?" she asked.

He stood, turning a roguish smile on his daughter. That was unsurprising. It had likely never occurred to him that his only daughter might not be happy to see him. "My wee bairn," he said, stretching his arms wide. "Give yer da a hug."

His face fell as he saw Edward enter the room.

"Alastair," Ed said grimly, taking a spot by Fiona's side, his arms crossed.

"Bite ma bawsack, ya fucking walloper."

Edward flinched and Fiona instinctively stepped between the two men. "Why are ye here?" she asked again before Edward could reply with a duel, or however dukes answered such insults.

"Can a faither nae simply wantae see his daughter?"

"Ye saw me last week. Back home."

"I wanted tae see how yer business interests wur faring. I

see ye'r dressed for th' part. Th' wig's a nice touch. Clever, clever." He settled back onto the settee, stretching his arms out along the top, one ankle crossed over his knee, and a smarmy look on his face as he threw Edward a challenging stare.

Edward, to his credit, didn't respond but neither did he leave. She was caught between two stubborn, arrogant patriarchs, both of whom she'd rather say good-bye to.

Instead, she answered her father's question, hoping for a quick end to the conversation. "Establishing the patent is proving more difficult than anticipated. The clerk seems to think a woman couldnae be the true owner."

She wasn't sure what reaction she was hoping for from him. Outrage on her behalf would have been nice given he had plenty of outrage to spare. Instead, he shrugged, and with a shake of his head he said, "Och weel. Ye'r a smart lassie. Ye kin come up wi' some aught else."

Disappointment flooded through her. She'd never been foolish enough to think he'd be her most vocal supporter, but she'd expected some sort of empathy, not this callous indifference.

"I'm nae coming up with a new idea, Da. I've worked hard on this an' I willnae be dissuaded."

He frowned slightly and then slapped his thigh. "Weel, that's mah lassie. Headstrong 'n' more than capable. I'm sure ye'll dae a stoatin job o' it." He pushed off from the settee and swaggered toward the door. "I'm off tae see a friend."

Edward shifted to the side to give her father room to pass. Alastair raised two fingers to his brow in an acerbic salute.

"Yer friend," she called out after him. "It's nae Charles Tucker, is it?" She didn't think her father had had anything to do with the rabble-rouser since Tucker scampered last year, but neither was she naïve enough to think Alastair had come to London for her.

He winked, and her anxiety doubled. "Dinnae fret, daughter. I will nae be getting intae any more trouble."

She'd be more inclined to believe him had he not given Edward a condescending pat on the arm on his way out. Edward made to grab him but her father, always slippery, ducked out of his reach and left the room whistling.

"Tucker?" Edward asked. "He's in London?"

There was no point keeping it from him. He'd no doubt be making enquiries the moment he got home. "Tucker was the actual target of that poorly thrown tomato."

Edward closed his eyes and rubbed his forehead. When he opened them again it was with an air of resignation, but there was a slight curve to his lips. "They shouldn't have arrested you. They should have given you a damn medal."

And, just for a second, she thought she saw Ed.

⁓

The ride to Edward's house was made in silence. She didn't have the inclination to fight anymore. What was done was done and, overbearing attitude aside, this situation she found herself in wasn't exactly his fault. In fact, one could say that she should be grateful for his intervention. Overbearing attitude aside.

But nonetheless she was not inclined to make small talk with a man who walked in and out of her life as he pleased, so instead, she kept her eyes firmly focused on what lay outside his richly appointed carriage.

By the time they reached his residence on Mayfair, it was a different London to the one she'd been through that morning. The people who walked the street—even the servants in their simple clothes—were plump, their faces smiling.

They stopped outside Wildeforde House, a large ornate

home that occupied nearly the entire block, waiting for a nanny and children to walk past before the carriage could turn into the long driveway that swept in a curve and ran the length of the home.

The door opened and a footman flipped down the carriage steps.

Edward exited. He turned and lifted his hand, as if to help her out, but then dropped it with a grimace. No doubt his conscience was warring between what was "right"—helping a lady out of a carriage—and what looked "proper"—which was definitely not giving his spotless hand to a dirt-covered, jail-worn lad.

She made it easy for him and hopped down without assistance, trailing him up the stairs. He stripped off his gloves and handed them to a sturdy, bald-headed man with thin spectacles.

She was vaguely aware of the butler saying something to her, but she was too stunned by what she was seeing to hear.

The marble floor of the foyer was flanked by curving marble staircases on either side. The walls, which felt as if they went up and up for days, were covered in art piece after art piece, no doubt each one worth more than every home she'd lived in combined.

The one time she had been to Edward's estate in Abingdale she'd just been blindsided by the news that the Karstarks were planning to turn her home into a hunting ground. She hadn't paid much attention to the grandeur of where he lived. Her focus had been on her shoes or on the tails of the butler's coat, and eventually, on Edward's face as she begged for help—the last thing she wanted to ask of anyone, let alone him.

But. This.

Her jaw went slack as his wealth belted her up the back side of the head.

Stupid, stupid, stupid.

How idiotic she'd been to imagine a future with the two of them together. When they'd been lying together in her father's hayloft, making constellations out of the knots of wood in the roof, she'd been thinking of them lying together in their bed, in a house with at least three rooms, with a fire in every hearth and food always in the larder.

Her wildest thoughts didn't even align with the reality of his foyer.

He'd been right to hide his true self from her. If she'd known that this was his life—this obscene pomp and grandeur—she would never have fallen for him. Only a foolish girl would swap a regular life for one like this. To be mistress of such a place would come at the expense of freedom she was not willing to give up.

Edward's pace slowed as he approached an older woman with iron-grey hair, a perfectly starched dress, and a stiff, expressionless face to match.

As he spoke, the battle-axe woman's eyes zeroed in on Fiona's hips, her chest, her hairline. Fiona's outfit had fooled dozens of men, but she had no confidence that she was fooling this woman.

Edward faced her and she shook herself, forcing her senses to catch up. "This is our housekeeper, Mrs. Phillips. She'll show you to your room." He turned to Mrs. Phillips. "I'll be dining at the club tonight. Send one of the more prudent maids with a tray to *Finley's* room at eight. We'll discuss this further when I return."

Within a handful of seconds, before she could make any coherent objection, he'd walked back out the front door, clearly making good on his promise not to see or speak to her.

Arrogant, pretentious bastard.

Twenty-year-old Fiona had been a naïve twit to have fancied herself in love with him. The overbearing, controlling duke considered himself above everyone except the king. But she had to thank him. For a few weeks he'd convinced her that maybe she could rely on someone else, that it didn't have to be only her against the world. Then he'd ripped that illusion away.

She wouldn't make that mistake again.

She'd overcome barriers an entitled lord couldn't even dream of. He thought himself stone and granite. But he was soft, like all of the upper class. Edward had no idea what real life was truly like, which meant he'd never truly understood her. She clearly hadn't known him, which meant they'd never truly been in love.

She was best avoiding him wherever possible. If she could get through the month without having another conversation with him, that would be a success.

Mrs. Phillips ran an assessing eye over Fiona, probably wondering what kind of criminal the esteemed Duke of Wildeforde would bring home to stay in his guest quarters. "Come with me, miss...?" The accusation hung.

"McTavish. Fiona McTavish," she muttered.

The housekeeper crossed the foyer at a quick clip to one of the grand staircases that flanked the hall.

Fiona looked back to where Edward had gone. When she turned forward again, Mrs. Phillips was frowning. "Guests are in the *east* wing. If you think you might get lost, don't."

Chapter 8

A̶nd so, it's decided then? We'll vote yes on next week's resolution." Graham, Viscount Dunburton, asked as he put down his napkin and looked at the men gathered.

Edward had gone to White's with the express purpose of getting away from Fiona. The entire carriage ride home she had stared out the window, clearly wanting as little to do with him as possible, and he had surreptitiously watched her and the emotions that played across her face as she took in all the good and bad that was London.

That artlessness, the complete lack of guile, had transfixed him years ago. He rarely banked on the expressions on a person's face. Yet, Fiona's true feelings had never been a mystery to him. Today he'd seen hurt and anger and mistrust and he'd known he deserved every bit of that.

So he'd left. Partly to give her room and partly because he yearned to do something to make it right—to undo the damage he'd caused—and it was best that he didn't. It was cleanest if she continued to loathe him.

So he'd gone to the place he was most comfortable. No sooner had he arrived than Graham and Lords Jeffries, Buchanan, and Haddington joined him, and they'd quickly gotten into a discussion about what relief measures could be put in place to alleviate the burden on the working classes while King George insisted on driving up taxes.

The discussion eased the knot of guilt that sat heavy in him. The development of new laws, crafting the direction of the country in such a time of turbulence, these were good, worthwhile things he was passionate about. They were things that felt familiar, that he felt sure about. Unlike the maelstrom of confusion buffeting him since setting eyes on Fiona again and the trepidation that gripped at the thought of her under his roof.

A footman cleared the plates so quickly and quietly Edward barely noticed his presence.

"I think we can all agree that this is the best move for the country," Haddington said. "Although we do need to be prepared for opposition from some landowners."

"Aye," said Jeffries. "And those bloody protests outside Westminster aren't helping to ease the tension. Yesterday's gathering got completely out of hand. I heard a full dozen men were arrested."

Edward's hand tightened on his glass. *A dozen men and a woman.*

Not that anyone could discover that. The information would destroy any chance Fiona had of selling her matches, and it would cause a scandal at least as great as his failed engagement to Amelia. One scandal in a decade was more than enough.

"They say Charles Tucker was seen at the gathering," Graham said. "The sooner they can find a reason to ship him off to Australia, the better."

All the men gathered nodded in assent. Tucker, here in London and no doubt planning on trouble. He'd been traveling around the country for years now. A powerful orator, he left nothing but destruction in his wake. Last year was proof of that. He'd whipped the village of Abingdale into a frothing beast.

Edward had done what he could to quell the rising storm but it hadn't been enough to stop the loudest, drunkest, angriest of them from marching on Asterly's house with pitchforks. Fiona's father among them. Only the explosion of Asterly's steam engine—a blast that knocked men from their feet a full five furlongs away—had ended the strife. The rioters scattered. One of them, a young lad, had died.

By the time the watch arrived, the villagers had sobered up and Tucker had vanished. He hadn't stopped, though. There were still reports of a short, bulldog-looking man speaking at village taverns across the country, sowing dissent. Edward wouldn't be shocked if Alastair McTavish had entangled himself in Tucker's web of subversion.

Alastair who, in another life, might have been Edward's family. Had he not broken his engagement to Fi. Had he not broken his promise to never leave her.

Buchanan rose. "Well, gentlemen. Should we retire to the card room for a hand of faro?"

"Not for me," Edward said, though he doubted Buchanan had anticipated a yes. It was widely known that that Duke of Wildeforde did not gamble.

Buchanan chuckled. "It's a shame you're not your brother. I could use the extra blunt."

While the men around him laughed, Edward clenched his jaw, putting on a tight smile to conceal his frustration. This tone taken about the Wildeforde family was exactly what he was trying to avoid. But William's blatant disregard for the family's reputation often threatened to undo all of it.

"Will we see you at the Macklebury ball?" Jeffries asked as he pulled his chair back.

"I'll be there," Edward said. "My sister will be in town by then, so I'm unlikely to miss a ball for the next few months." With any luck, he could get her married off this year and go back to his regular routine of showing up to just enough gatherings to satisfy the masses and no more.

"And it has nothing to do with you being on the hunt for a new fiancée?" There was a speculative edge to Jeffries's tone.

Edward grunted. He didn't want to discuss his hunt for a wife because it wasn't news he wanted broadcast to the *ton*'s marriage-minded mothers. But when Haddington hung back while all but Graham went to the tables, Edward knew exactly what conversation was coming.

"Are you truly thinking of marrying this season?" Haddington asked, turning his glass in circles on the tablecloth.

Edward debated answering. It was no one's business, but Haddington had been a longtime friend and ally.

"It's not something I want widely known, but yes. The plan is to marry soon. The older I get, the younger all the marriageable misses seem. If I wait much longer, I'll feel like I'm marrying an infant."

Haddington nodded. "That's fair. Commendable. Plenty of men don't think twice about saddling a young girl with their old, decrepit arses. Not that you're old, mind you."

Next to him, Graham coughed.

"Just say it, Haddington."

His friend leaned forward. "My Marianne is a lovely girl. Well behaved, no scandals, mature for her age, and more than capable of managing a household. And sharp as a blade, a fact that works against her with most men but I think you'd appreciate."

It was worth considering. A woman with unconcealed intelligence was a rare thing in society and he didn't have any reason not to consider the chit.

"I'll save a quadrille for her Friday. But for God's sake, don't go making her any promises."

Haddington smacked at the table. "I wouldn't want to get her hopes up. But with any luck, this could be an extraordinary union." He excused himself and followed after the others to the card room.

"I'm sorry about that," Edward said to his cousin.

Dunburton twisted his glass, his eyes on the wavering scotch. "You don't need to apologize. I lost my wife; that doesn't mean you shouldn't seek one."

"Still, you don't need the reminder of it."

Graham's chuckle was dark. "The reminder? There's not a day that goes by when I don't think of how spectacularly I failed her."

"It wasn't your failure," Edward said. Graham had loved Eliza. He'd spared no expense trying to make her happy, and yet she'd been so desperately unhappy that she'd done the unthinkable.

"I fell in love with a shopgirl, and instead of letting her live in the safety of her bookstore, I insisted she marry me. I thought I was giving her the fairytale."

Instead, Eliza had married into a nightmare. The thought sent shivers down Edward's spine as it always had.

A fish out of water dies gasping.

Graham's wife had been the punchline to every joke and on the receiving end of endless criticism. The vultures didn't try for discretion; the hurtful comments were always said just in range of Eliza's hearing. She'd been ridiculed and isolated, just as Fiona would have been had he been selfish enough to marry her.

No, there was only one option for men like them—to find a wife that fit society's mold.

On arrival home, Edward had meant to go straight to his rooms. He truly had. But nostalgia gripped him, and he couldn't shake free of it. He had mastered the art of not thinking about her years ago. He could go days, weeks even, without her crossing his mind.

Now that she'd crashed back into his life, he couldn't go seconds without the desire to see her.

Apparently, with Simmons's reluctant approval, Fiona had taken over the blue drawing room as her makeshift laboratory. Edward stood to the edge of the open door watching as she poured liquid from different beakers into a wide, shallow dish. She was in fresh breeches and a cotton shirt but no jacket or waistcoat, giving her the freedom to work unencumbered.

Her hair was no longer concealed by a cropped wig. It was tied in a simple queue that barely contained her curls. The lamplight turned the red tresses into a blazing halo of flame. He wanted to sink his hands into it, to breathe it in. It would smell of jasmine, a scent he'd banned from the house for the way it stirred up memories.

This was the Fiona he loved—industrious, whip smart, driven. There was no simpering from this woman intent on changing the world. There was no pandering. She cared not a whit for what society expected of her.

It made her fascinating. It made her captivating. And it left him feeling hollow.

Chapter 9 —————————————————

Fiona smoothed her heavy grey skirts, taking comfort in the weight of the bag on her lap. Mr. Duchamp was the first of four distributors she was meeting today and the first of fifteen she was meeting this week. She stilled the nervous drumming of her foot, but each time her eyes traveled to the clock on the wall, the *tap, tap, tap* started up again.

A clerk entered from a back room, pausing when he saw her, before taking a seat behind the desk. "May I help you?"

She stood, the bag swinging heavily in one arm. She grabbed the handle with her second hand, bringing the bag to rest in front of her—a leather shield hiding her nerves. "Miss Fiona McTavish from Asterly, Barnesworth & Co., here to see Mr. Duchamp. I have an appointment."

The clerk gave her the same condescending, top-to-toe inspection she'd experienced in the patent office. She worked hard to keep a pleasant smile on her face as he gawked and, not for the first time, she wished she'd taken Amelia's offer for a lesson on delivering a charm offensive.

At the time, she'd been convinced her work would speak for itself and that charm wasn't necessary. But Amelia could have taken the clerk's patronizing look and turned him into a stumbling mess. Instead, he lifted a single, sarcastic eyebrow. "I'll enquire as to Mr. Duchamp's availability."

She breathed in deeply, tamping down her frustration. "Yes, but as I said, I have an appointment. At nine this morning. It's nine, so I suspect he's available." She widened her plastered-on smile.

The clerk didn't even bother with a response before he disappeared through the doors behind his desk.

Fiona focused on her breathing as she waited. It was ridiculous, this tightness in her chest. She had survived homelessness in a Scottish autumn. She'd traveled on her own from Ballater to Abingdale with barely half a crown in her pocket to make the trip. She'd been thrown in prison twice in two days and managed to wangle herself out of sure disaster.

This was a conversation. She was offering him an opportunity he'd be mad not to leap at, so there was absolutely no good reason to be nervous.

Except she was.

Because if she sold her matches today then her future would be secure. She would never again live under the threat of being evicted. She would never be at the mercy of a landlord's whim. Nor would she ever have to worry about whether or not her father had paid the rent that month. She would be the one person responsible for her.

The clerk returned after less than a minute. "I'm afraid Mr. Duchamp is unavailable."

The flutter of nerves became a stampede and she struggled to keep her tone calm. "I am happy to wait for him," she said, as brightly as possible. As long as she didn't have to wait too long. She did have another appointment in ninety minutes.

"I'm afraid Mr. Duchamp is busy for the remainder of the day."

Oh. The thudding nerves devolved into bubbling, roiling anxiety. "I can come back tomorrow. I have time free after two."

Smug. That was the only word that adequately captured the clerk's expression. "I'm afraid Mr. Duchamp is busy for the remainder of the week. Or rather, the month. However, if Mr. Asterly or Mr. Barnesworth would like to make an appointment and appear themselves, he may look past this"—the clerk waved his hand at her—"and be willing to consider a meeting."

Look past this? As though her presence was an insult or a misstep. "But these are *my* matches. Nobody is better able to describe how they work or what kind of asset they'll be."

"Have a good day." The clerk sat and focused on the page in front of him, licking the tip of his finger and flipping it with a sharp snap.

Fiona took a deep breath in and let it out, picked up her suitcase, and left.

She had not expected it to be easy. She had fully expected to have to justify herself to these distributors. But she had also expected that they would at least give her the chance to do so.

Well, that was his mistake, and when her matches were being used in every home in Britain, rich or poor, she'd be able to rub his nose in it.

Andrew was leaning by the door, scuffing circles in the pavement dust with his foot. He straightened when he saw her, an expectant look on his face.

In her recent efforts to convince herself of her imminent

success, it appeared she'd convinced him too, which gave her failure an additional thorn, sharp and blood-drawing.

"How did it go, miss?" he asked.

"Not well, Andrew. Not well at all. I wish I could see his face the day he discovers what he missed out on."

"What do we do next?" he asked with confidence she'd have to match in appearance even if she didn't quite match in feeling.

He expected her to have the answer, because in their small village that's what she'd become known for—having all the answers.

"We move on, Andrew. We have ninety minutes to reach the Tarly offices. We can make it a leisurely walk instead of rushing."

She unlatched her briefcase and pulled out a map of London. The cab driver had dropped them off at the exact address for their first stop, but they were going to need to find their own way around the city from here.

"I think it's this way." She pointed down the road. Not wanting Andrew to sense her discouragement, she set a brisk pace, though truly, she was not paying an awful lot of attention to where she was going. Her mind was running over the events that had just occurred.

How. Bloody. Frustrating.

The earlier tightness in her chest hardened into a coal-like lump of fear. What if no one agreed to meet with her? When she had written to the distributors to arrange a time, she had signed her name F. McTavish from Asterly, Barnesworth & Co. She hadn't deliberately set out to mislead anybody, but she also hadn't felt the need to advertise her sex.

Because, surely, that shouldn't have mattered. Business was business and a good deal was a good deal.

The fact that she wasn't paying attention to where she

was going was why she didn't see Edward until it was too late.

He pushed off the wall that he was leaning on and into her path. Hands in his pockets and a look of extreme displeasure on his face, he stood so close that she was forced to tip her head to look at him. Her heart thudded at his nearness. He radiated an energy that could not be explained by science. It raised her temperature and quickened her breath and befuddled her thoughts with base instincts that followed no logic.

"What are you doing here?" she asked. Perhaps her words came out a touch surly, but shouldn't that be expected when one was accosted in the street by a man who'd previously sworn to avoid her?

"You took off in a cab."

"I told you I had business in town this morning."

"But you took off in a *cab*," he repeated loudly, "with only a young boy"—he waved toward Andrew—"to look after you." He looked over her shoulder at Andrew. "No offense intended."

"None taken, m'lord."

Edward fixed his stare on Fiona. "Do you know what could have happened to you?"

His outburst was a complete overreaction and one more indication that the duke was not at all like Ed, the man she'd known. "It was a hackney cab, not a random stranger."

He crossed his arms, staring her down as though she were an errant child. "I have carriages at your disposal."

She smirked in a way she knew would annoy him. "I didn't think you'd want the Wildeforde crest displayed through the working boroughs." In truth, she didn't want his help at all, not even his transport. He'd had the right of it yesterday when he'd insisted they keep well away from each other. She didn't need the discombobulation that came with his presence. There was serious business to be done and she couldn't accomplish it while she was distracted by the way her insides curled when he was near.

"I have *unmarked* carriages at your disposal—that one in particular." He pointed to a carriage that had pulled up across the street from Mr. Duchamp's office. It was relatively unassuming, for a duke's equipage. A far cry from the gilded monstrosity they'd ridden in yesterday.

She rolled her eyes. "Of course you do. Well, thank you for your concern, but I'm quite well. Andrew and I have decided to walk. We have plenty of time and it's good for the constitution."

"You two are not walking through London alone."

Damn insufferable despot. Had it been Andrew traveling alone, the duke wouldn't have batted an eyelid. But because she was a woman…"You're welcome to join me, if you wish," she snapped. "Although that makes some mockery of your decision to stay well apart from one another."

He massaged the spot between his eyebrows as though her very presence was giving him a headache. Which was needling. If either one of them should be giving the other a headache, it was him.

"Let's go," he muttered, and held out his elbow for her to grasp.

Damn. Her invitation had not been sincere. Surely, he'd sensed that. "You don't have anywhere more royal to be? Parliament? The king's court? In a room being fed roasted pheasant while you lord over all your subjects?"

Behind her, Andrew snorted. Edward pierced him with a withering stare. "Tenants, not subjects, and I have plenty of places where I ought to be. Luckily for you, a gentleman puts a lady's safety first. Even if that lady is being a bullheaded twit insisting on traipsing around London on foot rather than accepting a perfectly comfortable carriage."

"Walking is good for the soul," she said as she stepped around him, ignoring his outstretched arm. It wasn't untrue. The worst days of her life she'd spent walking alone in the cold, examining her life. It was on that long walk that she'd come to the realization that everyone was in this world alone. That even those who were supposed to look after you could not be counted on. Not really. Not when it mattered.

It was that realization that had driven her to step out of the confining construct men had created for women and drove her to take on a career.

It was that realization that had spurred her through the late nights and failed experiments in order to reach the holy grail—complete independence.

It was that realization that had protected her from the worst sting of Edward's betrayal all those years ago, because if she hadn't already known that no one could be counted on, she would have learned that lesson then.

The meeting with Tarly & Sons didn't go any better than her first meeting. The clerk was somewhat more apologetic but still firm in his refusal to admit her. Ninety minutes after that, the situation played out again at Portman Industries.

By that time, Fiona's feet were hurting from the nonsensical ladies' walking shoes she was wearing instead of the boots she wore day-to-day at the firm. She forced herself not to look longingly at Edward's carriage, which still trailed them. She got here under her own steam; she would continue that way. This wasn't even the toughest of the walks she'd made.

At some point, though, she'd stopped rejecting Edward's

proffered arm. She only had so much energy for argument and that was being spent trying to gain an audience with men she had already scheduled time with.

As the day went on, that first reluctant touch became firmer; she found herself wrapping her fingers tightly around his sleeve and—later—leaning into him, her shoulder against his arm as they walked. She found herself being unexpectedly, unreasonably, braced by his nearness.

As the rejections had gone on, his criticisms had lessened to the point where they walked in complete silence, a choice she was grateful for. Toward the end, he placed his free hand on hers. That support between battles might have brought tears to her eyes, if she let it. If she didn't need to continue on projecting false optimism in the face of defeat.

As they approached the final stop on the agenda, her heart rate picked up, which was surely a result of all the walking and not at all because she was about to face yet another rejection. She worked to wipe the emotional impact of the day from her expression. She needed to present an image of confidence and capability if she wanted a shot at speaking to the man in charge.

That said, she was fairly sure Edward could see everything she was feeling. He'd always had an uncanny and infuriating ability to do that. As they stood outside the brown-brick building, she swallowed hard.

Edward put a hand on her shoulder and squeezed. "I could come in with you," he said.

She knew exactly what he meant: *They'd take me seriously.*

"No, thank you. That's not necessary." She didn't want to partner with someone who was choosing to work with the duke and not her. His presence could not be more valuable than her efforts. She squared her shoulders as Andrew opened the door for her.

There wasn't just one person in the reception room. An older man in a simple but clearly expensive suit stood behind the counter, handing over a sheaf of papers to a young clerk whose fingertips were stained blue with ink. The man straightened as she entered.

"Good morning, miss. Are you lost?" His voice held genuine concern and he came around the side of the desk to stand in front of her.

There was a kindness about him. Her hopes soared. "Not lost at all. I have a two o'clock meeting. I'm a touch early, my apologies."

"Two o'clock? Your name is?"

"Fiona McTavish, from Asterly, Barnesworth & Co. I'm here to discuss a new tool that could change the fabric of society and I'm hoping you'll consider partnering with me." This was it. This was where he would sneer, or worse, turn his back and pretend she didn't exist.

He frowned. "I take it you're the Co. in Asterly, Barnesworth & Co.?"

"I am." She didn't let her voice waver. "Are you Mr. Pottinger?"

The man nodded and cleared his throat. He hemmed again and made no sign of inviting her into his office. He threw a look over his shoulder to the lad behind him, who was staring at Fiona, jaw dropped.

She couldn't let him escape. This was her chance. All morning she'd not gotten past the front desk gatekeepers. Here she had the man she wanted to see right in front of her and he hadn't run or thrown her out.

She leaned into that small miracle with all the bullheaded-ness she could muster. "Shall we discuss this in your office? I've brought a working prototype with me."

Mr. Pottinger pulled at his cravat. "This is, uh, singular."

It was the second time in two days she'd been described as such and it didn't improve her mood.

"I agree. I may not be what you're expecting. But if you would just give me a chance to show you my product..."

He took a step back, looking behind him as though the rail-thin, nervous-looking man at the counter was going to somehow rescue him from this overly forward female.

"I like women. That is, I like my wife and my daughters. I like my mother. I don't really know any other women, but as a group they're pleasant enough." Mr. Pottinger seemed to notice he was rambling and ran his hands through his hair, rubbing the back of his head.

"Well, then. I can be the next woman that you know." She forced a sense of cheeriness into her voice that she did not feel. Pottinger looked like a mouse cornered by the kitchen cat.

Lord, please don't let him run.

His face had gone beet red and he wrung his hands as he spoke. "It pains me to turn you away. It does. But the truth is, I wouldn't know how to go about working with a woman."

"It's not too unlike working with a man," she said encouragingly. "Here. Let's start again. I'm Fiona McTavish." She thrust her hand out to him.

He paused, eyes darting to either side of him, before taking her hand and hesitantly drawing it to his lips and giving it a perfunctory kiss.

Everything in her deflated and she drew her hand back.

He seemed to sense that he'd done the wrong thing, because he sighed and tugged again at the neck of his shirt. "You see? I can't work with a woman. What would we talk about?"

"The product?" She hadn't realized that small talk would be a necessary part of any bargain made.

He shook his head. "A good working relationship is a meeting of the minds. You don't come to understand a person by solely talking about a product. What if I cursed in front of you? I'm not used to watching my language unless I'm at home with the missus. And where would we go to do business over lunch? None of the clubs would admit you and I'm not taking a woman to a tavern."

What an unbelievably ridiculous reason to lose her dream—a bloody pub lunch. "I don't *need* food. I've gone days without it. And I work in a factory, so I can curse with the best of them, you old swag-bellied numpty."

She'd meant it as a jest, to put him at ease, but Mr. Pottinger took another two steps backward until he was butting up against the solid wooden desk behind him.

The deal was slipping away and try as she might, she could not hold on to it.

"I wish you the best in your endeavors. I truly do. We just aren't a good fit." He bowed and shuffled to the side until he was no longer trapped by the desk. He bowed again before fleeing through a door.

The clerk, who had spent the past few minutes watching in awe, suddenly found great interest in the tip of his quill.

Fiona swallowed and picked up her bag. The bag that held her proposal and test results and a working prototype. The bag she'd been lugging around London all day, all for naught, apparently.

~

The Fiona that exited the nondescript brown town house was not the Fiona that Edward had watched enter. Her shoulders sagged, and she'd lost the determination she'd strode in with. Her hands clutched the handle of her satchel as though it were a lifeline, and as she got closer, he could see a suspicious shine in her eyes that made him want to storm into that building, find whoever had made her cry, and drop them out the window.

"How did it go?" he asked as he settled himself next to her, matching her dejected pace. They didn't seem to have a set destination as they walked but Fiona had never been someone comfortable being still. She was always moving, and on the occasions that her body was still, her mind was skipping from one place to another.

She didn't look up at him; her focus seemed to be firmly on her slippers. "His nae was kinder than the others. But still nae."

"What will you do next?" Hopefully, she would call it quits and send Barnesworth or Asterly to do the business side of things. The sooner she was done traipsing about London the better for his sanity.

How the devil was he supposed to concentrate on his responsibilities knowing she was swanning through London with only a scrawny young footman to protect her—not even the proper parts of London, but the rougher parts where a lady shouldn't set foot?

Not that Fiona was a lady, and that was the problem.

If she were a lady, their story would be very different.

If she were a lady, even just a third daughter of a baron, he could have married her without subjecting her and his family to cruel gossip.

But she wasn't, and so here they were.

"I guess I'll just start again tomorrow."

Which was the response he should have expected. He'd never met anyone—man or woman—as stubborn as she was. She would keep pushing forward despite the obstacles and with no regard for the pain he knew it caused her.

There were plenty of places Edward was supposed to be that didn't include walking through working London with the woman he had sworn to avoid. He could justify it when he was looking out for her safety, but now that her meetings were finished, he really should send her back to the house so that he could get to parliament, where he was currently missing an important session about the king's latest taxes.

But the crestfallen look on her face, the listless walk, the desperation with which she grabbed her bag...They tugged at his heart too much to leave. As much as he wanted to be anywhere but next to her, he wanted to drive away her heartache more.

"Come." He signaled to the driver who'd been following them the entire day. "I have something to show you, and it's too far to walk."

Swinton pulled the carriage up beside them and a footman leapt from the back and opened the door.

"I dunnae like surprises." She made no move to get in.

He refrained from rolling his eyes. "That's because when it's a surprise, you're not in charge. Get in." He offered her his hand to help her up. After a long pause, she accepted it.

He faced her footman and gestured to the empty spot at the back of the carriage. The lad took a deep breath, as though he was about to protest, but then made his way to the dickey seat.

Once Edward was inside, an uncomfortable silence descended. Fiona slumped against the seat and her gaze traveled to the window, which she would stare out of wistfully until she'd jerk and return her attention to him and then to her lap.

After this occurred for the third time, Edward decided that he could not bear to watch her disappointment any longer. She needed something to keep her occupied until they reached their destination. "So, have you named them?" he asked.

"Pardon?"

"Your matches. Do they have a name?"

Her brows furrowed. "I have nae thought about it."

"You could call them Quickfire."

Fiona's eyes came alight with thought. She pursed her lips as she always did whenever she mulled over a puzzle. He felt a tug of satisfaction at the change in her, that he had been the one to give her a moment's relief from her sadness, even if she hadn't noticed.

She wrapped a stray auburn curl around her finger before tucking it behind her ear. That small movement, one she'd made over and over during their time together, snagged around his midsection. She was the most beautiful creature he'd seen, if not in a strictly fashionable way. She was too vibrant and raw to blend in with society's beauties. That copper lock of hair that had escaped the confines of her coiffure was the barest hint of the wild, fiery curls that he would give his soul to bury his hands in.

Edward shifted in his seat, the heated thoughts giving rise to unexpected twitching. "Redheads," he said. "You could dye the tips red to show which end lights, and it would be a subtle nod to the creator."

She liked that suggestion. He could tell from the way her eyes softened and a slight smiled formed. She cocked her head, studying him. The suspicion and hostility with which she'd viewed him the past few days was replaced by a tentative appreciation.

"You muddle me, Your Grace. I don't know what to make of you minute to minute."

He couldn't say the same. She was exactly who she always had been—the woman he'd fallen in love with. If she was confused, it was because he'd kept so much of himself hidden.

He took a fortifying breath. "You have me at your mercy for the next half hour. Ask me whatever you wish." He steeled himself for the question he thought would come: *Why did you leave?*

"Did you truly read Rousseau's work because philosophy called to you?"

That was not what he was expecting, though he shouldn't be surprised. They had spent hours discussing the work. It had formed the nexus of their first debate. "It was a text my professor had set," he admitted.

Her face fell.

"But that does not mean my views on it are any different. I think he is absurdly pessimistic."

Her disappointment quickly morphed into exasperation. "I can see *now* why you think so. Rousseau argues that mankind will never truly escape oppression and unless you're one of the oppressed, it's difficult to see his point. Only the privileged get to have such optimism."

⁓

Fiona had been so sidetracked by their debate that she'd paid scant attention to where they were going. But when the door swung open and Edward's footman flipped forward the step, all breath escaped her. She sat there, frozen, her fingers gripping the leather seat.

"You know that you're supposed to alight before I do," Edward said, but it wasn't true sarcasm in his tone. It was the kind of light teasing that made her throat fizz and lips form into an unbidden smile. She scrambled from the carriage. Once both feet were on solid ground, she looked up, holding her bonnet to her head with one hand, to take it all in.

The Royal Society. It was the epicenter of the finest minds in Europe. For centuries, the birth of scientific discovery began in this building.

She'd been here before. By here, she meant she'd been across the street, looking up at Somerset House from farther away, with its cream-colored façade, Grecian columns, and row upon row of tall glass windows. It had been the first place she'd visited when she arrived in London. She'd been too overawed to come any closer.

That Edward, the duke, would bring her here was entirely unexpected. It was the kind of thoughtful gesture she associated with Ed, the everyday man who didn't exist. But it was the duke who stood next to her, and the duke was not a man who longingly stared at a building from across the street.

No, he was a man who owned them, managed them. *Entered them.* That's why her stomach had erupted into dancing flames.

"It's beautiful," she whispered. It was quite possibly the most progressive, critical building in all of London. But it wasn't somewhere that women were welcome. In fact, only one woman had ever been admitted, and that was almost a century ago.

"It's not the only thing that's beautiful," Edward said.

Her pulse quickened at the compliment, but she didn't take her eyes off the building in front of her. "What are we doing here?" Because surely, surely, it couldn't be what she was thinking.

"I thought you might want to look inside." He put a hand on her lower back. Even through gloves and her velvet pelisse she could feel the warmth of his fingers. Inexplicably, the sensation flowed across her skin and a red heat crept up her neck.

She stepped away from him, fanning her face in an effort to quell the desire snaking through her. She could not entertain this want for him, no matter that she knew well what his touch could lead to, how he could make her toes curl and her skin shiver. "But I'm nae allowed in there," she said. With any luck, Edward would chalk her flustered countenance to excitement about the building in front of them.

"I am the Duke of Wildeforde; I'm allowed anywhere, and I will bring whomever I please."

It was wrong for one person to have such absolute power but in this moment, she would be grateful for it.

She let Edward guide her as his footman opened the gates. Together they strolled up to the door. He handed his card to the butler, who looked over Edward's shoulder at Fiona and grimaced a little but nevertheless, he stepped aside for both of them.

"I'll notify Sir Joseph of your presence, Your Grace. Would you like to wait in the conversation room?"

Sir Joseph. As in, *Sir Joseph Banks*. Renowned explorer, botanist, and current president of the society. The flickering of flames in her stomach transformed into wild bushfire.

"No need. I'm taking Miss McTavish on a tour. We'll be starting with the labs. Sir Joseph can meet us there if he chooses." Edward took Fiona's arm and led her past the stone staircase and down a corridor. She ran her fingers along the wallpaper. How many of her heroes had traversed these halls? What conversations had they been having as they did so?

Edward took another turn, guiding her again with a hand on the small of her back. She shivered at the touch. "I know you're a duke," she whispered. "But how, exactly, do you have free rein here?" And how did he know the place well enough to give her a tour?

He paused in front of a large portrait of Sir Isaac Newton,

somehow sensing that she would want to stop to take it in. "It is The *Royal* Society," he said while she gaped. "My cousin is the king and patron, and I donate generously."

She wanted to be taking in the magnificent work in front of her; she truly did. But her attention snagged on his words. Ed had never mentioned The Royal Society, despite their long conversations about science and philosophy.

"How long have you been doing this?"

"Roughly five years," he said, keeping his eyes trained on the painting.

Five years. He'd ended their relationship five years ago. She was not fool enough to assume that was a coincidence. But why? When he left, she'd assumed that she'd been nothing more than a brief liaison. A distraction soon discarded without a backward thought. But if she'd meant nothing to him, why his involvement here?

She turned to demand an answer, but he propelled them onward before she could voice the words. They stopped by the last door. Edward rapped sharply.

"Enter."

Her heart thrummed at the words; she held her breath in anticipation. The duke *winked*—dukes didn't wink—and opened the door.

Sir Humphry Davy was standing at a bench in the center of the room. Fiona recognized him from her issues of *Philosophical Transactions*.

He approached Edward and bowed, his smile the one of friends reacquainting. The juxtaposition should have been odd, these two very different parts of her life in the one room. But as they turned to her, she was struck by their similarities. Both intelligent men with purpose. Both accustomed to a certain level of influence.

Edward gave her a reassuring nod. "Miss McTavish, may

I present Sir Humphry Davy. Sir Humphry, Miss McTavish is an old family friend with a keen interest in chemistry."

Sir Humphry's eyes widened in surprise. "It's always a pleasure to meet a young woman with an interest in science." He brushed his lips against her glove and she nearly swooned.

"It is an honor to meet you, Sir Humphry. Your safety lamp was a product of pure genius."

"Truly?" Sir Humphry's eyebrows shot up. "I'm pleased that you found it so interesting. Are you a chemist?"

Like an eager student wanting to impress, she outlined her work. "I've created a compound that ignites when kinetic energy is applied. They're essentially matches lit by friction."

His demeanor changed from polite interest to genuine enthusiasm. "Another fire wrangler—how delightful."

Quite unbelieving that Sir Humphry Davy would have an interest in her work, she quickly told him of her research and her tutelage with John.

"Barnesworth is a remarkable fellow. If he's taken the time to teach you, you must be equally remarkable."

Delight fizzed through her, like sherbet on the tongue. Sir Humphry just called her remarkable. The man whose redesigned miners' lamp had saved thousands of lives.

It was instinct, the way she grabbed hold of Edward's hand. A sudden need to share her excitement. His bearing didn't shift; it was still duke-ishly reserved. But as he interlaced his fingers with hers and squeezed them gently, she knew he understood. And, surprisingly, there was no one else she'd rather share this moment with.

Bringing her here had been a massive miscalculation. All Edward had wanted to do was give her a happy moment to erase the disappointment of the day, and it had worked. She was as happy as he'd ever seen her.

But watching her converse with one of the brightest minds in England—holding her own entirely—just reminded him of how intelligent she was, and how vibrant and engaging and full of life she could be. His soul ached for her.

He was supposed to be moving on with his life and marrying a proper society lady. Reminders of her effervescence were not making that job any easier, and yet he couldn't take his eyes off her.

Fiona sat her briefcase on one of the long benches that ran the length of the laboratory and unlatched it.

He moved closer to see the match that she'd been talking about. His senses prickled at her nearness and he inhaled deeply—and gagged, turning away and bringing his fingers to his mouth to keep the sudden need to retch at bay. "What *is* that?"

Fiona looked up at him, her eyes dancing. "It's the sulfur," she said. "You get used to it."

"I'd rather not, if we're being honest." Yet, he was utterly unsurprised that she had. Where the women of his acquaintance would likely swoon, Fiona got her hands dirty.

There was a chuckle from Sir Humphry, and the older gentleman passed Edward a handkerchief, thankfully scented with sandalwood. "A hazard of the profession, Your Grace."

Fiona removed a metal box from her satchel and opened it. Within were a handful of long, thin sticks of straw-colored wood—not much thicker than his widest hat pin—half the length of which were covered in a thick, brown metallic coating and the tips of which had been dipped into a black substance.

Fiona pulled the match through a tube of gritty paper. It popped and hissed and a cascade of sparks showered the bench. At the center, her fingers held one tip of the wood. At the other was a small but steady flame.

She held it up so they could better see it, the flame reflected in her eyes. The red light in them glowed and all breath escaped him.

She was magical. She was brilliant. She was not of his world.

Sir Humphry clapped heartily and Edward jerked at the sound. He'd been so transfixed by her and her achievement that he'd forgotten anyone else was in the room. He joined the applause. "Brava," he said. "That is a most remarkable stick of fire."

Before he could say anything else, Sir Humphry peppered her with questions as he picked up a match and studied it— sniffed it, rolled it between his fingers, pinched it—all the while maintaining a stream of conversation that Edward had no role in. But he was more than happy to stand there quietly and watch.

An hour later, as they walked out of the quadrangle and onto The Strand, Fiona was letting her briefcase swing animatedly, a little too animatedly given Edward now knew what it contained.

She had exchanged addresses with Sir Humphry and promised him a tour of the firm, should he ever visit Abingdale. The clod-headed imbeciles she'd spoken with that day may not have been able to appreciate her genius, but the country's preeminent chemist did and she practically danced to the carriage.

When he climbed in after her, her feet were tapping away as though she were dancing a joyful jig. He couldn't match her enthusiasm, nonsensical jealousy still nagging at him.

She didn't notice. Instead, she leaned over, took his face between her hands, and kissed him. It was quick and firm and full of impulsive celebration. Before he could respond, before he could wrap his hands around her and sink into that kiss like a man happy to drown, she pulled away.

"Thank you," she said. "I will never forget what you just gave me."

There was no logical excuse for what happened next. He was simply an idiot fueled by envy and a desire to keep the moment alive: "I could get it for you. I could make them give you a contract."

Chapter 10 ⸺

Her elation was snuffed in a heartbeat, all of the last hour's excitement extinguished by his block-headed arrogance. "You did not, in earnest, say that?"

Of all the witless offers he could have made, nothing could have infuriated her more—a fact he clearly couldn't understand judging by the confusion on his face.

She climbed back out of the carriage.

Heedless of the danger he was in, the duke continued as he followed her. "You need a sale and I have the means to get it for you."

Exasperating man. "I dunnae want you to *get it* for me. I want to get it on my own."

He threw up his hands, looking at her as though she were a mad creature. "Why? What is the point of fighting and failing when you don't have to?"

Exasperation turned to fury. She jabbed a finger into the costly fabric of his coat, causing him to take a step back. "Ye do not ken what it's like to be told ye cannae yer entire life.

Ye cannae go to university because a woman has no need of books. Ye cannae live alone, because it's not 'proper' for a woman. Ye cannae dress as ye please because, och, we don't want to offend a man's sensibilities."

With each point she made, she pushed forward, until he was butting up against the lacquered wood. "I'm tired of being told that I cannae because I'm a woman, when I bloody well can. I made these matches. I can sell them. I don't need or want yer help. Is that clear?"

He opened and closed his mouth a few times before finally responding. "It seems foolish to risk all your effort for your principles."

"For some of us, principles are all we have." But as she said the words, they rang false. She would give up her principles in a heartbeat if it meant being able to put her own roof over her head. The truth was, she didn't want *his* help. She didn't want to owe him anything. Even today was too much. She had been a fool to accept it.

"Come on, Andrew." She reached into the carriage, grabbed her bag, and then marched off.

"Where are you going?" Edward called.

"Back to the house," she snapped, without even turning in his direction.

"Well, you're going in the wrong direction."

When she turned around, Edward was leaning against the carriage with his arms crossed. He had a smug look on his face that made her already heated temper flare. She resumed marching, this time in the opposite direction. Andrew trailed after her.

She was ten feet past the duke when he started walking behind her. She stopped. "What are ye doing?"

"Escorting you home." He held out an elbow for her to grasp.

Instead, she put both hands behind her back. "I don't need an escort."

"You're an unmarried woman walking through London. You need an escort."

In Abingdale she walked miles home by herself each night, yet in London couldn't walk six feet on her own. How had the women of high society not rebelled? The lack of autonomy over their own movement was abhorrent. Thank God she would soon be out of London, away from this ridiculous expectation.

"Andrew is escorting me."

The duke fixed Andrew with an intimidating stare and the tips of her footman's ears turned bright red.

Andrew rubbed his hands together, staring determinedly down at his feet. "She needs a chaperone, Your Grace," the boy mumbled.

Edward frowned. "Chaperones are dowdy old spinsters. Are you a dowdy old spinster, Andrew?"

Andrew's voice was steadier now and he almost met the duke's stare. "No, Your Grace. But I'm better than nothing."

Fiona wanted to cheer. Edward's face suggested that he'd never had a footman challenge him in his life. Andrew, a touch pale from the encounter, nudged her forward, seemingly keen to put distance between himself and the duke.

"Well done, Andrew," she murmured. "That was smashing. Once we get to the end of the street, do you ken which way we turn?" Fiona whispered, flicking her gaze over her shoulder and seeing that Edward still followed them.

"No, miss."

"Well then, let's just turn left."

The next street was a long one and was taking them

in roughly the right direction. She walked briskly, Andrew matching her furious pace.

He was right. That fact was almost as frustrating as what Edward was right about: today she'd been rejected over and over, not because of the quality of her idea, but because she was *Miss* McTavish, not Mr.

Well, to hell with the men who couldn't see past the dress she was wearing. Their rejections weren't a reflection of her talent or her worth; they were illustrations of how murky the lens of social perception was. She could be the most intelligent person in a room, and she would be thought less of because she was a woman. The quality of her product would always be marred by the sex of its creator.

If she was going to succeed, she needed to remove that lens from the equation.

She needed to be a man.

Fiona will become Finley.

So far, no one—not the magistrate, not the constables, not the prison guards—had guessed that Finley was a woman. The only man who'd fathomed it was that fellow inmate, and even that was only because she'd forgotten to lower her voice.

She could do this. She could pass herself off as a businessman.

Once her matches were in production and were changing the world, she would reveal herself as a woman, and in doing so, change the world in a different way. She would prove that women scientists—women in general—had something to offer beyond tea and conversations about the weather.

But first, she needed to enact her charade.

They walked in silence up Pall Mall, Fiona's new plan running through her head at breakneck speed. They turned right down St James Street, and right again until they were thoroughly lost. Frustrated, and with the blisters on her heel rubbing raw, she came to a stop and sighed.

"Andrew, please go ask the duke which way we need to go."

There was no need to ask. Edward had caught up to them the moment they stopped and was looking down at her with a gratified smirk. "It's left down here. Are you sure you don't want to take the carriage? You're limping."

"I'm perfectly well, thank you," she said.

"Stubborn mule," he muttered. They walked—she hobbled—in burdened silence until they reached the inter-section of Berkeley Square and Mount Street, where traffic had come to a snarling halt. An overturned cart had scattered barrels of lamp oil across the sidewalk, which was now coated with the thick liquid.

"Take my hand," Edward said. "You can barely walk as it is."

And that was the problem with the duke. It wasn't an offer or request; it was a demand. If he'd asked, then perhaps she would have accepted. Heaven only knew her feet were killing her. But it was the principle of the thing.

In hindsight, she should have looked past his arrogance this one time. Or asked Andrew for help. Or at least have let the footman take her bag rather than wallowing in her snit.

As she lifted her skirts with her free hand and tiptoed her way through the slippery mess, her feet gave way beneath her. Instinctively, one arm hugged the satchel, protecting its contents as she went down. She fell hard on her hand, her hip, and then her head, which smacked on the pavement with a heavy thud.

Ouch. Ouch, ouch, ouch, ouch, ouch, ouch, ouch.

She exhaled sharply, hoping the breath would take with it some of the pain. She couldn't tell what was worse—the throbbing of her skull or the shooting pain in her wrist.

Edward was by her side instantly, his hands going to her head and feeling her skull gently with his fingers. She winced as they found a swollen egg.

"Can you sit?"

She nodded, then immediately regretted the movement for the throbbing it triggered.

He tucked an arm behind her shoulders and helped her sit upright. The movement, the pain, the god-awful stench of whale oil—she swallowed hard in an effort to withstand the nausea.

"You should have just let me help you across."

"Thank ye. That's very helpful," she muttered.

He sighed. "What hurts?"

Everything. But that wasn't precisely the truth. "Everything from my hip upwards." She shifted a bit, testing the different muscle groups. "But my wrist. Definitely my wrist."

Edward gently undid the buttons of her soiled glove and those on the wrist of her definitely destroyed pelisse, heedless of the stains he was getting on his own attire. Softly, he turned the sleeve up. The swelling had already started.

"Can you stand?"

She nodded gently and let him help hoist her up, too sore to be embarrassed. She wobbled as she stood, almost toppling face-first into him, and he grabbed both of her arms.

"Take the bag," Edward said to Andrew, who was standing there with his mouth open in abject horror. "The carriage is stuck in the traffic. It'll be quicker to carry you home," Edward said to her.

"Whoa, whoa, whoa." She recoiled and almost ended up on her arse again. "I can walk." She was *not* about to rest in his arms again. No way, no how, not going to happen.

He sighed. "I'll carry you over the oil slick at least," he

said and then scooped her into his arms without seeking any further permission.

The sudden feeling of being swept off her feet set her pulse racing. They were close enough for her to feel his warmth and to catch his scent—that hint of ink and leather that had imprinted itself onto her nucleus. She inhaled—for the relief from the stench of oil only, of course—and immediately felt her heart rate slow and a sense of calm descend that did not mask the pain, but somehow dulled it.

While part of her was eager to be back on her own feet, another part wanted to burrow into him. And *that* realization was worse than the blisters, the fall, and the rejections combined.

Chapter 11 ——————————

Edward stalked in circles at the bottom of the stairs in the great hall. Fiona had tried to walk home, but a minute after he put her down, her knees had buckled. Luckily, he was close enough to catch her before she hit the ground again. He ignored all her further protests and carried her home.

The doctor had arrived a quarter hour ago and promptly shooed Edward out of Fiona's bedroom. So here he was, pacing, with the memory of his misstep circling in his mind.

She had come to life in that laboratory. As the scientist had enthused over her work, her smile had shone brighter than the flames she created. Their discussion went deep, quickly, far beyond what Edward's understanding of chemistry could follow. As she'd scrawled her postal address on a blank page of Sir Humphry's notebook, Edward had seen green.

She *liked* Sir Humphry. She was genuinely pleased to be in his company. What's more, she could be in his company without facing the wrath of the *ton*, and he'd felt stupidly, boyishly, jealous.

So he'd offered to solve her business problems for her, which had gone down as well as he'd have expected had he taken one moment to think it through. But he hadn't thought and now she was injured, which was not actually his fault, but he still felt responsible.

Just as Edward was ready to storm back upstairs, the doctor appeared.

"Well? Will she be all right? How serious are her injuries?" Edward asked once the sawbones had reached the foyer.

"It's a minor concussion. She'll be fine. Make sure she's drinking lots of fluids and that a maid is around to keep her awake for the next few hours."

Edward hadn't realized just how tightly his body was drawn until the doctor's words loosened it. Fi should be fine. "And her wrist?"

The doctor removed his spectacles and rubbed his handkerchief over the lenses. "Her wrist is mildly sprained. A compress and immobilization are all it needs. I'll be back in the morning to check on her."

Edward had to batten down the temptation to force the doctor to spend the night in the corridor outside Fiona's room. Even in his current state, he could see it was unnecessary. After seeing the doctor out, Edward went down to the kitchens. The bustling room stopped still as he entered. Scullery maids stood there, slack-jawed, hands submerged in dishwater. There was a *thud* as a kitchen maid dropped a lump of dough on the long wooden bench.

It had been a while since he'd ventured downstairs. Half of the faces staring at him were unfamiliar. Mrs. Price, after taking a quick moment to compose herself and check the pins in her cap, bustled up to him, wiping her hands on her apron. "Your Grace," she said as she curtseyed. "How may I be of assistance?"

"Miss McTavish is upstairs, injured."

"I heard, Your Grace. The doctor ordered a poultice for her wrist and one for the bump on her noggin."

"Is it ready?"

The cook hesitated, unused to his presence, let alone his interrogation. "Just about, Your Grace."

"And has dinner been sent to her room?"

"We were planning on sending it up with the poultice."

Edward nodded and clasped his hands in front of him. "Very well."

Mrs. Price looked over her shoulder at the pot boiling on the stove, then back in his direction. "Is there something else I can help you with, Your Grace?"

"Not at all." But he didn't move.

Edward was fairly sure she didn't mean for him to catch her exaggerated eye roll as she turned back to her staff. With a swish of her wooden spoon, she got the kitchen back in production. As they chopped and kneaded and tidied, the maids continued to send him furtive, speculative glances. Used to such attention, Edward didn't outwardly shift, but inside he was conscious of the stir he was causing. Downstairs gossip was the most sought-after chatter in London, simply because there was always a kernel of truth to it. What his staff would make of his interest in Fiona, he didn't know. But he paid them well enough to keep their thoughts to themselves. Simmons hadn't so much as batted an eye when Edward had asked them to conceal the truth about Fiona.

After a few minutes, the cook pulled the bell cord and one of the housemaids entered, stumbling over thin air as she realized Edward was in the room. Half her attention remained on him as she was handed a tray with two covered dishes and thick poultices that lay across it. Warily, she came to stand in front of him.

"I'll take it." He accepted the tray from the housemaid, ignoring her widening eyes and open mouth. A duke carrying a food tray might be unusual, but it was his house, and he could do what he liked.

He got more than a few odd stares from the footmen as he made his way to Fiona's bedroom but met each one with a raised eyebrow. Their curiosity quickly shifted to their shoes or the ceiling.

Outside Fiona's room, he set the tray onto the hall table and knocked softly. After a moment, she opened it. Her unbound hair fell in loose waves. She was wrapped from neck to ankle in a thick, serviceable robe, and from beneath the hem her stockinged feet showed. There was no reason for the sight to suck the breath from him, but it did.

"Why are you not in bed?"

"Because ye knocked on the door," she said.

"Why is your maid not answering?"

She sighed. "Because I don't have a maid. Honestly, Ed, I have a splitting headache; church bells are ringing in my ears and I'm nae entirely sure that I'm not aboot to vomit on your feet. Are you here for a reason other than to interrogate me about who opens my bedroom door?"

"I...yes. I am." He picked up the tray from the table.

She blinked in surprise. "You brought me supper? Did you go downstairs? Yourself?"

The constant implication that he was doing something he shouldn't by visiting his own kitchen was beginning to rankle. "Is that a surprise?"

She cocked her head, one hand on her hip. "When was the last time you were in the kitchens?"

Not since Mrs. Price's birthday six months ago. He made a point of visiting senior staff personally for their birthdays, but other than that once-a-year trip, he hadn't ventured into that room since his father had passed.

Dukes didn't spend time in their kitchens, even if they'd practically lived there as children.

"They're my kitchens. I can visit if I want to."

"Of course." She held out her hands to take the tray. Her wrists peeked out from beneath her robe, the left one still clearly swollen and turning a deep purple.

"You're not carrying the tray, you obstinate woman."

Sighing once again, she stepped aside and motioned for him to come in. That simple movement appeared rickety and off balance and if he'd had a free hand, he would have steadied her with it.

"Bed," he said as he took the tray to the dressing table by the window.

She did as he'd asked, probably because she was about to collapse and not because he'd suggested it. She sat against some pillows, her head leaning back against the headboard.

"How are you feeling?" he asked.

"Like a right dunce. I've never claimed to be the most graceful of women but ending up on my arse in the middle of Mayfair is a touch beyond my usual clumsiness. Thank you, by the way, for carrying me home."

There was a softness to her voice, and the lamplight illuminated her copper hair with layers of gold. The combination lit a warmth within him, the heat unfurling in his belly.

He coughed, hoping the sharp movement would disperse the pooling desire. "The sawbones says you're going to be fine. I have the poultices."

Edward picked up one of the two strips of cloth covered in a green, pungent paste and took it to her, grateful the smell was abhorrent enough to overwhelm his senses. Otherwise his body may have reacted to the scent of jasmine and honey that infiltrated his nose in the way it had infiltrated his mind these last five years.

Perching on the edge of the bed, he placed the poultice in his lap and motioned for her to lean forward. Thankfully, she complied without argument, but it meant she was within inches of him, her head almost resting on his chest.

Holding his breath, he gently felt for the bump, doing his best not to add to her pain. Once he found it, he gently separated her hair into two long ropes and began to knot them into braids.

"Where did you learn to do that?" Fiona asked, as he tied off the first one with a short ribbon that sat on her bedside table.

"You wouldn't believe it to look at her, but my sister was a devil child when she was younger. Refused to let the nanny touch her hair, and our mother certainly wasn't going to do it—that would require too much interaction with her children—so it fell to me." He gently tugged at a knot, teasing the hair apart.

"Did she struggle with you?"

"Strangely, no. It became our evening ritual. Then she got older and my skills were no longer needed." He'd felt the loss, when Charlotte had reached an age where she'd finally wanted a lady's maid. "But apparently those skills are still there." He tied the second ribbon and hung the braids neatly over her shoulders.

"It feels nice," she murmured as she leaned back. "No one has done my hair since Mother died."

Fi's mother had died when she was only ten. Had it truly been that long since she had help getting ready? His already low opinion of Alastair McTavish dropped even further.

Edward applied the poultice to the back of her head, wincing as she winced. He wrapped it around her forehead loosely before tucking the edges into the side.

"Now give me your hand."

There was no response. Her eyes were shut, her breathing settled. The doctor had been very clear. *Do not let her sleep.* He squeezed her shoulder. "Love, wake up."

Her eyelids fluttered for a moment before settling once more.

With both hands, he shook her gently, but she still didn't wake, so he took her chin in his hand and tipped her face toward his. "Love, wake up," he said more sternly.

Still nothing. His pulse quickened. His eyes crossed to the pitcher of water by the bed. *A terrible idea. Or is it?* He poured a little—just a few drops—on her forehead.

Her eyes opened with a start and she lurched forward, raising her hand to her head as she did. "What? What?"

His heart rate resumed its normal rhythm. "You can't sleep, Fi," he said. "The doctor said you must stay awake for the next few hours."

"But I'm so tired." It was the tone one would expect from a child complaining about having to go to bed.

"I know, love. Give me your hand." She held it out and he loosely wrapped the second poultice around it. "Sorry about the aroma."

"It stinks?" she asked.

He chuckled. "Like Hades. You honestly can't smell it?"

"Nae." She shook her head and then yawned, wincing as she did so.

With no more excuse to sit so close to her, he dragged a chair from the dresser to beside the bed. "I brought a book with me. Something to keep you awake for the next few hours."

Minutes shifted into one another and blurred into hours, only defined by the occasional tolling of the grandfather clock from elsewhere in the house. Fiona watched him as he read, taking advantage of how his gaze was trained on the pages in front of him. She let her eyes roam from the black curls that had escaped his queue to his aquiline nose to the soft pink of his lips. The way they curved and thinned and pursed as he spoke mesmerized her.

Every now and then he looked up to make sure she was still awake. Their eyes would catch, and she could feel her color rise. No, staying awake would not be a problem.

The resonance of his voice, the melodic rise and fall, bore with it memories of their time together in Abingdale, where they'd sat together in the back pew of the local church, empty on a Tuesday afternoon, and read *Conversations on the Plurality of Worlds*.

Then, like now, she'd been captivated by his hands. She'd shivered as long fingers grazed the page edges, as though those same fingers were grazing her skin. When he absently touched a fingertip to his tongue before turning a page, her sex became warm and wet as she imagined that tongue caressing her neck, his breath hot in her ear.

"Fi? Are you with me?"

She shook her head. What on earth had he just said? "Aye?"

"It's late; you should be safe to sleep now." He closed the book and uncrossed his legs. As he rose and approached the bed, her breath caught. He leaned over to place the book on the table beside her and he was mere inches from her. A frisson of energy crossed the space between and her heart skittered off rhythm.

His fingers flinched, ever so slightly, and for a moment she thought he would reach for her. Her head turned in his direction in anticipation; her tongue licked her lips as she waited for him to bend toward her.

But his hand fisted, and he cleared his throat as he stepped back.

Disappointment buried her. The brief escape from their current lives was gone. In the morning, he would once again be the Duke of Wildeforde, and she would be a working-class commoner, and their lives would be on different paths.

"Good night then," she said. A silence stretched between them. Either of them could break it to address the tension that hung in the room like a mid-winter fog. Neither did.

He nodded, proper, gentlemanly, as though he wasn't in her bedroom. "Good night. I'll send one of the maids up in the morning."

Edward had not slept well. He'd been tormented by vivid memories of Fiona, ones that had followed him for years.

The way she tasted, the way her body felt under his hands, the way she smelled, the slight mewling noise she made as they kissed. His cock went hard at the heat of the recollections.

Even once he had drifted into slumber, he couldn't escape her. Memories became fantasies, where he did more than just press her to him and ravage her with kisses. In his dreams he crossed the line he had honored in life.

He undid each button of her dress, exposing her skin to his lips. He ran a trail of kisses down her spine as his hands reached around her to stroke her silk-soft skin. She arched, her hips pushing into his groin. As she dug her fingers into his back and called out his name, his body found sweet relief.

He woke to wet sheets and the smell of sex that made his cock stiffen. Instead of fading as his eyes opened, the visions of her trailed him through the day, accosting him every time his mind wandered.

Which made focusing on budgets terribly difficult. No sooner had he read to the end of one page then he would need to go back to the top and start reading all over again as the numbers escaped him. Her presence in his house was a cursed nuisance. He had things—pressing issues—to concentrate on. How could he devote his attention to his work and his search for a wife when she was there, infiltrating his thoughts, reminding him why he had been ready to upend his life in the first place?

The arrival of his sister was a welcome interruption from his lustful woolgathering.

"Char," he said, holding his arms out as she stepped through the front door.

"Ned!" Charlotte-Rose threw herself into his arms, wrapping hers around him and squeezing tight. "I've missed you," she said into his chest.

Edward dropped a kiss on the top of her head. It was good to have her home. He stepped back, cupping his hands around her shoulders to get a better look at her. She looked healthy, if perhaps a bit tired. There were shadows under her eyes and fatigue in her movements. Her clothing had deep creases, and strands of hair had escaped from her usually flawless coiffure.

"I wasn't expecting you today. I thought you were arriving Friday."

Charlotte unfastened her pelisse and handed it to Simmons. "The inn was full, so we rode through the night."

"Did you tell them who you were? What inn was it? I'll write to them."

She rolled her eyes and unbuttoned her gloves. "I'm sure they would have found me rooms had Gunther mentioned my name, but they would have tossed someone out to do so. It's no one else's fault that I left for London earlier than expected and with no proper planning."

"No wonder you look tired," he said as he indicated to Mrs. Phillips for some tea. "You should have a bed, whether you'd sent ahead for one or not. I don't like the thought of you sleeping in a coach."

Charlotte yawned, patting his shoulder as she did so. "Relax, brother dear. I am perfectly well. There is no need to fret."

Concern for his sister's well-being was hardly fretting, but he let the aspersion pass. "Why don't you head up to your rooms? I'll have Mrs. Phillips send dinner with the tea."

"Don't be silly." Charlotte threaded her arm around his and steered them in the direction of the yellow morning room. "I haven't seen you in months. I want to know everything. How are you? How is William? Is he here?"

Edward gave a footman a nod, a signal to fetch William from his chum's residence.

As they settled into the yellow room, Charlotte regaled him with stories of her semester at Barrow House School for Ladies. In truth, she didn't need to attend. Her education had been flawless. She was fluent in four languages, played the piano, the harp, and the violin, was an adequate watercolorist, and at eighteen years old was proficient in every skill she needed in order to run her own household.

But the alternative to boarding school was to live with their mother, a fate he didn't wish on anybody.

"I swear, Edward. Two weeks with that woman was enough to drive me batty. I don't see why I couldn't have come straight to London."

"Because she is your mother and, naturally, she wants to spend some private time with you."

Charlotte slumped back in her seat, limbs sprawled

carelessly. "Well, I don't want to spend time with her. If you thought she was bad before, you should hear her now that she is unwell. I was waiting on her hand and foot. Her poor lady's maid. I don't understand how Annabeth survives in that house."

"I pay her exceptionally well." His mother's lady's maid was one of the most highly paid staff in his employ. He considered it his monster tax.

His sister continued. "The doctor says she's on the mend and will be ready to travel in a month. So let's enjoy the freedom while we have it." Charlotte straightened into a more ladylike deportment as Mrs. Phillips entered with a tray. With perfect grace, Charlotte poured his tea—black, no sugar—and passed it to him before making her own. "How are your marriage plans coming along?" she asked as she stirred.

Edward coughed, choking on his drink. Liquid sloshed over the rim of the cup as he placed it back on the table. "What"—cough—"marriage plans?"

"Don't be coy with me, Ned. I know Mother sent you a list. Hopefully yours is somewhat more palatable than the one she gave me." Charlotte grimaced.

He didn't blame her. He shuddered at the potential matches for Charlotte that his mother had sent him. That the duchess thought he would allow Charlotte to marry one of those crusty septuagenarians was absurd. Worse, even, than the list of potential duchesses his mother had given him. At least the ladies all had their teeth.

"My list was not as bad as yours," he said. "Although I was hoping for someone not so young, or so . . . bland."

Charlotte shook her head. "Well, if you don't like any of those, I'm telling you that you had best find your own bride before Mother arrives. Or she'll be choosing one for you."

That was just like his mother. The woman had ruled his

childhood with an iron fist and thought she could do the same now. "I'm the duke. I will choose my own bride."

Charlotte's eyebrows raised. "Truly? Is that how it went last time?"

No. That was definitely not how it went last time. Edward had been only fourteen years old when his mother insisted he find a bride to cover up the scandal of his father's death. He had rebelled, obviously. What fourteen-year-old wanted to tie themselves down with a fiancée?

His mistake had been voicing that objection to his mother without thought. Three days later, he found out about his own engagement in *The Times*. To the five-year-old daughter of the Earl of Crofton. A child he'd never met.

His mother's argument had been that an engagement with Amelia would give him plenty of time to sow whatever oats he needed to and gave her plenty of time to mold Amelia into the perfect duchess. While her logic may have been sound, the lack of autonomy vexed him. It was, after all, a decision he would sit across the table from his entire life.

That was not a situation he was willing to repeat.

"I have it in hand. Her assistance is not required."

Charlotte lifted the teacup to her lips and took a long sip. "Actually, about that," she said afterward, "I may have convinced her that without her help you'd make a complete mess of it."

"Why would you do that?" Oh, his sister could be diabolical.

Charlotte sighed, her expression extremely apologetic. "If she's focused on you, then she won't have time to focus on me. It was self-preservation, brother dear. Think of the list she gave me. There wasn't a man on there under sixty!"

His mother's machinations had been unnecessary. Edward would have handled it all once Char arrived in London.

"I've seen your list," he said, "and I'm not going to let you marry anyone on it. I will find you a suitable match. One that will make you happy."

Charlotte tugged at her sleeve. "I would like at least one season where I am able to meet men on my own without you or Mother marching them into my path."

"And so you turned her attentions toward me? That was your solution? Thank you. Much appreciated." His mother was an added complication he could do without.

"I *am* sorry."

Edward rubbed the spot between his eyebrows where he could feel a headache forming. "You think she'll try the same methods she did last time?"

"Oh, I know she will. She *said* she will. I'm surprised she hasn't already." Charlotte snorted.

His mother. The woman was the only person on the British Isles other than Fiona who cared not a whit for his position. "Well, I'll simply tell the editor of *The Times* not to publish anything without my direct consent." That was how he'd kept the Wildeforde name out of the paper after he ended his engagement with Amelia, and how William's antics were kept from public knowledge now. It wasn't cheap, but it was effective.

"And you really think she won't find another way to shoehorn you into an engagement you don't want?"

The sentence sent his heart thumping. His mother was absolutely capable of manipulating the situation, knowing that he wouldn't risk the scandal of another broken engagement. "Then I will find an acceptable wife before she arrives."

"Good," Charlotte said. "We have a month to find a woman that you would want to marry. I will devote all my efforts to finding you the lady of your dreams. Who do you currently have your eye on?"

Chapter 12 ──────────────

Long ago, Fiona had discovered the importance of appreciating the small things—a tree with ripening pears when her belly started to rumble, the ever-present light from the forge as she made her way through the factory at night, and now, Edward's open front door when she hadn't the energy to push it.

"Thank ye, Simmons."

"May I take your coat, Miss McTavish?" He truly was an exceptional butler. Nothing in his expression or tone gave any indication that he thought her appearance odd, despite the fact that she was dressed once more in breeches, morning coat, and wig. He must have some opinion; he seemed even more traditional than the duke.

What did *he* think of Edward's visit to her rooms last night? He must have known. Downstairs knew everything. Always.

"No, thank ye. I can put it away myself." Standing in the middle of the foyer, she had a choice—to take the stairs to the right to the guest wing and her rooms, or to go left and see Edward.

She should go right, take a long, hot bath, and wash the day off her. That's what her reasonable brain knew was the correct decision, especially given she'd kissed him yesterday and wanted to kiss him again last night. That desire had left her rattled all day—so much so that she'd barely uttered a coherent sentence at any of her meetings. Thus, she'd made it past the gatekeepers, but still it had been a "no" at every turn.

But the guest wing felt like a mausoleum—immaculately kept, but clearly not lived in. After a day of relentless disappointment, experiencing one rejection after another, she felt like company.

Perhaps it was foolish to want to see him. His attention last night could mean anything. She was, after all, a guest in his house suffering a head injury. Reading to her may have been nothing more than a host doing what he could to prevent a death from occurring under his roof.

Even if his interest had been romantic, nothing could ever come of it. Completely beside the fact that he'd already left her twice and she could never trust him, they were ill-suited. She had no interest in becoming a duchess and he had no interest in making her one.

So the stairs to the right it would be. Except somehow, she found herself veering to the left, climbing the steps with an imprudent eagerness.

In the west wing, she found more life than existed near her rooms. A footman stood at each end of the corridor and she could hear a piano coming from one of the rooms. She recognized the song. Edward had played it for her on the rickety church piano the night they had broken in.

She opened the door.

And stopped dead.

"Wilde!" a loud voice called. "You should hear—" The man speaking trailed off as he turned to face her. The music stumbled to a halt.

It was not Edward standing in front of her. It was his brother, William. Beside him, fingers still resting on the keys, was his seldom-seen sister, Charlotte-Rose.

"You're not Edward," William said. "Who are you?"

Fiona had no idea what to do other than cross her fingers and hope they didn't recognize her. There was no reason why they should. She'd never actually met them. She'd simply seen them on rare occasions at church where they sat in the first pew, reserved for the major church donors. And when at church, she wore a dress.

"I...uh...Finley McTavish. A friend of yer brother's. A pleasure to meet ye." She sketched a quick bow, praying they didn't notice the ungainliness of the movement.

"William Stirling. This is my sister, Lady Charlotte-Rose."

The resemblance between the siblings was uncanny. They both had thick, midnight-black hair, just like their brother. All three shared the same stubborn set to their jaw. *Their poor nanny.*

Their eyes were the same shade of cerulean blue ringed with dark sapphire. Unlike their brother, though, their features were softer, lending a welcoming cheeriness to their expressions.

"My lady, ye perform beautifully," Fiona said. Charlotte's playing had eclipsed Edward's, and Edward played very well.

Charlotte blushed. "Thank you, Mr. McTavish. How very kind." She stood and held out her hand, clearly expecting Fiona, *Finley*, to take it.

Good God. What do I do now? She'd not interacted with women when she was masquerading as a man. Only men.

Tentatively, she accepted Charlotte's hand and pressed it to her lips. It was a nice hand...Paler and softer than her own. The kind of hand that only proper young ladies who never undertook menial tasks managed to achieve.

Kissing it felt awkward.

Not to Charlotte, apparently. Her cheeks flushed prettily, and she looked up at Fiona through fluttering dark lashes.

Is she flirting?

Why the hell didn't Edward warn her that his siblings were coming to stay? This added a whole new level of complication. Should she reveal her true identity? Should she keep it secret? The staff had seen her in both guises, but she'd also heard Edward asking for their discretion.

Fiona was about to turn tail and head to her rooms—Ed could answer any questions his siblings had—when William picked up a pool cue and tossed it in her direction. By some holy miracle, she caught it with her uninjured hand.

"Here, take this," he said. "Edward is out, and I have no one to play with."

"Ye cannae play with yer sister?" She couldn't keep the arch tone from her voice.

He screwed his face up, as if the thought were sour. "Girls don't play billiards," he said, as though Fiona was daft not to know it. "That's why we have the piano in here. Wilde moved it so that we could be together while we played."

Edward's consideration for his sister's feelings tugged at her insides two ways—it was touching, that the Wilde-forde siblings chose to spend their time together. As an only child, Fiona spent her evenings alone. But moving the piano presupposed that as a female, his sister couldn't play billiards. When really, it was hitting a ball with a stick. The game was just physics and geometry. How hard could it be?

"I have nae played in a while," she said. "Remind me of the objective?"

"Hit that ball"—he pointed to a white ball at one end of the table—"with this cue stick, so that it hits both the red and other white ball."

Fiona quickly assessed the situation. She'd have to hit the ball at twenty degrees. She bent over the table, pulled the cue stick backward across her bandaged thumb, took a deep breath, and—

"What on earth?"

Her cue stick hit the white ball at the wrong angle, sending it off to the side, well away from her target. William snorted and his sister dissolved into giggles.

Fiona turned to face Edward. His lips were pressed tight against each other, his gaze disapproving. The duke was back. How disappointing.

"That was hardly sporting, Your Grace," she said. "I very nearly had that."

"You have an injured wrist. You shouldn't be aggravating it."

She was about to protest his high-handedness when William stepped in. "I think Finley can make his own decisions. He's a grown man, after all."

Edward gave her a *look*. But rather than correcting his brother, he addressed her. "I see you've met the family."

It cut a little, the displeasure in his tone, as though by meeting his siblings she'd delivered some kind of insult or threat. Perhaps she was to stay quiet and hidden. A secret, just like she used to be.

Ha. Good luck with that.

She settled her hip against the billiards table, presenting an appearance of comfort that she didn't quite feel. "Aye, we're becoming quite well acquainted. Does that concern ye,

Your Grace? Are ye worried about the scandalous stories we might exchange?"

Edward's lips thinned further.

"There are no scandalous stories," William huffed as he lined up his ball and took a shot. "Wilde is dreadfully dull. He's not deserving of his moniker."

Charlotte-Rose gave her brother a scowl. "William, that's not fair. Ned's not dull. He's simply interesting in a perfectly respectable way."

William snorted.

"If you're done talking about me as though I'm not in the room…"

He was getting annoyed. Good. "I don't ken that yer brother is *that* respectable," she said, delighting in the way Edward's eyes widened as though he thought she'd reveal their affair. "Did he tell ye about the time he broke into Mrs. Duggan's bakery in Abingdale?"

Discordant notes sounded as Charlotte's hand dropped to the piano in surprise. William sent a ball careening into the wrong corner of the table.

"Fi…nn." Edward's voice carried a thread of warning.

"Or the time he opened the gates to Farmer Murdoch's paddock so the sheep would get loose an' block the road to London?" At the time, he'd suggested it as a lark. Now Fi didn't know if it was perhaps his way of prolonging their affair. He had, after all, ended it the moment he returned to the capital.

"Finley, that's enough."

Charlotte didn't agree. "Finley, you are a treasure," she said. "Tell me why we haven't met before."

"You're not often in Abingdale, my lady."

"Well, I never knew I had a reason to be there." Charlotte-Rose fluttered her eyelashes again, causing heat to creep up Fiona's neck. Fi diverted her eyes.

Again, William snorted. "Don't mind Charlie, McTavish. She flirts with everyone."

He may have been trying to set Finley at ease, but it made Fiona flush deeper. Next to her, Edward cleared his throat. It was remarkable, really, the amount of expression he had in two quick coughs.

This was his displeased, this-conversation-needs-to-end cough. It was worlds away from his embarrassed, I-don't-want-this-attention cough or his we-should-find-the-nearest-quiet-corner-to-kiss cough.

Judging by the exasperated look his sister threw in Edward's direction, she was more than familiar with her brother's range of throat clearances.

"So what are you doing here, McTavish? You're far too interesting to be one of Wilde's friends," William said. He nudged her with the end of his cue stick and gestured toward the table.

"I'm in town for business." Her throat tightened at the reminder of just how bad her day had been and her voice came out slightly strangled.

Edward shot a concerned look in her direction, one she ignored because, to be honest, it stung a little, this sudden glimpse into the life she may have had, had Edward not ended things. The Stirling siblings seemed rather kind and funny, and their playful banter was not something she'd ever experienced. It was something she would have enjoyed, had Edward not been the duke and their engagement not been a sham.

She took another shot, and did at least manage to hit the red ball, even if it went nowhere near the other white one.

Oblivious to any fraught undercurrents in the room, Will clapped her on the shoulder. "Smashing. You must join us at the Macklebury ball on Friday night. These soirees are as dull as my Latin professor, and with Charlotte out this season, I'm actually going to have to show up to the respectable ones."

Edward's frown deepened. "As Mr. McTavish said, he's busy with business. I'm sure he appreciates your offer."

Fiona was sure that if Edward spoke for her once more, she'd throttle him.

"In the evenings, though?" William asked. "What kind of business is done in the evenings? Except the business of finding a spouse." William turned in her direction. "You're not in that kind of business are you, chap?"

Fiona flushed. "Nae, I most assuredly am not." She had her work, that was enough. A man would expect things from her, like her being home at a reasonable hour to cook instead of her working into the late nights. And any spouse found in London would be worse. Expectations of a common woman were onerous enough. Expectations of a lady were detestable.

"Capital. Then you can come with us Friday night."

Fiona looked to Edward. It was clear he didn't want her to attend. Whatever spark she'd felt between them the previous night had burned out. "I don't think yer brother wants me there, but thank ye for the invitation. I should go wash up."

There was a dejected slump to Fiona's shoulders as she left the room, and the look Charlotte gave Edward was mildly reproachful. He felt bad, of course he did, but it was a terrible idea for Fiona and his siblings to engage with one another. If they were seen being friendly and her ruse was discovered, Charlotte and William would be considered guilty of deception by association.

And society was unforgiving when it felt wronged. If he had to hurt Fiona's feelings a little to protect his family and their name, he would do it.

Charlotte shifted on the piano bench to watch William as he carefully lined up the three balls and struck them with marksman-like precision. Why Will couldn't manage his own life with the same care and rigor he gave to billiards, Edward couldn't fathom for the life of him.

"Finley seems like a lovely fellow," Charlotte said. "Although I do not for the life of me understand what he's doing *here*."

Edward couldn't blame her. They rarely had guests in their London residence and when they did, those guests were not working men. "He's a partner in Asterly, Barnesworth & Co."

"As in, John Barnesworth? Your friend from school?" Charlotte asked, her eyes brightening. "You haven't mentioned him in an age."

Edward hedged. He and John had been friends, until John had discovered his affair with Fiona. Now they were barely on speaking terms.

"Yes, that Barnesworth. And Finley is here because I'm doing Asterly a favor." It wasn't untrue. If Asterly had known of Fiona's assault charges and that the only way to keep her from prison was to have her as a guest, he would have insisted Edward step in.

William snorted. "Because Asterly married Amelia for you after you cast her aside and now you owe him one?" William's voice may have been light, but the sharp bite of his words was intentional.

Charlotte frowned as she always did when her brothers fought, which was why Edward insisted William reside at Wildeforde House whenever Charlotte was visiting, so she wouldn't know the extent of her brothers' estrangement.

"Asterly is my friend and friends do favors."

"Well"—Charlotte clapped her hands together—"I, for one, am looking forward to getting to know him. My interest is quite piqued."

Edward ran a hand through his hair. His sister could be tenacious when she'd taken a shine to something. "I'd prefer it if you both kept as far from Finley as possible. He's a nice enough lad but doesn't belong here."

That was the hard truth of it. If Fiona had belonged, if there had been any chance of bringing her into the family without simultaneously hurting all involved, he would have done it.

"Edward, that is quite possibly the least charitable thing I've heard you utter in a long time," Charlotte said. "Just because a person hasn't been brought up as a member of our society doesn't mean we can't show them good manners as a host."

"Hear! Hear!" William said with a smirk. "I would think the perfect Duke of Wildeforde would want us to demonstrate the graciousness that befits a family of our standing."

Will could be an utter pestilence. He wouldn't have paid a second's notice to Fiona if he hadn't seen how much Edward didn't want him to. "Don't push me, William. *Finley* is here because I don't have another option. But the moment he sells his matches and finalizes his other affairs"—that blasted trial—"he's gone and we won't see him again."

Chapter 13 ————————————

Fiona left Faulkner and Sons on her third day of visiting distributors feeling as dejected as she had on the first.

True, her disguise had meant she was at least bypassing the gatekeepers that were the front-end secretaries, but the initial pitch was as far as she was getting.

In a good meeting, the businessmen would ask a handful of questions before rejecting her. In a bad one, it was a "many thanks, but no" before she'd even finished.

Their excuses varied.

I'm not looking to expand into new industries.

It's an untested product, thus too great a business risk.

Mass production of a product that spontaneously combusts is an unjustifiable hazard.

And her favorite:

Why on earth would I invest in a product that makes life easier for chambermaids? They don't have the blunt to make purchases.

Through each excuse she'd maintained a polite façade and

put forth what she thought were relevant counterpoints and assurances. But it got her nowhere. She had one more day of meetings lined up. If she couldn't close a deal then, she wasn't quite sure what to do next.

"Finley!" A hand closed on her shoulder and she spun around, heart racing at the sudden bellowing in her ear.

William stood, hands on thighs, puffing. "I've been calling your name for half a block. Could you truly not hear me?"

"I...uh..." It was not so much that she was hard of hearing and more that she was unused to responding to a name that wasn't hers. "Sorry. I was deep in thought."

He wrinkled his nose briefly. "Huh. Can't say that I've ever been that deep in thought, but to each his own. Where are you off to?"

"Nowhere in particular." Fiona had no more meetings scheduled for the day and had planned on returning to Edward's to distract herself with a letter that had arrived from Amelia that morning.

"Capital," William said. "Come with me to White's."

"White's?"

White's was an incredibly exclusive male-only club that only the crème de la crème of society had membership to. Some men—lords, their sons and brothers—had membership practically at birth. Others languished on the waitlist for years.

White's was the epitome of everything that was wrong with a society that favored men above women and titled men above all. But some sick fascination in her couldn't pass up the opportunity to agree and take a peek inside.

William hailed a cab and made the kind of jovial, light conversation Fiona hadn't known she'd been craving. He didn't ask any questions of her, and instead he regaled her with stories of the numerous pranks his posse had inflicted on the scholars of Oxford.

She took some pleasure in the tales, particularly given these scions of political and scientific endeavor worked so hard to keep women like her outside of the academic community. By the time they'd reached St James Street, she was in a fit of laughter.

William exited the hackney cab and strode past the dual lampposts and up the short flight of stairs to the plain brown door of White's with its gleaming brass knocker and handles.

As William reached the top step, an older man in dignified livery opened the door, greeting him with a bow and Fiona with a respectful nod.

She nodded in response, holding her breath as she waited for the man to spot her as a fraud as quickly as the staff at Edward's home had. But there was no grand denunciation and as she crossed the threshold, she released her breath with a *whoosh*. Unfortunately, her sense of foreboding did not escape with it.

At the register, William signed his name, the date, and in the "guest" column—*Finley McTavish of Abingdale*.

It was the first time she'd seen her alias in writing and the flowing text further fueled her anxiety. For the past few days, she'd fooled people only out of necessity: for her safety or to get past the barriers that Fiona couldn't.

This—visiting White's purely for entertainment purposes, exposing herself to a group of the most powerful men in England, making a mockery of one of their most hallowed spaces—it suddenly felt a little daft.

The consequences of being found out, the inevitable black-balling of her career, didn't seem quite worth her curiosity. But it was too late to back out. William was striding down the corridor, without pausing his conversation, assuming she followed.

She increased her pace to keep up with him, trying to refrain from feeling the edges of her wig or adjusting the bands that kept her breasts bound. She didn't want to do anything that might give the game away.

They would stay for a drink and then she would make some excuse to leave. Hopefully, she could be in and out without anyone noticing, and then she would store the memory away someplace special.

Another footman opened a set of double doors that led into the morning room, where men sat in groups on plush chairs, servants stationed in intervals along the perimeter, ready to respond.

And there, at the tables by the wide double bow windows looking out on the street, sat Edward. The light that streamed through the window caught the peaks and valleys of his curls, creating pockets of silver within the midnight black that her fingers itched to explore. It emphasized the furrow between his brows and the straight line of his jaw, and for a brief second she imagined running her hand along it, reaching his throat, shifting and cupping the back of his neck.

He was deep in conversation, his gestures graceful and restrained but carrying a confidence that was uncomfortably appealing, that stirred something inside her that she wished had stayed dormant.

He turned, his mouth cocked in a half smile that disappeared when he saw her. His lips thinned and his eyes widened. Even from this distance she could see him stiffen.

So much for going unnoticed.

"Yer brother does nae look too pleased to see us here. Should we go?" she whispered to William as he scanned the room.

"Ignore my brother," he said quietly. "He's dining with Liverpool. Dreadfully dull fellow."

Fi's heart stumbled at the mention of Liverpool's name. Disappointment flooded her, quenching any spark that had just ignited. "I did nae expect His Grace to be friends with the earl. I thought his political views were somewhat more progressive than that."

During their brief affair, they had strongly debated many social and political issues. But while Edward had always been more moderate in his ideas for achieving reform, they had always agreed on the principle need for it.

She had never anticipated that he would dine with the Tory leader, a man who advocated for fewer rights for the working class.

"Ah! Dunley, old fellow." William waved to a group of men seated in the corner of the room. "We have a new pal."

Fiona dragged her gaze from the duke and his companion. She had never seen a more vivid riot of color in one place. Each of the men lounging in the chairs had at least three hues to their outfit, in silks and lace no doubt worth more than her entire wardrobe combined. These were the type of men Amelia called dandies.

Swallowing, she allowed herself to be towed in their direction. When a footman pulled out a chair for her, she mimicked the cross-legged affections of the party, resting both hands on her knee.

"May I present Mr. Finley McTavish," William said. "He's a country boy staying with Wilde while in London and I'm determined to see him thoroughly ruined while in town."

Oh, God.

Fiona ducked her head, a hot flush creeping up her cheeks. "Gentlemen. Pleased to make yer acquaintance."

"Tell us," one of the dandies said. "What are you doing in

London? And why are you residing with the *Anti-Wilde*? I couldn't imagine a more tiresome host."

Her instinct was to defend Edward. He was arrogant and overbearing, but he was a man who'd moved his sister's piano so the family could be together, and was a conscientious estate owner—even if she hated being his tenant. He'd walked into last year's riots with nothing but his presence to defend him. He was far from tiresome.

But she also couldn't look past the person he was currently associating with. Whenever she thought she was finding scraps of Edward beneath the duke, something like this would crop up to show her just how wrong she was.

The men were staring at her expectantly. She'd forgotten to answer their question. "I've developed a tool to make it easier to light fires. It's safe, easily portable, and will significantly shorten the time it takes a chambermaid to prepare a room."

"Why on earth would anyone buy those?" The derision in the dandy's voice matched the tone she'd been dealing with these past days. It was frustrating, this complete disregard for the humans who made their privileged lives function.

But if the distributors she'd spoken to had no care for the working class they'd sprung from, she was mad for thinking these flouncing, insubstantial sugar puffs would.

"A chambermaid's day is eighteen hours long," she said through gritted teeth. "With this device they have an extra two hours' sleep in the morning."

There was a collective eye roll from the men in front of her. One of them—ridiculous in his purple-and-blue paisley waistcoat—turned to William. "I thought you had brought us someone fun to play with."

William colored slightly. "Finley is fun. At least, he has the potential to be, and you can't criticize a man for wanting to better himself—what's the last useful thing you accomplished, Cossington?"

"Better question, has Cossington ever accomplished anything?"

There was rolling laughter around the table. Paisley Waistcoat grimaced. "Yes, yes. Very droll. My wife throws a better party than all of yours." He finished his drink and motioned for another.

One of the other men, whose morning coat was edged in gold thread—real, no doubt—turned to Finley. "I hate to be the bearer of bad news, chap, but no one is going to pay good money to make a chambermaid's life easier."

The impact of his comment was softened only because Fiona had come to the same conclusion that morning. Hence her pessimistic woolgathering when William had ambushed her.

"Well, seems like the businessmen of London agree with you. Can I get a drink?" Whiskey would be preferable, but at this point she'd take anything. Her eyes drifted back over to Edward, laughing with the man who stood so solidly and immovably in the way of crucial electoral reform.

A nearby footman appeared with a crystal cut glass and poured Fiona a dram of whiskey from the decanter on the table.

She swallowed it in one go.

One of the dandies—whose costume was less ornate but no less expensive—took pity on her. "You know, you might get a better result talking to someone like the Earl of Livingworth. He's got plenty of spare blunt and a bleeding heart. Insufferable to be around, though."

"True," one of the other men said. "Or you could try Viscount Chester. Less a bleeding heart and more of a betting man. He's been known to take a gamble on new business ventures. Sometimes it pays off; he was one of the lucky bastards that invested in the Andaman Silk Company."

"Didn't he lose a thousand quid trying to manufacture a ventilating hat?"

For the first time that day, Fiona felt a little bit of hope. She pulled a notebook out of her satchel and wrote down all the names the men threw out, ignoring the scorn and jibes that went with them.

Yes, a distributor would have been ideal—someone with connections in London households who could help her scale her product quickly and successfully. But her matches had proved to be too much of a risky endeavor for men who needed to balance the books every month.

A lord with those same connections and enough wealth to invest? That's what she needed. A little voice in the back of her head threw out its own names. Benedict. John. Edward.

She discounted Benedict; he had the money but not the London connections. The same could be said for John. Edward had both, but she wasn't about to ask for his help. Especially not while he was consorting with the enemy.

"So, what are the plans for tonight, gentlemen?" William asked the men at the table.

"Boodle's for a meal, a few hands at the Black Dwarf, and then rounding off the night at Madame Leverie?" Gold Thread asked.

"A solid plan," Paisley Waistcoat responded. The men around her raised their glasses and murmured their assent, so she raised hers and grunted.

"You with us, McTavish?" William asked.

Was she? A night drinking and gambling in London with a strange group of men? For one, she had no money. For another, it seemed rather risky. The more time she spent with these men, the more likely it was that one of them would discover her secret.

But what could she possibly say to get out of it?

"Aye. I'm with you."

From behind, Edward's voice sounded. "No. You're not."

Chapter 14 ────────────

She hadn't heard Edward approach and the sound of him directly behind her made her lurch up straight, whiskey sloshing over the glass rim and onto her pants.

She twisted in her chair, a move that put her face-first into his crotch. His breeches hugged him tightly, showing off the hard curve of his hips, the long firm muscles of his thighs, the sizeable bulge behind the fall. She swallowed hard and dragged her eyes away from the body parts in front of her to his face. From the arch of his eyebrow it appeared he was aware of where her thoughts lay. Thank God for her shirt and cravat. They hid the worst of her blushing.

"I think Finley can make his own decisions," William said, coolly. "Or does your iron fist extend to your guests also?"

The tension that radiated from Edward was almost palpable, but rather than confront his brother, he simply said: "I promised Charlotte a family dinner, and she wants Finley to attend. You as well."

Fiona had no idea whether or not that was the truth, but

it was the excuse she needed. However irked she was about his high-handedness, she appreciated the out. "I did swear to Lady Charlotte that I'd join her this evening."

The dandies around her groaned. One even booed. Gold Thread looked up at Edward. "What concessions did you wrest from Liverpool today, Duke? How many more of our rights have you eroded?"

Fiona's ears pricked up and she looked at Edward. A muscle ticked along his jaw. "If you want to have an opinion, Mallen, I suggest that you make an appearance in chambers once in a while. Otherwise, let the men work."

Gold Thread's face turned an unhealthy shade of red but, surprisingly, he didn't respond. She guessed there was only so far you'd push the boundaries with a duke.

Unable to help herself, she grasped at the hope that her earlier assumption was false. That Edward hadn't been betraying all they'd talked of. "Are ye working with Liverpool, then?" She hoped no one else could hear how the lump in her throat strangled her voice.

His sober gaze gripped her. "I *am* working with Liverpool." Her heart sank, but before she could turn away to hide her disappointment, he grasped the back of her chair. "I believe the only way to enact meaningful change is through working together, even when each other's perspectives seem so...faulty. Protests and pitchforks cause a lot of harm for limited gain."

There was a haunted look to his eyes, and she realized that she'd never stopped to consider how that night—fronting an angry mob with nothing but his size and his title to protect him—had impacted him. She'd been so lost in her own grief at Jeremy's death and Edward's sudden departure that she'd never thought of his pain.

That felt incredibly selfish and unkind now.

"And once again the Wildeforde manages to suck the fun out of a conversation," Gold Thread said. He turned to Fiona. "I look forward to seeing you at Macklebury's tomorrow night, Finley. We'll extricate you from this dullard's grip and show you a proper good time."

Edward's fingers flinched almost imperceptibly on the back of her chair, but he said nothing to Lord Mallen. "Finley, I need to grab some notes from my study before heading back to Westminster. Do you need a ride back to the house?"

She couldn't tell if he'd phrased it as a question because it genuinely was one, or if he didn't want to be seen as dictatorial in front of these men. Either way, she was keen to leave. As much as she found her current company shallow and insensible, they had given her the seed of a new strategy. She *was* going to attend the Macklebury ball and she was going to approach these Lords Chester and Livingworth.

She stood. "Gentlemen, you've given me much to consider. Thank ye for yer help." She bowed, gathered her satchel, and turned on her heel, forcing Edward to follow her.

She stopped at the dining room exit.

"To your right," he said from behind her with a sigh.

Doing her best to appear to the liveried footmen around her that she knew exactly what she was doing, she strode down the corridor with her head high.

"Mallen's an arse," she said as they got to the steps outside. "I quite enjoyed watching you skewer him."

Edward didn't chuckle or even clear his throat in an amused way. Instead, he leaned in, a furious expression on his face. "That was a blasted foolish thing to do, setting foot in that building."

It was the truth. She knew it. But the unfairness of it all made her blood boil. In the short time she'd been there, she'd seen business and political dealings all around her along with a gaggle of aimless barnacles who cared not a whit for the privilege of admittance. All the while, she couldn't even manage to secure a second meeting for her actual hard work.

She was in no mood for Edward's lecture. "You make it sound as if the walls were about to cave in around us," she snapped. "That my mere presence could prompt such a disaster."

"In 120-odd years, no woman has ever set foot in that club."

"That you ken." Fiona sniffed, quickening her pace.

He kept up easily. Damn his long legs. "Pardon?"

She stopped abruptly, forcing him to turn around and face her. "*I* just stepped foot in that club. Hell, I had two glasses of whiskey in it, and I'm a woman. What's to say other women have not also snuck in under the guise of a man?"

His eyes narrowed. "Because all guests must be backed by a member, and every member knows that allowing a woman in will get you blackballed for life. And likely kicked out of every other club in London."

"Oh, boo-hoo, you need to find somewhere else to drink and play whist."

Edward leaned closer, his voice quiet but furious. "Lives are built in that club. The country's most important political decisions are made there. Men create business empires between those walls. It is far more than a place to drink and gamble, and you risked William's access to all of it."

"And you don't see a problem with that? A problem with the foundations for success being built within a building women cannae even enter? That in order to succeed, hard work is nae enough unless there's a hanging member swinging between yer legs?"

Edward stared at her, mouth agape.

"Think on that, Your Grace."

⁓

The force of Fiona's words almost felled him. Rarely was he so sure he had the moral high ground and then been proven so obviously wrong.

His instinct had been to dismiss her comment. After all, a woman's success did not rely upon conversations that were had at his club. A woman's success was judged by her ability to marry well and run a household. A woman's success was determined in the ballrooms of Almack's and the houses of Mayfair.

But he also couldn't deny that, for Fiona, success meant something different than it did for most women of his acquaintance. Objectively speaking, her endeavors were to be admired. She had shown more grit, determination, and intelligence in the development of her matches than many of the men whose entrance to White's went uncontested.

So was it fair that she lacked this key tool for success?

No. She had earned the right to be treated with the same dignity and respect as a man.

But did that mean that centuries of tradition should be overturned because one unusual female was out of the mold?

No. He couldn't agree with that either.

Which meant that, as Fiona marched stubbornly forward, he followed behind, addle-brained—not entirely sure what the answer was. His sense of right and wrong had always been his guiding star and now it led him in opposite directions.

Fiona had paused at the end of Piccadilly Street and pulled out her map of London. She unfolded it, turned it, and folded it again.

"Where are we going?" he asked.

"Stratford Place."

"We keep walking straight," he said.

She looked up at him, her earlier annoyance not assuaged by his help. "Aye. I ken."

He held his hands up in surrender. "We could take my carriage. Swinton does know the way." He gestured to the carriage bearing the ducal crest that had been following them since they left the club. What his driver thought of spending the past few days shadowing them as they walked, Edward didn't want to know.

"No thank you," she said with a clipped tone, her satchel swinging in large arcs. "I'm perfectly capable of getting there with my own two feet."

Of course she was. At least this time she was wearing proper boots and not those mincing slippers, though he suspected her earlier blisters still rubbed. "As you wish. What's on Stratford Place?"

"Bessie Bleufleur. She's been seeing to my wardrobe since I arrived in London, and if I'm going to attend tomorrow's Macklebury ball to talk with Lords Chester and Livingworth, I'll need something to wear."

Edward suppressed the eye roll he felt with his entire body. "I told you, I have a dressmaker on staff."

Fiona stepped around two men walking in the opposite direction. "And I told you that I don't need your help. Besides, I checked with Simmons. Your dressmaker doesn't reside in the house. I don't know about you, but I prefer to have as few people ken Fiona-is-Finley as possible. If she's taking my measurements, there's no way she can miss my breast bindings or the lack of, you know, in my pants."

His cock twitched like a green boy's at the thought of

"in her pants." "And this Bessie that we are going to knows about your ruse?"

"Not exactly, but she's from Abingdale and I trust her to keep a secret."

They arrived at the modiste's, a discreet shop with MADAME ALLARD on the sign outside. The jinglejangle of bells sent a heavily painted woman bustling into the main room. She looked at Finley, and then she looked at Edward, her gaze traveling from his boots to the trim of his morning coat, to the jeweled stickpin in his cravat, and she gave him a deferential smile.

"Bonjour, my lord," she said in an atrocious French accent. "I am honored to have you here." She edged to the side and flicked what he assumed was supposed to be a subtle glance through the front windows, where his carriage and its crest could be easily seen. Her eyes widened and then sparkled with ambition.

"I'm here to see Miss Bleufleur," Fiona said.

From out the back, a young girl walked into the room, her mouth full of pins, her eyes trained on the swatch of fabric in her hands. She looked up.

Edward saw the flash of recognition when she looked at him and she sank into a deep curtsey. Then she looked at Finley. In the moment that she recognized Fiona behind the wig and breeches, her mouth dropped and pins scattered across the floor.

"His Grace and companion are here to see *you*, Bessie," Madame Allard said, jealousy creeping through her tone. "*Comme c'est curieux.*"

"We were neighbors," Fiona said, "before Bessie left for London. She had quite a reputation for her speedy yet exceptional work, so she seemed like the obvious choice for an urgent job."

Fiona's heaping of praise on a junior seamstress was doing nothing to quell the store owner's displeasure or the potential for gossip. He stepped in, keen to have their business resolved as quickly as possible. He might not agree with Fi's decision to go to the Macklebury ball, but he wasn't fool enough to think he could stop her.

"Mr. McTavish needs a set of evening attire altered and ready to wear tomorrow evening."

"*Tomorrow?*" both women said in unison.

"Not from scratch," Fiona added. "I'll send over the clothes to be altered this afternoon."

"*Hmph.*" Madame Allard pursed her lips for a brief second before plastering a smile on her face. "Well, Bessie should probably measure you up then." The shop owner herded Finley and Edward ahead of her toward a side room, richly appointed with a cluster of soft chairs, a small dais, and a ring of mirrors that circled the room.

It was clearly meant for high-paying clientele to *ooh* and *ahh* over each other in private.

"Here's a seat for you, Your Grace," the modiste said, indicating a chaise longue. "I suppose *I'll* be the one to bring the refreshments in," she muttered on her way out the door.

Bessie followed quickly behind, leaving Edward and Fiona alone.

"What are you doing?" Fiona hissed, waving her hands toward the door. "Get out!"

"I can hardly loiter in the main shop instead of sitting comfortably. That's a dead giveaway that something is amiss."

Fiona crossed her arms. "Then go to another shop."

That was a fair suggestion. There was a gunsmith across the road who sold exquisite hunting rifles. Edward nodded and was about to exit when Madame Allard reentered with two glasses, a decanter, and a beaming smile. "I've opened my best brandy, just for you, Your Grace. I've been saving it for years, but if you won't open it for a duke, when are you going to open it?"

Blast. He looked to Fiona. Leaving now would be exceptionally rude. The woman had just opened her best brandy. The set of Fiona's jaw suggested that she didn't care.

Bessie reentered, dragging a screen with her. "Mr. McTavish has always been shy, ma'am," she said to her shop owner. "It's probably best you leave."

The girl had her wits about her. She'd managed to oust the curious shop owner and protect Fiona's modesty without setting off any alarm bells.

As soon as Madame Allard had left the room, Edward stood to help Bessie position the heavy screen.

"Thank you, Your Grace."

"Thank *you*, Miss Bleufleur. I appreciate your discretion in this matter. You shall be compensated accordingly."

Fiona rolled her eyes. "Good God, Ed. Nae everything needs to be solved with money."

He looked at Bessie, who was in turn looking at Fiona as though Fi had sprouted three heads. "It's not a payment for her silence. It's a token of my appreciation. I assume it's welcome?"

Bessie grinned. "I appreciate the appreciation, Your Grace. I won't say no."

Edward settled himself onto the chaise longue, taking a sip of the special-occasion brandy and wishing that he was not so special. But he would drain every drop purely because Madame Allard had been so absurdly pleased to give it to him.

His shoulders were tight, the tension of the past few days making itself felt in the stiffness of his muscles and a general ache that ran from his shoulder blades to his skull.

He leaned his head to each side, enjoying the pull that gave him momentary relief. When he arrived home, he'd send for his healer to massage the area.

He twisted his neck to the left, and then to the right—and that's when he saw it. The plethora of mirrors placed around the room to give the model a view of all aspects of their outfit also provided a clear view of Fiona, despite the screen in front of him.

Despite knowing better, he couldn't look away.

She shrugged off her jacket, Bessie helping to guide it past the bandage on her wrist. With her left hand, she clumsily unbuttoned her waistcoat, allowing the seamstress to remove it for her.

Beneath the simply knotted cravat, which came undone with a simple flick and tug, the lace of the shirt neck was open, likely because she'd been too stubborn that morning to ask one of the maids for help. He would send Mrs. Phillips to attend Fiona the next morning.

Then Bessie lifted Fi's shirt, and Edward's mouth went dry. He looked away, but not before catching a glimpse of her creamy skin, only a shade darker than the thick, white bandage wrapped around her breasts and scattered with orange freckles. The binding might hide her breasts when covered with a shirt, but two soft mounds and the deep crevice of her cleavage were visible.

He counted folds in the fabric that hung off rolls in the corner of the room, but it didn't erase the image from his mind. She was every bit as beautiful as he remembered. They had not made love—he was not in the habit of taking a young lady's virginity—but there had been nights, hot passionate ones, when they'd shared more than a kiss.

And the sight of her in nothing but a wide bandage and men's drawers had his cock straining against his breeches.

He turned his attention to the backs of his hands, which were rubbing against his thighs.

But just because he couldn't see her anymore didn't mean he didn't have a perfect mental picture. His skin prickled and he was keenly aware of every sound that came from the women's direction. He imagined what those sounds were attached to. How she was moving. What that would do to her figure.

He needed different thoughts before these ones got him into trouble. He needed a distraction.

"Why do you insist on walking?" he asked. There. Banal. As unprovocative as conversation could get.

"I like walking."

"I like hunting, but that doesn't mean I feel the need to kill my own meat for every dinner."

She paused, and after a moment, he couldn't help but look at her reflection.

Her lip was between her teeth, as if the answer was not straightforward and she wasn't sure how much of herself to give up.

So he stayed silent. She would tell him or not. It would be her choice.

Bessie kept her mouth closed and went about the business of measuring her client. Eventually Fiona spoke. "It was a few years before you and I met. Father had already left Scotland. He'd been in trouble with the law and so he disappeared. I was living with my aunt and uncle on their farm in Bandeforde. The soldiers came at daybreak." She faltered there, as though the words were more than a memory. As though the soldiers were before her and the shock had stolen her breath.

"We were given two hours to collect our belongings and leave. The laird who owned the farm wanted the land for sheep grazing—it's a better business investment, ye ken—and we were simply in the way.

"There weren't many options. We gathered our things and took my uncle's wagon to Aberdeen. We sold what we could, including the cart, but could only scrape together enough money for four tickets to the Americas, and so they left. They felt bad. I ken they did. But they had my cousins to think of, so they left me there with just a few coppers."

He pictured it, this flame-haired woman standing on a dock, with all her belongings at her feet, watching what was left of her family sail away. The thought ignited a small lick of anger within him. "And yet you're here. You're not still in Scotland," he said. *Thank God for that.*

"I knew my da had moved to England; the last I'd heard he was in a village in the south. So I gathered what clothes I had with me, rolled it into a pack, and began to walk."

The shock of her words stunned him. It took a long moment before his brain could form words again. "That's got to be six hundred miles."

She gave a small, wry smile. "Almost. I didnae walk the entire way. I took main roads in the hope that somebody would pick me up and take me closer in a cart. There was no money for the mail coach."

Edward's heartbeat thundered in his ears, the rushing and thumping akin to the worst of storms. A young woman traveling alone. Anything could have happened to her. Then a sick feeling formed in the pit of his stomach.

Maybe something did happen to her. "That's not the safest of situations for a young **woman to** be in," he said quietly. He couldn't bring himself to put **his q**uestion into words. He hoped he didn't have to.

He fixed his gaze onto her reflection in the mirror. He

had to know the truth. He wasn't sure what he'd do with the knowledge but he had to know. Quietly, Bessie rolled up her measuring tape, gathered her notes, and exited, giving her client the space she clearly needed.

Fiona swallowed hard, the muscles in her throat working. She didn't seem to notice the seamstress leave, so lost was she in the memory. "I learnt quickly when not to accept a ride. And there were nights...when I had to barricade the door to whatever room or barn I'd been able to barter my cleaning services for."

Edward's fists clenched. He wanted to wrap his hands around the throats of the men responsible and throttle them. Assaulting any woman was a bastard act. Assaulting *his* would be a death sentence. But luckily for them, he would never know who they were.

"That should never have happened to you." He worked hard to keep his tone neutral. She had her own feelings to bear. He would not add to them with his own rage and terror.

She shivered. "The cold was the worst part—especially on those nights between villages. It was warmer to climb a tree than stay on the ground, but then I couldnae sleep. Most nights I couldn't start a fire. You need dry wood for a spark to catch and it was not always available."

And so she had created friction matches. A young woman with nothing to her name, nothing but fury and resolve, had taken all of that fear and anger and trauma and had channeled it into a tool that could change the world. "I am sorry that you had to go through that."

She shook out her arms, as though the cold still nipped at her. "It's nae your fault," she said. "You don't need to apologize."

And there was his Fiona—not wanting anything from

anyone. Not even condolences. "I'm sorry, nevertheless. But still confused. After all of that, why would you *choose* to walk?"

She gave a soft, sad smile as she stepped down from the dais and took her shirt from the back of a nearby chair. "That journey taught me an important lesson. That if I wanted security, I would have to create it for myself. I cannot count on anyone else. I couldn't count on my father to stay out of trouble. I couldn't count on the lord who owned our farm not to kick us out. I couldn't count on the person offering me a lift to be doing so without ill intent."

"And you couldn't count on me." He'd promised her a home together, a marriage, a life—and then he'd reneged. He'd known he was hurting her when he ended things, but he'd had no idea that he'd been the final bit of proof she needed that she could rely on no one.

"And I could not count on you." There was a tremor to her voice, and she carefully slipped her injured arm into a sleeve and then pulled the shirt on over her head.

"I'm sorry that I broke your trust."

She laughed cynically as she fumbled with the laces. "If it makes ye feel any better, by the time I met ye, I had no trust left to break."

"I loved you, you know." He needed her to know that. To know that she hadn't been a mere dalliance. That despite how he'd betrayed her, she had meant something to him.

She caught his eye in the mirror's reflection. "I wish I could say the same, but I never knew you. I knew a boy called Edward, nae the Duke of Wildeforde."

His chest constricted at her words. They weren't the truth. She was the only one who actually did know him. Every-one else knew the curated version—the perfect image he'd worked so hard to create. Even his siblings. Only Fiona had ever seen him cry. He missed being truly seen almost as much as he missed her.

She came out from behind the screen, her shirt and waistcoat on, her jacket hanging over her uninjured arm. She held her wrist out to him. "Would you mind?"

"I'll never mind." He took her hand in his, trying to ignore the frisson that shot through him as his hand cupped hers. Her skin was soft, but he could feel a scattering of small ridges on the backs of her hands. Her fingers were scarred, some rose pink from recent burns, others a white so pale they almost blended in with her skin, only the slight sheen of them indicating past accidents.

He tamped down the urge to press them to his lips. Instead, as gently as he could, he fastened the buttons over her bandage, leaving the outer one open so as to not press the knot into her wrist. He took her jacket and held it out for her as she slid awkwardly into it.

She winced as she pulled her left arm through, and his eyes closed in fellow feeling. When they opened, she'd turned— still within the circle of his arms—and faced him, her own eyes clouded as though she too felt the bond between them, once strong then shattered, now intensified beyond what it ever had been.

He couldn't help graze a hand along her cheek, and as she leaned into his palm, his heart thudded and his cock hardened and his other hand reached for her waist.

The jinglejangle of the front door sounded. Fiona colored and stepped back, putting a good foot between them. The loss of her nearness chilled him. He cleared his throat to mask the awkward moment.

"Here." He reached out for the cravat that hung around her neck, but she waved him off.

"Let's just leave it undone," she said. "It's a bit roguish, don't you think?"

It was a valiant attempt to change the mood, so he played along. "Incredibly roguish. I might have to beat the ladies away from you."

She snorted, the least ladylike noise a woman could make, yet the sound made him smile. As they exited the modiste's, Edward's carriage was still waiting outside. "You can go back to the house, Swinton. McTavish and I will walk."

Chapter 15

Staring at her reflection in the oversized mirror that hung in her guest dressing room, Fiona tucked a stray hair under her wig. Wilde and his siblings would have already gathered in the billiards room, but Fiona was dragging her feet.

What had come over her? She'd never discussed her journey from Scotland to Abingdale with anyone. Her father hadn't bothered to ask how she'd gotten there, and when John had enquired years later, she'd glossed over it. It was done and dusted. Nothing was going to change her experiences of those weeks, and sharing them would only result in criticism or pity. She didn't want either.

Which was why telling Edward the truth of those days had been an unexpected choice for her to make. An unconscious one too. Something she hadn't realized she was doing until the words were out. In that moment, she'd felt inexplicably safe.

His reaction had been just as unexpected. If you'd asked her beforehand, she'd have suggested he'd call her foolish or stubborn or damnably arrogant to think she could have gone on such a perilous journey on her own.

But he seemed to have understood that she'd had no choice. He hadn't criticized her or smothered her with pity. He'd simply expressed empathy and care—even when she'd described how perilous some moments had been. His voice had steeled, and for a moment she'd expected to witness the wrath of the duke.

Instead, she'd witnessed the Edward she remembered: kind, curious, sensitive. Someone who listened rather than dictated. But there had been more to it. There was something about the self-assurance of the duke that made her feel secure—so secure, she'd almost kissed him again.

She sighed and tugged on the bottom edge of her waistcoat. It was so much easier to engage with him when anger fueled her, but she couldn't honestly say she was angry anymore.

Confused? Yes. She didn't understand why today's Edward, the one that seemed to genuinely care for her, would have broken their relationship off so abruptly. But angry? No. That emotion had burned out.

She buffed her shoes with a bit of spit and a handkerchief until they shone. Tonight, she would do her best to make friendly, polite conversation. When Charlotte and William were otherwise occupied, she would find a moment to thank Edward for all he'd done for her since he'd sprung her from jail, and she would let him know that she'd forgiven him for everything that came beforehand.

And what could come next? It was daft to even consider anything other than them going their separate ways after the trial. He did not want her as his duchess and she didn't want to be one, because she was an independent, intelligent woman.

But not wanting to be a duchess didn't preclude her from wanting *him*. As much as the logical part of her brain resisted, the illogical organ in her chest was drawn to him.

The hammering of her heart increased as she walked down the hall connecting the two wings. Just to the side of the open door, she paused, willing herself to get her nerves under control. That's when she heard Charlotte.

"So, that's what I want to do," Charlotte said. "I want to volunteer at Miss Marcham's school for underprivileged women. I can teach them deportment and help them transition into real jobs. They could be nannies or housemaids, maybe even lady's maids if they have the skills."

Fiona smiled. The plan was bold. A young woman of the *ton* spending her time with that part of society was unheard of. Charlotte clearly had her brother's confidence. It must come with being part of royalty—wealth, power, assurance. Charlotte was using that privilege to subvert the establishment that gave it to her. How impressive.

Fiona was about to walk in and congratulate the youngest Stirling sibling, perhaps offer some help with the strategy, when Edward's firm voice stopped her.

"No."

"But Ned—"

"It's out of the question. While it's a kind and well-intentioned thought, it's not appropriate for a young lady to have such close dealings with the masses. There are more fitting ways for you to spend your time."

"But no one is championing these women and someone must."

Fiona could not continue to stand here, eavesdropping.

She either needed to leave and return in a half hour when the squabbling was over or enter and choose a side.

So she chose her side. "Good evening," she said as she entered. "Lady Charlotte, I could nae help but overhear yer conversation. What a brave and progressive plan."

Her eyes went straight to Edward as he lounged in one of the armchairs. He'd changed for dinner, the amethyst patterned fabric swapped out for simpler attire—light greys and charcoals that gave his blue eyes the appearance of a winter storm. His gaze zeroed in on her as well, studying her expression and then lightly—so fast she almost wasn't sure it happened—dropping to her lips, before he shifted in his seat and refocused his attention on his sister.

The hairs on the back of Fi's arms stood at attention.

Charlotte was grinning as she looked at Fiona, completely oblivious to the undercurrent that swirled around them. Her blue eyes flashed with passion. Judging by the square set of her shoulders and energy in her bearing, her argument with Edward was only just getting started.

"I'm glad you approve," Charlotte said. She leveled a disapproving look at her brother. "Ned seems to think that it will lead to my deflowering."

William choked on his drink. A muscle ticked along Edward's jaw. "I did not say that."

"It's what you implied," Charlotte shot back.

"I'm certain yer brother has more faith in yer good judgment than that," Fiona said, trying not to laugh.

Edward rested his elbows on his knees, his fingertips drumming against one another.

"If you were proposing financial support only, then I would acquiesce. It's a noble cause and deserves our patronage. But you actually want to *go to* these places. In the flesh. You want to spend your days in a, frankly, unwholesome environment, and quite beyond the fact that it's dangerous and you'd likely be hurt, the gossip mill would have a field day. I will not have the Wildeforde name besmirched when the poor can be assisted in other ways. Char, you need to care about your family as much as you care about these women."

Charlotte inhaled sharply, her fists firm at her sides. The way her lips thinned and her eyes narrowed, the jutting out of her jaw and militant look on her face—she was the spitting image of Edward, and the dead-calm resonance of her response echoed his.

"I know that you didn't just suggest that I don't care for the family name, because given I follow all of your many decrees *to the letter*, that idea would be preposterous, wouldn't it?"

The prospect of Edward having to deal with a younger version of himself was frightfully entertaining. From the filthy look he gave Fi, she hadn't quite managed to suppress her smile the way she'd intended.

"We will discuss this later," he said, standing and taking a cue stick from the stand on the wall.

Charlotte plastered a false smile on her face and settled on the piano bench, fanning her skirts out around her. She looked the picture of innocence, but Fi couldn't believe that Char would give up the fight so easily.

"Have you heard from Abingdale since you arrived?" Charlotte asked Fiona with a flutter of her lashes. "I do so much miss *Amelia's* company. She is much fun. One would have to be *block-headed* not to see it."

The notable force with which Edward struck his ball suggested his sister's insult had landed.

Hesitant to get caught in the skirmish, Fiona chose her words with caution. "Amelia is currently about fifteen months pregnant, so I doubt she's the fun ye remember."

Fiona did wish her friend could be there, though. This entire situation would be easier with Amelia's caustic, unvarnished advice to guide her.

"Then you will have to make up for it. I expect no less than two dances from you tomorrow night, Mr. McTavish."

No. No, no, no, no, no. Tomorrow's ball was a mechanism for meeting potential investors. That was it. There would be no casual socializing with the *ton* and certainly no dancing. "I'm afraid I dunnae dance."

Charlotte shook her head, as though sitting out was not an option. Good God, this family was autocratic. "Pish. It would be rude to go to a ball and not dance *at all.*"

Fiona would rather be rude than caught out in her lie. "Truly, my lady—"

"Call me Charlotte." She ducked her head and looked up through her lashes, a move that had surely felled many an objection. It had no impact on Fi at all.

"Truly, Charlotte. I am nae a good dancer. I would be an embarrassment to us both."

"Well, that's something that can be rectified. We have time before dinner." She stood, taking the gloves that lay on the top of the piano and pulling them on. "William, help me push the chairs aside. Ned, you're on music."

William shrugged and got to work. Edward simply rolled his eyes, a gesture Fi had seen plenty of times from Ed. This was the first time she'd seen it from the duke.

Fiona's heart rate quickened as Ed's sister stood and smoothed her skirts. "Charlotte, I dunnae think this is a good idea. I've never been to a ball, and I've only been to a handful of assemblies." Fiona had barely managed to get the steps correct when she danced as herself. There was no possibility of her managing to reverse her lefts and rights without stumbling all over the place.

But Charlotte would not be dissuaded, and the younger Stirling siblings made short work of the furniture, clearing a space for dancing where a set of comfortable armchairs used to sit. Every time Fiona tried to intervene, she was quickly hushed.

Was this how all siblings acted? Launching into assistance, whether you wanted it or not? It was overbearing and a lifetime of it would send her mad.

Yet at the same time, watching Charlotte and William needle each other fondly, seeing how they gently teased out a softer, more relaxed version of Edward, left Fiona with an odd sense of lacking, as though there had been something missing—the absence of which she'd never noticed—and now the echoes of her childhood memories sounded hollow.

She was adrift in that unwelcome longing when Charlotte took her hand.

"We'll start with the waltz."

"The waltz? Surely no one will expect me to dance something so intimate."

Charlotte laughed. "Finley, I had no idea you were such a prude. Here. Your left hand goes here." She took Fiona's hand and guided it to her waist. "And your right hand goes here. Edward, play, please."

As the notes began to sound, Fiona froze. She'd forgotten how talented he was. He imbued the music with heart and soul that simultaneously arrested her and yet had her blood vibrating. It was as though all feeling and expression that he shuttered away as the duke found its release through the keys.

He'd played for her on the rickety church piano the night they'd broken in. The intensity of it had toppled her affection for him into the deepest longing. Tonight, following a day that had muddled her sense of who this man was, his playing threatened to do the same.

"Finley," Charlotte barked.

Fiona shook her head. "Pardon. I lost myself for a minute." She tried to focus on the woman in front of her, not the man to the side, who was utterly wrecking her heart.

"He is very good," Charlotte acknowledged. "I can understand your surprise. It's a shame he won't play for anyone but William and I."

Fi looked at Edward. "Ye don't?"

Over by the billiards table, William snorted before striking a ball. " 'The Wildeforde men are not frivolous,' " he said in a falsetto tone that she assumed mimicked their mother. " 'Music is too trivial a pastime.' "

" 'Wildefordes have duty to attend to,' " Charlotte jumped in with the same mocking voice. " 'They should not be spending time on such fanciful diversions.' "

William flicked his hand in a dismissive movement, his nose wrinkled. " 'Wildefordes are not monkeys, performing for the entertainment of lesser *ton*.' "

Fiona looked to Edward to discern his reaction to his siblings' jesting. He'd stopped playing. He shrugged, but his Adam's apple bobbed and his face tightened. Charlotte and Will clearly found their mother's decrees amusing, but Fiona didn't believe Edward's nonchalant mask.

"You play," she said to Charlotte.

"Yes, but we ladies *are* performing monkeys and performing is our duty," she quipped. "So, I have that freedom."

Was it freedom, though? It sure as hell didn't sound like it. Charlotte was *allowed* to engage in frivolous pastimes such as music and flower arranging but not allowed to turn her hand to anything more substantial. Goodness, she wasn't even allowed to participate in charitable endeavors that weren't firmly within what was expected of a young lady, and it was Edward making that decision.

Before she could challenge any of them on their completely mad perspectives, Edward resumed playing and Charlotte grabbed her hand. After a quick rundown of the steps that Fiona didn't need, they began to move.

And she promptly stepped on Charlotte's foot.

"My apologies."

"It's nothing."

A few more attempts and only one more crunching misstep later, and the two of them were moving around the room in a relatively graceful rhythm. It was peculiar dancing with a woman. To begin with, Charlotte smelled like a summer garden and Fiona wanted to know where the scent was purchased. Then there was the gentle curve of Charlotte's waist, which her brother didn't have, and the slenderness of Charlotte's fingers around hers.

The scientist in her was too busy noting her observations to pay close attention to her movements.

"You must *lead*, Finley. You dance as though you're expecting *me* to."

Frustration snagged at Fiona's fraying patience. "I'm nae used to—"

"You're not used to what?"

Sigh. "—dancing," Fiona said before the word *leading* left her lips. "I'm nae used to dancing." This whole enterprise was tempting fate and she began to wonder if perhaps she shouldn't put an end to it. Women were more observant than men. There was no possibility of fooling them all in such close quarters. If she was as intelligent as she prided herself, she'd be avoiding other people like the plague until her matches were sold and her trial was over, and she could return to Abingdale.

But there were potential investors at tomorrow night's ball, and she couldn't let the opportunity pass.

"Three dances, Charlotte. That's it. And please find me partners who will nae mind if I tread on their toes."

Charlotte nodded. "Will do." They completed another turn of the room, and Charlotte looked over Fiona's shoulder. "Edward, I hope you're ready to dance tomorrow night."

"I'll dance with you, as always," he said, not missing a beat.

"Don't be silly, you won't have time to dance with me. You'll be looking for your future fiancée."

With those words, Fiona's heart stopped.

Chapter 16 ———————

"My goodness, Mr. McTavish, are you all right?"

Fiona had tripped over her feet, stumbling into Charlotte's arms. "I'm fine. Just rusty." Her face burned. With any luck, Charlotte and William would put it down to embarrassment over the fall, and not what it was—the shock at hearing that Edward was actively looking for a wife.

Shame coursed through her. Of course he was. She had always known this day would come; the timing was simply unexpected. They had spent a not inconsiderable amount of time together in the past week, and he'd never mentioned it.

They'd had moments—at least she thought they'd had moments—but clearly they hadn't.

Stupid, featherbrained halfwit.

What had they truly shared since he'd freed her from jail? One quick kiss. Conversation. A book. True, she had bared her soul to him that afternoon in a way she never had, but he hadn't asked her to do that. He hadn't sought that vulnerability out. She'd offered it to him, idiotically.

She righted herself, schooled the hurt and humiliation from her face, and stepped back into her dance with Charlotte. Still, she couldn't help but sneak a glance at him.

He had the good sense not to be looking in her direction. The jackass clearly had some survival instincts.

"That's not something we need to discuss right now," Edward said, not taking his gaze from the keys in front of him. The notes had become sharp and distracted.

Charlotte stopped mid-turn and gave Fiona an apologetic look. Fiona did not care. She made directly for the decanter of spirits on the side table.

"If not now, then when?" Charlotte asked her brother, arms akimbo. "You're out all day and we must have time to strategize before we venture out into the whirl."

He stopped playing. "Mr. McTavish doesn't need to be here for this conversation."

Fiona nodded her assent as she poured a generous glass of brandy and wished that it were a good Scottish whisky. The last place she wanted to be was here, for this conversation. But she had no cause to leave his siblings abruptly. Besides, this was where the spirits were.

"Finley doesn't mind, do you, Finley?" William said, coming over and nudging her in the ribs, as though she were a willing sidekick in this farce. "You can laugh with the rest of us at Edward's misfortune."

"It's hardly a misfortune that he has to marry," Charlotte said. "It will only be misfortune if he has to marry one of the women that Mother has planned. I'm sure between the lot of us we can find someone more suitable."

So he'd not yet picked a duchess. Relief flashed through her. Self-loathing swiped back. She did not *want* to want him. He'd lied to her; he'd abandoned her just as her father had; and he'd made it clear she was not the kind of woman he'd marry. This yearning inside her was an embarrassment.

She knocked back her drink in one gulp, eyes watering as the brandy burned the back of her throat. Good. She would take the physical discomfort over this emotional turmoil any day. "What are ye looking for in a wife?" she ground out, when it became clear the younger Stirling siblings were waiting for her to join the conversation.

Edward glared at her, eyes narrowed in frustration.

"She needs to be attractive," William said. "Can't have some hideous chit joining the family."

Fiona stepped back from William. "Is that *actually* yer criteria?"

He sniffed and raised his brandy glass. "Not the only criteria. She should come from good breeding stock. Think of the children."

If anyone else in the room thought that a magnificently horrendous comment, they didn't show it. In fact, Charlotte was excited as she chimed in. "Oh. She needs to be able to host parties and balls, et cetera. Edward needs a wife who will complement his political dealings. If she can't plan a menu then she'll be a liability."

"That's enough," Edward barked. "I don't need any help finding a bride."

Charlotte rolled her eyes. "That's not what our conversation was yesterday."

Edward flicked a look toward Fiona, full of guilt and apprehension.

Charlotte continued to tick off her fingers. "She needs to be agreeable. The last person we need to join the family is someone always in the mood for an argument."

William nodded. "Oh yes, I concur. None of these overly

progressive types who can't seem to get through a meal without harping on about the plight of one unfortunate or another."

Fiona drew in a long breath, preparing to deliver William an education. Edward stepped in before she could begin her lecture on the necessity of "progressive types."

"That's entirely inappropriate," he said. "And demonstrates a remarkable lack of empathy for those we have a moral obligation to support."

William cocked his head, looking at his brother with his brows furrowed. "So you *want* to marry someone divisive?"

Edward closed his eyes and rubbed the spot between his brows. "I didn't say that. I simply said that there wasn't anything wrong with a woman who has such ideas."

Oh. How comforting. The Duke of Wildeforde tolerated women with opinions.

"Then we can be agreed," said Charlotte. "Such women are perfectly acceptable in society but not as a duchess."

She could keep her tongue no longer. "What of intelligence? So far Edward's wife needs to be pretty, amiable, able to plan a menu, and not have any radical ideas. She sounds awfully insipid. Should she have a mind?"

"Oh, I don't know if that's a good idea," William said with not a hint of sarcasm as he shook his head.

"No," Charlotte said, tapping her cheek. "I agree with Finley. Ned's wife should have a brain. What say you, Edward?"

Edward's eyes were cold flint. "Yes," he bit out. "I would like my wife to have a brain."

Charlotte clapped her hands. "Then we are agreed. Edward's wife is to be pretty, social, and have intelligence so long as she doesn't apply it to anything controversial."

"Hear! Hear!" William raised his snifter in mock toast.

With a grim smile, Fiona filled her glass again and knocked it back. Dinner was shaping up to be delightful.

Edward knocked on Fiona's bedroom door, his chest tight, dreading the conversation that was about to happen.

"Who is it?" Her tone was clipped and angry. No doubt she knew exactly who it was.

"It's me." He wouldn't be surprised if she refused to open the door. Tonight's dinner had been brutal. Charlotte and William simply hadn't let go with their matrimonial teasing.

While Charlotte seemed genuinely determined to find him a wife, William had used the opportunity to get whatever jabs in he could.

Neither of them knew that the person they were most likely hurting wasn't him. It hadn't ended until he had lost his composure entirely, yelling at them to mind their own blasted business and be quiet when he said to be quiet.

Dinner had been relatively silent after that and he chose not to attend afterward while Charlotte continued with Fiona's dancing lessons.

"I want to apologize," he called, resting his forehead on the door, his arms braced against the frame on either side of it. He should have put a stop to the conversation much, much earlier. He should never have allowed her to be in that situation.

The door opened and he straightened. Fiona was looking at him with an expression he hadn't seen before—part hurt, part confusion. Her usual self-assurance had vanished. This was the face he'd never seen, yet had still haunted him. Her feelings were writ clear across her face, and five years ago, she would have had the same expression. She'd had no warning then, and no warning tonight either.

While she still wore the breeches and shirt of Finley, she'd removed the wig, her long red hair cascading across her shoulders. Her cravat had been discarded and the collar of her shirt hung open, exposing the gentle curve of her neck and the hollow at her throat. She stared at him, waiting.

"I'm sorry." The words felt small and inconsequential; three syllables couldn't adequately convey the anguish and remorse he felt. He rubbed at the back of his neck, the muscles there rock hard.

After a minute of steady examination, she quirked her lips and stepped back from the doorway, opening it a fraction farther. "For someone obsessed with not creating scandal, you certainly show up at my bedroom door on a regular basis."

Scandal was the last thing on his mind. Nothing he'd been through following his father's death had felt as gut-wrenching as this.

"I just want to see that you're well." He entered. The last time he'd been in her rooms, it had been with a purpose. He'd had food to deliver and medicine to administer. He'd been able to tell himself that he was exactly where he ought to be—overseeing the well-being of a guest. Now he stood, with nothing in hand, uncertain of his place.

She closed the door behind him and strode to the chair, which had been returned to its place by the dresser, and cleared the coat, jacket, and waistcoat that hung over its back. "I'm fine," she said, tossing the clothes in a heap by the corner. "Why wouldn't I be fine?"

The slight crack in her voice rent his already failing armor. "Because my blasted siblings spent the past three hours discussing what I need in a wife?"

"And?" She crossed her arms, daring him to say it.

"And it couldn't have been pleasant to hear, given our history."

"You mean, given I don't meet the criteria?"

He ran a hand through his hair. This was his reckoning, the moment he paid the price for his past mistakes. The moment where his selfishness for entwining his heart with hers so long ago finally bore consequences. "I guess. Yes. Given you don't meet their criteria."

It was a simple word change. *Their* not *the*. And he hoped she'd recognized it. Because if he hadn't been the duke, if he needed a wife and not a duchess, if he'd been free to follow what he wanted and not what was expected of him, then the whole of her—every quirk, every seeming flaw, every trait that made her entirely unsuitable—would be his only criteria.

But she didn't notice that small change. Instead, she flung her hands in the air. "And the bar is nae even high! She must be pretty and amiable with no opinions?"

"Fi…" No woman would ever meet the standards she set. No woman would ever take complete hold of his heart the way she had. The bar was impossibly high for whoever it was he eventually married. They would always pale in comparison. It was a cruel and bitter thing to do to a woman. Deep down, it was the reason he couldn't go through with his engagement to Amelia, and he felt sick that he was about to enter an engagement with a nice enough woman— whichever one he picked—and he'd never be able to give her all of him.

Unaware of the declaration his soul had whispered but his body could not, she shook her hands, as though trying to fling off the memory of their time together.

"Nae," she said. "Nae, it's *bonny*. Now I ken *exactly* why you ended things. And I'm glad ye did, because if that's what ye need in a wife, then I am most unsuitable for the position."

"Fi…"

"Nae. It's fine. Really. Ye can go to bed now and sleep well." She crossed to the bed where she sat and began to unbuckle her shoes, pulling at the leather with an angry tug. Swearing, she changed hands, resting her still-swollen and wrapped wrist in her lap.

He should've done as she said.

He should have closed the door and gone back to his own rooms.

Instead, he stepped forward to stand before her. She didn't look up from her feet, and perhaps that was a good thing. He probably couldn't have said the next words if he'd been forced to look her in the eye as he did so.

"I need to marry." The words cut, like a blade through his skin. He had no wish to take a wife that wasn't Fiona. But he was a duke. "And I need to marry soon. Before my mother has a hand in it and chooses someone dreadful. Before the gossips start to spread rumors about why the duke has not yet chosen a duchess and produced an heir."

He had a duty. He'd been irresponsible putting it off this long as it was.

She looked up, flinging her hair over her shoulder. Her green eyes sparked with a hot fury. "Good. You should marry, and Charlotte has the right of it; ye should choose somebody who's able to manage your dinner parties and flutter about charming yer guests without being a constant risk to yer reputation."

"I wanted to marry you." It was probably unfair to say it. They were words that he needed to utter but that she didn't need to hear. But if this blasted situation had taught him anything, it was that he was more like his father than he'd care to admit. Selfish and greedy. Irresponsible and uncaring of the pain his actions would cause.

"Aye. Ye wanted to marry me. But ye didnae." She turned her attention back to her boot, struggling to pull it off with her uninjured hand.

He knelt in front of her, taking the heel in his hand.

"It's *fine*," she said, pulling her slipper from his grasp.

"Just let me help."

She sat stiff as he tugged the first shoe free. Then he pulled at the buckle on the other, keeping his eyes trained on the leather in front of him, because if he had to look at her, he wasn't sure he wouldn't cry.

"I would never have married ye anyway." Her words stung like a reed against his bare back. "Nae once I found out what you were." *Crack.* "If ye hadn't broken it off, I would have." *Crack.*

And now the torment of rejection was his to endure. As he sat there on his knees in front of the woman he loved but could not have, he could understand what drove his father to follow his heart somewhere so inadvisable, because the pain of this was almost unbearable. Almost.

Chapter 17 ——————————

He'd barely slept. He'd wished for the relief of slumber, but when it came, it did so with the same dream repeating over and over. She made love to him and then dismissed him, and he would wake up calling out her name. Every time he succumbed to sleep, he'd been compelled to endure it again.

Which was why forcing himself to smile this morning as he walked toward Charlotte's drawing room took more effort than usual, because he knew what awaited him, had agreed to it two days ago when Charlotte was outlining her plan to find him a bride, but now it felt as though he were walking into purgatory.

At the other end of the corridor, William appeared. At least Edward wasn't in it alone.

"Will." He couldn't keep the frost from his tone. It wasn't fair to blame his siblings for last night's exchange with Fiona. But they sure as hell hadn't made the evening easier.

"You also received a summons?" Will asked. "Did Simmons tell you what it was about?"

Edward raised his eyebrows. "Char didn't inform you?" Well, at least he got this revenge. He pushed open the door and the two brothers entered the room.

"Oh, hell no." William turned on his heel and walked back out the door.

Edward was tempted to follow, but such a move would certainly reach the ears and lips of London's gossips, because in front of him was a semicircle of debutantes, each seated in front of an easel with watercolors on a tray beside them.

At the front of the semicircle were two chairs and an array of fruits, books, and other props. He had not agreed to the props.

"William!" Charlotte called as she hurried after him, leaving Edward alone facing the group of girls with varying degrees of nervousness on their faces.

"Ladies." He bowed a touch deeper than normal, taking the extra second to determine what he could possibly say in this utterly absurd situation. "You all look lovely" was the best he could muster.

Charlotte reentered, hands on her hips, with an annoyed expression. "My apologies, ladies. It seems my younger brother has a pressing engagement that I was unaware of. But for now, His Grace is here." She smiled widely at the women present.

Charlotte turned to Edward. "I was just telling our guests how excited you were at the opportunity to be their muse."

Excited was not the adjective he would use. However, his sister had suggested it as a way to get to know some of the latest crop of marriageable women outside of a ballroom setting, and if it would help him find a suitable duchess sooner, then he would grit his teeth and bear it, despite how ill it made him.

"Yes, my sister is full of ideas. I *love* her for them." He walked into the center of the room and took a seat in one of the two chairs. "No fruit," he muttered to his sister as she brushed his shoulders and adjusted his cravat.

Charlotte ignored him and placed a pineapple in his lap. "There," she said to the women. "We are almost ready. We are just waiting on—"

Fiona entered, her attention on a notebook in her hands. "William said you wanted to see me?"

A lump formed in Edward's throat and he skipped a breath.

She looked up and stopped dead in her tracks once she realized what was waiting for her. Slowly, she started to back out.

Not willing to let another model off the hook, Charlotte took Fi by the arm and guided her toward the chair next to Edward. "Thank you so much for volunteering, Mr. McTavish. Helping one's friends is such an important endeavor, don't you think?"

From the look on her face, Edward was fairly sure that in this situation, *no*, Fiona did *not* think. But she was also not about to embarrass Charlotte in front of these women.

As Charlotte delivered a quick explanation to the gathered debutantes, Fiona settled into the chair next to him. The tension between them was palpable. Fiona leaned away from him, with her ankles and arms crossed in a clear demonstration of exactly how she felt about the situation. Edward leaned one ankle on top of his knee and held the blasted pineapple as formally as he could.

Smile, Charlotte mouthed silently as she peered over her easel. He stretched his lips wide, but considering the shake of his sister's head, it did not resemble a smile.

With the ladies all engrossed in early sketches, he took a moment to survey the chits in front of him—that had, after all, been the purpose of this hellish situation. A couple were from his mother's list, a couple were suggestions his sister had made, and one was his own request, Lady Marianne Haddington.

All of them paled in comparison to Fiona. They were traditionally lovely—pale skin, delicate features—but they were very, very young. Not one was past the age of twenty, he was sure of it. Which was the norm, he supposed, when it came to society marriages. But the thought of bedding one gave him no pleasure.

Miss Ashby was turning splotchy pink merely from looking at him.

Lady Anne was notoriously political—a rare and admirable trait in a woman, but not when her politics were the complete opposite of his.

Lady Eva simply looked bored. She was by all counts an eligible young lady, but in three seasons she'd yet to show any hint of interest in the marriage mart.

Lady Marianne was the only one who looked as though she was genuinely enjoying herself. She even managed to induce a shy giggle from Miss Ashby. When Edward caught her eye as she looked at him, she didn't blush and turn away. She gave him a smile and a small nod, as though she could sense that this was every bit as awkward for him as it was for them.

If only she knew the half of it. Luckily, from their angle, none of the women would be able to see the red flush creeping up the back of Fiona's neck.

"My brother is very much looking forward to hosting dinner parties," Charlotte said. "Lady Anne, you hosted several on behalf of your father last year, did you not?"

Lady Anne's pink splotches turned a violent shade of crimson. "I did. I've also held three dinner parties in the past month to welcome various members of the family as they return to London."

"And what did you serve?" Charlotte asked.

Fiona shifted in her seat so that she could lean close to Edward. "Is this an interview?" she hissed. "Are you interviewing these women for the role of duchess? *In front* of each other?"

"It was Charlotte's idea," he muttered. Though it hadn't seemed quite so harebrained when she'd suggested it.

The door opened, and Simmons entered followed by two footmen toting another easel and paintbox.

"Lady Luella Tarlington," Simmons announced, stepping aside as the young woman entered. She wore a simple yet elegant dress that had been expertly tailored to emphasize her height and the delicate curve of her collarbone. The watered silk perfectly suited her skin tone, and she moved with a practiced grace many young girls tried for but couldn't master.

To most, she was considered perfect. Since Amelia's departure from society, Luella had been crowned the *ton*'s diamond, which was no doubt what put her at the top of his mother's list. But Edward saw her ruthless ambition. He'd kept her at arm's length because of it. She was beautiful the way a fox was beautiful, stunning but quick to devour any animal smaller than her.

And by the look she threw Fiona, she had her prey in sight.

Next to him, Fiona stiffened and Edward remembered. The two women had met last year at Amelia's blasted dinner party. When Fiona had been herself and not Finley. He ran an eye over Fi—her wig, her figure widened at the shoulders with padding, her male attire and worn knee boots. He'd never been fooled by her costume, but plenty of others had been. Would it be enough to fool someone who'd met her before, though?

As Luella set up, half her attention always on Edward, Charlotte continued interrogating the other ladies. "Lady Eva, what would you say your greatest talent is?"

Lady Eva looked Charlotte straight in the eye and replied in the most deadpan tone, "Conversation." And went back to her painting.

Edward coughed to cover his snort. Perhaps Lady Eva was more interesting than he had gathered. Fiona smiled.

Luella, hand poised in the contrived expression of an artist about to work, looked at Edward. "I would say, the mark of a truly great wife is not what her strengths are, but how she nurtures and highlights the strengths of her husband."

"Bollocks," Fiona muttered, not quietly enough.

Luella's gaze sharpened, fixed on Fiona like a blade held at a throat. "I don't believe we've met."

Fiona inclined her head casually, but her fingers dug into her coat sleeves. "Mr. Finley McTavish, at yer service."

Luella raised an eyebrow. "*Finley* McTavish? I believe I've had the pleasure of meeting your sister. You look very much alike."

Blast. She knows. It wasn't her words, exactly. It was the threat her tone carried. The rest of the girls were oblivious to it. To them it must have seemed like polite chitchat, though Lady Marianne watched the exchange with interest.

"We both take after our father," Fi replied coolly.

Charlotte, the ever-involved host, chimed in. "Isn't familial resemblance uncanny? Why, I've had complete strangers ask if I was related to William. People thought us twins when we were younger."

Luella's smile turned cunning. "How interesting it would

be to make a direct comparison. Is your sister in residence? Perhaps we could call her in."

Edward's stomach tightened. Before he could intervene, Fiona responded.

"She's nae currently in London. But I will pass on yer regards."

"Hmmm." Luella considered Fiona and continued to sketch. "How interesting. I was certain I saw her on Grosvenor Street a few days ago. In the arms of the duke. That was her, was it not, Your Grace?"

Curse it. He hadn't thought twice about carrying Fiona after her fall. His only goal had been to get her home safely so he could summon the physician. But he'd been a fool not to realize the Duke of Wildeforde could not carry a woman in his arms through Mayfair without being seen by those who knew him, and who would want to know more.

Every girl in the room turned their attention away from their easels and to him.

"That sounds far more salacious than it was," he said. "Miss McTavish was injured, and traffic had come to a stop. For her health, I helped her home."

"How kind of you," Luella said.

From Charlotte's expression, it was clear that she was realizing that there were undercurrents to this situation that she was unaware of. "My brother is the kindest of souls. Lady Marianne, why don't you describe how you've managed your father's household since your poor mother passed. I'm sure my brother is keen to know of your skills."

For the next hour Charlotte, with the help of Haddington's daughter, kept the conversation on utterly inane matters related to managing a household and engaging with society. It served as both a buffer between him, Luella, and Fiona, and a reminder of his responsibilities—to marry a woman who would bear him an heir, run his household, and support him in the execution of his duties, both political and social.

Any of the women in front of him could fulfill those duties with ease. They held no appeal to him, but they were perfect examples of what a duke should be looking for in a wife.

Not the woman beside him who could barely contain her contempt for the conversation. Who could never fit that mold.

Relief washed through him when Charlotte announced that the morning's activity had come to an end and that it was time to leave. She would send a footman around with the easels once the paintings had dried.

Each of the debutantes curtseyed deeply as they left, although by the hurried way they packed up their things, it seemed they were as eager for the event to be over as Edward was. Only Lady Marianne stopped to exchange a few words with him before she left.

Luella was the last to leave, and she held her arm out to him. "Will you escort me out, Your Grace?"

Despite wishing to have nothing to do with her, he took her hand. She was the only person outside of his household who knew of Fiona's deception, and he needed to discover exactly what she planned on doing with her information.

"The rest of society may be fools, Your Grace, but I am not," Luella said once they were in the hall and out of Charlotte and Fiona's earshot.

Fear and anger were twin beasts waking inside of him. "You've always struck me as an intelligent woman, Lady Luella. One who knows better than to make unnecessary enemies." Advice. Warning. Threat. He didn't particularly care how she interpreted his words, only that she heeded them.

She turned to face him. "I'm merely concerned, Your Grace. I'd hate to see your good name ruined by a woman who'd found a novel way to sink her claws into you."

Luella's faux concern turned his stomach. "Fear not. My decisions are my own."

Simmons appeared with her coat and parasol. She stood there, unmoving, until Edward took the coat and held it for her. With a satisfied nod, she turned and threaded her arm through the sleeve. "We will eat her alive. You know that, don't you?" she asked in the same sweet, polite tone someone might use when discussing what flavored ice they wanted. "She will be the subject of scorn in every house in London."

Her words chilled him. "Sheath your claws. *Finley* is in town for business only."

Luella faced him, smiling as she buttoned up her coat. "And I'm sure that business won't go well if *his* deception is revealed. Neither will your complicity in fooling the *ton* be viewed favorably. It might well be the biggest scandal since...oh, I don't know. Your father?" She accepted her parasol from Simmons, who, despite his impeccable training, could not keep the scowl from his expression.

"What do you want?" Edward asked. Her response did not surprise him.

"I need to be a duchess, and I don't really care how."

⁓

After Edward and Luella had left, Fiona's instinct was to make a quick exit, but she couldn't resist visiting each easel. It was disconcerting to see her face replicated so many times. It was especially disconcerting to see such masculine versions of herself, for each of the debutantes—subconsciously or not—

had strengthened her jaw slightly, gone heavier on the brows than was true, and thinned her lips just a touch.

It was as if they saw only what they expected to see.

Except the last painting—a beautifully rendered image of her and Edward leaning toward each other, mid-conversation. No, this painting did not skip over her feminine features, but rather enhanced them. Anyone looking at it would see the truth of the subject—a woman disguised as a man, and not very well at that.

Looking to the bottom corner, she saw what she expected to: Lady Luella's name elegantly drawn.

With a quick glance to make sure Charlotte's attention was on packing up her own work, Fiona picked up the painting, folded it in quarters and stuffed it in her morning coat, then she crossed to the window where she could watch Luella leave.

"That was an interesting afternoon," Charlotte said, coming up beside her as Luella climbed into her carriage. "I must confess, I'm not sure I had all the information going into it."

A thread of guilt wormed through her. "No one ever does, Char. We just make the best choices we can with what we have." She'd certainly not had all the information when she and Edward met. Falling in love was the only thing she could have done, under the circumstances.

"And have I made the right choices, do you think?" Charlotte held out the sketch she'd been working on. She'd done a lovely job. The boy on the page was captured mid-smile, a cheeky, friendly look on his face. It was a flattering likeness and beneath in an elegant hand, two words: *New Friends*.

"Have I missed anything, do you think? Have I got anything wrong?"

Fiona swallowed, wishing she could tell Charlotte every-thing. Both the Stirling siblings would be hurt if—when—they discovered the truth, and Fiona was coming to care for them a great deal, just as she cared for the duke. And look at the damage she'd done to him last night.

A week ago, the thought of being "even," the score being "settled," would have given her some measure of satisfaction. Instead, it made her stomach roil.

"No, Char. Everything is perfect."

Chapter 18

To Fiona's frustration, she'd not had the chance to speak with Edward alone that afternoon. No sooner had the young ladies and their painting sets vanished than her father arrived. He was *displeased*. Apparently, not even the threat of jail time was a reasonable excuse for residing under the same roof as that "black-hearted, self-serving toff."

At least he hadn't said it to Edward's face. But walls had ears and she was sure the duke would hear about Alastair's arrival, and his insults, soon enough.

In an effort to avoid further conflict, she'd done as her father asked, showing him around the makeshift laboratory she'd created from one of Edward's rarely used receiving rooms. She didn't know why he bothered feigning interest in her work now, when he'd never visited her permanent lab at the firm back home. He didn't even question her continued appearance as Finley. No doubt he simply wanted to see inside a ducal manor, to find more evidence of inequity to fuel his constant fire.

By the time she'd managed to get him out the door, Edward had left once more and her chance to talk to him had vanished. And she needed to talk to him. His words had plagued her all night. She had been surly that afternoon while their portraits were painted in part because she'd not slept.

I wanted to marry you.

She'd been so hurt by that evening's conversation that she'd lashed out. Now, every time she closed her eyes, the way he'd recoiled from her words played through her mind. She'd hurt more than his pride; she was sure of it. But she didn't know what that meant for them.

So a cloud hung over her, making it all the more difficult to focus on what mattered. Tonight's ball was crucial. Both Viscount Chester and the Earl of Livingworth would be there.

William's old clothes had been tailored to fit Fi perfectly. Bessie had added subtle shoulder padding to the blue tailcoat to create a masculine silhouette. The wide lapel and voluminous frill served to hide any hint of swelling around the chest. Fiona was grateful for the design. It allowed her to loosen her chest bindings a fraction so she could dance without fainting from lack of air.

The breeches had been sewn to snug tightly to her legs, as was the current fashion. As she sat in the carriage, thigh to thigh with Edward, Fiona hungered for the layers of skirts and petticoats that would have provided a more stringent barrier between them.

She could feel the tension in him. It seeped into her bloodstream, causing her heart to thrum and the hairs on the back of her neck to rise. Sitting so close, his scent was pervasive, occupying her nose, her lungs, her brain—fogging up her thoughts to the point that the practiced words of her pitch scattered like birds following a gun shot.

I would ne'er have married ye anyway.

Was it even the truth? She didn't want to be a duchess, but back then, in the full bloom of passion, would that have stopped her? Or would she have trusted in their love to see them through? Even now, her body ached for him—as though he were a missing part of her—not caring that it betrayed her in the process.

It had ached for him that morning as she was forced to sit there and watch while his potential wives vied for his approval. They had every trait Charlotte and William had stipulated. All traits Fiona lacked.

"Finley, you seem nervous," Charlotte said, a concerned expression on her face. "You shouldn't be. Your dancing is perfectly acceptable. A few more hours and you'd out-dance most men of the *ton*."

Fiona tried to give a smile, though it felt distorted. "Less nervous about the dancing and more fearful of bollocksing up the pitch to Lords Chester and Livingworth. It's hard enough remembering each point when I'm in the quiet of an office. I can't imagine how badly a ballroom will distract me."

She had been trying to practice her case all day. In her earlier meetings she'd had test results, sketches, and a working prototype. Tonight, she would have nothing. All she had to rely upon to convince these men to invest thousands of pounds were her words.

"You'll be fine," Edward said—the first words he'd uttered since they'd entered the carriage. "Livingworth likes to be reminded of how benevolent he is, so be sure to mention that you've heard of his reputation for taking on worthy causes. And Chester hates sycophants. Be casual in your approach with him."

Rather than easing her nerves, the information agitated them, because neither of those points had been in her plan.

She suddenly felt very, very foolish. Edward had had a wealth of information. If this went wrong tonight, it would be her fault for refusing to tap into it.

"Well, I can introduce you to the Earl of Livingworth," Charlotte said, "but William or Edward will need to introduce you to Lord Chester. He's not one debutantes spend time with."

"Not me," said William, shaking his head. "I...uh... Chester and I aren't speaking. I might have...Never mind. Edward, it'll have to be you. Just don't tell him I'm here."

Edward looked at Fiona. The small smile he gave her was encouraging, both that she might actually succeed tonight, and that he might one day forgive her for her words the night before.

Charlotte patted her on the knee. "You'll be in good hands with Ned. You'll see."

The butler announced them. His Grace the Duke of Wildeforde, Lord William Stirling, Lady Charlotte-Rose Stirling, and Mr. Finley McTavish.

All heads swiveled in their direction. The general hubbub of a room talking quieted for a moment and then broke out in furious whispers. As Fiona looked around, she could see women at the back of the room craning their necks to see the newcomers, the feathers in their hairpieces bobbing and weaving like a flock of mating flamingos.

"Do you always attract such attention?" Fiona murmured to Charlotte.

"It's Edward. He attracts attention all the time, but no doubt word has gotten out that he's looking for a wife this season. Be prepared for the onslaught."

Just as Charlotte predicted, the four of them were mobbed within seconds. A horde of middling-aged women appeared, each towing at least one daughter in their direction—young women dressed in various shades of white, some with their heads gracefully high, others trying their best to hide behind their marriage-minded mothers.

Charlotte was like a torch that had ignited. Her eyes gleamed and her smile shone bright on every person she looked at. She pressed people's hands, bestowed on the congregated masses breathless air kisses, and let her infectious laugh roll over every person who approached. Clearly, she was in her element.

While each of the girls was gracious as Charlotte introduced Fiona—Finley—they each had their attention fixed on Edward, whose smile was oddly frozen in place. He responded to their flirtations with acknowledgments that felt forced in their jauntiness.

"He doesn't seem to be enjoying this," Fiona murmured to William, who had stepped beside her.

William snickered. "He doesn't have to enjoy it. He's the duke. It's his duty."

Damn his duty. If he hadn't been so beholden to it, perhaps she could have convinced him to live a different life, with her. And damn these women and the predatory way in which they circled.

"Right," said William. "I'm off before his dance card fills up and they come after me instead. The gaming room is at the back. You should join me when you're done with your business whatnot."

And just like that, he was gone, ducking and weaving his way through the crowd, managing to brush off every woman who tried to hail him. Fiona wished she could follow. Instead, she was left to stand beside Edward as his potential future brides lined up for the opportunity to flatter him.

"Your Grace," one of the debutantes said with a slight whine in her voice, "surely you don't mean to keep us all in suspense. At least ask *one* of us to dance." The look she gave made it very clear who she thought that "one" should be.

"Actually, I promised Mr. McTavish that I would introduce him to Lord Chester, who is over there. Excuse us." He bowed to the ladies present, and in a synchronized wave they curtseyed. Not one of them wobbled, despite the depth of the bend and the weight of the jewels that were proudly displayed.

Edward smiled tightly as he broke through the ring of silk, sighing as more than one lady refused to move, necessitating his brushing close past them.

"How can you stand it?" Fiona whispered to him as they reached open waters.

"They mostly left me alone while I was engaged to Amelia," he muttered. "It's been a deuced nightmare since. Every woman wants to be a duchess." He flushed, grimacing slightly. A muscle ticked along his jaw. "Almost every woman."

The pain in his tone tugged at her heart, and she had to remind herself that whatever her feelings about his words last night, the reality was he'd decided she wasn't fit to be a duchess a long time ago. So she tried to put aside the guilt for the cutting things she'd said and focus on the task at hand. Her business deal. But the constant fawning interruptions— by women and men—as they crossed the ballroom set off a jinglejangle of nagging thoughts in her mind.

"How do you know who likes you for you and not your title?" she asked eventually, after Edward had extricated them from yet another bootlicking encounter.

His shoulders stiffened. "I don't."

It was as brutal a response as she could receive. They were walking the perimeter of the room. As they passed a cluster of potted palms, she grabbed him by the arm and towed him to privacy behind the giant green leaves.

"I'm sorry," she said, cupping his cheek with her hand, and she was. She was more than familiar with the inability to trust others, but at the very least she had a good sense of who felt what for her. To not be certain about the very nature of one's relationships was bleak indeed.

He pulled away and looked up at the ceiling, his head shaking slightly as if arguing with himself. "I'm fairly sure my sister loves me," he said eventually. "I'm fairly sure my mother doesn't. Everyone else has a question mark above them. Except you. At least, back then."

"Because I didn't know you were a duke." The world tilted slightly, shifting her view of the past. He hadn't been mocking her when he hid his identity. He hadn't been trying to take advantage of her. He had just...

He caught her gaze, his stare burning into her soul. His expression was raw, vulnerable. "The relief I felt when I realized you had no idea I was the duke was visceral—like the burden of the title was this great weight that had suddenly lifted. It was wrong not to tell you. But I saw the opportunity to be known, to be liked, for me, and I latched on to it."

It had been wrong, and it had caused her incredible harm, but she could understand it. She, too, knew the pain of wanting to be loved—wasn't that why she'd chased after her father as she had? She took his hand and squeezed it.

"I know you say that you never knew me," he continued. "But it's not true. You're the only one who ever has." His voice cracked as he spoke and the look in his eyes was so bleak, so desolate, so hurting, that it was all she could do not to wrap him in her arms. Instead, she tightened her squeeze and his fingers wrapped around hers as though they were a lifeline.

He had loved her, and if she truly looked at all the evidence—the way he tried to make her smile even when she was furious with him, the way he cared for her even when that meant being an overbearing arse, the way he'd crumbled at her words last night—it was possible that he still did. And yet he'd kept himself away from her.

"How do you live your life like that?"

He answered the question he thought she'd asked. "I don't have a choice." He pulled away from her, disentangling their hands and stepping back, once more putting on the mantle of the lord. "I can't not be the duke, and that comes with certain expectations I must live up to. To do otherwise would subject my family to the worst kind of gossipmongering. I won't put them through what my father did."

And there was the crux of why they could never be together. He couldn't join her in her world without abdicating his responsibilities to his family, his tenants, and the people who relied on good men to enact change from the top. She couldn't join him in his world without giving up the essence of who she was and risking Charlotte's and Will's happiness.

"I forgive you," she said. "I can grasp why you did it."

"And you don't hate me for it?" he asked, raising a hand to her cheek, stroking it softly with the backs of his fingers.

She shook her head, scared that if she opened her mouth, how she really felt about him would spill out. Scared she'd tell him she loved him, and that would accomplish nothing but hurt. Because it wouldn't change anything.

He caressed her cheek and she breathed in deeply, leaning into his palm, her heart rate slowing as her senses wallowed in his touch, in the comfort it brought.

She swayed toward him and him toward her. His hand moved from her cheek to the back of her head. But as his fingers brushed the edge of her wig, he pulled back.

Stupid, stupid, stupid.

As she raised a hand to her chest to quiet her beating heart, Edward looked around them. Yes, they were obscured by plants. But they were in the middle of a ballroom and the palms would only protect them from a casual glance. It wouldn't hide them from anyone actively looking for him, and he was the Duke of Wildeforde, the most eligible bachelor in the room. Someone was bound to be looking for him.

He cleared his throat and worked his jaw, tipping his head from side to side as he constructed the façade of the unfeeling duke once more. With a sharp inhale and long exhale, he stepped around the potted palms and back into the maw.

Mortified, she followed.

How do you know who likes you for you and not your title?

The question haunted him with every step and turn he took. His dance partners were all polite and agreeable, some he would even describe as engaging, but he was under no illusions: they saw him as the duke first, and Edward not at all.

It irked, that sense that his title was more valuable than himself as a person, but then the sense of his own hypocrisy irked more, because what were these women to him other than their titles, their training, and their ability to do the job he needed them for? He'd be lying if he said he was looking to fall in love. He'd done that once. That had devastated him enough.

He looked to Fiona, who had just joined the line of country dancers with Charlotte as her partner. Her eyes were alight and she was grinning. Her discussion with Chester had clearly gone well. That was good. He wanted her to succeed. She deserved to.

Edward had introduced Fi to Chester, subtly praising her intelligence and business acumen, before leaving the two alone. She had been more than capable of making her case without his help.

So he'd focused on his own goal and went about filling out his name on dance card after dance card, trying to avoid the shrewish, the vapid, and the vain. It was unfathomable that within the small circle of the *ton* he would find a woman with Fiona's ambition and drive. But perhaps he could find one with her intelligence and honesty.

Lady Marianne was looking over at him from the edge of the dance floor. This dance was hers and he'd yet to appear. He forced a smile to his face and crossed to her. "Lady Marianne."

"Good evening, Your Grace," she said as she curtseyed. "You've had a busy night. I had not realized that you were such a keen dancer." Her tone was teasing, and he found himself enjoying the respite from the simpering he'd endured all night.

"It is a recently discovered joy."

She grinned. "As recently discovered as your need for a wife?"

He held back a snort. It was the first time that night one of his dance partners had managed to make him laugh. "I cannot confirm nor deny that allegation. Shall we dance?" He offered her his arm.

She slipped her arm into the crook of his elbow, but rather than heading toward the lines of people ready to dance, she paused. "Why don't we take a stroll around the room? It's not healthy to indulge one's newfound passions at all times, Your Grace. God forbid you're danced out before the week is done."

He raised an eyebrow. Whether Haddington's daughter was as perceptive as her father was and could sense his disdain for hopping about like a bug, or she was simply cunning enough to angle for a way to differentiate herself, he couldn't tell. But she was his most promising prospect for a wife and joining in another dance was the last thing he wanted. "A turn about the room it is," he said, negotiating their way through the crowd.

"So, why are you looking for a wife now?" she asked once they'd cleared the throng that ringed the dance floor.

The girl continued to surprise him. "That's an unusually forward question."

She patted his arm. "You and my father have been friends a long time, Your Grace. He appreciates how forthright you are and notices how you tend toward others with a similar honesty."

"And he has loose lips, I take it."

She gave him a cheeky grin. "He has a desire to strengthen the bond between our families, so yes, he may have suggested that I speak my mind."

"And what is on your mind, my lady?"

"You were engaged to Lady Amelia for sixteen years. By all accounts, she would have been the perfect duchess. You didn't marry her when you had the opportunity and you didn't appear particularly affected by your broken engagement. Yet here you are, looking for a wife."

The candid appraisal made him uncomfortable. It was part of the title, to have his actions scrutinized by his peers in drawing rooms across the country, but few people dared share their frank assessments with him in person. "Is there a question in there somewhere?"

Lady Marianne pursed her lips. "I've seen the women you're choosing to spend time with—I'm flattered to be one—but I cannot see what any of us offers that your previous fiancée did not. I see no indication that you're expecting a love match. So, what *are* you looking for?"

He could not help but flick his gaze toward the dance floor, where Fiona and Charlotte were laughing as they bobbed and weaved. He had not married Amelia because she'd had such high hopes for their union, and his soul would always be with the red-headed firebrand who'd taken up residence in his heart.

"I'm looking for a wife who is content with managing my house and bearing my children, and won't desire any more from me." *Someone with no further expectations.*

Lady Marianne's lips pursed thoughtfully and a crease appeared between her brows. "While I appreciate you being honest, Your Grace, I do hope that you're being honest with yourself. That you will truly be happy with the arrangement you're describing."

He would never be happy with a life that wasn't spent with Fiona. But then Luella's words came back to him. *We will eat her alive.* They echoed his mother's. *A fish out of water dies gasping.*

No, he would simply have to settle and learn to be at peace with it. "It's the only arrangement I can offer."

She nodded decisively and slipped her hand from his arm. "In that case, Your Grace, you may dance with me a second time tonight." She curtseyed and excused herself, and he was left feeling atilt. He hailed one of the passing footmen, taking a brandy snifter from the tray, and knocked back half the glass. It burned on its way down.

His cousin sidled up next to him. "Liquor?" Graham asked. "I haven't seen you drink spirits in an age. But I haven't seen you forced to enter the marriage mart either. Has the gaggle of young, willing women overwhelmed you?"

He hadn't been overwhelmed, but he did feel as though he stood upon a precipice. Lady Marianne was candid, intelligent, and in possession of all the requirements to be the Duchess of Wildeforde. She was young—so very young—but it was otherwise a good match. She would do an excellent job.

But rather than feel satisfied that he'd found a suitable candidate—and before his mother could arrive and make a mess of it all—he felt as though he'd suddenly lost something. That a big gaping chasm had just appeared inside him.

He turned to his cousin, the one man who should be a cautionary tale against the very thing that hole was yearning for. "Can I ask you a question?"

Something in his expression must have indicated the seriousness of his thoughts because Graham moved closer and lowered his voice, frowning. "Of course. You can ask me anything."

"Before you proposed to Eliza, did you consider what the worst of society might do?"

Graham swallowed, his lips pursing and the furrow between his brows deepening. "I considered. I found my own needs more pressing." His voice was tight and his eyes shone more than they had a moment ago.

It was unfair of Edward to bring up memories of his cousin's wife, but he had to know. "Was there anything you could have done to protect her?"

"Yes. I could have not married her, and she would be fine."

Edward nodded and finished his drink in one gulp, fixing his gaze on Fiona and wondering which, if either of them, was ever going to be fine. Wondering if he had the strength to do what Graham and his father couldn't.

⌒

Fiona was elated. Lord Livingworth was not interested in her matches, but in just over a week she would have the opportunity to show Viscount Chester what they could do, knowing that he already approved of the concept and now just needed to see proof it worked.

It was intoxicating, being so close to the dream. Her heart jittered and her head spun, and it had nothing to do with the punch or the circles she was turning as she exchanged one partner for another in a country dance. She was enjoying herself more than she could ever have expected.

The only cloud to the evening was watching Edward dance with one fine-looking miss after another. On the rare occasion he wasn't on the dance floor, he was at the epicenter of female fluttering. She wanted to believe that he hated the attention—that's what logic and everything she knew about him would suggest—but his smile didn't falter once. She knew because she had her attention on him all evening.

Which was why she didn't see the danger coming until partners changed mid-dance and Luella took her arm with a viselike grip. Fiona's heartbeat shifted from excited jittering to a panicked stampede. She could feel perspiration beading across her hairline, just at the edge of her wig.

"What a pleasure to see you again, *sir*. You certainly seem to be making the most of your time here in London."

Fiona was tempted to take up arms against Luella. She was the epitome of everything that was wrong with the aristocracy, and the fact that people like her thrived off the backs of the working class made Fiona's blood boil.

But a war of words would solve nothing and would only jeopardize what Fiona had set out to achieve—financial independence and bettering the lives of others. So she would be meek, if that's what it took to succeed.

"I'm enjoying my time, my lady. As brief as it will be. I plan to return home shortly. Alone." *I have no interest in the duke.* That was the message she was trying to imply.

"It won't work," Luella whispered as the music came to an end. "This scheme of your *sister's*. He will never make a common girl his duchess. Not after what happened to the Viscount Dunburton."

Fiona stilled. Around them gentlemen escorted their dance partners off the floor. Fiona found herself at the sharp end of annoyed looks as couples navigated around her and Luella. Manners dictated she take Luella's arm and guide her to her next partner. But Fi's feet were rooted to the floor.

"I've nae heard of the Viscount Dunburton," Fiona replied. She knew whatever Luella had planned was a trap but she was too intrigued to avoid it.

"Truly?" Luella asked with an innocent flutter of her lashes. "It was quite the scandal. I would have thought even a country bumpkin such as yourself would have heard of it."

"London gossip does nae tend to make it that far south."

Luella thrust open her fan, using it to shield her face from view as though she and Fiona were friends sharing titillating gossip for amusement. "Wildeforde's cousin married a *shopgirl*. A woman with no breeding and no experience. A base commoner instead of a lady more deserving of the title."

Fiona's heart plummeted. How had Edward not mentioned it? Because he didn't want to admit that a girl like her could be a viscountess but not a duchess? Or was it just that a girl like her couldn't be Edward's duchess?

Luella took her arm and propelled her into motion.

"Society gave her the welcome she deserved," Luella continued with saccharine sweetness. "She only lasted a month before she took her life."

All the air rushed from Fiona's lungs. Her breast bindings felt as though they were constricting all on their own. Blackness crept into the edge of her vision. "When was this?" she managed to ask, hating the way she leaned on Luella's arm for support.

Luella screwed up her nose in contemplation. "About five years ago?"

Chapter 19

If it was going to be any of them, it would be Lady Marianne Haddington. She would meet Charlotte's approval and Graham's. Likely William's and maybe even his mother's. The sooner he proposed, the sooner he could be done with it all.

And yet he couldn't bring himself to feel any kind of enthusiasm at the prospect of perhaps having found the perfect future duchess. He couldn't bring himself to feel anything at all.

The strains of a waltz started. He sighed. Lady Luella had demanded a waltz and until Fiona was safely gone, he would have to placate her. She was at the edge of the dance floor, watching him. Waiting expectantly. But in between them was Fiona, approaching quickly. She was white as a ghost, her face stricken.

"What's wrong?" he asked as she got close.

She didn't break stride. "Come with me."

Confused, concerned, he followed her as she tore out of

the ballroom. Upon reaching the foyer, she growled as she eyed the many servants and guests present, and then turned down the corridor.

"Fi!" He grabbed her arm. "Where are we going?"

"An empty room," she said. Her voice was so urgent and so full of hurt and anger and disbelief that he snapped into bodyguard mode, taking her by the shoulders and guiding her to safety. "Fourth door on the left," he said. "It's Macklebury's library."

Fiona opened the door, waited as he passed her, and then slammed it shut behind them.

He took her by the shoulder with one hand, the other coming to her cheek, searching her face for a clue as to what was wrong. "What happened? Are you well?" He would pulverize whoever hurt her.

"I ken." Her voice cracked as she said it.

"You know what?"

She raised a hand to cover his, pressing it into her cheek. "About your cousin. About the viscountess. That's the real reason, isn't it? Why you broke things off?"

Fuck. This wasn't how he wanted her to find out. He hadn't ever wanted her to find out. He dropped his hands and turned away, raking his fingers through his hair. Guilt, fear, regret— they all warred through him. He should have told her earlier. He should have told her when he broke off their engagement. She'd had a right to know the true reason he'd left.

But she was so good, so amazingly self-assured. Back then, he'd worried that if he told her, she wouldn't accept it.

"Good God, Ed. Did ye really think that would be me?"

His concern was clearly well-placed. She could not fathom the depths of the cruelty she'd be subjected to. She would have approached it with her usual energy, and she would have been crushed. "You don't know this world. It looks all sugar and sparkle, but parts of it are vicious and cruel. Had we married, you would not have been safe."

She threw her hands up in disbelief. "Safe? From cruel comments? From being ostracized and ignored? I have been thrown out of my home, traveled the length of England with only a kitchen knife to protect me, and had to barricade myself against drunk and ill-intentioned men. And you were worried some scornful comments might harm me?"

She didn't understand, the way he'd known she wouldn't. "You say it like it's nothing, but the love of Graham's life *died*. I would rather have broken your heart than stopped it."

She sagged back against the door. The furious energy drained from her expression, leaving quiet, solemn examination. She watched him for a long moment. He could see thoughts ticking over, but he had no idea what they were. Eventually, she asked, "Why did ye go back to London that week?"

He leaned on the chaise that sat opposite the fireplace. "To break the news to my mother that I was about to marry someone wholly unsuitable to be a duchess."

She swallowed. "Ye were willing to live through the scandal, despite what it would cost yer family?"

"To have you? Yes."

She looked away. The tears in her eyes reflected the flames from the fireplace. And he waited, silently, for her verdict.

At last, she nodded. Then, faster than his mind could process, she crossed to him, took his face in both hands roughly, and kissed him.

It was like he'd been wandering a desert for five years and had now found himself home. He drank her in, his thirst for her insatiable. He pressed at her lips with his tongue—wanting more, needing more—and with a groan she opened for him.

The taste of her, the way her tongue met his with equal fervor, the need with which she pressed her fingers into the back of his head, holding him to her—it made his cock stiffen, straining against the fall of his breeches.

Without breaking their kiss, he stood, one arm wrapped around her, grabbing her arse in his hand and pulling her hard against his groin. The other hand snaked up her spine, over her neck, to where it found the edge of her wig.

Desperate fingers sought and removed the pins that held the wig in place, tossing them carelessly on the floor. The wig came next, dislodged as his hand sank into her silken-soft curls. "Oh, God, Fi," he murmured, breaking their kiss in order to rest his head against hers and inhale deeply.

He'd missed the scent of her, that sweet jasmine and honey that had haunted him every time he'd walked through the wrong garden or past the wrong flower stall.

With her here, he breathed in deep. He'd never thought they would have another moment like this. Never thought she'd once again be in his arms. This was where she belonged. This was where everything made sense.

"Ed." His heart thundered at the use of his nickname. She tipped her head back, her hand coming to his jaw, and caught his gaze. In her eyes he saw a flame that matched his. A fire that had smoldered for years but now flared into its fullest fury. "Don't stop," she said.

And so he didn't. Desperately, he took her lips with his.

With both hands he picked her up and spun around to sit her on the back of the chaise longue. She wrapped her legs around his waist and sank her fingers into his cravat, pulling and yanking until the knot came free.

Desperate to feel her body beneath his palms, he ran his hands up her sides, his thumbs grazing her stomach, her chest. But instead of a neckline and soft, soft skin, there were folds and folds of fabric—the edge of her waistcoat, the frill of her shirt, the soft linen of her cravat.

Thank God, because if fingertips had grazed skin, he wasn't sure he'd be able to stop. And he needed to stop. This was madness.

They were in a library with hundreds of his peers just outside. She wasn't Fiona, she was Finley, and being caught in this charade would be disaster.

"We can't," he said. "Not here." Dragging himself away from her was the hardest thing he'd done in years. His body stiffened in protest. His cock pressed hard against his breeches, straining to be free.

Her chest rose and fell, over and over, and he could tell the moment her mind cleared. Her cheeks, flushed pink with desire, reddened and her pupils focused as she realized where they were and what they'd been doing. "Um…help me find my pins?"

Together, they gathered the hairpins Edward had tossed on the floor, and haphazardly constrained her curls until she could shove them beneath her wig.

"Do I look all right? Do I look like Finley?" she asked.

"Every man who looks at you and doesn't see the beautiful woman beneath it is both blind and stupid," he muttered. She was the sun, and if she were to enter a London ballroom as herself, every lord of the *ton* would fall to his knees in worship.

When her costume was back in place, he cupped her face in his hands, kissing her gently. "This isn't over," he murmured, his forehead resting against hers. He didn't know what that moment meant; he just knew that he couldn't carry on as if it hadn't happened. There was no moving on with his life this time.

She curled her fingers into his shirt frills. But he would

never know what she was about to say, because at that moment, the door to the study opened. "Ned? Are you in here? You've always said it's rude to—" Charlotte stopped in her tracks as her gaze landed on Edward and Fiona, leaning against each other.

He sprung backward, but it was too late. Charlotte's eyes narrowed. They focused in on Edward's untied cravat, traveled to his rumpled hair, then shifted to Fiona, who was staring steadfastly at her shoes, her cheeks aflame.

"Well," Charlotte said, closing the door behind her and turning the lock, which in hindsight would have been a good thing for Edward to have thought of earlier.

"I can explain," he said, not entirely sure what the explanation would be. They would have to come clean to her at some point. But right here, right now was probably not the best place.

Charlotte approached them with a leery expression. She took Fiona's chin in her hand, raising it so the two girls were eye to eye. She turned Fiona's face to the right and then the left, studying it.

Fiona swallowed.

Charlotte smiled, and then she tucked a scrap of Fiona's hair that Edward had missed underneath Fi's wig. "I must say, this is starting to make more sense."

Chapter 20 ————————————

They didn't remain at the Macklebury ball much longer. Fiona watched Edward dance with two more debutantes while she stood by the refreshment table and feigned interest in a conversation about horses. Soon after, Charlotte—unsatisfied with her brother's promise to explain the situation when they returned home—complained of a headache and the family left. Just in time, according to William, who had apparently had a run-in with Lord Chester.

Thud. Thud. Sitting at the dressing table, Fiona tossed her slippers into the growing pile of clothes in the corner of her room. She had refused Edward's offer of someone to attend her but was beginning to see why the upper classes required valets and lady's maids. The constant changing of clothing, the intricacies of each outfit, they all contributed to the pile, and she'd had no time to clean or press them herself.

She pulled and tugged at her cravat before sliding it off and laying it flat alongside the wig she'd removed as soon as she'd gotten home. Then she started on the buttons of her waistcoat.

In another room, Edward would be doing the same thing. Her pulse quickened at the thought of him slipping one button after another. Of him pulling his shirt from his waistband. Of him unlacing the fall of his breeches.

A hot flush crept up her neck. Their kiss had ignited a fire within her. All the physical sensations of their time together had lain dormant for so long but now bubbled up to the surface—the rasp of her fingertips through the coarse hair on his chest. The feeling of his breath, hot against her ear. The warmth that pooled between her legs.

During their first affair, they had never taken it too far beyond the bounds of propriety. Their clothes had stayed on, even if their hands roamed beneath. He'd been quite resolved in that manner, to her frustration.

That same wanting, that same desire that consumed her then thrummed through her now, as if no time had passed.

She considered going to him. There was no reason not to. She was twenty-five years old, a true spinster, and she'd decided long ago that marriage wasn't for her. She would have her cottage and her work. If she chose to take a lover to fulfill other needs, then that was her business alone.

She and Edward would never have a happily ever after; their lives were too different, but there was no reason they couldn't be happy for now. Just until her matches sold and her court case was over. Then she would return to Abingdale with wonderful memories of him.

Knock. Knock. Fiona's heartbeat picked up pace. "Who is it?" She struggled to keep her voice even.

"It's me."

The breath whooshed out of her. She stood and looked quickly around the room. She took a blanket from the reading chair and threw it over the pile of clothes. She gathered her papers—haphazardly strewn over the dressing table—and smooshed them into a stack. On her way to the door, she knocked her trunk closed with her foot and adjusted the neckline of her shirt.

Taking a deep breath, trying to calm the flutterings of her stomach, she opened the door.

Edward had an arm on either side of the doorframe. He loomed forward, over six feet of powerful, duke-ish energy that radiated from him making her knees weaken and her breath come in short, shallow gasps.

His hair was damp and tousled, as though he'd run his hands through it over and over before coming to her. He wore no coat, no waistcoat, no cravat. Instead, his shirt hung open at the neck, revealing the sharp edge of his collarbone and a smattering of dark hair that led down, beyond the edge of the fabric to where her mind strayed. A hot flush crept up her neck.

"I want you," he said and the words sent pleasure coursing through her. "I want you so much I cannot think of anything but you. I cannot bathe without going hard at the thought of you wet beneath me. I cannot work without wanting to clear the desk and take you upon it. I cannot go to bed because of all the things I want to do to you in it."

"Oh…" The intimate place between her legs began to tingle and heat at his words. As she looked at him—the wildness in his eyes, the tense stance, the bulge in his breeches where his cock pulled them taut—the tingling spread through her core.

He was magnificent, and if he didn't come inside soon, she would accost him in the hallway.

Edward gripped the doorframe, his knuckles white. "If I enter, it will be to make you mine. But I will not enter unless you invite me in."

Good God. Her body moved before her brain could catch up. She stepped forward, wrapped a hand into his damp curls, and pulled his lips to hers, the heat inside her intensifying. She slid a hand around his side and up his back, and he groaned.

She broke off the kiss just long enough to say, "You should come in."

The words were barely out of her mouth when he put both arms around her arse and lifted her. Reflexively, she wrapped her legs around his waist, drawing them together to get closer to him.

"Fuck me. Fiona," he murmured. He entered her room, kicking the door shut behind him. She flinched at the bang and he paused until she relaxed against him.

He crossed to the bed, and slowly she uncurled her legs, sliding down him until her stockinged toes hit the floor. She was barely steady before he had both sides of her face cupped in his palms, and he bent his head to capture her mouth in a kiss. It was like a burning fire after a freezing walk, a good meal after too long without food. It nourished her body and soul in a way she hadn't know she was lacking.

She moaned and ran a tongue along the edge of his lips until he opened up and she touched her tongue to his, exploring the depths of him. She'd missed this with every molecule of her being.

He tugged at her shirt, pulling it from her waistband, and then his hands were roaming her naked back, leaving a trail of heat wherever they touched.

Not to be outdone, she grabbed his shirt in her hands and eased it from his waistband. She pulled away from their kiss and leaned back so she could push the fabric up his chest, revealing a toned and muscular physique. The interlocking muscles at his midsection were dusted with wiry black hair, which grew thicker farther down his body.

Edward grabbed the edge of his shirt from her and pulled it off over his head. He was stunning. His body dipped and curved, the lamplight creating shadows and highlights that made him look like a perfectly crafted statue—so incredibly hard, yet when she ran a tentative hand across his chest, he was silken soft.

Everywhere her fingers touched, goose bumps formed on his flesh. His fingers flexed; she could see that he wanted to reach for her. Instead, he stood still and let her peruse him, exploring every inch of him with her hands. When her fingers reached his throat, he swallowed hard, the muscles working. She wanted to run her tongue along it, to taste him, to feel the thrum of his pulse against her lips.

When she stepped forward to do just that, he put a restraining hand out. "Your turn."

She swallowed, shy as he took the edge of her shirt. Tentatively she raised her arms, allowing him to pull the shirt off her. As the soft linen grazed her skin, she shuddered.

He cast the shirt onto the floor at the foot of the bed and hooked a finger into the bindings that held her breasts down. With a gentle tug he freed the end that had been tucked into her cleavage. He pulled on it, and she turned in circles, letting him slowly unwrap her.

With every turn, she became that much closer to being exposed before him. Her heart thumped and her desire shifted into nervousness. She stopped, facing away from him, when the band fell away. She reached her hands up to cover herself.

Yes, she wanted this. She wanted him. But during their previous time together his hands had roamed while her clothes stayed loosely on. Standing bare-chested in front of him felt so brazen. She should have snuffed out the lamp. She was about to when he stepped close behind her and she stilled. They didn't touch, but she could feel the heat of his skin on hers. An electric energy pulsed between them, skittering across her.

He drew her hair to one side and bent so close his hot breath on her ear made her wet down below.

"You're beautiful," he whispered. He grazed the back of his fingers along her side, and she gasped. Those same fingers skimmed across her stomach and the heat between her legs began to pulsate.

He reached both arms around her and pulled her against him, encircling her in his warmth. With nimble fingers, he unbuttoned the fall of her breeches, then the column of buttons at her waistband. He dipped his fingers into the mound of curls between her legs and she sucked in a breath in anticipation.

His fingers pushed through the curls, skimming the skin beneath them.

"I want to see you," he said, pulling his hand back. She arched her body, begging his hands to return to their task, but he stepped away from her. Facing him may be daunting, but that hesitation was no match for her need to have him touching her now.

She turned, her hands falling away from her breasts—one to her breeches to prevent them from falling, the other to her stomach.

Edward's eyes widened and his pupils dilated as his gaze traveled the length of her. He pressed his lips together. "You're beautiful. More so than I ever imagined, and I've been imagining for a long time."

It had been a long time. She didn't like the reminder of it, so she kissed him before her thoughts could venture in that direction. He groaned and picked her up, her breeches falling to her ankles. She kicked them off as he lay her upon the bed. She reached down to the blanket resting at her feet and pulled it up to cover her nakedness.

His lips quirked but he didn't comment. Instead, he went to work unfastening his own breeches. From this angle, he looked all brawn and sinew. He pushed his breeches down his legs and over his knees. Her eyes grazed over his strong, muscular thighs to his cock, large and erect and pulsing.

"Good God." She snapped her mouth shut, which had embarrassingly dropped open, and took a deep breath in. It was—odd. He would be loath to hear her say it and it was likely not the most appropriate thing to think in this moment. But this thing in front of her…It was thick and muscular, appearing from a wealth of wiry, curly hair. A large vein meandered down its shaft and at its head, the shaft swelled. Right at its tip, a gap from which dripped a single bead of liquid.

Tentatively, she reached out to touch it. His cock recoiled as he groaned. She tried again, this time grasping the full circumference of it. When she looked up, Edward's head was tilted back, his eyes were closed, and his lips pressed together. She ran her hand down the length of him, and he clutched her wrist, focusing his eyes on her.

"Not just yet," he said through gritted teeth. He pulled the blanket back and climbed into bed with her, thankfully repositioning the fabric to keep her covered. His cock pressed hard against her thigh; instinct—common sense—made her spread her legs, prepared for him to mount her. She nodded, resolved. "I'm ready."

He chuckled. An all-knowing, infuriating chuckle that doused her flames with frigid water. "Do not laugh at me," she warned.

Immediately, the chuckles stopped, and his expression

became more serious. "I apologize. I simply—" He paused. "Let me show you what ready feels like."

He caressed her inner thigh, and her desire quickly leapt back to life. His fingers found their way to her curls and he gently explored them until his fingers reached her crevice. He slid one finger in, stroking her gently. The strokes became smoother as she became slick beneath him, and his finger found the nub at the center of her. The one she used to find her own personal satisfaction. He stroked it, over and over, and small waves of pleasure rocked over her.

But she couldn't relax. He was right *there*, his deep blue eyes focused on hers. She could feel the pleasure on the peripheries, but his face so close to hers, watching her with such expectation—she couldn't relax. So the pleasure remained where it was—hinting and teasing at her but ultimately out of reach.

"Close your eyes," he whispered, and she did so.

Without the pressure of his expectation, the pleasure blossomed in her body and mind. Over and over he stroked. With each caress her consciousness drifted farther away, her breathing becoming heavier. Just as she felt ready to cry out, he stopped.

She panted, gulping in air as she opened her eyes, and the present rushed back at her. His expression was dazed as though her pleasure had muddled his mind. He'd gone tense, every muscle at attention.

She raised a hand to his face, stroking her thumb across his cheek. "Please," she whispered, half of a mind to push his hand out of the way and finish on her own.

The befuddled look on his face sharpened into a grin. He leaned down, pressing his lips to hers. As he did so, his attention didn't return to where she so desperately wanted it. Instead, he circled her opening with his finger.

He wasn't going to... Surely...

Slowly, he entered her.

Her breath caught, her mind reeling at the unexpected touch. The peculiarity of it. It was not *bad*, per se. In fact, it felt quite good. Muscles she'd never known existed clenched tight around him. It was simply *unusual*.

She opened her eyes; the rapture had slipped. Edward was looking down at her in reverence. That's when she realized the blanket had shifted under her writhing. A flush of embarrassment crept up her, turning her pale skin pink. He noticed—clearly, how could he not notice with his eyes fixed on the naked skin that was flushing—and his gaze returned to her face. His eyes captured hers, but she could not divine the emotion in them. It was less lust than it was adoration and that both terrified her and made her glow.

"Is this what you want?" he asked, and his finger returned to her clitoris. The ecstasy returned immediately, but this time stronger, more intense, as though his finger entering her had heightened her sensitivity. He caressed her, over and over with the rhythm of an engine, bringing her to the edge of climax. She clenched the sheets in her hands as she gasped and then she collapsed as he pulled his hand away, returning his attention to her entrance.

The pattern continued, his bringing her to the edge and then entering her. Each time he penetrated her, it was harder, faster, and she became more slick. Each time he returned to her pleasure center, the bliss intensified.

Just as she thought she could stand no more—when her hands were fisted in the sheets and her back was arching, he tipped her over the precipice. She bucked and moaned, her hand going to his to keep it in place. She rode his fingers as wave after wave of pleasure rolled over her, far more than she had ever achieved alone.

When it stopped, she felt dizzy. Stars danced at the edge of her vision and she drew in ragged breath after ragged breath. Edward looked down at her with a look of utter satisfaction.

"Now you're ready."

He was going to marry this woman. As he watched her writhe beneath him, her mouth forming a delicate, desperate O and her fingers gripping his wrist like a drowning man gripping a lifeline, a door in his soul slammed shut. It was done. There would be no other woman underneath him. No wife in his bed that wasn't her.

It wouldn't be without its problems, lord only knew, but no problem would be as intolerable as letting her go again. Not now she'd been his.

"Now you're ready," he murmured. He braced himself on both hands, nudging her gently with his knee until her legs were wide open and waiting for him. He settled between them, the feeling natural, as though this was already a habit, a position they'd sought a hundred times.

The sated, post-climax haze on her expression cleared, and she caught her bottom lip between her teeth as she looked at him uncertainly. He dipped his head, capturing her mouth in a long, deep kiss. Her hands reached to caress his back, her fingers pressing hard into muscle, and it took every ounce of self-control not to plunge himself into her, knowing how hot and slick and ready she was.

But this was her first time making love, and he would make it perfect for her. The wild abandon could come later. He moved his lips from her mouth to her earlobe, licking and nibbling at it until he could hear her mewling beneath him. The sound made his cock throb, and she gasped as he grabbed her arse with both hands and pulled her against him, the base of his cock pushing against her sex.

"I need you." He groaned as he spoke, and with his cheek pressed against her, he felt her nod.

"Yes," she gasped. "Please."

They were the words he needed, the acknowledgment that she felt the same unshakable desire. He lowered his hips, positioning the tip of his cock at her entrance. Damnation, she was so hot and so wet.

Beneath him, she stiffened slightly. Her fingers, which had been gripping his forearms, tightened a fraction. She needed a momentary distraction. He leaned forward and captured a breast in his mouth.

"Oh," she gasped as he suckled on her nipple. Her hands reached for the sheets and gathered them firmly in her fists.

He sucked harder and as he did so, he inched forward so the head of his cock slid inside her. Spasms of pleasure shot through his entire body. His own fingertips curled into the sheet by her shoulders.

He forced himself to keep his eyes open, to watch the awe on her face as he moved forward another inch. "Is it all right?" he asked, fully preparing to withdraw but praying to God he wouldn't have to.

"Yes," she breathed. "It's odd. I don't know quite what it feels like. But good."

He swallowed back a chuckle. Ever the scientist trying to observe and classify. But if she had room in her brain to think, then he wasn't doing his job well enough. He returned his attention to her breasts, this time using his teeth to graze the nipple, taking deep satisfaction in the way they peaked into firm nubs between his lips.

He gently bit her again and her body arched, bringing him

deeper within her. That was the edge of his resolve. In fact, it was a step past it. He buried his head into her soft hair, the scent of jasmine and honey his only earthly connection. The rest of his senses were lost into the feeling of her, the tightness of her as he slid all the way in, burying himself within her.

She felt so damn good. It wasn't just his cock or the wave of physical pleasure that crested over him. It was the way the cracked pieces of his heart seemed to heal. It was the foreign sense of fullness, as though for the first time in his life, nothing in his soul was missing.

Slowly, careful to ease her body into the experience, he pulled back. She gasped on the withdrawal and he paused, but the look on her face was one of bliss. Before his body could fully leave hers, she pressed her hips toward him, grabbing his waist as though to keep him from leaving.

Edward had never experienced the animal need that he did as her hands grabbed him. Faster this time, he entered her. Faster, he withdrew. And then again.

Instinctually, she met him thrust for thrust. Their bodies established a rhythm and he found himself sinking deeper and deeper into her. With every drive forward, the tension inside him grew until each muscle in his body was rigid with raw need.

"Edward." Half spoken, half moaned, the word undid him. When she reached up to grab his hand with hers, his climax, which he'd been holding at bay through sheer bloody-mindedness, began. His thrusts became harder, faster, frenzied, and her moans deepened.

Just as he was about to peak, he pulled himself away, collapsing onto the bed next to her, spilling his seed on the sheets. This time. Once they were married, he'd relish every opportunity to finish inside of her.

Every muscle in him was weak and useless. Just throwing an arm across her required the effort of a sparring match. But he managed to pull her close to him, cradling her body with his, curling a hand around her stomach, and breathing the scent of her.

"I've dreamt of having you beneath me," he murmured, arm squeezing. "My imagination was colorless in comparison."

"I dreamt of this too," she whispered, running her fingers in swirls across his arm. "As much as I could, given the limitations of my knowledge." The words were enough to rally him. His cock began to harden once more at the thought of her, dreaming of him. Goose bumps ran along his flesh and his hands pulled her tighter against him, all of their own accord.

But she was new to this and he wouldn't risk her comfort by going again tonight. Besides, they would have a lifetime to experience each other. Despite Graham's warnings, Luella's threats, and his mother's expectations, she was going to be his duchess.

And Fiona was not a gentle, sheltered, naïve bookshop assistant like Graham's wife. She was fire and steel. She'd been forged by experiences unimaginable and had endured more than most. She'd not faltered once as she strode through society as Finley.

She was an intelligent, strong woman. She would make an uncommon but excellent duchess. Her care for the working classes would translate into empathetic service of their tenants. Her passion and understanding of politics would make her a hostess whose value went beyond the menu and instead helped establish effective change.

Most important, she would be here beside him as a sounding board for ideas or an avenue to express his frustrations.

She could support him where he truly needed it—helping to guide and protect his headstrong siblings.

She would not be a duchess in the usual sense. She would be so, so much more.

Five years ago he had proposed to Fiona in an abandoned church, no ring, no flowers, no planning at all. It had been a spontaneous suggestion made by an infatuated boy with no sense. This time, as much as he wanted to call the archbishop tonight and be married in the morning, he would propose properly, with all the care and thoughtfulness she deserved.

After all, they had a lifetime together. As long as they could put an end to her deception quickly and keep the charade a secret, the only controversy they faced was her birth. There would be scandal, but he would see his family through it. He would protect them. After his father's death there had been no one to shield him from society's venom. But he was not his parents. He would not abandon his family to it. Together, they would come through unscathed.

Chapter 21 ———————

Fiona lay on her side, Edward's body pressed against her back, one of his arms thrown across her waist, a thumb gently stroking her midsection. The warmth and smell of him enveloped her, and she could feel her heart rate slow to match the steady, calm *thump*, *thump*, *thump* of his.

She could fall asleep like this. Tonight. Every night.

She hadn't felt this safe since her mother passed. There was something about his slow breath in her hair that created a sense of comfort and peace. It was the very opposite of the lively, bubbly infatuation she felt five years ago. That had been a girlish reaction to a man she barely knew. This was her entire body calm, complete in their connection.

Things had shifted. The pieces of him that had felt so disparate that they couldn't possibly connect: the duke, the musician, the autocrat, the sounding board had all coalesced into one figure—the lover.

She finally knew this man, and she was willing to love him for whatever brief time they had together.

A lump formed in her throat at the thought of their parting, even though there was no other reasonable ending to this situation. Her mind told her to enjoy the time while they had it. Her business deal was almost done. Her vision of owning her own home was becoming more tangible every minute. And, for the moment, she had Edward's love. Any feelings of discontent were both illogical and extraordinarily privileged.

Determined to distract herself, she turned over so she was facing him, her eyeline at his throat, so close she could see the faint flicker of his pulse. Gently, she traced lines in the coarse hair on his chest as it rose and fell evenly.

He was beautiful in his sleep. All the pretense of the duke was gone and instead he was simply Edward, a man whose responsibilities had worn a crease between his brows that had not disappeared with slumber, whose stubble was flecked with grey but whose lips were soft and relaxed into a half smile.

She lightly ran her finger across them and the steady thump she could feel through his chest faltered before resuming its normal rhythm. Curious, she tried again, this time running a finger along his jawline.

His heart skipped a beat. She couldn't help but smile to herself. Moving her hand to his bare waist, she turned her head so she was once again looking at the hollow in his throat, and she planted a soft kiss at its base.

His heart rate picked up, but this time it didn't settle back into its sleeping rhythm. She kissed him again, and then gently sucked at his skin. The arm around her tightened, drawing her closer to him. She grazed his skin with her teeth and felt his cock stiffen.

"God, Fi..."

She broke off from the nibbling at his neck to look up

at him. His eyes burned with desire. She was stoking those flames, and the fire was catching.

He reached for her, his arms gently pushing on her shoulders, trying to lay her on her back, but she resisted. With her bottom lip caught between her teeth, she shook her head, turning the tables on him, taking delight in the surprise on his face as she straddled him.

Leaning over, her hair hanging over her shoulder, she captured his mouth in a kiss. "My turn."

When she woke next, dawn light was beginning to creep under the curtains. Edward was at the foot of the bed, peeling a pair of breeches down his calves. "Yours," he said, holding them up and tossing them to her. "I'm looking forward to never being in the position to make that mistake again."

"I've been wearing breeches as long as you've known me."

He sighed. "True."

"You're leaving," she said, sitting up in bed, pulling the blanket to her chest and watching him pull on clothes that were actually his.

Edward gave a small smile and crossed to her, cupping her face in his hands and kissing her. "It's almost daylight. I should go before the maids catch us."

That made sense. Edward's staff had proved loyal. Nary a word of her ruse had escaped the confines of the house. But she had no desire to have the people who brought her tea know about her sexual exploits.

But despite the sense it made, what she wanted was to curl back up in bed with him. They had weeks together, at most. She didn't want to waste any of it. But she wasn't going to beg. "You're right. Take the book with you," she said, indicating the copy of *Plurality of Worlds* by her bedside. "If you run into anyone, you can say you were retrieving it."

Edward grinned as he buckled his slippers. "Yes, because I'm sure that will fool them." Scooting up the bed until they were hip to hip, he sank his hand into her hair. His fingers grazed the back of her scalp.

Then a loud boom sounded from below and the floor beneath them shook. It took half a second for her to process what she'd heard. The blood drained from her face.

"My lab."

Chapter 22 ───────────────

They ran down the hall at full speed. She didn't stop long enough to put on shoes. She simply needed to get to the drawing room she'd converted into a laboratory as fast as humanly possible.

Her heart raced, and she couldn't tell if the pounding in her ears was blood rushing through her head or echoes of the explosion that had rocked them. She grabbed the balustrade as they thundered down the stairs so as not to lose her balance. Simmons and three footmen joined them in the race.

As they approached her lab, she could see the flickering orange reflections on the marble floor of the doorway. "Goddamn it."

"Fiona, wait." Edward grabbed at her shoulder but she shook him off, raising an arm against the heat as she entered the room.

Thankfully, the fire was contained to her workbench and the wall above it. She'd cleared all other furniture and decorations away from the area when she'd first set up, limiting how far the flame could travel.

"We'll go for water," one of the footmen said, dashing out of the room.

"Nae. Water won't help," Fiona said over the crackle of the flames. Sitting at each side of the bench were four metal buckets filled with sand. "Take that one," she said to Edward, pointing toward the end closest to the door. She hefted a bucket on the other side, dumping the sand across the base of the flame. The movement sprained her hurt wrist and she winced. She grabbed a second bucket as Edward, following her lead, grabbed his own, throwing the sand at what remained of the fire. Within seconds it was out.

Fiona sagged against the wall, bent over, hands on her knees, her loose hair falling in front of her face. She heaved in breath after breath, not sure if she was winded from the run or from the panic at seeing her work on fire.

Her work. Good God. She was meant to be presenting to Lord Chester in a week and a month's worth of work had gone up in flames.

"Are you all right?" Edward asked from the other side of the bench where he, too, was dragging in deep breaths.

She slid down the wall until her arse thwacked on the floor. Her hands rested on her drawn-up knees. "Fine. You?"

He nodded. "Fine." He looked at the debris on the floor, the shattered glass, strewn sand, and puddles of chemicals. Then he looked at her bare feet, a frown appearing.

He crossed to her, bending down on his haunches to examine the soles of her feet.

"Truly, I'm fine," she said, drawing them away.

He cleared his throat in the I'm-not-actually-listening-to-you manner that drove her mad. "Fetch Miss McTavish a pair of slippers and a bandage," he said to one of the footmen standing by the door, whose mouth was agape with astonishment.

"I dunnae need a bandage." There were only a couple of cuts on her feet and they were tiny. They'd already stopped bleeding.

He sighed. "A fresh handkerchief then."

The footman nodded and tried to exit with his eyes still fixated on the scene in front of him, which was why he collided with William as Will barreled into the room. Charlotte, wrapped in her dressing gown, was close on his heels.

"What the devil was that?" William asked as he straightened from the collision. He looked at the charred wall and sand-covered workbench, and then to Edward. And then to Simmons. And then to Fiona, his eyes widening as he took in her state—hair loose from its wig, in a thin shirt, collar open, cleavage no longer bound. "Again. What the *devil*?"

"Surprise?" she said weakly.

"Finley?" Will asked.

"Fiona, actually," Charlotte said, her tone superior. No doubt she had interrogated the staff the moment she returned from the ball to find out just who the woman she caught kissing her brother was.

"You *knew*?" William looked more affronted at his sister's knowledge than he had at the sight of Fiona's deception exposed.

"You *didn't*?" Charlotte asked, as though she'd known all along and hadn't, in fact, found out only a few hours earlier.

"I think I need to sit down." William staggered to the chaise longue at the other end of the room and collapsed into it, fingering a hole in the fabric where glass from the explosion had lodged into the arm. He dug out the fragment and held it up to the light, Simmons having lit the lamps in each corner of the room.

Charlotte joined him, looking at the walls closely as she moved. "The wallpaper is ruined. We'll need to redo this room." She sat next to her brother, spreading her skirts out neatly, and looked expectantly at Fiona and Edward.

Technically, this debacle was Fiona's fault. She was the one who'd dressed up and then failed to reveal herself to the siblings when she met them. But she was going to let Edward handle the situation. That's what he liked, wasn't it? Control of a situation?

The sardonic look he gave her called her a coward. "The emergency is over," he said to his staff. "Everyone as you were." He crossed to Fi and took both her hands in his to help lever her up off the floor. The footmen trailed out, Simmons closing the door as he left.

Fiona dusted off her pants and readied herself for the inevitable interrogation.

"You're a girl," said William.

"I am."

"But you came with me to White's."

"I did."

"And we played hazard."

"We did."

"And…you're a *girl*?" He fixed his eyes on Edward. "And you knew?"

"I did."

William gestured to the burned-out workbench. "Then who made all of this stuff?"

Fiona found it hard to withhold her eye roll. "*I* did. Being a woman does nae preclude me from also being a chemist."

"A chemist that destroyed our third-best drawing room," Charlotte said, snippily.

William nudged his sister. "Come now, Charlie. It wasn't our *third* best. More like our fifth or sixth, and she ruined that god-ugly portrait of Great-Aunt Gertrude. Nice work there, Finn." William paused. "Can I still call you Finn?"

"If ye wish," Fiona said. She crossed the room and collapsed into a nearby armchair. It had been one hell of a night. Edward stood behind her, a comforting hand on her shoulder.

"How did you learn how to do it? All of this match stuff?" Charlotte asked, her face alive with curiosity. "My governess never taught me anything useful."

"Lots of reading. But mostly my teacher, John. When he wasn't working on his engines, he was teaching me math, physics, chemistry."

"John Barnesworth?" Charlotte asked, her voice cracking.

"Jealous, Charlie?" William asked, poking her in the ribs. Charlotte flushed a crimson red.

Fiona cocked her head, caught off guard by the sudden shift in conversation. Behind her, Edward cleared his throat, displeased.

"Charlie has had a crush on John since she was eight years old," William explained.

"William!" Charlotte slapped his arm. "That is a complete fabrication. How dare you concoct such a falsehood."

He chuckled. "I read your diary."

Charlotte gasped. "You fiend."

While the two bickered, Fiona mulled the pairing over. *Charlotte and John.*

She had never pictured John with a love interest. Where Benedict and the other men at the firm would playfully flirt with the barmaids at the local tavern, John didn't go to taverns. He worked. He was at the firm at least twelve hours a day, often longer.

"What do you think, Finn?" William asked. "Has Charlie got a shot?"

"John is not an acceptable match," Edward said sharply. "Not for you."

Pardon? John was the second son to the Viscount Harrow. He was a kind and thoughtful man. Where most men would have dismissed Fiona outright, John took the time to teach her. She would still be sweeping floors if it hadn't been for his generosity.

Before she could come to her mentor's defense, Charlotte leapt in. "I thought you liked John," she said. "He's your friend."

Edward rubbed his brow. "John is one of the best men I know. But the two of you are complete opposites. He's a man who seeks quiet. You are the furthest thing from that."

Charlotte's mouth dropped open, her cheeks ablaze with outrage. "Are you calling me a loudmouth?"

William snickered, clearly enjoying his brother's discomfort as Edward turned his eyes toward the ceiling.

"No, Char. You are perfect."

William snickered even more loudly, but Edward ignored him. "You're simply not perfect for him."

Charlotte's expression took on the muleheaded stubbornness Fiona had seen on Edward many a time, so Fiona interjected before the argument—which was over an entirely hypothetical situation—escalated.

"Regardless, John's in America and is nae likely to come home soon. According to his letters, he's quite enjoying life over there." And she was happy for him; she truly was. And if it hurt that he, too, had left her . . . well, at least he'd said a proper good-bye beforehand and wrote regularly.

"And with any luck," William said. "He hasn't blown anything up. Unlike someone else . . ."

Edward scowled. "That isn't funny."

William shrugged. "I mean, it's a little bit funny. The glass sliced right under Great-Aunt Gertrude's nose. It looks like she grew a proper mustache."

"And if anyone had been in this room at the time, a sawbones would be busy digging glass fragments from their body."

Oh. He was angry. Guilt settled in her stomach. He was right to be. She'd just destroyed one of his drawing rooms and endangered his household. Someone could have been seriously hurt.

Edward squeezed her shoulder. "Tell me this won't happen again."

But she couldn't, because she had no idea why it had occurred in the first place. It made no sense. "I dunnae ken what happened," Fiona said, standing up and walking over to her work area. "I've had accidents before but never spontaneous combustion. When I packed up yesterday afternoon, I checked it all. There were no open flames; all the chemicals were put away. I can't see a cause."

The stool she usually sat on had been knocked over. The bookshelf she had repurposed to hold jars of chemicals still stood but was covered in glass fragments and pools of sharp-smelling liquid. Only a handful of bottles on the bottom shelf remained unscathed.

Beneath the bench was the scorched remains of the box that held the finished prototypes. The soot-covered metal box was hanging open and all that was left was a pile of ash at the base—her diagrams and test results gone.

Absolutely, for certain, she had not left that box open, and it had been tucked away under the bench where no explosion would have knocked the lid off. "Someone has been in here."

"Impossible," Edward said. "This house is full of staff. Someone would have noticed an intruder."

She turned to him. "Full of staff or nae, someone has been in this room since I left it."

William sank farther down into the couch, his usual confident expression faltering. It did not go unnoticed.

"William," Edward said.

The younger Stirling brother held up his hands in surrender. "Look, I'll admit I was in here last night, after the ball."

She sighed. "Good God, Will." She pressed her hands together, tapping her fingers on her lips. It was all gone. All the prototypes, most of the materials required to make new ones. Thank God the formula had been burned into her brain, because her notebook was included in this pile of ashes.

She had nine days to create a new set. Not impossible, but if she was going to succeed, she needed to get started immediately. She needed to seek out a supplier of the raw materials. The sun had continued its rise while they were attending to the accident. Businesses would open soon.

Edward rounded on his brother. "Curse it, William. What in the blazes did you think you were doing coming in here?"

Will stood, hand on heart. "I was just looking. I swear. I put everything back exactly the way it was. There was no chance that this is because of anything I did."

Fiona took a deep breath in. "Just looking" would certainly not have created an explosion. Especially not one of this size.

The thought pulled at the knot of unease that had twisted up inside her from the moment she'd heard the blast. She turned back to her bench. Almost all of her stock had been destroyed in the fire. "Huh."

"What 'huh'?" Edward asked.

"There were at least thirty bottles here this morning and

now there's only five. Given how much was destroyed, the fire really should have been bigger than that."

The information made Edward even angrier. "You could have killed somebody," he yelled at his brother. "What if Charlotte had been in the room? What if one of the servants had been in here?"

William flushed red. "This isn't my fault, somebody else must have been here."

"I'm done with your excuses," Edward said. "Get out of here. Charlotte, you too. I don't want you down this hallway until Fiona's project has been cleared out."

The siblings left, William with his hands balled by his sides, his eyes shining—whether with tears of anger or embarrassment, Fiona wasn't sure. "Because Wilde is so bloody perfect," he muttered on his way out.

Edward turned to Fiona, who was accepting a pair of slippers from a footman who looked like he could not get out of the room fast enough.

"I don't know what I'm going to do with him." Edward sighed. "It doesn't matter what I say, what punishments I mete out, I just can't get it into his head that he is no longer a boy. There are consequences to his blasted actions."

Fiona righted her stool and grabbed one of the empty sand buckets. "He needs a purpose in life. He's flailing. Nae wonder he knocks things over." She squatted down, collecting the larger pieces of shattered glass and dropping them into the wooden bucket with a sharp *ting*.

Edward grabbed the broom that usually rested between the bench and the wall but was currently lying on the floor. With short, sharp strokes he began to sweep the debris into the center of the room. "I've offered to purchase him a commission or find a suitable parish, but he refuses to enter the military or the clergy."

She paused and looked up at him. "Are there truly no other options? Because I can see how neither would appeal to a man like him."

"There are no other options suitable for a man of his station. The pathway of a second-born son is clearly set."

"I imagine the path of a duke does nae usually include sweeping a floor, but yet here you are. Perhaps you can bend that same way for yer brother somehow."

Fiona bathed and then dressed and then dragged William out by his rumpled coat lapels to a precinct near the Thames that was just beginning to come to life, scullery maids and boot boys out moving quickly to complete their chores.

She didn't care for Will's protest that he hadn't yet slept or eaten or even changed clothes since the Macklebury ball. If he was going to reduce her laboratory into shambles, he was damn well going to help her fix it, regardless of how tender he felt after a night of drinking.

Despite his complaining, however, he did as she asked, porting cases from the store to the carriage. By the time they'd returned to the house, she felt pity for him and sent him to get a few hours' sleep. But at noon, Andrew would be at the foot of his bed with a bucket of water and at ten past, William would be dressed and in the lab ready to help Fiona remake the matches he'd destroyed. In the meantime, she had another task.

Edward was in the breakfast room, his plate full of sausage, eggs, and kidney. He was reading *The Times*, and a copy of *The Morning Post* sat ironed at his elbow.

Copies of both newspapers had been included on her breakfast tray each morning since she arrived, and she wondered if he'd always had two copies of the paper delivered, or if he'd ordered the second especially for her.

He smiled and stood when she entered. The cocked eyebrow and the long gaze that traveled slowly up her body made her tingle. He gestured to the seat next to him and she felt a nervous fluttering at the thought of being so close, despite being as close as two bodies could get just hours ago.

She took a plate from the side table and filled it.

"How did you fare this morning?" he asked, returning to his seat as she sat.

"We had to visit four different establishments, but we managed to secure all the elements we need. William is getting a few hours' rest before I put him to work." She ate quickly, putting more food into her mouth at one time than she should, she knew. But old habits could not easily be dismissed. Her body never truly forgot the hunger she'd experienced.

"Thank you, for taking him," Edward said.

"You're welcome. It's a good idea. Perhaps some time spent working on this will inspire him to find something, anything, useful to do with his time. Goodness knows, he owes me."

Edward picked up *The Post* and handed it to her. "There's a story on page six that I think you'll find interesting."

No doubt it was interesting, page six usually was, but she'd come to breakfast this morning with a specific conversation in mind. It wasn't an easy one to have, and if she looked at the paper, she would find all the excuse she needed not to have it. So she placed it beside her breakfast plate.

"Actually, if you have time, I have a question."

He folded his newspaper and set it aside. "I have all the time in the world."

Good. That was good. Really. She took in a deep breath.

"I need help," she said on the exhale. There. That wasn't too difficult. She bit the inside of her lip as she waited nervously for a response.

He raised an eyebrow. "That wasn't a question."

"Oh. Of course." *Stupid, stupid, stupid.* "Could you please help me?" That didn't make much sense either. Bother. It had been so long since she'd willingly asked for assistance, she'd quite forgotten how to do it.

"You see, I met with ten distributors this week, as Finley, and I could not convince one of them that coming on board was a sound idea. I know the product is good. My presentation obviously isn't."

"And you want help finessing your business case."

"I want help with all of it. My business case, my presentation, my mannerisms. I want to be as impressive in my meeting with Chester as you are when you meet with your political opponents."

He gave her a gladdened smile and gestured to the footman to bring another pot of tea. "That, I can help you with."

Chapter 23 ─────────────

Ten days later, Edward hummed as he made his way out of parliament chambers. He knew he was humming; he knew he was getting odd looks from his colleagues as he did so, but he didn't care. He didn't care that it was frivolous. He didn't care that there were more important things for the Duke of Wildeforde to be doing than playing the piano. He didn't even care when the Earl of Gloucester paid a visit and caught Edward composing an original work in the second-best drawing room. He felt music again.

So he hummed as he descended the stairs quickly, eager to make his next appointment. The jeweler had sent word that morning that the work Edward had commissioned was ready. Some would consider less than a fortnight to design a ring, source the stones, and assemble it an unreasonable request, but what was the point of being a duke if one couldn't make unreasonable requests and have them met?

He'd considered giving her one of the family rings, but that wouldn't do. Not only had his mother worn them, none of them were quite Fi. She worked with her hands; she couldn't have a ring with a large stone. It would get in her way. No, she needed a simple band that she could wear every day without it catching, set with three small stones that sat flush with the metal—little red licks of flame surrounded by gold.

"Your Grace," came a voice from behind him.

Edward stopped and turned, frustrated by the interruption. It was not uncommon for him to be approached in the halls of Westminster. He was, after all, one of the more notable figures in this circle and plenty of men wanted to avail themselves of his influence. But this morning was not the right time for it.

The man in front of him did not have the polish of a man who belonged in the building. He was expertly nondescript—plain faced, plain clothed. He stood out here for his lack of finery and the trousers he wore instead of formal breeches. But everything else about him was designed to blend in. "Can I help you, Mr. . . ."

"My name is Mr. Nigel Patterson, from the Home Office."

The disquiet that had settled in his stomach at the sight of the man began to churn. It was rare that Edward had anything to do with the group of men responsible for maintaining the nation's safety. He could not think of a good reason why this man would be seeking him out. "How may I be of service?" he asked, ensuring that his tone was smooth and showed no signs of his disquiet.

"I wanted to discuss a young man that you recently helped release from jail."

The churning picked up pace. Fiona had been picked up for throwing food. The Home Office didn't waste their time on petty misdemeanors. Even the upgraded charges of assault weren't worth the time of a department that often focused on international espionage.

"You're better off directing your enquiries to my man. I barely know the lad. I stepped in as a favor for a friend." It was better the Home Office think Finley unimportant, beneath the notice of a duke.

"So you do not know the character of the man you've brought under your roof?"

"A deuced idiot is who I brought under my roof. Someone whose curiosity put him at the wrong place at the wrong time."

Mr. Patterson shook his head and clasped his hands in front of him. "I'm afraid it's a bit more serious than that."

Edward paused for a long moment to push back the rising nausea. This was not the first time he'd been approached by the authorities—William had been in trouble with the law on several occasions—but it was the first time he'd felt more sick than angry.

"Mr. Patterson, I think it's better if we met elsewhere to discuss this. I can meet you at the Lucky Penny in an hour. It's the grey building on the corner of Long Acre and Endell Street."

The investigator cocked his head, an interested expression on his face. "I wouldn't have thought you'd be familiar with the Lucky Penny."

Edward was *very* familiar with the establishment. The proprietor could be counted on for his discretion. Edward paid him well every month for the sole use of a private parlor and a private entrance. Paid him *very* well.

"The rabbit stew is exceptional. They don't serve rabbit at White's."

Chapter 24 ————————

The next sixty minutes was the longest hour of Edward's life. What the devil had Fiona done to end up a target of the Home Office? Being arrested for disorderly conduct wasn't enough to warrant such investigation—tomato throwing be damned.

His heart galloped in his chest, but externally he retained the same bland, impassive look he wore when dealing with more trivial matters. He had learned as a boy not to show fear. Fear only inspired bullies to push harder, knowing they were close to the kill. Like wolves tasting blood. The *ton* was no different. Nor London's law enforcement. Any hint that Edward was uncomfortable would tell his adversaries exactly where to push the knife.

He arrived a few minutes early and ordered two tankards of ale and bowls of rabbit stew. By the time the investigator arrived, he was dunking fresh bread into the thick, brown soup.

Patterson grunted as he slid into the booth.

Edward waved his hand at the meals in front of them. "I took the liberty," he said. "It really is very good."

Patterson hesitated. To not eat would be rude. To eat would be unprofessional. The inspector seemed flustered by the loss of control of the situation so early in the conversation. Which was exactly as Edward had planned. Pressing his lips together, Patterson pushed the bowl to the side.

Edward shrugged. "Your loss." He continued to eat, nonplussed.

"What do you know of Mr. McTavish?" Patterson said.

"Nothing more than that he is the son of one of my tenants." A lie. Mr. McTavish didn't exist, but *Miss* McTavish was his future wife. Patterson had no idea the ground he was skating on.

Patterson pulled out a notebook and flipped it open. "Mr. Alastair McTavish is your tenant, yes? The same Alastair McTavish that was responsible for the Abingdale uprising last year?"

"I wouldn't call it an uprising," Edward replied.

"What would you call it then?"

The crackle of flame and the acrid, burning smoke. The scythes and pitchforks. The yelling. The way he'd been forced to dodge bottles of beer and pats of mud as he called for calm. Oh, it had been an uprising. Only the explosion of Asterly's steam engine had stopped blood from being spilled. But death had occurred anyway. The vision of that young boy, bleeding and burned, still showed up in his dreams some nights.

He gave a little shrug. "It was more . . . a heated discussion about how to move forward."

The inspector gave him a disbelieving look. "The watch were called, were they not?"

Edward rolled his eyes, the very image of a bored

nobleman. "An overreaction on behalf of Lady Amelia Asterly. You know how women can be."

Patterson flushed. "Regardless, it's clear that the McTavishes have political inclinations that may pose a danger to our nation. Especially when they ally with men such as Charles Tucker, who has been seen with the McTavishes in recent days."

Edward put his spoon back on the table and pushed his meal aside. If Patterson wanted to get serious, they'd get serious.

"Alastair McTavish is too pickled to pose danger to anything. Finley *is* political. I give you that. And I can't say that I agree with all of his views. But he's just a boy with a vision for a better world. He's not a danger to anybody."

Patterson leaned forward. "But Finley's associates are. We've been monitoring them for a long time—watching where they go and who they visit. Alastair has even been seen at your home. Now Finley has joined the scene with his new incendiary device. Fire at one's fingertips."

Her matches? That was what had the Home Office in a snit? "The lad is making it easier for chambermaids to light fires, not creating bombs. Good God, man, be reasonable."

The inspector's expression soured. He pursed his lips and raised one eyebrow in the kind of condescension that no smart man unleashed on a duke. Especially not the Duke of Wildeforde.

But Edward remained silent and let the fool talk.

"We have it on very good authority that revolutionaries, Charles Tucker in particular, have been using smaller protests against the rotten boroughs to discuss plans for further, more extreme, action. Our investigations found that Mr. McTavish was arrested at one of the protests recently. Your Grace, this is very serious."

Curse it. "I can understand the need to take this seriously.

Charles Tucker is a blight on society. But I can't believe that Finley is involved. The boy is barely out of his leading strings. What evidence do you have otherwise?"

This blasted business was worse than he expected. It was one thing to save Fiona from charges of disorderly conduct. It would be something else entirely to extricate her from charges related to explosives. Edward started flicking through his mental address book, wondering who in the justice system he could contact in order to put an end to this without causing a scandal.

Patterson shifted. "So far the evidence is circumstantial. That's why I'm talking to you."

The inspector was a fool if he thought the Duke of Wildeforde would actively participate in any criminal investigation, let alone one that featured a houseguest. The Duke of Wildeforde did not court scandal. The Duke of Wildeforde took every measure possible to distance the family name from such activity. Fiona could have been this generation's Guy Fawkes, and Edward would have kept the entire, ugly mess away from his family.

Sensing that he wouldn't get the cooperation he wanted, the inspector moved on to threats. "It won't be long before we manage to uncover some hard evidence against this group. The entire resources of the Home Office are being thrown behind this. If Finley McTavish is a party to these activities, we will learn of it."

Edward signaled to the servant, who was positioned by the door, to clear away their plates. This conversation was over. "I'm sorry that I can't help you. I don't believe that Finley is involved in this, and I have no further information that can assist."

Patterson smiled at the young girl who reached across him to grab the uneaten stew and then looked back at Edward.

"It seems odd that you would so strongly defend an insignificant country boy, unless there was some special relationship between you."

Edward knew very well what the man was insinuating, as did the maid, given the sudden widening of her eyes and the added haste to her movements.

He seethed with anger. "I'm doing a good deed for a tenant whose welfare I am responsible for. That's what gentlemen do."

"In that case, I'll take my leave," Patterson said, digging a coin out of his jacket pocket and putting it on the table's edge. "But if you can think of anything else or if you notice anything suspicious over the coming days, please inform me."

Fiona leaned forward in the chair, legs wide, elbows resting on her thighs, fingers tented together. It was the same intense, dominant pose Edward used whenever he was trying to get a point across. He'd demonstrated it to her.

When he did it, he seemed authoritative, controlled, determined. When she did it, she felt awkward and gangly. But her experiences of recent weeks had shown her the world made way for men of power. Men of power didn't ask. They didn't pitch. They didn't fuss with their color-coded papers laying out the proposal in an effort to convince people.

So today, with all of her training, she would channel Edward.

With no apparent effect.

Fiona swallowed the lump of frustration that stuck in her throat. "The point of technological innovation," she argued, "is to increase efficiency in a way that improves the lives of the working class. Why in twenty, thirty years working days will shorten considerably, with no impact on productivity."

One of Chester's cronies shook his head. "The point of technological innovation is to increase profits, period. Otherwise, why would anyone bother investing in it?"

She wanted to yell. She wanted to tell him just how important social change was and how if something wasn't done about it, then the divide between the rich and poor would lead to violence and anarchy.

But she wanted to make the sale more.

And not because of the chambermaids and their extra hour's sleep in the morning, or the mothers with eight children who just need that extra ten minutes.

No, she needed the sale because she needed the money. Money that would leave her independent from anyone else. If she was truly honest, it was money that drove her to create the matches, not some noble crusade to make the world better. It wasn't enough to be a duchess and have access to Edward's money. She wanted her own. She wanted true self-sufficiency, and she would not get it as long as she relied on a man.

"If ye want to focus on the financial benefits, those chambermaids could spend the extra time sweeping the floors. Households may even be able to let some o' their workers go." And she did her best to ignore the hot crawl of shame up her neck.

"I disagree with my man of business in this," Lord Chester said. "I believe there may be a market for such a product and it's something I'm willing to take a punt on."

Relief washed through her. "Thank ye, my lord. Ye won't be disappointed. Our Abingdale factory is ready to launch into production at yer earliest convenience. I have quotes from the suppliers of the raw materials, and they can deliver the necessary materials within a month."

Chester shook his head. "Hold up, McTavish. You're getting ahead of yourself."

Fiona took in a deep breath in an effort to restrain herself. She was so close to the dream. It was almost assured. She simply had to calm down and work through these final steps without scaring her prospective business partners off. "Of course. We'll need to negotiate the contract first. I've taken the liberty o' drawing up a draft that we can use as a starting point." She reached into her satchel and pulled out the sheaf of papers John's lawyer had put together. She offered it to him, but he declined to accept it.

"First, you need to confirm that you have a patent for this." The mood turned cold, quickly.

Drat. Damn that stalling patent officer. If this deal was delayed because of him, she'd strip his hide. "The patent is pending. All the necessary documents are with the office, and they have assured me that it will be approved shortly."

"And there are no disputes?" The men exchanged pointed looks, as though they knew something she didn't. A spark of unease ignited inside her.

"Nae. No one else is working on friction-based matches. There is some headway being made on chemical matches, however, they're more volatile an' more difficult to transport. They won't go anywhere once my product hits the market."

"That's interesting," Lord Chester said, "given we met with another Scotsman this morning, whose product is identical. And he assures us that his patent is on the cusp of approval."

Unease flared into outright fear. Her stomach dropped and her mouth went dry. It couldn't be. The scientific community was small. John would have known if there was someone else working on a similar product. "Who is he?" she demanded in a tone that probably didn't help.

"We're not at liberty to share that information. All we can tell you is that he approached us this morning. The test results he presented were thorough and the sample he showed us looked somewhat more finessed than yours."

The only reason her samples weren't finessed was because she'd had to make a new set at such short notice. Through gritted teeth she asked, "And what is his background? What proof do ye have that this is in fact *his* work?"

"About as much proof we have that it is yours," one of the men said sternly.

She clasped her hands together so tightly her fingertips would likely leave bruises. But it was that or thump them on the table in righteous fury and *that* would not be viewed well.

"I cannae believe it." Her words came out calm but clipped. "There is nae another person in England working on this." John would have known. He'd have heard some kind of whisper. "Please. I've worked on this product for a very long time. I've devoted every waking minute to it for years."

Chester neatened the papers in front of him and handed them to his man of business. "If this is truly your work, then you have a week to bring me the evidence. We will delay our decision until then."

Once again, Andrew fell into step beside her as she exited the building. She'd suggested he stay back at the house, but he'd insisted on coming with her, despite there being little reason for Finley to be chaperoned. It seemed the pomp and rigidity of the duke's household was overwhelming the young footman. Not even Amelia's household had the same heavy sense of hierarchy and stringent formality. Following Fiona around London appeared to be a much-needed escape.

"How did it go, miss?"

"Badly, Andrew. Very badly."

"They didn't like your matches?"

"Oh, they liked them. They want to go into business. Just not necessarily with me."

Confusion flittered across Andrew's face. It matched the confusion she was feeling. "They were approached this morning by a man who had the exact same product."

"Is that likely?"

"No."

"The timing is quite coincidental."

"It is."

There was only one thing that made sense to her. Someone else had gained access to her matches—the research, the samples, the business case—and was passing it off as their own.

Confusion shifted, melded into fury. Whoever he was, he would not win. She had a week to identify the criminal and collect the evidence she needed to prove to Lord Chester that the matches were hers.

As they walked, her mind ran through all the people who could know enough about what she was working on to be able to execute a deception like this.

"Andrew, is there anyone you can think of back home who would want to sabotage this venture?"

"Sabotage? No, miss. Especially not after..."

Especially not after last year's riot. Jeremy's death had stunned their small village. It had brought them together rather than driven them apart. No. It wouldn't be anyone from home.

She sidestepped a woman towing three kids in a line behind her. There was Sir Humphry. He was intelligent enough to see the true value of her work and would understand how it operated. But she couldn't believe that a man of science would blatantly steal someone's discovery. The theft of intellectual property was against their code. Besides, he wasn't a Scotsman.

"What of His Grace's staff? Could ye see any of them stealing my notes? Sharing them with others?"

Andrew shook his head. "They're loyal folk, miss. Near worship the duke. Working against you would be seen as betraying the family."

Family. Was that how the staff saw her? She wasn't, though.

Family. An ice-cold shiver ran down her spine. A Scotsman with access to her work. Surely not. What possible reason could he have?

Money. Her father had been complaining about money for as long as she'd known him. Even when she'd pointed out ways in which their lives were rich, he'd been fixated on how poor they were. It was the sight of those lords and ladies in expensive carriages pulled by fine horses that had triggered his desire to start a riot last year.

Yet he hadn't mentioned money once since arriving in London. Not even when he was surrounded by the extravagance of Edward's home. That certainly should have set him ranting. And if he had been spending time with Tucker as she believed...

It wouldn't have been the first time Alastair had chosen an illegal venture over her. It was why he left her back in Scotland, after all.

Ye'r a smart lassie. Ye kin come up wi' some aught else.

She should have suspected then—the moment he'd shown

such sudden interest in her and such little concern for what was happening.

"Andrew, has my da been around th' house recently?"

"Not since you took him through your lab. Before, you know"—he gestured with his hands—"boom."

Boom.

The fury already writhing through her veins began to boil. "Hail Swinton please, Andrew. We're going to visit my father." And she'd be damned before she walked to him again.

Chapter 25 ————————————

The crumpled scrap of paper on which her father had scrawled his address was still in her bag, where she'd stuffed it in frustration after their last conversation.

Andrew's face when he opened the carriage door to exit was hesitant and mildly alarmed. When she alighted and got a good look at the neighborhood her father had chosen to reside in, she could understand his reaction.

It was old. The street was narrow. More refuse than expected lined the gutters and the pavement. There was a sharp odor of urine and horse feces and rotting fruit. The buildings were covered in soot and the windows were dim, as though no one had bothered to clean them in decades.

She could hear angry shrieking from inside a building, but outside all was quiet save for the barking of dogs. The entire street had come to a halt, all eyes on Ed's very fine ducal carriage and on her. Some of the expressions were benign—merely curious about the well-dressed lad who'd arrived. Other expressions were more speculative, and Fiona felt more vulnerable than she had since that long walk from Scotland.

"I'll go with you, miss," Andrew said.

"That's not necessary." After all, it was her father she was visiting. He was idiotic and selfish and ofttimes criminal, but he would not hurt her. Not intentionally. Not physically.

"I *will* go with you, miss." His hands were fisted by his side and a crease had formed between his brows. Behind him, Swinton bore a similar demeanor.

"Very well."

The inside of the boardinghouse where Alastair was staying was dark, cold, and dingy. They climbed a set of narrow stairs, her gloves sticking to the banister until she released it and held her satchel with both hands.

When they reached his rooms, she heard muffled voices. He had company, then. Company would not be ideal for the conversation she needed to have. She turned around; she would confront him later.

But as she took steps back across the landing, Chester's words came to mind. She had a week to prove that her work was her own. If the thief wasn't her father, she needed every second of that week to track him down.

Taking in a deep breath, then immediately regretting it as she inhaled a thread of acrid tobacco, she returned to the doorstep and knocked thrice, sharply.

Behind her, Andrew shifted.

The door opened. A cloud of smoke swirled. She waved it away from her, her eyes watering. "Wee bairn," her father said. "Whit are ye daein' 'ere?"

"Da. May we enter?" she asked.

He stepped to the side, allowing her to pass. He clapped Andrew on the shoulder with enough force that the boy stumbled as he followed. The room was small, bland, and grimy—how her father's cabin had looked when she'd first made her way to Abingdale. It was as though he didn't notice the mess.

There, sitting in one of the two chairs in the room, was a man who had been burned in her memory. Charles Tucker sat relaxed, his ankles crossed, a glass of liquor in one hand and a pipe in the other. He fixed Fiona with a jaunty grin.

"Well, hello there, *Finley*." Tucker winked conspiratorially.

"Och. Nae need fur that here," her father said. He gestured for her to sit in the spare chair, but she couldn't bring herself to get that close to Tucker, partly because she was currently holding herself back with every shred of restraint she had. She'd love nothing more than to rake her fingers down those ruddy, pocked cheeks.

"What are ye doing with *him*?" she asked. "He killed Jeremy."

"Oi—" Tucker straightened and her father stepped between them, putting a restraining hand on her shoulder.

"Now, Jeremy's death was an accident. An awful one at that, but an accident. We had no idea the engine would explode the way it did."

We had no idea. She sucked in breath. The comment hit like one of Ben's steam engines. Behind her, Andrew started forward, and she threw a hand out to stop him passing her.

"Tell me ye didn't know, Da. Tell me ye never had the chance to stop a sixteen-year-old boy from sabotaging the engine boiler the way he did." Because if he had known, then her father had been equally responsible.

She'd looked past his flaws. She'd forgiven him for the way he abandoned her. But if he had used Jeremy for his own purposes, if he had pushed the boy into the factory that night of the riot, she wasn't sure she could forgive him for that.

Her father rubbed at his nose, suddenly finding the wall behind her fascinating, and she had the answer she needed.

Her throat closed. All this time, she'd thought Jeremy acted on his own, spurred on by Tucker and the poison he'd been spreading but ultimately making the rash decision for himself.

Shame flooded her, shame for her father's selfishness, for his myopic view of the world that left no room for empathy or kindness or decency. He was so caught up in his anger and his fire for revolution that he didn't care about the people burned along the way.

But there was a deeper shame, one that sat like poison in her gut. She still loved him. He had done terrible thing after terrible thing, yet she still loved him. Her cheeks seared at the wrenching of her heart and her eyes stung with tears.

Then the man she wanted to hear from least stood. "The boy's death was a loss," Tucker said. "He had great potential. But at least he died for a good cause."

There was a roar, and then Andrew barreled past her, tackling Tucker to the ground. He raised a fist and planted it into the revolutionary's face with such force that Fiona heard bone crunch.

Tucker yelped and put his hands over his face, but Andrew continued to rain down blows, his fists finding any unshielded spot.

Her father looked at her to stop the assault, but she couldn't move. After a few moments, Alastair grabbed Andrew by both arms and hauled him off. Andrew scrambled to his feet.

Tucker sat, cursing and trying to stem the bleeding from his nose, but Fiona had eyes only for her father. "What else are you doing 'for the cause,' Da? Who else are ye sacrificing?" *Me? Are you sacrificing us again? Do you have such little care for your daughter?*

Guilt washed across his face, and his eyes flicked to the

desk on the other side of the room. No doubt its drawers held her match samples and the paperwork to go with them. Shaking her head, she marched toward them.

"Fiona." Alastair moved quickly. Faster than she could have anticipated. He shoved her away, and she stumbled to the floor.

Oh. She gasped as she sat. Her father had actually struck her.

"Oi!" Andrew rushed to her side, giving her his hand to help her stand. She couldn't say anything. Her mouth opened and closed but no words would come out, as though shock had stolen her voice.

Standing in front of her, his arms crossed, Andrew said: "Miss and I are going home. Stay away from us."

Edward didn't return to parliament following his meeting with the inspector. He didn't manage to make his way to the jeweler either. He had more pressing matters to attend to.

His first move had been to contact the informants he used whenever he needed intelligence about what was actually happening on the working streets of London. Whatever Tucker's machinations were, he wanted to know all about them. What, when, where, and most important—how Fiona fit in to them.

Fi wasn't fool enough to knowingly involve herself in a situation like this, but that didn't mean she wasn't somehow connected to it. Perhaps she'd delivered a message for her father. Perhaps she'd spoken to one of the conspirators at that blasted rally she'd been arrested at.

Whatever the link was, his people would find it.

Then Edward had requested Lord Barr join him at White's.

He needed someone else to make enquiries at the Home Office about this Nigel Patterson. Barr could be counted on for both his contacts and his discretion.

Needless to say, by the time he arrived home, he was in less than a fine mood. When he saw the large traveling carriage at the end of the drive, with footmen carrying trunk after trunk up the stairs like a parade of insects, his foul mood darkened further.

"Blast."

He stripped off his gloves as he stormed up the steps, shrugged off his coat, and handed it to Simmons without a word. His erstwhile butler knew better than to say anything.

He turned right into the first morning room.

"Mother."

Charlotte had said the Duchess of Wildeforde would be at their Erstforde estate for at least another fortnight. What could have persuaded the woman to travel this far while unwell?

Edward had one idea, and he didn't like it.

The duchess was in pride of place by the window overlooking the front garden, with Charlotte-Rose seated across from her. At first glance, Char seemed perfectly put together, but then she shot him a brief, panicked look.

"Duke." His mother raised her hand.

Edward crossed the room to lay the barest kiss on it. "I wasn't expecting you for a few more weeks. I trust your trip was pleasant."

Stepping back, he could see changes in the duchess since he'd last seen her. She'd been drawn and brittle for as long as he could remember, but now there was a frailty to her frame and a ghostly pallor to her skin that stood out against the bright green fabric of her dress.

"The trip was excruciating. The worst thing I could do in my condition." She coughed.

"Then why didn't you stay in Erstforde?"

His mother pinned him with the kind of stare that made kings squirm. "I received word that you are receiving *interesting* guests. I wanted to see for myself since both you and Charlotte-Rose had neglected to mention houseguests in your letters."

He and Char exchanged glances. He certainly hadn't mentioned Fiona or Finley to his mother, and it was no surprise that Charlotte had had the good sense to omit that information too.

"Tell me more about this Finley McTavish."

Tell me more about this Fiona... The words, an echo of her words five years ago, sent a shudder down his spine.

"It was me," Charlotte blurted. "I invited him to stay. He dropped by to deliver a package to the duke from Mr. Asterly and we began talking and he is *such* a diverting young man. And he was all alone in Asterly House, Mother. And I thought, well, we cannot have that—you know how much I hate people to be lonely—and so I invited him to stay."

Edward didn't know if he should be pleased with the lifeline his sister had just thrown, or terrified that she could lie so easily.

"And what is he doing in London?"

Charlotte clapped her hands together, the very picture of excitement. "Well, he is here on business. He's very talented. He has invented little fire sticks. They're truly extraordinary. I imagine they'll become quite the entertainment at parties."

Despite the enthusiasm with which Charlotte prattled on, the duchess looked far from convinced. "*He* has, has *he*? Funny. I didn't know that Alastair McTavish had a son. I knew he had a daughter..."

Edward's chest constricted. She knew. Or, at least, she was almost sure. If she knew for certain, there was no telling what she'd do to Fi.

He plastered a neutral smile on his face. "Given how much attention you pay to the tenants on our estates, Mother, I'm surprised you knew of even one of the McTavish children. Exceptional work."

The duchess's lips thinned. "And what of his sister? Has she graced us with her presence in town?"

"No," Edward said, praying his mother hadn't heard of the red-headed woman he'd been seen carrying through Mayfair.

"I haven't seen her," Charlotte added.

And then, with impeccable timing, William entered. "I say, have either of you seen Fiona? She said she'd be back by no—"

William stopped dead in his tracks at the sight of Her Grace. "Mother," he said coldly with a perfunctory bow. He didn't cross to her. He didn't take her hand.

"You were saying, dearest?" the duchess said.

"I was looking for Miss McTavish. Never mind."

Edward shot William a murderous look.

"What?" William flinched under the glare.

Once again, Charlotte jumped in. "What I meant to say, Mother, was that I hadn't seen Fiona *today*. She's residing at Mr. Asterly's residence as is proper and her brother, Finley, who *is* staying with us, as a *completely separate person*, is in a business meeting, is he not, brother?"

Finally, William twigged. "Oh. Yes. Finley. Lovely chap. I've never met a nicer man. Or a smarter one. Male, that is. Definitely a great addition to *man*kind."

And for the first time, Edward wished his brother was a better liar.

"I'd like to meet this Finley," the duchess said. "Since he comes so highly recommended."

Edward was going to do everything in his power to keep Fiona out of his mother's clutches. "As Charlotte said, I'm not sure he's home."

"Do you know," William said. "I have somewhere to be." And with the slightest of bows, he left the room. He wouldn't return until well after dinner, once their mother had retired for the evening.

"You have yet to teach your brother proper manners, Duke," his mother said. She turned to watch William walk down the drive, and with timing that rivaled Will's in its travesty, Fiona, as Finley, passed him on the steps.

Will grabbed her arm and shook his head. His lips moved in some kind of warning, and Fiona, curse it, looked up at the drawing room window. Her face fell as she saw the duchess.

His mother picked up the bell from the table next to her and shook it with furious fervor in Fiona's direction. There would be no escaping the meeting now. If Fiona didn't join them in the drawing room, his mother would hunt her down.

Fi must have sensed that, because a moment later she stood in the doorway, her shoulders squared and her head held high.

Edward's mother motioned her inside. "You're Mr. Finley McTavish?"

"Aye, Yer Grace." Fiona bowed, a move she'd become surprisingly fluid at in these past weeks. When she looked up, Edward was rocked by the sadness in her eyes. The defeat. His mother made people frustrated, furious, sometimes anxious, but not sad. Fi's meeting with Chester might have done, though, if it had not gone well.

But before he could seek the truth from her, they needed to deal with the witch in front of them.

"Tell me the circumstances under which you came to reside under this roof, boy."

Blast. If his mother started interrogating Fiona before they had time to get their stories straight, they would be in serious trouble.

"I told you, Mother," Charlotte said. "I invited him to stay with us after he'd dropped off some doobywhatsit for Edward."

"Aye. That's exactly how it happened," Fiona said.

"And your sister? What's her purpose in London, if you're here for business?"

"My sister..." Fi looked at Edward. "...is here to visit friends?"

The duchess's lips pursed and her eyes narrowed. "And she no doubt drops by to visit her brother, who has been taken in by the most eligible bachelor in England. How convenient." The cloying sweetness of his mother's tone was a trap.

Warily, Fiona asked, "What, exactly, are ye implying?"

His mother poured a cup of tea, pretending that this was a normal, polite conversation rather than the interrogation it was. "Why, nothing at all. Only that I'm so very glad to have arrived in time. To meet her during her stay, that is."

Fiona met his mother's saccharine smile with her own. "I'm sure she'll be flattered by yer attentions, Yer Grace. If you'll excuse me."

She bowed once more, then spun on her heel and marched out of the room. Edward made to follow but stopped at the door when his mother called out.

"Duke, I expect Miss McTavish to join us tomorrow night at Augustus's soiree. Her brother too."

Edward nodded curtly. "Excuse me, Mother."

Charlotte jumped up. "Excuse me also, Mother. Your unexpected arrival has flooded my senses with joy, and I fear

I must lie down." She crossed to Edward and took his hand. "Brother, escort me to my rooms?"

Together they walked silently out the door and down the corridor until they were out of earshot.

"You said we had a month," Edward hissed.

"I thought we did! Do you think she suspects Fiona and Finley are the same person?"

"If she didn't before she does now."

⁓

"Why didn't ye tell me yer mother was visiting?" Fiona threw open the trunk that she'd dragged to the end of her bed. She had to get out of his home. It was too risky to stay.

First Luella. Now Edward's mother. Both of them knew or suspected the truth of her deception. Both were more than happy to see her life implode. And if Lord Chester discovered her lie before the contract was signed, there was a chance it wouldn't get signed at all.

"I was as shocked as you were to see her here, I promise. I wasn't expecting her for another fortnight."

She began to pick up her items and toss them into the trunk. Another two weeks and everything would have been over. She'd have sold her matches, the trial would be concluded, and she'd be back home in Abingdale.

If Abingdale was still home. It would take time before money from the matches started coming in—not until they'd been produced in bulk and purchases were made. Until then, her home was with her father. But she wasn't sure she could even face him now, let alone live with him.

Her heart ached at the thought, and tears filled her eyes. Perhaps she could stay with Ben and Amelia. Maybe she could live in John's cottage until he returned home from America.

"This is a disaster," she said when she realized Edward was waiting for a response. "She kens who I am."

"She probably suspects. Would you put down the boot?" Edward grabbed her hand, and she realized she'd been gesticulating wildly with the footwear. She dropped it into the trunk on top of the crumpled shirts and balled up stockings.

"The only thing that we can absolutely count on is that Mother won't risk the Wildeforde name. She won't expose you, publicly anyway."

That did nothing to assuage any of her concerns. The duchess could still do a lot of damage privately. "If she won't expose me, then what?"

He sighed, massaging between his brows. Whatever it was, he didn't want to tell her. "She'll use the information to destroy any chance you have of making your business a success and she'll manipulate me into marrying a girl of her choice."

"Oh. Is that all?" Fiona couldn't help the bubble of horrified laughter that escaped her. "Well, that's just grand." She picked up the boot's twin and tossed it into the trunk. Then she grabbed her night rail from the end of the bed and began to roll it.

Edward put a gentle hand on hers and this feeling that she had, that she might suddenly fly apart, settled at his touch. "You can't leave," he said.

Was he insane? She couldn't *stay*. No, she had to leave. It was better for all of them if her connections with the Wildeforde family were severed, especially given her father was likely responsible for the explosion, putting Edward's entire family at risk. If it came out that someone under his roof was connected to men like Tucker? It would cause a scandal even greater than her charade being discovered. It would ruin him.

No. She'd return to Benedict's town house until she could solve her business problems, and then she'd go home.

"It's best if I go," she said, trying to ignore the painful lump in her throat. "Coming to live with ye was a terrible idea in the first place." Losing him twice had been hard enough. This third time might actually break her.

"You can't leave. Residing here is a condition of your parole." She made to interrupt but he put up a hand. "And the Home Office is investigating you," he said quietly. There was a leaden timbre to his voice that caused even more dread than the words *Home Office*.

"It's *what*? For throwing a tomato? This is unbelievable." She had been a wretched fool to go to that bloody protest. All her problems—well, almost all her problems—could be traced back to that one moment.

"They think you're associating with Charles Tucker."

"I— Uh—" The words lodged in her throat. It was a scant hour ago that she'd seen him. Surely news couldn't have made it to the Home Office and from there to Edward in such a short amount of time.

She looked up at Edward. His expression held nothing but compassion tinged with worry. He was here for her. He would do anything to protect her.

This would be the moment to tell him that she'd seen Tucker, to recount everything that had happened that afternoon, from the moment Chester had told her that an unknown man was trying to steal her work to the subsequent realization that it was her father, and that he was likely responsible for last week's accident.

But she couldn't bring herself to say the words. She was angry, so angry with Alastair. He'd managed to hurt her in a way she thought no one could again. But he was her da, and that same compulsion to find him after he'd abandoned her in Scotland drove her silence now.

Because if it was true, then he'd been responsible for jeopardizing the safety of Edward's siblings, and she couldn't see Edward, overprotective at the best of times, letting that pass without consequences. There was a good chance he'd find a way to pack Alastair off to Australia, and that—that didn't bear thinking about.

So she lied.

"If lobbing a bloody vegetable in his direction is associating, then they're not wrong. But otherwise, I have nae seen hide nor hair of him since last year."

She collapsed onto the bed, face in her hands, unable to look at him. How had this all gone so wrong? He sat on the bed next to her and put an arm around her shoulders, and she sank into him, turning her face into his chest. The scent of him, that ink and leather, helped to slow her racing heart. His touch, the firm rub of his hand up and down her arm, kept her mind from spinning in all different directions. The feeling of his breath, hot in her hair, gave her own breath a regular rhythm to follow. His kiss, firm against her head, grounded her.

"It will all be fine," he murmured, completely unaware of just how dire the situation was, and how terribly her father had betrayed her and how guilty she felt at keeping it from him. "It would be better if we could be honest with Patterson about who Finley really is. If you get caught out in this lie, they'll not believe you when you tell them the truth about your relationship with Tucker."

She shook her head. "No. I just need a few more days." Once they'd told the Home Office, there was no guarantee that the truth wouldn't escape and find its way to Lord Chester. If she could just nail down the patent and convince

Chester to sign with her, then she could be honest with the Home Office and the magistrate. She would give them everything she knew about Tucker—as little as that may be—once she'd had a chance to warn her father.

Edward frowned, unhappy with her choice but accepting it with a nod. "Then we just have to be utterly unremarkable and give them nothing to see. How did the meeting with Chester go?"

"Well," she lied, shocked at how easy it was. "I just need to resolve the patent issue and the contract is as good as done."

His chest, the arm around her, all loosened somewhat. "Thank God something is going the way we intended. Is there anything I can do to help with the patent?"

Her first instinct was no. It was on the tip of her tongue without a second's thought. But there was something he could do, as much as she hated it. "Yes. The patent office requires a man to write a letter confirming that the work I've done is my own. I could use your help with that."

It was stupid. Utterly unreasonable. They didn't require men to have another man sign off on ownership, but apparently a woman capable of achieving anything significant beggared belief. She could have asked Benedict for such a letter when it was first requested but from sheer stubbornness, she hadn't. She'd been determined to do it on her own.

She could tell from Edward's expression that he knew how much the request cost her. "Consider it done. Is there anything else?"

"Nae. There's nothing else. Unless you're sure ye dunnae want me to leave?" she asked, pulling away and searching his face for the truth. All she found was weariness.

He sighed, cupping her face with his hand and resting his

forehead on hers. "No. I don't want you to leave. I would keep you here forever."

Forever. Her soul yearned for it. Her body wanted to cleave to his and never part. Her heart wanted to see him over breakfast every morning for the rest of their lives, and spend every night in bed together always.

He would kiss her good-bye and go spend his days running the country, while she'd work away in her laboratory on whatever project came next. They'd meet as a family before dinner for as long as William and Charlotte wanted to live with them, and their nights would be spent making love.

She tipped her head back until her lips were against his, soft and honorable. She hadn't realized she'd been crying until she opened her mouth to his and tasted the salt of tears.

He pulled back, wiping her cheeks with his thumbs. His brow was furrowed in confusion but she didn't want to talk about what was wrong—how the anticipation of their end was breaking her heart and she didn't know how she'd survive it when it actually came to pass.

Because there was no other future. He couldn't not be a duke and she couldn't be a duchess. He opened his mouth to speak and so before he could, she wrapped a hand around the back of his head, her fingers sinking into his hair, and she pulled him to her, kissing him desperately, forcefully, furiously.

She teased at his lips until they opened, and she slid her tongue into his mouth. He groaned, one hand going around her waist, tearing at her shirt until it was free from her waistband. The other pulling out the pins of her wig, tossing them to the floor. The wig followed.

She stood, facing him, and hooked her hands around the hem of her shirt, lifting it over her head. There was no longer any sense of embarrassment at being naked before him—just a spine-tingling sense of anticipation. She could already feel the apex of her thighs heating.

Edward, still on the edge of the bed, curled an arm around her and yanked her forward until his lips were pressing against her lower rib cage and his hands were cupping her arse.

His breath against her skin was hot and moist and she braced herself on his shoulders to keep her knees from buckling, fingertips digging into muscle.

He raised one hand to the binding around her chest, tugging at the knot until it came free, pulling at the fabric until it was loose enough for her to shimmy out of it. He nipped at the waistband of her breeches with his teeth. The way they grazed at her skin ignited a spark of raw need. She kicked off her slippers as one by one he pulled at her buttons and one by one they came free until the fabric needed little more than a nudge for her breeches to fall in a heap around her ankles, leaving her there in just her knee stockings.

Edward fell to his knees on the floor, his hands grazing the length of her legs, as though she were a deity to worship. The great Duke of Wildeforde genuflecting before her. Goose bumps prickled across her skin. Every ounce of passion she had for him, he matched. In this, at least, they were a perfect pair.

He undid the bow of her garter and peeled her stocking down. As each new inch of her was exposed, he nibbled and licked at it. It was quickly, too quickly, that she was standing there naked before him, and he was standing there, far too dressed.

She wrapped a hand into his collar and tugged upward until he stood. She made short work of his clothing, desperate to feel his bare skin beneath her fingers. Then, when he too was stripped, she gently pushed him backward, the backs of his knees hitting the bed, and he went down softly, his eyes wide in surprise as his head hit the pillow.

She climbed on top of him, her sex pulsating. A raw need was building there. She could feel herself get hot and slick. The sensitive bundle of nerves that he'd used to bring her to collapse called out for his attentions. She sank her hips toward him, grinding herself along the long, thick edge of his cock. They groaned in unison.

Without conscious thought, she continued to rock her hips back and forth, rubbing her clitoris on his shaft over and over, feeling the swell of pleasure but never the crest. She closed her eyes, channeling all of her senses to that building exhilaration.

"Fiona," Edward groaned. "Please." His hands found her hips and she knew what he wanted. She lifted a little, positioning herself over him. He reached down a hand and gently guided his cock so it sat at the entrance of her, a thrill going through her body at the feel of him.

Slowly, she lowered her hips, shuddering as she stretched to fit him. Edward's sharp hiss and the way his fingers dug into her thighs as she sank down made her heart beat double time. When she took those last few inches—seated herself fully on his cock—a pleasurable pain pushed at the very core of her.

She resumed her back and forth motion, once again grinding against him, the wiry strands of his hair creating an almost-unbearable friction. The fullness of him was what she'd been missing. With him deep inside her, the wave of pleasure quickly dwarfed anything she'd felt previously. She collapsed forward, bracing her arms on his chest as she continued to ride him hard.

"Oh, God." He thrust his hips, driving himself farther into her, and she cried out at the intensity of it. Again and again.

His hands held her firm against his cock and she rubbed herself over him.

Eyes closed, lost in a sea of flames, the blaze built until she was a raging forest fire, and then she exploded, wave after wave of pleasure causing her toes to curl and fingertips to dig into his flesh. She could feel her sex clenching over and over as she spasmed.

She collapsed fully this time, her head resting in the hollow of his neck, her hands wrapped into his hair as he, too, found release, grabbing her arse and thrusting into her. Beneath her, she could hear the wild staccato of his heartbeat and the pant of his breath, the damp coolness of his sweat at her lips.

She could stay like this forever, with nothing between them. Not even clothes. Not even space.

But she didn't have forever, and the salt of his sweat mixed with the salt of her tears until she didn't know where she ended and he began.

Chapter 26 ———————

Despite all that was weighing on her, despite the dangers posed by the duchess and Luella, Finley still joined Edward and Charlotte that night at a ball. Edward's logic, which she reluctantly agreed with, was that not attending Lady Mottram's event would raise his mother's suspicions further, and they would be better served by pretending all was well.

All was definitely *not* well.

The duchess's interrogation of Finley lasted the entire carriage ride. Where she could, Fiona told the truth. The fewer lies she had to keep track of the better. But even the truths were told with as much brevity as possible, because there was a constant low level of nausea that threatened to rise each time she opened her mouth.

Once they'd entered the ballroom, she was flinching at shadows, waiting to be accosted by Lady Luella, sure that tonight she would be publicly exposed.

She was too distracted to dance, too fearful to flirt, and when she tried to escape into the card room, she was faced with Lord Chester. There was no making light conversation over the tables with the man who held her entire future in his hands.

Every moment she was there, the nausea increased until she was breathing with short, shallow breaths. She could not play at this life while her actual life went up in flames. Not when there was something else she could be doing to rescue her deal with Chester.

After a scant hour, she feigned a headache and excused herself. "Stay," she said, when Edward went to leave with her. "No one will miss me, but your departure will raise eyebrows."

Grudgingly, he agreed, which left Fiona free to do what she needed to—break into her father's apartment and steal back her matches, sketches, and reports. She'd racked her brain all day for another solution but couldn't see one. Alastair had made it clear familial loyalty meant nothing to him, and she'd seen enough of Tucker to know that he couldn't be reasoned with.

Once back at Wildeforde House, she donned black trousers, comfortable black boots, a black shirt, and an oversized black coat. She crept through the hallways, keeping to dark corners and shadows where she could. She took the back stairs to avoid being seen by Simmons and any Home Office investigator that might be watching out front.

There was no moonlight, just the flickering of lamps guttering in the wind. A light rain started to fall, and she wrapped her scarf tighter around her neck. In the shadows, she waited for a cab to come past while running through tonight's plan.

1. Have the driver deposit her three streets from her father's apartments.

2. Make her way to his building without being seen.
3. Find a way to break in.
4. Take back her work so that Alastair couldn't use it to arrange a false patent.
5. Go to Lord Chester so she could make the deal. So she could stop lying to Edward. So she could stop lying to everyone.

Number three might prove difficult. She had no idea how to pick a lock.

She was so intent on getting her plan just right, she didn't realize someone had crept up beside her.

"What the devil are you doing?"

She whipped around. Her heart raced until she realized it was William standing there, arms crossed, leaning against a tree. He had one eyebrow raised in question.

"Nothing," she said. "None of yer business. I'm just going out."

"Nothing? None of your business? I'm just going out? I've spoken those words so many times that I *know* you're up to something. A devious something. Something that Edward would not approve of, given that you lied to him this evening."

"It's nae his concern. He's not my keeper." Damn. That was too defensive.

William chuckled. "A feeling I know only too well. My brother—the despot." He pushed off the tree and planted himself in front of her. "If you're planning to defy Edward's high-handedness then I volunteer to be your accomplice." He doffed his hat and bowed.

"My accomplice?" She had toyed with the idea of asking Andrew for help and dismissed it half a second later. She'd almost gotten him arrested at the protest march. She wasn't going to jeopardize his future again.

"Precisely. I also had to leave the Mottram ball—slight issue in the card room—which leaves me with nothing else to do tonight. Except join you on whatever mad scheme you're running. What scheme are you running?"

She wasn't sure if she could trust him, but she was sure that tonight would be easier and safer with a six-foot bodyguard. Perhaps it was time to start trusting someone. For all his faults, William was a good man.

"My father, and the scum he's working with, stole my matches and is trying to sell them as his own."

William's eyes widened and he let out a low whistle. "So, what then? We're off to break his legs?"

The rain increased and Fiona stepped beneath the branches of the tree. There was no need to lower her voice, but she did anyway. "I'm going to steal it back."

William nodded thoughtfully. "When you go rogue, you go rogue. Have you ever broken into anything before?"

"Nae." There was that one time, five years ago, when she and Edward had broken into Abingdale's church hall. But that had been Edward doing the breaking. She had only done the entering.

"Then you're going to need me." He rubbed his hands together, a grin on his face. "It's an art form and I know it well." At that moment a hackney cab made its way down the street. William hailed it, giving her only a few seconds to make up her mind.

She shouldn't involve Edward's siblings in her nefarious activity. Edward would be furious. But William also had a point... This was not a moment for amateurs, and Will was much better at devious behavior than she was.

He yanked the cab door open and motioned her inside. When she hesitated, he quirked his lips. "Either I come with you, or I go inside and tell Simmons."

Who would no doubt inform Edward and send half the manservants after her. She had no real choice then. "Very well. Let's go."

By the time they reached her father's apartments, Fiona's heart was thumping out of control. She shouldn't do this. It was absolute madness. If they were caught, then she might go to jail again. This would be an *actual* crime, rather than the farce she was currently charged with.

If she were alone, perhaps she would have changed her mind and made her way back to Wildeforde House before anyone knew she had left. Perhaps she would have tried to talk with her father again and convince him to see reason.

But she wasn't alone, and William's enthusiasm for the project made it that much more difficult to leave without trying.

Maybe they would be able to pull this off. The area was quiet. There were a handful of lights on upstairs above shops, but blessedly, the building they were after was dark. This end of the street was black, with the exception of one lone streetlamp. The rain had stopped, but clouds still obscured the moonlight.

They crept down the alley that led to the back of the building. The door was locked but there were two small windows. Fiona placed both palms against one, pushing hard, and tried to slide the glass pane up using friction and force. It was locked, and even if it weren't, the rain made it impossible to get a good grip.

She leaned over, hands on knees, and looked for other options. William, however, didn't bother with the ground floor windows. After she'd pointed out the room they were after, he scrambled up a nearby tree as though he were a sailor used to climbing rigging.

Once he reached the height of the second story, he began

to inch his way along a branch that almost brushed against the building.

Fiona held her breath, praying that he wouldn't slip. The closer to the window he got, the more the branch bowed under his weight. She bit her lip, waiting for the telltale crack of wood snapping.

Instead, there was a soft "Whoop" as he got his fingers under the window frame and slid it open. About a minute later, the door in front of her swung open and she hurried inside.

The foyer was pitch black. She reached into her coat pocket and pulled out a candle, passing it to William, and then the box with matches and sandpaper. She struck the match across the sandpaper, feeling her usual rush of satisfaction at the hiss.

When she developed this product, she had imagined it being used for good, helping out those in times of need. Funny then, that its first proper use was a crime. She took the candle from William and lit it.

They climbed the stairs, quickly reaching her father's front door, which William had left slightly ajar. She hadn't brought a spare candle as she hadn't anticipated having an accomplice. So she took the risk and touched the flame to a lamp by the door, illuminating the room.

William went straight for the windows and pulled shut the curtains to stop anyone on the street from seeing the light. Fiona made directly for the desk her father had been so keen to keep her from. Crouching down, she lifted the lid off the first of the hat boxes.

Jars of sulfur. She hefted it aside and opened the box below it. Potassium chloride and, stuffed between the jars, glass powder in bags.

"Bastard," she whispered.

William whipped his head around as she swore, eyes wide in shock. But she didn't care. Alastair was a bastard. "Here," she said. "We need to take these."

She stood and rattled the desk drawer but it didn't open. She stepped aside as William joined her.

"Oh, that's easy," he said. "I've broken into Wilde's desk many times. Do you have a hairpin?"

She pulled out one of the pins that secured her wig and gave it to him. Within a few seconds the drawer snicked open.

"Don't tell Wilde." William grinned.

"And reveal how I ken about yer secret talent?" The words came out lightly, but her shoulders sank a little under the weight of yet another lie. They were starting to pile up and the more mistruths she made, the more secrets she kept, the harder it would be to ever come clean.

I guess it's a good thing we're going our separate ways. He'll never have to know any of it.

The papers inside had been stuffed in, in no identifiable order. There were not even piles, just a single large heap. Here and there she could see the deep blue of her preferred ink and her loopy, uneven hand.

She pulled out a handful of pages and passed them to William. "Look for anything that says matches, sulfur, or glass, or anything with my handwriting." She held up an example.

Quickly, efficiently, she sifted her papers from the rest, snapping each down on the top of the desk. With every sheet her anger grew. William was not nearly as efficient. In fact, he'd hardly made headway through his pile at all. Instead, he had turned toward the lamp and was examining a document.

"For goodness' sakes, Will. You can read them when we're home."

"It's not that." He passed a leaf of paper to her. It wasn't her writing. It wasn't her ink. The hand was lighter, the strokes thinner and sloping at a more acute angle.

And the content—that was certainly not hers. It was a cipher—one her father had used with his friends back in Scotland before he'd been run out of the country by the law. She'd cracked it as a child, out of curiosity more than anything.

He hadn't changed, clearly. He was still planning revenge on the upper classes. The document didn't go into too much detail, just today's date and that they would be laying supplies in preparation for their final mission. There were instructions on where to meet and where to reconvene should the group be separated. "Oh, Da. What th' devil are ye doin'?"

William held up a map. "This is Westminster Palace. I've been there before. The king is my cousin."

Fiona cursed. Her father had always been angry and volatile. He didn't think before he acted, and he certainly didn't consider the consequences for himself and his family. But this? This was a whole new level of recklessness. Tucker was surely to blame.

At William's concerned look, she relayed the contents of the coded paper. "Bloody hell," he said. "He'll hang for sure. At the very least they'll pack him off to Australia for good."

Her throat constricted at the words. She loved him. He wasn't even remotely deserving of her loyalty, but he was all the family she had left and she couldn't bear the thought of being alone in the world. She paused, desperately racking her brain for a solution.

William picked up the papers she'd let drift to the floor and sorted through them, separating her documents from the rest. When he'd made a neat pile of everything that was hers, he folded it and stuffed it into his coat. Everything else he shoved back into the desk in the same haphazard manner in which they'd found it.

Fiona remained frozen.

He took her by each shoulder, forcing her to look up at him. "We could do it, you know," he said. "We could break into Westminster Palace."

"Are you mad?" Breaking into her father's rooms had been risky enough—the palace was unthinkable. "What would it achieve?"

"We go in, intercept your father, convince him he's being an addle-pated, harebrained lunatic, and lead him out. If the guards catch us, I'll pass it off as a prank on my cousin."

It might work. It might be an utter disaster. "Maybe we go and get Edward. I should have told him the truth this afternoon. I just— He just— After last week, I don't know if he will help."

William's expression flattened. "The explosion?" He huffed, and she waited for the yelling to start. Instead, he just pointed a finger at her. "I told you it wasn't me."

He had, and both she and Edward had been so willing to assume otherwise. "I'm sorry. Does it change your offer to help him?"

William shook his head, dropping his finger. "No, but I am going to thrash him when we're through."

"Fair enough." She sagged against the desk, rubbing a hand over her jaw. She did not want to tell Edward about her father and Tucker. Yes, it was becoming a better and better idea, but it would also mean admitting that she hid the information from him in the first place.

But this as an alternative? "Breaking into the palace is idiotic. I feel idiotic just listening to the idea."

William shrugged, raising his hands in an I-don't-know-what-to-tell-you manner. "It's your choice. I just don't know that there's time for anything else. If they catch him, he's done for."

The sensible, rational, reasonable part of her knew that this was foolish. On the unlikely chance they did manage to intercept her father before he was caught, there was no guarantee he'd abort his mission—not with Tucker encouraging him.

Her heart latched on to William's reasoning: if they were caught, his name, his relationship to the king, would keep them from harm, and potentially save Alastair also.

"Fine," she said, straightening her shirt and coat. "God, I hope this works."

William's expression was jubilant. He bounced on his toes and rubbed his hands together, looking so confident that she thought maybe, maybe, this could work.

⁓

From under the deep shadows of one of the trees that lined the street, Fiona and William stared up at Westminster Palace. All the confidence that had built up on the long walk there dissipated once she saw the tall fence topped with spikes, the plentiful and evenly spaced lampposts that flooded the area with light, and the pair of guards with long rifles who were walking the perimeter.

Even William seemed hesitant, his previous enthusiasm extinguished. "You know, Edward probably would have a solution to get your father out of this scrape. He does it for me all the time."

And perhaps that's what she should do. Perhaps this was

where she needed to confess to her secret keeping and ask for Edward's help. But then she would also have to confess to her actions, to leaving the Mottram ball so she could commit felony break and enter. That wasn't an argument she was willing to have.

"Ye dunnae have to come. Da has done nothing to earn yer help."

William exhaled. "I'm hardly going to leave you to do it on your own."

Thank God. She didn't think she could have done it on her own. At the very least she would need his help carrying the stolen supplies home from where they'd stashed them on the way to the palace.

The patrolling guards turned a corner. "I guess it's now or never." He raced to the fence and wrapped each hand high around iron posts and began to walk up the fence. When he got to the top, he straddled it awkwardly between two spikes and offered her his hand.

With blood rushing through her ears, she accepted it and let him pull her up the fence. Instead of straddling it, she toppled over, landing hard on her still-tender wrist. She couldn't help the yelp of pain that escaped her.

William dropped elegantly to his feet beside her. "Finn? You all right?"

She sat upright, gingerly moving her hand. "I think so. Aye." Thank goodness for the thick wool of her coat. It had saved her from grazing herself, though tomorrow she would be covered in bruises.

William gave her his hand and she stood, brushing dirt off her pants.

"We should move," William said. They had gone no farther than three steps when the barking started. A pack of six dogs—huge, snarling brutes whose bared teeth glinted under the lamplight—came hurtling around the corner. Fiona and William looked at each other. His expression was as horrified as hers must have been.

"Bad idea," Fiona said.

"Fucking bad idea."

Chapter 27 ————————————

I have never moved with such haste in my life." Fiona said, sinking into the billiards room armchair with a very large glass of whisky in hand.

"I legitimately shat myself. That's why I changed," William said, pouring himself a glass. "Christ, that was fun."

"Fun?" She choked on her drink, coughing and spluttering until William leaned over and thumped her on her back. She winced at his enthusiasm. Once she gathered herself, she looked at him with utter disbelief. "It was stupid and foolhardy, and I cannae believe we even attempted it. No one can know about this."

"Agreed," William said raising his glass. "To partners in crime, may we always be there for each other."

Fiona raised a glass, too, but the toast stung. William was a good man. Foolish and reckless, obviously. But he was a good brother to Charlotte and had been a good friend to Fiona. When he said "be there for each other," he meant it.

Which made her feel like rubbish, because she genuinely

cared for the Stirling siblings. They'd shown her a life she hadn't known existed, let alone craved. Getting tangled up with them was selfish and unkind when she knew she wasn't going to stay in their lives.

She should tell him. Warn him that she was not someone who could be counted on. She was just about to say so when Andrew entered the room. She straightened. Andrew had been asked to stand watch over Alastair's residence.

"Your da is back home, miss. Stumbled out of a cab and staggered into his building."

She breathed a sigh of relief. "Thank you, Andrew. You should head to bed now. It's getting late."

Andrew nodded. "Good night, miss."

"Sleep tight," she replied.

She turned back to William, who was regarding her thoughtfully, more serious than she'd ever seen him. "You're an odd duck, Finn."

She snorted. "Because I said good night?" But her cheeks reddened. This was yet another example of how little she fit into this world.

"You should marry me," Will said.

Fiona spat out her mouthful of scotch. "*Marry ye?* What the devil are ye talking about?"

He shrugged. "You are more interesting than any Mayfair miss I've met. They can't seem to discuss anything other than the weather, who is wearing what, and the latest gossip. What man actually *wants* to marry that?"

Fiona took a measured sip from her glass, giving herself time to form a response. This was Will, after all. She had no desire to hurt him. "It's a big leap from 'I like talking to you' to 'let's get married.'"

William snickered. "It would really piss off Wilde. I think he has a tendre for you."

And there was the crux of it—why the younger Stirling brother had interest in her. She sighed and cocked her head. "Why do ye hate him so much? He is the one who raised you."

William tossed back the rest of his drink. "Because he's a controlling bastard who has dictated or tried to dictate every aspect of my life since Father died. What I wear, who I associate with, the subjects I take at school. It's suffocating."

"Why does he do it?" Edward confused her. Sometimes he was the man that William described; other times, he was someone completely different. Perhaps his brother had an explanation for the dual personalities.

Will leaned over to the table that sat between their chairs and poured himself another drink. He drank a lot. Fiona hadn't noticed it earlier, but now that she thought back, she couldn't remember him without a drink in reaching distance.

"Brother wants the family to be paragons of virtue. Reputation is all that matters to him. He's just like our mother. The family name is worth more than the actual family."

"Will." She gave him her very best mother hen look. "That's nae true. You matter a great deal to him."

William snorted. "I suppose that's why he's intent on pushing me into a career then."

"Is that a bad thing?" she asked. "Careers can be more rewarding than days spent drinking and gambling. It could give you purpose." Maybe that's what Will needed. She could see why Edward was pushing him in that direction. No one could live such a frivolous life for long without devolving into a pickled-livered sluggard.

"Your career might be rewarding," Will said. "It's deuced interesting what you're doing. I've got two options—the clergy or the military. He wants me to devote myself to God or die in a foreign country just so we can look the part. Well fuck that and fuck him. I'm happy with my life."

The pain on Will's face was so raw Fiona had to look away. That's when she saw it. An Edward-sized shadow in the doorway. It was fleeting, but it had been there.

She knew down to her soul that there was more than one brother hurting right now.

"I'm not a monster." Edward stood at the window of his study, staring out into the darkness. The light from behind him caught the rivulets of rain that tracked down the glass. He heard the door click shut but he didn't turn around.

"I know," she said.

"I love him." Edward's voice cracked as he said the words. From the moment William had been born, Ed had loved him. He'd spent his entire life working to protect him—first from the fallout of his father's misdeeds and then from himself. There was nothing he wouldn't do for his brother, and yet Will couldn't see that.

She crossed the room and wrapped her arms around his waist, pressing her cheek into his back.

"I know."

His fingers curled around the window frame, his knuckles going white. "I'm not my mother. I care for him. I'm *protecting* him."

She sighed, her chest rising and falling against his coat. "I ken ye believe so," she murmured.

He stiffened in her arms and then pulled away. She had no idea what they had been through. Had no idea how cruel society could be. "He was too young," he said, running a hand through his hair. "He didn't experience what I did. If he had, he'd know the danger of not living squarely between the lines."

"At the expense of happiness, though?" She stepped backward, propping herself against his desk.

"*Yes.* If the choice is to indulge in personal pleasure or protect your family, you protect your family. It shouldn't even be a question. He risks all of us for his diversions."

He leaned against the wall next to the curtains, hands shoved in his pockets. He didn't look at her. Instead, he stared at a point beyond her.

"What happened?" she asked softly. "This is nae about gossip and rumors. The hurt is too deep."

Edward pressed his lips together and nodded. His eyes stung and watered. It was a long moment before he could continue. "Did John ever tell you how we met?"

"Nae." She pulled out the chair and sat. "Just that you and he were as close as brothers when you were younger."

They had been. That relationship had fractured when John found out about his affair with Fiona.

Edward rubbed at the back of his neck, still unable to meet her gaze. "I was thirteen and at boarding school. I had been cornered by some of the other students, stripped naked, and stuffed into a trunk."

"Oh." Her mouth dropped open.

Oh was an understatement. He'd been a duke for a whole of two months when it happened. Once he'd returned to school following his father's funeral, it was clear that word of the duke's death—not only the fact of it, but the manner of it—had reached the prestigious college.

Up until then, Edward had been admired; other students deferred to him, sought his approval, because he was the future Duke of Wildeforde and position was everything.

Until it wasn't.

He'd been grabbed after the candles had been snuffed. The shock of it had given his attackers the split second they needed to overpower him. As they held him down and stripped him of his clothes, they mocked him. They called him depraved. They insinuated that his father's penchants must be his own.

Then they shoved him in a trunk and dragged him out into the cold night.

To this day, the memory made him shrivel up inside. He looked to the ceiling, refusing to let the tears come. He had thought that his father's death was the worst thing that could happen to him.

He was wrong.

The worst of it was that it was his father's fault. His father had taken his pleasures where he wanted with no thought for the scandal it would cause if he were caught. No thought for the damage it would do to his family if he died in the wrong bed.

He had thought his father loved him. But didn't you protect the ones you love? And weren't you honest with them?

He clenched his jaw and blinked. As it always did, anger overruled the tears. Fiona was still looking at him, waiting for him to continue.

"I don't know how long I was in there for. It felt like hours. Barnesworth and Asterly were returning from the prefect's room when they saw my attackers gathered around the trunk and decided to investigate. They heard me whimper."

It was the last time he would ever make that sound. It wasn't the last time the bullies came for him but it was the last time he gave them satisfaction.

"John and Ben freed ye?"

"Asterly was a giant, even then. He was mocked

relentlessly for his parentage, but very few were willing to confront him physically."

"And ye became friends."

"We became brothers."

Three outcasts—Barnesworth for his stutter, Asterly for his lineage, him for his father's scandal—united through suffering and scorn.

It had taken over a decade for Edward to repair the family name and rebuild the esteem in which his family had been held. Every move from that wretched night onward had been carefully crafted—from the bills he supported in parliament to the dresses Char wore—all to protect his family. To ensure they never went through the trauma that he had.

Edward became aware of his foot tapping on the wall behind him, and he shifted, standing upright. She noticed. She always noticed the little things about him. She was the only one who ever saw.

"It was just as awful for my mother. She left London and went into hiding in the country. I'm not trying to defend the person she is. The woman is poison. But I understand why she became so bitter."

"Is the pursuit of perfection, the avoidance of all things scandalous, really worth the sacrifice, though?"

He looked at her, this common-born woman in men's clothing with liberal opinions who created fire. Marrying her was the very opposite of what he was trying to achieve in life.

"No. If it means losing you, then no."

~

Once again, Edward snuck out of her rooms just as day broke, leaving her sated, her limbs sinking heavy into the mattress, her breath drawing long and deep. But while their lovemaking had left her body in a bliss-like state, her conflicting thoughts nagged at her from all directions, each with its own particular worry to champion.

There was only one thing each thought agreed upon. She was in love with Edward. She loved the way he loved his family. She loved the way he took care of his people. She loved the way he used his position to enact real change. She loved the way he loved her mind and never tried to make her conceal it.

In the time that had passed since the Macklebury ball, Edward and the duke had both shown up, day after day, and she'd found the truth of him somewhere between the man she had known and the lord that everyone saw.

Fiona tapped at her temples as though she could physically push all the thoughts into line. It worked sometimes, when she was on the brink of a scientific insight. But no matter how hard she tapped, they kept circling.

Being with Edward now. Being with him tomorrow. *Not* being with him in a month. What had been a clear decision— to love him for whatever time they had left—now felt murky. What was logical—that once her trial was over, they said their final good-byes—was perhaps not right. And that made no sense.

She huffed and threw back the covers. She didn't want to be a duchess. That was the primary, salient point and that hadn't changed. All of the thoughts that were suggesting otherwise could go jump into the Thames.

She pulled on her stockings, then breeches. Her energy would be better spent contemplating the day ahead, not the conundrum that was her relationship. She'd retrieved the stolen plans and matches last night, but there was still work to do. She needed to confirm her patent so that any further attempt to take credit for her work would come to nil. And maybe, if she could bring herself to do it, she would once again try to talk to her father.

She took a deep breath in and then shook it out. She could do this. She'd broken into the grounds of Westminster Palace, for goodness' sake. She could have a conversation with the man who sired her.

But not without a fortifying breakfast. She kept an eye out as she made her way to the dining room, keen to avoid the duchess and any of her staff, who had joined the bustle of Wildeforde House.

For the past week she and Edward had fallen into the habit of breakfasting together. Her, because she had always been an early riser, and Edward, because he had work to do for his estates before going to parliament.

It had become a pleasant ritual. When they weren't in the middle of a debate, Edward would read *The Times* while she'd read *The Morning Post*, and once they were both done, they'd swap.

Neither Charlotte nor William had ever appeared before midday, so it was unexpected to see them at the breakfast table this morning. It was not unexpected to see them slumped over the table, bleary-eyed and gripping desperately to their chocolate.

As always, Edward stood as she entered. "To what do we owe the pleasure this mornin'?" she asked the siblings as she filled a plate from the offering on the buffet table.

"Mother is in town," William said. "And if the choice is between rising at this ungodly hour or having breakfast with her, I choose to rise early." William grunted his appreciation at the footman who had just placed a large plate of greasy meats and toast in front of him.

"What William said," Charlotte added, lifting her head

from the table. She graciously accepted a single piece of toast. "Except it's also time for a war council."

"War council?" Fiona asked as she sat. "My, that sounds dramatic." She tried to sound light and unconcerned, but good God, what new problem had befallen them? Surely Edward hadn't told his sister about the Home Office, and William would have been mad to tell Charlotte about last night's adventures.

She glanced at Edward, his gaze connecting with hers over the newspaper. He looked as confused as she was.

Charlotte straightened, drained her chocolate, and signaled for another cup. "The mission was to find Edward a fiancée before Mother arrived in London. For whatever reason"—she leveled a disapproving glare at her eldest brother—"that mission has not yet been accomplished."

Fiona squirmed. No doubt Charlotte had been expecting an announcement, given the scene she'd walked in on at the Macklebury ball. She couldn't know that neither Edward nor Fiona saw that future.

If William hadn't been there, she would have defended Edward against Charlotte's censure. But thankfully—hopefully—William knew nothing about their liaison.

Edward sighed and folded the paper, clearly realizing that this wasn't a conversation topic he'd be able to dismiss quickly. "Finding me a bride is no longer the mission. Let it go."

"I am not about to 'let it go' when you are about to be trapped into matrimony."

He shook his head. "I'm hardly about to be trapped. Mother has other things to preoccupy her at the moment," Edward said, his annoyance clear.

Other things like taking me down. Fiona shivered.

His sister looked at him with a superior expression. "You have a letter from the editor of *The Times* sitting on the salver in the hall. He really should use thicker parchment if he doesn't want his correspondence read before it's opened." She bit into the toast daintily, fully aware of the chaos her announcement would cause.

"You read my correspondence?"

"Just the bit I could see when I held it up to the light."

"You are the worst kind of busybody." Edward gestured Simmons, who left to get the letter in question.

William gave a low whistle, regarding his sister with awe. Clearly, Charlotte had inherited the worst traits of both brothers—Edward's propensity to interfere and William's lack of moral compass.

"What did it say?" Will asked, suddenly more animated.

"Mother has placed an announcement in *The Times* of Edward's engagement. Mr. Barnes writes for Ned's approval before he publishes it." The look she shot her brother was a clear I-told-you-so.

"Damnation." Edward thumped his fist on the table. "That devil woman."

"Ned, did you just curse? You never curse," Charlotte said.

Edward's jaw tightened. "Apologies."

William raised his chocolate mug in a half toast to his brother's shift in language. "No apologies necessary. Welcome to the club."

Simmons entered and held the salver for Edward, who snatched the note and ripped it open, his expression darkening as he read the contents.

"Well?" William asked. "Who is my future sister-to-be?"

Edward passed the note to William.

"Ha! Lady Luella Tarlington. Better you than me, brother." He tossed the paper into the middle of the table.

Luella. Fiona pressed her nails into the thick tablecloth. Of course.

"Well, I guess we know who told Mother that Finley had come to stay," Charlotte said, accepting a second mug of chocolate. "Interfering, grasping parasite. Now, how do we prevent this?" She looked at Edward, William, and Fiona in turn. Despite Fi's ire, she felt a fuzziness at the way Charlotte included her as "just one of the family." A fuzziness that vanished when William opened his mouth.

"Assuming you want to prevent it," he said. He shrank back under Charlotte's glare. "What is that look for?" he asked. "She fits all the requirements for a duchess. She's beautiful, devilishly intelligent, and can surely plan a dinner party."

Nausea rose in Fiona's stomach at the thought of Edward married to that viper. The thought of him married to anyone made her feel ill. She bit down on that feeling. If she wasn't going to marry him, then he would have to marry someone else.

Just please don't let it be her.

"Oh, I believe we've moved on from those criteria," Charlotte said. "A rather shortsighted set of requirements. No, there's only one condition for the role now."

"And what's that?" Will asked.

"Just that Ned must love her." Over the rim of her hot chocolate, she gave Fiona a conspiratorial wink.

Fi shifted uncomfortably in her chair. She might have made her position clear to Edward, but his sister obviously had expectations Fiona couldn't meet.

Tears burned at the back of her eyes. When she left, she wouldn't only be leaving Edward. She'd be leaving two people who had embraced her in a warm fold unlike any other she'd experienced. Edward had taught her how to love, but Char and William had shown her what it meant to be family.

"I believe Lady Luella suspects the truth about Fiona,"

Charlotte said, unaware of Fiona's misery. "I could be wrong, but in hindsight, some of her comments while she was painting were suspect. I do think she's a liability."

"You say that like you're going to have her assassinated," Will said. "Bloody hell, Charlie. You sound terrifying."

Charlotte grinned, a sneaky, self-confident, wild grin that was so very like William. Fi's heart sank. Whatever Charlotte had planned, it was shaping up to be reckless.

"I don't want to assassinate her. I simply want to cut the legs out from whatever she has planned—and fool Mother in the process. I want Fiona *and* Finley to go to Aunt Augustus's ball tonight."

"No," Edward said. "Not an option. That's not going to happen."

Charlotte stood, holding her hands out to keep her brother from standing. "Hear me out. Fiona can't live a double life for long. Mother will ferret it out in a second, if she hasn't already, and the Lord knows we don't want to give her that kind of weapon."

"Agreed," Edward said cautiously. Fiona was hesitant to agree with anything Char was saying. It felt awfully like a fly agreeing with a spider.

"And then you have Luella."

Bloody Luella.

"If Fiona and Finley are seen at the same time tonight it will take the wind out of her sails completely. No one will believe her when she tries to spill your secret."

William was nodding as though it all made sense, but nothing added up to Fiona. "And how, exactly, am I supposed to be in two places at once?"

"Stand up."

Fiona stood and Charlotte walked to her side, slipping an arm around her waist. "Look," she said, gesturing to the mirror that hung over the sideboard. "We're the same height. We're practically the same shape. From afar, you couldn't tell the difference."

"There's just the small matter of your black hair versus Fiona's red," William said sarcastically.

"Not in a wig."

The penny dropped, as did Fiona's jaw. Edward made the realization just as she did.

"No. Absolutely not." He pushed back out of his chair. "You are not dressing up as a man and walking through a London ballroom." He crossed his arms and fixed a piercing stare on his sister.

Who didn't even flinch.

"I'm not going to be walking through the ballroom; be reasonable. The ruse will work at a distance but not up close. We'll simply have a couple of strategic moments, where Fiona is in plain view and Finley is further away. As long as a handful of people remember seeing them both, Luella has no ammunition against us."

William began to clap, his face lit with pure admiration. "Brilliant. Absolutely brilliant. This puts every one of my schemes to shame."

The look Edward shot his brother was murderous. "I'm not risking it. I will find another way to deal with Luella and the duchess."

Charlotte crossed her arms, a mirror image of her brother. "I've spent all night planning this. Listen. If you can find a fault with any of the details, then we'll call it off."

Chapter 28 ————————————

The challenge, Fiona realized, was not going to be wresting a signed patent out of the damned patent officer. The challenge would be escaping Charlotte's iron-and-silk-clad grip long enough to do it.

After she and Edward had reluctantly agreed to Char's harebrained scheme, the youngest Stirling sibling had promptly claimed Fiona for the rest of the day.

She'd barely managed to finish her breakfast before she'd been forced to put on one of the day dresses that were sitting crushed at the bottom of her trunk and sneak out of the house.

The modiste hadn't batted an eyelash when a footman carried in an armful of dresses and Charlotte asked for one to be altered and ready for the ball that night.

"If it's nae possible, I understand completely," Fiona said, hoping for an excuse to get out of attending.

"Pish," Charlotte said. "They're minor alterations."

Minor alterations they may have been, but it was still two

hours before Charlotte and the modiste decided which dress Fiona was to wear, and another two hours being poked at and squeezed into stays that pushed her breasts into unnatural positions.

Trying on dresses then turned into browsing Bond Street for bonnets, which then turned into looking at gloves, which then became having lemon ices at Gunter's Tea Shop.

By late afternoon Fi had spent a full day doing what she imagined most ladies of the *ton* did. While she was willing to admit that it had been fun, it didn't change the fact that she had a very serious business that must be done.

But she simply couldn't shake Charlotte.

When Charlotte announced that it was now time to look for an appropriate reticule to use that evening, Fiona snapped.

"Charlotte, I have business I *must* attend to," she said as their footman loaded the carriage with Charlotte's latest purchases. "I have paperwork to sign at the patent office."

Charlotte gave Fiona her usual, sunny smile. "Oh, that's not a bother. I'll have Swinton circle the block a few times until you're ready."

That was the best she was going to get, apparently. The upside was that Charlotte was too busy nattering away for Fiona to work herself into a bundle of nerves. It wasn't until she was marching up the stairs into the patent office that the butterflies started.

Her nerves were unfounded. Mr. Jones took one look at the missive from Edward and then signed her letter of patent. He didn't look happy about it, but neither did he seem willing to go against the duke.

Fiona folded the document into thirds and slipped it into the reticule she'd borrowed from Charlotte. There was only one thing left to do: show the patent to Lord Chester. Once the contract was signed, she and Edward could go to the magistrate and iron out this issue of the assault charges.

Then... Well, she wasn't sure what would happen then. It didn't quite bear thinking about.

~

Fiona and Charlotte had one unified goal when the carriage arrived at the house: to get Fi to her rooms as quickly as possible without being seen.

"Fiona" had yet to meet the Duchess of Wildeforde, and they wanted to keep it that way for as long as possible.

It wasn't just the duchess she was avoiding. Edward's staff had proved reliable, but Her Grace had arrived with her own retinue of people who would likely take any sign of her to their mistress in a heartbeat.

So they moved quickly. Simmons had the door open before they hit the top step, and as they entered, he, Charlotte, and two footmen formed a tight circle, masking her as they crossed the foyer.

"Thank you," she murmured. But before they could take the first step—

"Simmons!" The duchess's voice was nails on chalkboard.

The butler froze. Assisting Fiona was one thing, ignoring a summons from the lady of the house was something else altogether. He pivoted on the spot, a surprisingly graceful move that still managed to preserve Fiona's anonymity.

"Was that Miss McTavish I saw entering with my daughter?"

Dash it.

Charlotte broke away from the group. "Good afternoon, Mother." She curtseyed low.

"Who is your guest?"

Fiona stepped outside the circle of protection, not willing to make Charlotte lie for her. Fiona was telling enough lies for everyone.

She also curtseyed, taking the time to fasten a relaxed expression on her face. "Fiona McTavish," she said as she rose. "We met last year at Lady Amelia's dinner party."

Charlotte took a step forward, putting herself between them. "We assumed you must be resting, Mother, after your illness and the ordeal of your trip. Otherwise, we would have come to see you directly."

Her Grace arched a brow, clearly not believing a word her daughter said. "Come." She waved her fingers and made for the sitting room, turning with a frown when she realized the girls weren't following her.

Charlotte had Fiona's hand in a viselike grip, holding her firmly in place. "Fiona and I must be going. She doesn't have a lady's maid, which is why she's here, and so Grace is going to have to do both our hair and dress us for tonight. We should have started hours ago, truly."

The duchess stepped close to them, grasping her daughter's chin in her long, bony fingers. Charlotte winced.

"It's fine, Char." Fiona stepped forward, forcing the duchess to step back, releasing Charlotte. "I'm certain we can spare a few minutes."

Charlotte gave Fiona a wary glance and took her hand, giving it a small squeeze, before linking elbows. Like men to the gallows, they followed the duchess.

Steeling herself with a deep breath, Fiona entered the sitting room, fully prepared to face a dragon and instead finding herself facing a milquetoast-looking fellow whose gaze traveled the length of her, in clear assessment. He had not one single interesting feature but when his eyes met hers, she couldn't look away. He was dangerous in the way sulfur dioxide was dangerous—invisible yet capable of choking breath from the lungs.

"Let me introduce you to my guest," the duchess said. The dual thread of viciousness and glee made it quite clear why Edward and his siblings loathed her. "Inspector, Miss Fiona McTavish. Miss McTavish, Inspector Patterson, from the Home Office."

Fiona curtseyed again, wobblier this time, eyes on her feet. Ed had told her that she was—*Finley was*—under investigation. She hadn't taken it seriously enough.

A misstep.

"Miss McTavish. I believe I've had the pleasure of meeting your brother. On Bryan Road. Last week."

The blood drained from her face. Thank goodness for Charlotte's steadying grip because Fiona's knees almost buckled. She hadn't met the inspector, not as Fiona or Finley, but she had been on Bryan Road last week when she was trying and failing to engage with distributors. Which meant the Home Office had been following her for some time. Perhaps ever since her father had first visited.

"That's possible, sir," she said, trying to keep her voice steady. "Finley has been in town for several weeks now."

"And when did you arrive in town?"

Drat. The more lies she told, the more likely she was to be caught out. But how could she not answer him? "I arrived last week."

"What day?" the inspector asked, picking his notebook up from the table beside the chair.

"Goodness, this feels like an inquisition," Charlotte said. "Should I prepare an accounting for my whereabouts, also?"

The inspector frowned. "It's just a harmless conversation."

With a boldness she didn't feel, Fiona asked, "Do ye normally take notes during harmless conversations?"

He snapped his notebook closed and pressed it against his chest. She had annoyed him. She could see it in the thinning of his lips, the huff of his breath, the muscle ticking along his jaw.

"What is your brother doing in London, Miss McTavish?"

All pretense of conversation vanished. "Trying to sell his new invention. Some chemistry thing. I dunnae understand it."

The duchess sniffed. "No? A resourceful woman like yourself?"

"It's quite beyond me, I'm afraid." The words tasted bitter in her mouth, but she would say whatever it took to prevent Patterson from joining the dots between Finley McTavish and herself.

"What was your brother doing in New Palace Yard the day he was arrested?"

"I'm nae sure. Likely he was just there for a gander. Finley is too curious for his own good."

"Not protesting the current distribution of representation throughout the boroughs? I was under the impression you come from a politically minded family. Your father was an instigator of last year's Abingdale riots, was he not?"

She inhaled sharply. Sensing Fiona's shortening temper, Charlotte dug her fingers into Fi's forearm.

With a calm she did not feel, she said, "My father was protesting the eviction of nearly thirty farmers from the land they'd worked for generations."

She shouldn't be engaging with this man. She should end this conversation and walk right on out of this room. If he had more questions to ask, he could haul her back to jail.

"A boy died during those riots, did he not? And the factory your brother worked at was destroyed? Tell me, has anyone faced consequences for that night?"

She couldn't keep her mouth shut. "Jeremy's death was consequence enough for us all. There wasn't a person in our village who wasn't devastated by the events. 'Twas a lesson for everyone. Except the Karstarks. I dunnae believe they cared a whit."

Her emotion was getting the better of her, and the investigator could tell. He leaned forward. "Yes, I can believe that the boy's death would have been particularly hard for those who worked with him."

"It was." Her voice cracked and her eyes stung. Jeremy had just been a boy. A stupid, foolish boy who had gotten caught up in the web of dangerous men. She could not think of his death without contemplating her father's part in it.

Patterson's eyes lit up. "And who was that, who worked with him? Was it you or your brother?"

"I…" Oh, bloody hell.

Behind her, Edward cleared his throat in a murderous fashion she hadn't heard before. She hadn't noticed him enter but she was so very relieved he had.

"Mother. Patterson. What an interesting development to see you both here."

The inspector's face colored at Edward's tone.

"Duke," his mother said dispassionately. "I thought you were in session today."

"I was," he said as he took Fiona's other side. "But you've so recently returned and been so poorly of late that I felt the unexpected need to come home to attend to you."

His mother's mouth pursed, drawing tight as though she tasted something sour. "I'm perfectly fine. As you see."

"Yes, you are in your usual fine form." He turned to the inspector. "Do you make a habit of interrogating peers' households?"

The inspector's jaw tensed. "You were so bereft of

useful information, it made sense to seek information from elsewhere."

"Well, I hope you got what you were after." Edward gestured to the door, where Simmons was standing with the inspector's hat and coat.

Patterson nodded tersely and stuffed his notebook into his satchel. He turned to the duchess. "Your Grace, thank you for your insight." He turned to Fiona. "Miss McTavish, I'll be seeing you later."

The words sent a shiver of trepidation down her spine. As the inspector passed her, she couldn't help but shrink against Edward. He put a comforting hand on her hip. A move that was not missed by Edward's mother.

Just as she thought she was free, the inspector turned. "One last question, Miss McTavish. Where was your brother last night?"

Every muscle in her body tensed. He couldn't know, could he? About the foolish choices she and William had made? There had been no one in sight when they left Wildeforde House.

"Finley McTavish was with me, at the Mottram ball," Edward said. "There were easily two hundred witnesses. Would you like my man to send through their names?"

"That's not necessary." The inspector smiled at him and tapped his hand against his satchel before leaving.

Without taking his eyes off his mother, Edward said, "Charlotte, Miss McTavish, go upstairs."

It felt like the greatest form of cowardice, but Fiona fled.

Chapter 29

A fish out of water dies gasping.

His mother's words were all he could hear after Simmons told him Fiona was in with her and the inspector.

A fish out of water dies gasping.

He had run to his mother's sitting room, heart thumping in his ears.

A fish out of water dies gasping.

"What are you doing?" He struggled to keep a civil tone.

"What are *you* doing, Duke? Inviting criminals and strumpets into our home."

He clenched and unclenched his fists. "You will not talk about Fiona in that manner." It was hard to get the words out, his jaw was set so tightly.

"Why not?" The duchess fixed him with a challenging stare, daring him to declare his feelings.

Because she knew. *Tell me more about this Fiona . . .*

He should never have mentioned Fi's name. He'd damned her the moment he had. The duchess knew exactly what was happening when she'd received Luella's letter.

Welcoming Patterson into their home with arms wide open was just the first of her attacks, because there was no way that the duchess would accept a woman like Fiona as a daughter-in-law. She would do everything in her power to prevent it.

And God only knew what she would do next.

The duchess remained perched on the edge of the settee, sipping at her tea. Edward took enough steps toward her that she was forced to crane her neck to look at him.

"Let me be very clear, Mother. If you do or say anything to hurt Fiona, I am going to buy an estate at the furthest edge of Scotland, one with leaking roofs, where the wind howls through cracks in the walls, and there is no one within fifty miles to hear you complain, and I will exile you there."

With one hand still holding her teacup, she poked him in the stomach with the other, forcing him to take a step backward.

"Your mistake, boy, is thinking your words are law in this house. You may be the feared Duke of Wildeforde to every other person in this empire, but I birthed you. If you want to protect Miss McTavish, I suggest you pack her off back to the one-room cottage she crawled out of. Do you think jail is the worst thing I can do to her?"

Her stare didn't waver. Her expression was as confident as it was cruel, and he was reminded exactly why he chose to end things with Fiona five years ago.

But that was five years ago. He'd thought he'd been in love. The truth was, he hadn't really known her. Fiona— the woman who'd walked from Scotland on her own, who was more intelligent than the brightest men of his acquaintance, who'd worked so hard to master fire—she wasn't a woman about to crumble under the sting of harsh words.

Edward might have, all those years ago, but he'd been thirteen, a boy who'd just lost his father. Those same bullies could lob those same comments at him now—if they dared—and he could withstand it.

Side by side, the two of them could weather the storm of any scandal.

⌒

Fiona paced in circles around her bedroom. Charlotte, having received no responses from Fi to any of her questions about why there might be an inspector from the Home Office in their drawing room, sat on the bed and watched with an anxious look.

Charlotte, a perfectly sweet and kind girl who would bear the brunt of any scandal Fiona caused. It would be her who would be shunned by society and unable to make a good match. Fiona had to leave before that happened. She had to go home to Abingdale. London was fraught with too many dangers.

Lady Luella. The duchess. Inspector Patterson.

No, she couldn't stay. She would pull Lord Chester aside tonight and show him the signed patent and hopefully that would be enough for him. Then, parole conditions be damned, she would go to Ben's town house and hide there until the issue of her assault charges could be resolved.

By the end of the week, she would be on the next mail coach out of London.

She was staring out the window, her head leaning against the glass, when the door whooshed open and Edward entered. She could tell it was him even without turning around just by the way her heart skittered and the hairs on the back of her neck lifted.

"Charlotte, out."

There was a muted scramble, quiet footsteps on the floor, and then the door shut with a *snick*.

He sighed, long and weary, and she turned to look at him. The furrows of his brow were deeper, the lines around his mouth more noticeable. "I know you don't want me to reveal the truth about your sex to the magistrate until after you've signed your contract with Chester, but I think it's best if I go to the courthouse tomorrow, explain the whole situation—why Finley exists, your relationship with Tucker and Alastair—and ask him to dismiss the charges. All you did was throw a poorly aimed tomato."

She didn't hesitate. "Aye."

He looked up in surprise, no doubt expecting her to argue. But this situation was beyond her. It had escalated so far out of control she felt like a piece of falling ash, being buffeted in different directions.

She needed his help. She'd needed it weeks ago; she was only just now getting over her own pride enough to admit it. "I'll go with ye, though," she said.

"Fi," he said, his frustration seeping through. It would be easier for him without her. He could be all royal and demand rather than ask. God only knows what he'd say about her to get the magistrate to agree if she weren't in the room.

Foolish. Idiotic. Naïve. She could imagine all of those words coming out of his mouth, and he wouldn't be wrong.

"This is my mess, Edward. I agree that we need to resolve this as soon as possible and I'll accept yer help because, heaven help me, I need it. But these were my choices and I'll be the one to account for them."

He nodded, and even though she could see it went against all his instincts, he agreed. "Fine."

"I'll speak to Lord Chester tonight and insist his solicitor draw up contracts tomorrow. Hopefully we'll be able to sign before my charade becomes public knowledge." Because what man would want to go into partnership with someone who lied so easily?

Just as easily as she lied to Edward. He'd asked her if she'd seen Tucker and she'd pretended she knew nothing. If she was going to be honest with him, she would tell him about last night. The inspector had asked for her whereabouts, and she'd let Edward unknowingly provide a false alibi.

Edward, there's more you should know . . .

The words were on the tip of her tongue, and despite all the terrible things that were happening, she felt a sense of relief that the lies were about to be over.

"Ed—"

He crossed to her, gathering her in his arms and resting his cheek on her hair, cocooning her in his warmth. "It will all be well," he murmured. "I'll sort it all out, love. I promise."

Tomorrow. She would tell him the truth tomorrow.

Chapter 30 ———————

Edward waited alone at the bottom of the stairs. Fiona was running late, and his mother wouldn't appear until everyone else had arrived and was waiting.

There was still time to call off Charlotte's madcap scheme. His mother knew Fiona was Finley; this charade was no longer for her benefit. The biggest threat was Lady Luella and how she would react when tomorrow's copy of *The Times* reached breakfast tables without her anticipated engagement announcement.

It was highly likely that would be the impetus she needed to begin gossiping about Finley's true identity. Once she realized she was not going to be the new Duchess of Wildeforde, she'd have no reason not to start the scandal of the season.

Two weeks ago, that would have frightened him. His family at the center of the year's greatest scandal had been his greatest fear. Now, he couldn't give a damn. His only hesitation was Charlotte and how a scandal might impact her ability to find a husband. Once that was achieved, the *ton* was going to see just how little Edward cared for their good opinion.

But Charlotte's match was not yet set, and so Edward would allow tonight's shenanigans. Finley and Fiona in the same place at the same time—it was the only guaranteed way to circumvent the gossip firestorm Luella would try to ignite.

"My goodness." Simmons's appreciative murmur, so very unlike him, caused Edward to look up. Fiona stood at the top of the stairs, looking down nervously.

All breath escaped him. Her curls had been fashioned in a way that they now cascaded over one shoulder. Charlotte's crystal beads had been pinned throughout, so as she descended the stairs her auburn locks glinted and glimmered like flames.

Her lashes had been lined with the barest kohl, contrasting against her pale skin and highlighting the deep green of her eyes. Eyes that looked at him apprehensively as she stood before him.

"Well?" She looked down at her dress, a pale green silk that, despite its modest cut, did more than just hint at the figure beneath. He went hard instantly.

He took her gloved hand, bringing it to his lips. "You are beautiful."

She quirked her lips, wryly.

"No more or less beautiful than in breeches and shirt." He meant it too. This version of Fiona was breathtaking. But she was so when clad in trousers and was even more so when dressed in nothing at all.

He could not wait to marry this woman. That afternoon, he'd sent for the ring. It was currently in his dress coat pocket, next to his heart, where it would sit until tonight was over and they'd resolved the issue with the magistrate.

"Simmons, please call for the duchess."

"There's no need." His mother's thin and reedy voice came from the upstairs landing. From the look on her face, she hadn't missed his momentary lust-filled befuddlement. "Where is your brother, Miss McTavish?" the duchess asked as she joined them. "I expected to see you both tonight. Or is there a reason that won't happen?"

Fiona swallowed and curtseyed. "I'm afraid he's been detained, Your Grace."

"Is that so?"

Charlotte took Fiona's arm. Edward would forever be grateful for his sister's willingness to play the part of a human shield. A lifetime of the duchess's caustic comments had toughened her.

"Well, Mother," she said with her usual brightness. "Finley is with William, and you know how Will is. He'd much rather carouse with his friends than dance a waltz. But he has *promised* me that they will both attend, and he does not break his word."

That was a bald-faced lie; William was more than capable of breaking his word. But the duchess would hardly disagree out loud in front of the servants, so she simply *hmph*ed and made her way to the carriage.

Once they were at Aunt Augustus's ball, his mother joined her cronies on the settee by the balcony doors, where they could observe who went in and out and with whom.

The mob of young ladies who had trailed Edward like ducks at every event this season descended on him once again, seemingly not put off by Fiona, a stranger in their midst. This time, he was in no mood to indulge them.

"Your Grace, it's such a pleasure to see you again."

"Thank you, Miss Clarke. Excuse me."

"Your Grace, my father bid me to give you his greetings."

"That's very kind, Lady Violet. Excuse me."

"Your Grace, I've been thinking on this since our last dance; what is your favorite color?"

"Green, Lady Anne. Excuse me."

"Your Grace, I've saved a dance for you."

"For Christ's sake."

There was a collective gasp from the gathered debutantes. Their mouths dropped open and some even put their hands to their hearts in shock.

Blast. "I apologize for any mistaken impression I gave, but I am *not* in search of a wife." His statement rippled through the ballroom, carried on the lips of gossip-minded individuals, titillated by the sight of the always-calm and always-respectable Duke of Wildeforde losing his temper at a group of young girls.

One of whom burst into tears.

Edward breathed in deep, held it for a count of five, and exhaled. Tonight was going to be excruciating. The sooner he could tell the world that his heart was engaged, the better.

"Well, you handled that abominably," Charlotte said. "And you might as well dance. William won't be here for at least another two hours—not until they've stopped announcing guests."

Two hours. He had to endure another two hours of this. Fiona looked just as weary at the thought. She may have enjoyed herself as Finley; the young Scotsman was the subject of little attention when standing next to the eligible Stirling brothers. But as Fiona, an unknown woman standing next to a duke who had just announced he was no longer looking for a wife? She was suddenly the subject of every single eye.

Which was what they wanted, if their ruse was to succeed,

but it did not make her comfortable. She tapped her fingers on her skirts and the smallest of creases had formed between her brows. He wanted to stroke it away. He wanted to take those tapping fingers and enclose them in his so she knew he was in this with her. Neither of those things would help alleviate the cause of her anxiousness.

"Ned, if you cannot pretend that all is well, then I ask that you join the men wherever they disappear to and let Fiona and I be seen." She gestured toward the increasing crowd of gentlemen hanging at the fringes of their conversation.

He looked at Fiona. He would not leave her if she was not comfortable.

"I'm fine, Ed."

"All right," he said. "But once William arrives, we do this quickly."

The next few hours were excruciatingly slow. Charlotte was an absolute darling and didn't leave Fiona's side except during a select few dances, where she'd chosen Fi's partners for her—dull men with few conversation skills whose questions never got more difficult than "It's fine weather, isn't it?"

The rest of the time, the two women promenaded, arm in arm. Charlotte commandeered every conversation and by the time the clock struck ten, Fiona had met every person in attendance without divulging a single thing about herself.

And yet somehow, the fragments of conversation she overheard were about how "charming that Scottish girl is."

"You're incredible," she murmured to Charlotte. "They see only what you want them to."

"Well, I've been groomed to play the part of perfect lady

all my life. My mother may be many things, but incompetent is not one of them." Charlotte patted Fiona's arm.

It's not just Edward. Charlotte had already moved on to continue chatting when the realization fully hit. Edward was not the only sibling to build their entire identity around their mother's twisted notions of what was right.

It was remarkable, really, that Charlotte had developed as she had with a mother like the duchess as her role model. She could have turned into someone like Luella. Both girls were conniving, but where Luella's manipulations were vicious and self-serving, Charlotte's were a force for good.

Overcome with appreciation, Fiona leaned over and gave her a quick kiss on the cheek. "Thank ye," she whispered.

Charlotte's eyes crinkled around the edges as she smiled. "Yes, yes. Don't thank me yet. The hard part is just starting." She gestured toward the door, where William had just entered. "You're on your own from here."

As Charlotte made for one of the side doors, Fiona watched her leave with rising trepidation. From across the room, Edward caught her eye and gave her a nod.

In fifteen minutes, Charlotte would be upstairs on the mezzanine, dressed as Finley. She and William would be obnoxiously loud drunks—too loud not to be noticed, too far away to be seen with any real clarity.

Edward would ask Fiona to dance. Every woman in the ballroom would take note of the Scottish lass the duke chose to dance with. Apparently distracted, Edward would look up, repeatedly, at the scene unfolding above them. His face would darken. He would abruptly leave the moment the music finished, leaving Fiona alone in the middle of the dance floor.

And every person in that room would remember clearly Fiona and Finley in the same place at the same time.

There were so many things that could go wrong. William was absurdly confident that morning when she'd listed them all. "I have it all under control," he'd said. Only Char's nodding in the background had provided any comfort.

William and Charlotte entered the mezzanine just as the orchestra played the first strains of a waltz. The show was about to begin. Edward weaved his way through the crowd until he was standing before her. "Ready?"

She nodded yes but the answer was really no. This charade-on-top-of-a-charade was the beginning of the end of her time here in London.

She wasn't ready to say good-bye to Edward. She wasn't ready to remove herself from his family, one she had become part of so quickly and easily before she'd even realized it. Her heart already ached at the loss.

She slipped her hand into his and let him guide her to the middle of the dance floor. She put her other hand on his shoulder and shivered as his fingers touched the small of her back.

"You realize this is the first time we've danced together," he said, sweeping her into the first turn.

"I will try to let you lead."

He smiled. "I've given up expecting you to do as others do," he said quietly, moving them in a way that no other couple could easily overhear them. "Self-determination is your very essence. I wouldn't change it."

"Even if it made me the sort of woman ye could wed?" She so wished she was that sort of woman. She wished he wasn't the duke and she wasn't a singular creature with an objectionable father and that they were just two people unconnected to an actual time or place as they had been five years ago.

His fingers squeezed hers, the biggest sign of physical affection he could give, given they were the center of everyone's attention. "I love you for who you are, Fiona McTavish. I wouldn't want to be married to a different version of you."

His hand, warm and steady on her back, felt like their entire relationship captured in a single touch. It did not push her in any direction or force her to follow his lead, as she had presumed the duke would. It was simply there to provide a calm, grounded point amid the twirling. It was Edward, the man she loved. The man she was leaving.

William's laughing was loud enough to be heard over the orchestra and the general hubbub of the room. Snippets of conversation reached them.

"—and *then* she said, 'Come back when yer wearin' yer kilt and I'll toss yer caber for free—'" The rest of the sentence was unintelligible, thank God.

Fiona's ears flushed red with embarrassment. Edward did not need to fake the irate look he sent in Will's direction. "I'm going to kill him."

Fi was tempted to agree. "He is getting the job done, though." Around them, the crowd held a mix of expressions— astonished, aghast, appalled. Guests were most definitely looking from Fiona and Edward to Finley and William, just to see how the duke would react.

It had worked. There was no way Luella would be able to convince anyone that Fiona had been swanning around town masquerading as a man and staying in the duke's residence unchaperoned.

There was still the issue of his mother but otherwise, the threat had been quashed. There was only one part of the scheme left to go. Fiona and Charlotte would meet so Fiona could change into Finley's clothes. She would approach

Lord Chester with the patent and ask that he make the deal with her.

In a small sitting room off the hallway, door guarded from unexpected visitors by Edward, Fiona got to work on the buttons that secured Charlotte's dress.

"Wasn't that brilliant?" Char gushed, using her fingers to fix the curls that had been crushed under the wig. "I swear, that was the most fun I've had in a long time."

The words were a direct echo of William's just a few nights prior. What was it with the Stirling siblings and their penchant for intrigue?

"I will consider it brilliant only when we're all home an' curled up with a hot milk, with no one the wiser of our games." She did up the last of the buttons and stepped back.

"Spoilsport," Charlotte said as she turned. "Spin." Charlotte made short work of the buttons down the back of Fiona's dress, and she unlaced the stays that were highlighting Fiona's more feminine features. Fiona slipped out of both, handing the items to Charlotte to fold and place in the satchel Will had brought with him to the ball.

Fi was already wearing men's stockings beneath her dress. She pulled on the breeches Charlotte had worn, the shirt, the waistcoat, and the dress coat. They had opted for the fastest, most simple knot possible for the cravat.

"There," Charlotte said, adjusting Fiona's wig as Fi wiped the kohl from her eyes with Edward's handkerchief. "There are no pins, Will forgot them, so don't bow to Lord Chester when you see him, or all of this will be for naught."

"Nae bowing. Got it."

Charlotte cupped Fiona's face in her hands. "It will all be well, sister. In ten years' time when we're old and frightfully dull, we'll look back at tonight and remember how interesting we used to be."

Sister. Tears sprung to Fiona's eyes and she turned her attention to the buckles of her slippers so Charlotte couldn't see them. "I'd be happy to be a little less *interesting*," Fiona said. And God, was that the truth. She was going to miss Charlotte and Will, but she was also looking forward to quiet nights back home.

"I will spread the word that Fiona is unwell and has retired for the evening. Everyone will assume you were too mortified at being left alone on the dance floor to continue. Then I'll meet you at the carriage."

Before Charlotte could leave, Fiona grabbed her hand, squeezing it lightly. She was not fond of good-byes and she planned on leaving first thing in the morning, as soon as she and Edward had finished with the magistrate. This may well be the last moment they had alone together.

"Thank ye, Char, for everything. You are an intelligent, kind, and brilliant young woman. Don't let society force you into a box in which ye dunnae belong."

Charlotte cocked her head, her expression slightly confused. "I won't, Fi. Never you worry." She kissed her on the cheek. "Good luck with Lord Chester."

Chapter 31 ————————————

As the three Stirling siblings walked back into the ballroom, all eyes turned to look at them.

"Remember, you're irate with me," William murmured. He yelped as Charlotte stepped on his foot.

"That's not difficult," Edward replied. The two of them would have words. But not here. Right now he was focused on tying off loose ends and getting them all out before anything could go wrong.

Charlotte put a hand on his arm. "As much as I'm loath to interrupt this episode of brotherly affection, should we be concerned?" Charlotte nodded toward the balcony doors, where their mother was watching them with a gleeful look on her face. "She should be livid, not grinning like a child who just broke into the sweet jar."

The duchess gave Edward a smug, satisfied smile. The kind of smile that sent shivers to his core. "She's plotting something."

"Clearly," Char said. "But what?"

Destroy Fiona. Manipulate Edward into marriage. They were his mother's two focuses of late. But that gave him no firm picture of what she was intending to do in this moment.

Then Luella joined his mother, gave her a quick kiss on the cheek, and ran her hands over her skirts, the way his mother did before guests entered her sitting room. The way Charlotte did before walking into a ballroom.

"You don't think..." Charlotte's voice was wary. Her hand tightened on Edward's arm.

"Surely not. Mother's expecting her—my—engagement announcement to run in *The Times* tomorrow. She's not reckless. She'll take that safe win."

"*Oh.*" That single, horrified syllable from Will caused Edward's stomach to drop. His feet froze to the floor.

"William Stirling, what did you do?" Char demanded.

"I might have mentioned that you'd uncovered her plans. She wouldn't give me a moment of peace this afternoon."

Edward's feet were rooted to the floor as he watched his mother march determinedly toward the orchestra, Luella in tow. The girl had a sweet and happy expression on her face, but when she looked over at Edward, he saw a flash of triumph.

"I won't do it," he said. "I won't marry Luella simply because Mother announces that I will. She knows that." But even he didn't believe his own words.

"It would be one hell of a scandal," William said. "She knows you won't tolerate the Wildeforde name being besmirched like that."

He shook his head. "I won't do it."

"Ned, you'd be painted as the villain. You'd be completely ostracized," Charlotte whispered. "Two broken engagements in two years."

The orchestra launched into a final refrain. The duchess raised her kerchief to get the conductor's attention.

"Move. Move, move, move, move, move," Edward said. The three of them strode purposefully through the crowd, Charlotte in the lead, clearing the path with her charming smile and friendly hand gestures, literally towing her brothers along behind her.

The final notes sounded. They weren't going to make it.

Charlotte released Edward's hand and broke into a run, catching her mother and Luella as they climbed the stairs to stand at the front of the stage.

"I'm not sure a spat in front of the whole crowd is much of an improvement," William muttered.

But their sister surprised them both. She threaded an arm through Luella's and shot her a syrupy sweet smile, even going so far as to give Luella a quick peck on the cheek. His mother, stuck in front of the crowd, had no choice but to plaster on a fake smile as she looked at her daughter.

Edward's heart was in his throat. He continued to make his way to the front of the room, but with all eyes on his mother, he had to weave in and out of a crowd that was too distracted to get out of his damn way.

The usually loud hubbub of the room had died down to a quiet humming as everyone waited for the announcement.

He reached the platform, but by then it was too late. The music had stopped and his mother stepped forward. *Goddamn it.*

"Ladies and gentlemen," the duchess said. "It gives me such great pleasure to announce that—"

"Oh," Charlotte said loudly, raising a hand to her forehead. Her knees buckled slightly, and a loud murmur ran through the crowd.

The duchess scowled and ignored her daughter's outburst. "As I was saying, I am delighted to announce that—"

But Charlotte, the bloody heroine that she was, wouldn't be put off. Her knees buckled again, and this time she stumbled forward. The entire crowd gasped as she swooned. The men closest to the stage rushed forward just as she toppled delicately over the edge.

Edward's heart only slowed once he realized Lord Montford had caught her and she was safe in his arms. The murmur of the crowd swelled into a cacophony of frenzied gossip. His mother's face twisted in fury. She waved her arms to try and regain the room's attention, but they were still too titillated by Charlotte's "accident."

"She won't be put off," William said.

Indeed, their mother shook the conductor's arm. He motioned to his French horn, who blew a long, loud note.

The crowd hushed again.

"This is ridiculous." Edward strode forward. Dragging his mother from the stage would cause almost as much gossip as a fake engagement, but it would be infinitely more satisfying.

At least, it would have been—if William hadn't turned around and punched Lord Pallsbury square in the jaw, and then thumped Lord Alverton when he came to intervene.

The room went wild, all turning away from the stage to view the ruckus. The crowd surged toward the fight, a mix of busybodies aiming for a better look and men determined to either end or enter the fray.

No one noticed Edward climb the stage. No one noticed as he grabbed both women and dragged them down the steps.

He started with Luella, gripping her shoulders and looking her dead in the eye. "I will not marry you, no matter what scandal it causes, no matter how much your reputation will be damaged, no matter what society may think. I will not be a gentleman. Despite whatever my mother promised you, I'm not so scared of scandal that I would ever take you as a wife."

Panic crossed Luella's face. She did not cry, though. She held her chin high with the arrogance of a woman who had only ever known privilege. "You do not know what you're doing. You don't understand. I would be a perfect duchess for you. I swear it."

"But not a perfect wife."

Her eyes filled with tears and she pressed her gloved fist to her lips before fleeing to the nearest exit.

Edward turned to his mother. "I've quite acclimatized to the idea of a scandal, Mother. You will not manipulate me into an engagement a second time."

The duchess's face twisted into a sneer, showing the ugliness that was always there yet usually hidden. "You will marry a woman worthy of the title. Someone who has *trained* for the role. Who will bring esteem to our name."

"Fuck our name, Mother. She will bring love, and joy, and kindness, and that's worth more than a good reputation could ever be."

Fiona stood, mouth agape, at the teeming mass of color at the front of the room. While she was vaguely aware of William being restrained by three men and yelled at by no fewer than four old dragons of the *ton*, her attention was fixed on Edward, to the side, almost hidden by potted palms.

He was furious.

His mother was staring up at him, an equally furious, equally stubborn look on her face. Fi had a good idea what crisis had just been averted, but the feeling of relief that washed over her was not for Edward and the miserable future he'd managed to avoid. It was a selfish relief that, for now, he wasn't engaged to someone else.

It would happen, of course. He couldn't remain a bachelor forever. He was a duke. He had a responsibility to produce an heir. She simply hoped that by the time he did, her heart would be mended a little, so she could receive news of his betrothal and feel happiness for him rather than grief.

"Egad. What the devil is all of that about?" Lord Chester said, frowning at the ruckus.

"I'm sure I have no idea," she murmured.

"The boy has always been a hellion. Wildeforde really should take him in hand."

How hypocritical, coming from a man whose potential investment in her matches was because he loved a good bet more than anything else. "I think Will just needs to find his purpose in life," she said.

Chester shrugged. "Perhaps. Now, McTavish. You had something to show me that couldn't wait until tomorrow. I assume it proves the provenance of the matches."

"Yes, my lord." She nodded a little too hard and felt her wig slip just a fraction. Chester didn't seem to notice, so she ignored the itch to adjust it and instead reached into her inside coat pocket to retrieve the signed patent and pressed it into his hand. "So you can see, these match designs are mine."

His expression remained unreadable and her heart began to yammer as she waited for a response. She needed this to be over with. She needed the problem solved, the deal fixed, so she could go to the magistrate tomorrow and have this whole mess sorted out. Then she would go home and pretend that she hadn't fallen in love with a duke, effectively breaking her own heart this time.

Lord Chester frowned as he read through the patent details.

Behind her, she could hear the now-familiar swell of alarm and intrigue. She tried to ignore it. Nothing that was happening elsewhere in the room was as important as what was happening in front of her. Not even Edward.

Lord Chester turned his attention to the seal of the patent office. He held it to the light, as though he was checking for some sign of authenticity.

The buzzing grew louder.

She held her breath, waiting. If he accepted this as all the proof he needed, and if he was willing to act quickly...

His attention returned to the first few lines of the patent and his frown deepened. "So, tell me..." He trailed off as something behind her caught his attention. His eyes widened.

For God's sake. She turned around.

Oh heavens, no.

Six uniformed guards marched in her direction, not twenty feet away. At their head was Inspector Patterson, with a grim look on his face.

She froze.

"Fiona!" Edward's voice called out to her from the other side of the room. Somewhere behind the buzzing in her ears, she registered the fact that he'd used her real name. Whatever was about to happen, then, was worse than her charade being exposed.

"Get out of my way. Goddamn it. Fiona!"

She couldn't see him. All she could see was the wall of uniforms in front of her. Then Inspector Patterson was standing less than a foot away. His eyes were cold flint.

"Fiona McTavish. On behalf of his Majesty King George IV, I hereby arrest you on the charge of treason."

Her breathing stopped. The buzzing sound suddenly felt so very far away. She swayed a little. By the time two guards had circled her and pulled her hands behind her back, she couldn't feel their touch. It was as if she were watching the scene play out as a spectator from above.

Cruelly, Patterson yanked at her wig, tossing it to the floor, and her hair tumbled loose across her shoulders. The crowd took a collective breath in as the pieces fell together.

"Fiona!"

The crack in Edward's voice brought her back to her body. There was a sudden onslaught of noise. Every voice in the crowd loud and outraged. She could see him now, held back by two of the guards.

"Let her go! Now, Goddamn it. Let her go or I will destroy each and every one of you."

The guards behind her shoved her forward. She stumbled over her feet and would have fallen had one of them not grabbed the fabric of her coat.

And still, she could not breathe.

She locked eyes with Edward as she passed him, three men required now to keep him at bay. His furious, anguished yell brought tears to her eyes.

Suddenly, Charlotte was in front of her, hands on her hips, an incensed, mulish expression on her face. "I am Lady Charlotte Stirling, cousin to King George, sister to the Duke of Wildeforde, niece to the Duke of Camden," she said. Her voice held an imperiousness that Fiona had never heard before. "Release her immediately." There was no *or* just the assumption that her orders would be obeyed.

"Excuse me, my lady." One of the officers gently pulled her aside, ignoring the outrage on her face.

Fiona was pushed forward once again.

She stared in front of her, her face burning as the crowd parted. The looks on their faces suggested they were glad of the spectacle, glad to see her fall. She had, after all, deceived them and made them look like fools.

Then there was a friendly face. William stood by the ball-room door and caught her eye. She focused on him, trying to let all the other faces slip away. As she drew near, he said, loudly enough for his voice to reach her over the din, "Don't say anything, Finn. Not a word. Wilde will be there soon."

She swallowed, a ball catching in her throat, and repeated the words to herself in her head over and over and over again.

Wilde will be there soon.

Chapter 32 —————————————

It killed Edward not to follow the prison cart from the Alston residence to the jail where Fiona was to be detained. He wanted to storm into the governor's office and demand she be freed. Her spending even a single minute in a cell filled him with rage.

But he also knew that the man on duty was unlikely to release her on his say-so.

So instead he followed Patterson to King Charles Street, where the Home Office was located. The inspector was going to give a full accounting for his actions tonight, so help him God. And then he was going to face the full force of Edward's wrath.

Edward's carriage had barely stopped moving when he shoved open the door and leapt out. Patterson was just a shadowy figure retreating through the doors of the double-story building.

Edward followed, but by the time he entered the foyer, Patterson had disappeared. The night watchman escorted him to a small room with bare walls, furnished only with a long wooden table, scarred with age, flanked by two long, heavy-looking benches.

Edward took a seat that faced the door, heels knocking, fingers tapping on the tabletop. Every minute he sat there waiting—at least ten—the tension inside him built. Every minute he was here, Fiona was there—in a cell, alone. Hopefully alone. By the time Patterson arrived, Edward's entire body was quivering. He tried to suppress all signs of his anxiety by taking a deep breath, but the air wouldn't come.

As Patterson took the seat opposite Edward, his lips quirked as though suppressing a smile. The blasted inspector knew he had the upper hand. He placed a folder on the table between them, resting his hands on top of it. "Can I order you some tea?" he said mildly.

Fucking tea. Fiona was sitting in a prison cell and this bastard was offering tea. "No, Goddamn it. You can tell me why you have arrested Fiona McTavish on a spurious charge like treason."

The inspector looked at the officer standing at the door. "Just one tea, thank you, Donaldson."

Edward pressed his feet into the floor, anchoring himself to stop from lunging over the table. "I'm waiting for a response."

Patterson leaned forward, interlacing his fingers in front of him and regarding Edward over his hands. "As I mentioned when we last spoke, the Home Office has been investigating a plot to attack parliament for some time now. The protest Miss McTavish was arrested at was used as a distraction for the perpetrators to gather people for their scheme."

Edward shook his head. This was beyond belief. "There were almost three hundred people at that rally. Are you suggesting they were all plotting treason?"

"Not all three hundred were arrested and charged with assault."

"She threw a bloody tomato. It was stupid, not assault. I pay a king's ransom in taxes; trust me—the guards can purchase another bloody coat."

Patterson ignored his outburst and instead slid his hand into the folder and retrieved a sheaf of papers. Papers that looked familiar. He had seen ones like them in Fiona's laboratory.

"Do you recognize this handwriting?" Patterson asked.

"What of it?" And how the hell had they come into Patterson's possession?

"These papers contain a formula for an explosive device. Her Grace was kind enough to show me through Miss McTavish's laboratory this afternoon."

"A bloody match. It lights a fire the size of my pinkie finger. Be reasonable."

Patterson shrugged. "In the quantities suggested in these documents, true. But they could be scaled, and then you're looking at a dangerous weapon."

Edward rolled his eyes. "That is somewhat of a reach, Inspector. It's proof of nothing other than her intelligence and hard work."

The inspector looked at him, fist pressed against his lips, remaining silent. It was a strategy Edward was perfectly familiar with, and to have it used on him made his blood boil.

"Damn you, man, for locking up a woman on nothing but circumstantial evidence. For throwing my—" What was she? Not wife. Love? "—guest into prison because of your suspicions and nothing else."

He had enough anger in him to throw the entire table against the wall, which is probably why he had been directed in here, where the furniture was bolted to the floor. He satisfied himself by thumping his fist onto the wood.

"We've been watching Charles Tucker and his associates for some time. The chit was seen entering the building where he's residing yesterday. And last night..."

Damnably calm, the inspector opened his folder and methodically placed three images in front of him.

Sketches of a face—unmistakably Fiona's—wig askew, black scarf wrapped around her neck. Her eyes were too narrow in one, her lips too thin in another, but they were clearly the same person.

"This person was seen breaking into Westminster Palace. He—*she*—was run off by the King's Guards. They were each asked to describe the would-be intruder. This is the result."

Edward's heart stopped. An ice-cold shiver ran down his spine. Fiona had left the Mottram ball early. He'd come home to find her dressed entirely in black, drinking with William. What the devil had she been doing?

He swallowed. His reaction was being watched and it could be used against her in court. If he admitted to recognizing the face in the pictures, he would damn her in an instant.

So he sat there, jaw tight, saying nothing.

"She was seen with another person. Six foot tall, broad shoulders. None of the guards got a good look at him, other than that he was dressed in very fine attire and had black curly hair, somewhat like yours. Can you account for your whereabouts on Monday night?"

Anger settled over him like a heavy fog.

William.

Chapter 33 ———————

Edward strode into the billiards room, still reeling from his conversation with Patterson. On the journey home he'd tried to piece together what had happened. What could possibly have caused Fiona to lose her bloody mind. But nothing made sense.

William would have answers, though, and he would damn well share them.

Charlotte launched herself from the settee and rushed to Edward, grabbing his arm. "Where is she? Is she out?"

Edward set her aside, his gaze firmly on his brother, who, having divined some kind of warning from Edward's expression, had taken several steps backward.

"No. She is not out." Edward continued toward his brother, who had now moved behind the settee, putting the furniture between them as though it could possibly stop Edward from delivering the thrashing William deserved.

"She is not out, because there are at least three reliable

eyewitnesses who saw her and an unknown gentleman attempt to break into Westminster Palace last night."

The blood drained from William's face. Edward took bitter satisfaction from his brother's distress. In all their years of arguing over his scrapes, Will had never looked so apprehensive. Behind him, Charlotte gasped.

"Do you want to tell me, brother, what the hell you and Fiona were doing?" The two of them circled around the settee, William doing his best to keep distance between them.

"It was a terrible decision," William said.

"Whose decision?"

"The break-ins in general or Westminster Palace?"

Edward stilled, almost stumbling over his brother's words. "Break-ins? Multiple?"

William swallowed, his Adam's apple bobbing. "Her father had stolen her idea and was passing it off as his own. She was on her way to steal it back when I ran into her, so I tagged along."

Edward's ears rang, but not loud enough to drown out his thoughts. Fucking Alastair McTavish.

But Fi... She hadn't trusted him and then she'd outright lied to him. She'd chosen to put herself in danger rather than ask for his help. That blasted stubborn woman.

"You should have stopped her."

William cocked his head. "Have you *met* her? Fiona is as bullheaded as you are."

"Did you try?"

William stared at the back of the settee between them. "No," he muttered.

"And Westminster Palace?"

William looked up, meeting Edward's furious stare. Fear, regret, anguish—his expression held all three. "It was my idea."

Edward's heartbeat thundered in his ears. Rage engulfed him. He leapt over the settee, colliding with his brother, the two of them tumbling to the floor with a hard thump. William grunted as Edward landed on top of him.

"No," Charlotte yelled. "Stop it."

But Edward couldn't stop. He straddled Will and thumped his brother in the jaw. It had been one blunder after another since William had been in leading strings, and Edward had allowed it to happen, always hoping that each act of rebellion was the last.

Clearly, his brother was not going to learn, and this was the absolute last straw. For Will to put the woman Edward loved in danger—actual, life-ending danger—was unforgivable.

"Enough!" Charlotte grabbed Edward around the shoulders and tried to pull him back. She might as well have been a butterfly trying to move a boulder. After a brief attempt, she released him.

William didn't fight back. He had his arms up to protect his head, but he made no move to return the blows Edward continued to rain down.

Bigger, stronger arms captured him. Charlotte had called for two footmen to intervene. They grabbed hold of Edward and dragged him backward a few feet, putting William just out of reach.

Chest heaving, Edward sat on the floor, leaning against an armchair. The knuckles on his hand stung and he felt strangely hollow.

William sat up, gingerly pressing fingers against his cheekbone and the swelling that had already begun there. There were tears in his eyes as he looked at Edward. "I'm sorry. It was a stupid lark."

His apology didn't matter. They were beyond sorries. "Stupid doesn't even begin to describe your actions."

Charlotte went to William, using the hem of her skirt to blot away the blood from a cut to his brow. William flinched under her touch but didn't shift his gaze from Edward. "I didn't think anything truly bad would come from it."

"No. You didn't *think*. You should have protected her. Whatever your feelings for me, you should have been a gentleman and protected her. Even from herself."

"I'm sorry." William's voice cracked. The look Charlotte threw in Edward's direction was furious.

Edward didn't care. Both of his siblings needed to grow the hell up.

Edward dragged himself to his feet. "Stand up," he said to his brother.

Warily, William stood, raising his fists as if prepared for another round of blows. Charlotte stood between them, hands on hips, jaw set in determination, ready to physically block any further attack.

But Edward didn't want to fight anymore. He'd been fighting with his brother for years. It was over. He was done. If William wouldn't learn that his actions had consequences, couldn't bring himself to operate with the maturity required of a man his age, then Edward had no more time for him.

"Tomorrow I will be purchasing a commission for you. You will join the army. Perhaps they can teach you what I could not." Perhaps they could succeed where Edward had failed.

William shook his head, eyes wide. "I won't."

"You will. Because you are cut off. Your allowance is gone, your lines of credit will be closed. You are not welcome in any of my homes. I will contact White's and Boodle's and any other clubs you're a member of and instruct them not to admit you. You *are* cut off."

Charlotte gasped, her mouth dropping open. William stumbled backward. "You wouldn't," he said in disbelief.

"It's done. Pack your things tonight. General Hastings will be expecting you tomorrow."

William took several steps forward but halted just out of Edward's reach. "You would have me waste my life in battle?"

No. Edward would have William home and happy and whole. But if William continued on this path, it would only be a matter of time before he ended up a drunk, or worse, in another man's sights in a duel. "You're wasting your life here."

William shook off his sister's hand and marched out of the room, but not before Edward saw tears roll down his brother's face. It was not how he wanted things to happen, but there was no other choice.

Charlotte stepped close enough to him that she had to crane her neck to meet his gaze. "I will never, ever forgive you for this. You are dead to me." Then, with a swish of her skirts, she followed William.

If he had the time, Edward would listen to the sound of his own heart breaking and question his choices—his siblings' happiness had been his sole focus since the day their father had died.

If he had the time, he would think about how much it hurt to lose them.

If he had the time, but he didn't, because unless he could find a way to fix all this, Fiona would soon face a magistrate, charged with treason.

The noose that was primed to wrap around her neck, wrapped around his heart and tightened.

Chapter 34 ————————

Fiona shivered. She had been thrown into a small, dark cell with no light, no overcoat, and no blanket.

And she'd waited.

William's words echoed in her head: *Wilde will be there soon.*

Every time a footstep had fallen in the corridor that led to her cell, every time she heard a mumble of voices, her heart leapt. But it had been hours, and the longer the night got, the more the chill seeped into her bones, the more she began to doubt.

Yes, Edward was a duke, but maybe this problem was bigger than him. They were treason charges, after all. Maybe it was a problem he didn't *want* to solve. He hadn't come to court when she was charged with disturbing the peace. Maybe this scandal was a step too far for a man whose life had been dedicated to rebuilding the esteem of his family name.

Maybe Edward wasn't coming.

She had tried to sleep but sleep wouldn't come. The hiss

of the ballroom had followed her to her cell, setting up in her head and refusing to dissipate. Her chest felt tight, and she couldn't draw in a full breath. She tried to focus on dragging in a stream of air, but it felt thin, as if it lacked what was necessary to keep her alive.

Wilde will be there soon.

Yes. Maybe. Then, where was he?

There was a sharp clang of keys in the door, and with a rusty squeak, the door opened.

Edward. Thank God. He hadn't forsaken her. Who else would be here for her at this hour? Well past midnight but before the dawn?

Two guards entered—one stood with a baton held at the ready, the other knelt to unlock the shackles around her ankles. The shackles on her wrists remained in place. She was pulled to her feet roughly and almost stumbled. She could barely feel her feet from the cold.

Fiona kept pace with the guards. After three flights of stairs and more twists and turns than she could count, they led her into a small, windowless room.

There he was, sitting at a table, his head in his hands. He looked up as she entered. Worry lines were etched into his face. His eyes were grief filled. His hair was disheveled, and he still wore the clothes he'd worn at the ball, although his cravat was loose and there were small specks of blood on his shirt.

She was too tired and too scared to care what had happened in the hours previous. All that mattered was that he was there.

He was up and with her in seconds, gathering her into his arms. She buried her face into his chest, breathing in the scent of him, and then the tears started falling. She pressed her cheek against him and sobbed.

His arms tightened around her, and she felt the warmth of his breath as he kissed her hair. She cried harder. She wanted to wrap her arms around his neck and sink into him, but the shackles prevented it, so she clutched at the lapels of his coat.

"Shhhh, love. It will be all right. Shhhh."

His gentle soothing calmed her. The tears slowed, as did her racing heart. When he pulled back, his expression was soft and comforting, but it darkened quickly when he saw her wrists bound by irons.

"Take these off her."

"We've orders, Your Grace."

"Take these off her and leave us."

The guards hesitated, but they knew who he was, the power he had. Reluctantly, they unlocked the shackles and left the room.

Fiona immediately collapsed into him, her arms around his neck, pulling him into her like they could become one person. When she could compose herself, she stepped backward and wiped the tears from her cheeks.

She had been shivering for so long now, she barely noticed it, but he must have because he frowned and removed his greatcoat and placed it over her shoulders. She wallowed in the warmth. Wallowed in the calming scent of him.

"How bad is it?" she asked as she took a seat at the table. He took a seat on the opposite side, far, too far away, and took her hands into his. Quickly, he explained the evidence they had against her. With each point, her heart thudded, heavy and erratic.

"Oh, God. What did I do?" The words tumbled out, a quick, quiet staccato. "What did I do? What did I do? What did I do? What did I do?"

She wasn't guilty of the crimes they were charging her with, but it was her fault that the case against her was so strong. If she had just gone to Edward for help rather than stubbornly trying to solve the problem herself. If she had simply weighed the risks properly.

"They want Tucker and your father. The bastards were almost apprehended on the palace grounds—one was shot—but they had a boat waiting on the Thames. The authorities haven't seen them since."

Shot. There was a chance her father was dead and that she might hang, and while she should be furious, all she could think was that this time, he might be gone for good.

"Tell the inspector where they are and we might be able to arrange a deal."

"I cannae."

"Damnit, Fi. This is serious. I understand that he's your father, but surely you won't take the fall for him."

"I *cannae*. I dunnae ken where they are. Ed, I swear, I am not a part of this." She could understand why he thought she might be. What other reasonable excuse could she have for her actions? She'd been stupid, bullheaded, and stubborn. Most intelligent people would never let a situation devolve into *this*.

Edward racked his hands through his hair.

"I'm going to hang," she said, hands covering her mouth.

"No, you're not."

"Ye dunnae ken that." She dropped her head in her hands and pulled at her hair, taking comfort in the slight pain it caused. "This is nae William in trouble for racing where he shouldn't. We're talking about treason. They might nae hang a duke based on this evidence, but they'll sure as hell hang a girl from nowhere."

She was such an idiot. Her bloody pride. Her stupid,

bloody pride. She should have gone to him for help the moment she'd heard that someone was trying to steal her matches.

Edward reached out across the table. "Which is why we need to be married."

"What? *Nae. Nae, nae, nae, nae.* Ye cannae marry me because of this. Ye need a proper duchess."

Disbelief warred with fury on his face. "How could you think I *wasn't* already going to marry you? I'm not in the habit of deflowering virgins. I was simply waiting for the right time to propose. This is it, apparently." He reached into his pocket and pulled out a ring box, opening it to show a delicate gold band studded with rubies.

"I would make a terrible duchess." She couldn't do any of the things society expected for that role. Worse, she would slowly wither and die under their constraints.

He reached over and took her hands. "You are the most intelligent, most hardworking, most capable woman I have ever met."

She shook her head. "I cannae marry ye. Think of the scandal it will cause. Think of what it will do to Charlotte. This is nae what I want."

He thumped his fist on the table. "Fi, be reasonable. You've turned both our lives upside down with this charade of yours, all because you desperately want 'security.' What I'm offering you *is* that. As my duchess, you will never not have a roof over your head again. In fact, you'll have your choice of twenty-three different roofs, and if you don't like any of those, I'll buy you a different one."

The fury that thrummed through her was so charged she was shocked the air around her didn't crackle. "That's not the *point*."

He ran a hand through his hair. "It *is* the point. You say

you want safety and security, that's what I can give you. You'll never have to work for it again."

"I *like* working. I dunnae want to give it up."

He pushed back from the table, his cheeks blowing out in frustration. "You cannot work if you're dead. And without my name to protect you, you might be. For God's sake. Stop being so idiotically stubborn."

She couldn't be his duchess. He needed a wife who could play the part of society hostess. A woman whose grace and accomplishments made her an asset to his work. Someone who could plan a perfect dinner and hold proper conversation with lords and ladies and politicians.

She needed a life that didn't confine her into the tightly bound definition of what a lady ought to be. She would suffocate in that role. She knew it.

"There has to be some other solution. Find my da. He'll tell the magistrate that I was nae involved."

"He is gone. His apartments have been cleared out. I will not find him in time."

It couldn't be. Edward could do anything. He could find anyone. He was the bloody Duke of Wildeforde, for Christ's sake. "If I explain to the magistrate what an idiot I've been...If I tell him the truth about what happened..."

He rubbed his hands on his thighs, as though the friction were an outlet for his exasperation. "You *might* walk free. Or you might be convicted."

She tapped the backs of her fingers on her lips. *Think, Fiona. Think.* But she couldn't see an answer. "I cannae marry ye," she whispered, shaking her head and trying not to let the tears flow once again.

She could see the impact of her words as he flinched. His face slackened, as though he'd been dealt a heavy blow, and then it hardened. "Do you think I want to *want* to marry you?

I've worked hard my entire life to fix the damage my father did to the Wildeforde name. I've spent decades putting out my brother's fires, keeping his antics out of the papers and away from gossips.

"I've made every right choice, danced every right step, said every right word, and reached the point where our family's name is the most respected one in England. And in less than a month you've destroyed that." He dropped his head into his hands, his fingers digging into his scalp.

She had ruined him. He'd been right in leaving her five years ago, given this was the damage she'd wrought.

He looked up at her, his torment writ clear, and it killed her.

"Then that is every reason ye need not to marry me." She tried not to let her voice splinter as her heart just had.

"I will not have you hang. That is not how this is going to end. And if the only way to prevent it is to marry you, then that's damn well what I'm going to do."

There was a soft tap at the door before it opened. One of the guards stuck his head in. "You have fifteen minutes' visiting time remaining, Your Grace."

"Send the archbishop in," Edward replied. He had pulled back from the table, putting as much distance between the two of them as it was possible to achieve in such a small space.

"The archbishop?" Fiona said. "He's here? At this hour?" She could just imagine Edward hammering on the front door of the archbishop's London residence in the middle of the night. Few men could get away with it. The duke was one.

"I was never going to be given the option, was I?" she asked as realization dawned. "Regardless of what I said."

His lips thinned and he shifted in his seat. "There is no other way to ensure, without a doubt, that you will go free."

But it wouldn't truly be freedom. She'd be trapped into marriage with a man who no longer wanted her.

Chapter 35 ————————

For the two hours that she was in the dock waiting for the judge and jury to hear her case, Fiona pressed herself against the wall closest to the bailiff and tried to ignore the looks the other accused sent her way.

She wasn't sure if it was the quality of the dress Edward had sent over that morning—more opulent, even, than the one she wore to last night's ball—or if her story had gotten out to other inmates, but something was inspiring bitter, angry stares from the dozen men in the dock with her.

She recognized some of them from her first stint in jail. On the other side of the long bench they sat on was the man who'd come close to revealing her secret. Perhaps it was the weeks she'd spent free that caused these men to dislike her.

One by one they were taken from the dock to stand before the judge and jury while the officers who had arrested them presented their evidence.

One by one, each of the accused spoke their defense—

everything ranging from "I wasn't there" to "I was just walking past" to "I damned well did it and I'd do it again."

The jury, a group of twelve people with sour faces, sat and listened. At the end of the day, they would rule on each case. Until then, the accused sat and watched the rest of the trials.

How many of these men—if any—would walk free? How many of them would find themselves on a ship to Australia? None faced Fiona's charges, only breaching the peace and assault, all because they voiced their disagreement with how poorly they were represented.

"Miss Fiona McTavish," the bailiff said. "Your turn."

She wiped her sweating palms on her velvet pelisse and swallowed. Her heart thumped.

She stared at her feet as she was led to the main floor. *Look respectful*, she thought to herself. *Keep your voice low. Make them think you're simply a foolish woman.*

When they reached the desk opposite the judge and next to the prosecutor, she finally looked up from her slippers. Rollins, Edward's lawyer, stood there, a grave look on his face.

"Keep quiet and let me work," he said.

That didn't instill much confidence. The last time they had faced court together, her misdemeanor charges had been upgraded to assault.

She twisted to look at the gallery behind her. Edward sat in the first row of the packed spectator benches, right in the center where his presence could not be missed. He looked every inch the duke—perfectly presented with jeweled stickpin the size of a robin's egg. There was no mistaking who he was.

Even from this distance, she could see his displeasure; his jaw was set at an odd angle, his face in a permanent frown. His hands rested on his thighs, out of sight, but she could picture the frustrated tap of his fingers against his breeches.

There hadn't been this big an audience gathered at her first hearing. Clearly, the story of the duke and the treasonous, duplicitous scientist had spread. Those who weren't ogling her in clear delight were craning their necks to get a good look at him.

He would be hating every second of this. The perfect Duke of Wildeforde now a key player in the most melodramatic of storylines. She tried to feel sympathy for him but couldn't.

Despite what he must be feeling, he caught her eye and gave her a curt nod. A you'll-be-fine nod, intended to make her feel better but ultimately making her stomach roil further.

The prosecutor stepped forward. "Your Honor. Today we bring before you Miss Fiona McTavish. While she may look like a respectable woman, we have evidence that she has consorted with known extremists and supplied them with the knowledge and tools to create an incendiary device that could devastate our beloved city, putting its lords, its lawmakers, and even its sovereign at risk. In addition, we have three eyewitnesses from members of the King's Guard who can testify that she was seen breaking into the grounds of Westminster Palace. We will demonstrate that she poses a great risk to society and that her sentence should reflect the seriousness of her crimes."

The courtroom broke out in wild exclamations, and the magistrate was forced to bang his gavel multiple times to restore order.

The prosecutor looked as though he was ready to continue his opening statement, but Rollins spoke up. "If I may interrupt, Your Honor. Before the prosecution continues with their entirely spurious accusations, I ask that they at least use the plaintiff's correct name—Her Grace, the Duchess of Wildeforde."

A wave of nausea almost overcame her at the use of the title she didn't want, that she was forced into. Shocked gasps echoed through the chamber. The prosecutor sent Rollins a murderous stare. "This is naught but a ruse," he said loudly, trying to be heard over the din of the crowd.

Rollins waited patiently for silence. "I assure you, Your Honor, it is very much the truth. His Grace is also willing to testify that his wife was with him the night of the alleged palace break-in. One must ask, which eyewitness account holds more credibility, that of a royal peer of the realm? Or of three guards who viewed the suspect at night, in the rain, from thirty yards away for less than a handful of seconds?"

The magistrate took a long look at Fiona, clearly assessing the situation, then turned his attention to Edward. She watched as Edward gave a solid, deliberate nod to the man who held her whole future in his palm.

The magistrate cleared his throat. "My learned friends, I agree with the defense. I'm not satisfied that the prosecution will be able to deliver a compelling argument."

Fiona's knees buckled, and she reached out a hand to Rollins to steady herself. He didn't so much as glance in her direction as the prosecutor protested.

"The case is dismissed without prejudice," the magistrate said. "The prosecution is free to bring charges again when— if—it has more solid evidence. But mark me, the evidence must be overwhelming for you to waste my time with this case again."

She laughed shakily, her whole body trembling. She wouldn't be charged again—there would be no stronger evidence because she'd never been guilty. Now it was time to get the hell out of London. To get away from everyone in it. To put this whole, wretched experience behind her.

She and Rollins had to pass the dock to exit the courtroom. The angry clamor of the men there matched the clamor of emotions within her. Relief. Guilt. Anger. Grief.

Once they'd reached the corridor outside, the bailiff uncuffed her and she sagged against the wall, looking up to God in thanks.

Rollins turned to her, a bland expression on his face, as though they hadn't just been through the most harrowing moment of her life. "His Grace will be very pleased. He bid me to escort you to his carriage. It's waiting in the mews behind the courthouse."

Ha.

"Tell His Grace he can go to hell and that I dunnae want to set eyes on him again."

Fi!" Edward took the stairs to the guest wing two at a time. "Fiona!"

When the judge had announced her freedom, eighteen hours of blind panic had subsided. Suddenly free of the image of her swinging from the gallows, his brain had begun to process thought again, and the realization of how much of an arse he'd been crept in.

Why had he told her he didn't want to *want* to marry her, as though marrying her was anything other than a privilege?

Why had he said she'd ruined the family name when adding an intelligent, kind, hardworking woman to it could only be an improvement?

Why had he said such cruel things? Her rejection of him did not justify such words.

When he reached Fiona's room, the door was already open. Inside, two maids were packing up her things.

"Where is Fiona? Where is my wife?"

The maids shared a nervous glance. Edward waited in

silence, arms crossed, letting his displeasure show, until one of them was forced to speak. "She left a half hour ago, Your Grace. Took the mail coach back to Abingdale. We're to pack up her things and send them after her."

Edward thumped his fist on the doorframe. "The mail coach? On her own?" Sure, she had traveled from Scotland to Abingdale by herself. She was a supremely capable woman. But just because she *could* didn't mean she *should*. She need not do things on her own anymore.

"She had young Andrew with her, Your Grace."

That was something, at least. Not much—the boy could hardly be relied upon should a band of highwaymen attack, but at least she wasn't alone.

"Did she say if she was coming back?"

The maid grimaced. "I don't believe she intends to, Your Grace."

Blast. She wasn't even going to give him a chance to apologize. Maybe he could catch her. There was only one main road running in that direction. If he took his horse rather than the coach, he could probably reach her before she left London.

He ran to the family quarters, ignoring the startled looks of his footmen as he thundered past them. He could spare five minutes to change into attire more suitable for hard riding. Only the buzz of activity around Charlotte's room gave him pause. He slowed to a walk and then ducked his head into his sister's room.

A dozen maids were in the process of packing up trunks. Charlotte's clothes were strewn around the room, and she was going from dress to dress identifying which ones were to be packed away for storage and which ones were to go with her.

His heart sank. "What are you doing?" he asked, apprehensive of the answer.

"Getting away from *you*." The words, the loathing in her tone, were like a knife to his chest. First his brother, then his wife, and now his sister.

How did it all turn so bad so quickly? He entered the room and took his sister's hands. She narrowed her eyes but didn't pull away.

"Don't leave," he begged, not caring at the growing number of staff watching his display. "Stay. Even if it's just to yell at me daily. Stay, so I can fix this bloody mess I've made. Please, stay."

Her eyes narrowed further, and she pursed her lips. "I do want to yell at you," she said eventually.

The muscles in his chest loosened a fraction. "Then give me a few hours. I need to stop Fiona from leaving. Then I'll be back, and you can yell at me for as long as you like."

She rolled her eyes. "You arrogant, block-headed fool. You're going to go 'stop Fiona from leaving'? Great idea," she said sarcastically, throwing her hands up. "Because your high-handedness, your insistence on controlling everyone else isn't what got you into this problem *at all*. Pffft. Men." She indicated her maid to start unpacking the trunks and grabbed an armful of dresses from her bed to take to her dressing room.

He collapsed onto the edge of her bed, the mad rush of the past few hours wearing off and leaving nothing but exhaustion. "You don't think I should go after her?"

She turned to face him, head tilted, a slightly patronizing expression on her face. "I think you might have been able to force her to marry you, but if you try to force her to love you then she will be miserable for the rest of her days."

"So you don't think I should go?" he asked, hoping her answer would be different than it had been a second ago.

"You're an idiot."

~

Amelia looked at Fiona, shook her head, and poured each of them a cup of tea. "Well, I must say," she said. "I'm awfully disappointed to have missed the season. You seem to have caused quite a stir." She handed over the cup and saucer with an unladylike grunt as she leaned forward over her very pregnant belly.

Fiona ran a finger around the familiar chip in the saucer's edge. Appalled that the factory had been operating without a full tea set, Amelia had bought a brand-new one last year. It had remained intact for almost a month before the teapot lid went missing and the first cup cracked.

Asterly, Barnesworth & Co. was not a place for luxuries of the *ton*. It was hot, sweaty, and dirty with a constant symphony of blacksmiths' hammers, the *whoosh* of flames, and *chug* of the steam locomotives.

This was where she felt comfortable—with the bang and clatter of the factory in the background, in a lab stocked full of glass bottles, at a desk piled high with notepaper. Not in a duke's flawless manor where there were no scratches or dings, with a retinue of staff to ensure everything was polished to reflect the perfection of everything else.

"Causing a stir was nae my intention."

"Intention or not, you did it." Amelia rubbed her belly with both hands. "Benedict almost fell off his chair when he picked up the paper this morning."

Of course. Treason charges. Marriage to a duke. She had probably been the subject of every conversation for days. "I'm sorry. I should have told you."

Amelia arched a brow. "That you had been arrested? That the product we'd invested in was in jeopardy? Or that you were home?"

"All three?" She took a sip of tea, trying to avoid Amelia's stern look. It didn't work. It was clear from her friend's expression that she was about to receive a well-deserved walloping.

"Fi, you're a stubborn goat. You need to start asking for assistance. Especially from the people who love you. We *want* to lend a hand. You don't actually need to do everything on your own."

It was the same criticism Edward had leveled at her, and she knew they were right. But she also knew they didn't understand. It wasn't a switch she could turn off. She couldn't just wake up one day and be perfectly fine relying on others when she'd struggled to do it for so long.

"I ken. Believe me, I had that reckoning as I sat on the floor of that cell wondering if I was headed for the gallows because I wouldn't let Edward help me."

Amelia shuddered at the mention of Fiona in prison but then shook it off and refocused her attention on Fi. "And this is what you do with your newfound insight? Hide away in your office until I come to find you instead of coming to the house? Goodness, you're making *great* strides."

"I'm nae hiding." But Fiona didn't believe her own objection, and from the way Amelia *tut-tut*ted, neither did she, because if Fi truly wanted help, she wouldn't have retreated to her laboratory, which required climbing a set of very long, narrow stairs.

She hadn't counted on Oliver, the foreman, carrying Amelia up them.

"This is you tackling the situation head-on, with support? My apologies, I must have missed the part where you said 'Amelia, I'm in a bind and need your help.'" She took a sip of tea and waited for Fiona to respond. Because, good God, Amelia was not the sort of person to let bad behavior slide, which Fi generally loved about her. Not so much today.

"Fine. I need yer help. I married Edward but dunnae want to be a duchess."

Amelia rolled her eyes, passing Fiona her cup to put on the table. "I'm having the most remarkable sense of déjà vu."

"It is nae the same thing."

Ben's future title may have increased his responsibilities but it did not fundamentally alter who he was. It did not prevent him from living his life the way he planned.

"Truly? Benedict refused to be the earl and you refuse to be the duchess. Is there something in the water that I don't know about? Are these steam engine vapors muddling everybody's senses?"

"My senses are nae muddled. I'm thinking very clearly."

Amelia cocked her head, looking at Fiona with eyes that were searching for a deeper truth than what Fi was presenting. That was the best and worst thing about her friend—she saw everything. "Of course," Amelia said. "Turning down power, privilege, and wealth is such a rational decision."

Fi couldn't sit under that penetrating stare another minute. She stood and picked up the teapot, taking it to the stove. She dumped what liquid remained in the pot into the sink and poured water into the kettle.

"Nae power, privilege, nor wealth is worth locking myself into a gilded cage. I'm nae going to squeeze myself into stays and uncomfortable slippers so that I can make fake pleasantries over a twelve-course dinner."

"Granted, stays are not much fun, but have you ever thought that instead of making fake pleasantries, you could perhaps try *real* pleasantries?"

Fiona dumped a spoonful of tea leaves into the pot. "With the lords and ladies of the *ton*? Somehow I dunnae think they're interested in discussing the chemical properties of binding agents."

Amelia sighed. "Fiona, you are the most intelligent woman I know. Are you truly trying to tell me that you cannot hold a conversation about anything other than science?"

"Nae. That's nae what I'm saying," she said through clenched teeth. Of course she could hold a conversation about other things. Char and Will knew nothing of science, and they'd spoken at length for weeks.

"So other than stays, which with your figure you could probably forgo, and conversation, which we've just established you're capable of, what is the issue?"

Fi turned to look at her friend. Amelia's curls were perfectly set. Despite her condition, she dressed in the height of fashion. She spoke perfectly. She ran her household with the same military precision with which she ran the firm. She had been the *ton*'s diamond, raised to a life ruling the aristocracy. "Ye spent years training to be Edward's duchess. How much of that time was spent playing the pianoforte and embroidering cushions? Would you go back to that life?"

Amelia put both hands around her belly protectively. "No. But to be fair to Edward, I probably would have been perfectly happy had that remained my future. I didn't know any other kind of life existed."

Fi crossed to where Amelia sat and knelt, so their eyes were level. "But I do! And that's the point. How could I possibly become a society matron who plans dinner parties and arranges flowers when I could have a career?"

Amelia reached out a hand and cupped Fiona's cheek. "Remind me to bring you some geraniums and touch-me-nots tomorrow."

"Why? What does that mean in your language of flowers, my disdain for which is another reason why I cannae be a *lady*?"

Amelia's caress became a pat. A forceful one. "That I'm getting impatient with your stupidity."

"What?" Fiona asked, rubbing her cheek. It hadn't actually hurt physically, but the insult had certainly stung.

"I think you're making up excuses—pitiable ones at that. If you don't want to arrange flowers, pay someone to do it. Mrs. Phillips is more than capable of planning a dinner menu on her own, and I doubt very much that Edward has ever suggested you play an instrument."

Fiona recoiled from the inconvenient truth in those words. "He may nae have suggested an instrument, but he did say I would no longer be working," she said defensively.

If she had thought the eye roll Amelia gave her earlier was dismissive, it was nothing compared to the eye roll Amelia gave now at the news of her ex-fiancé's comment.

"Well, men say a lot of imbecilic things that are simply better to ignore. The truth is, you're both going to have to compromise. It's not going to be easy. But it's doable. And I know you already know that." Amelia grasped Fiona's hands. "So, what's the truth, Fi? Why did you really leave London?"

Fiona thought back to that night, to the realization that the archbishop was already there. That she had no choice but to marry Edward. "He took control of my life. I didnae even have a choice. He forced me to marry him when I'd already said no."

Amelia released her. "*Pish.* You were in control of every event that put you in that room. What you experienced was not powerlessness; it was consequences."

"*Oof.*" Amelia's censure felt like a blow to the midsection. This was why she'd chosen to hide in her office rather than visit her friend at home.

Amelia continued. "One might say that it was Edward who was left with no choice. That he had to marry you, despite how it would make you feel about him, or he had to watch the woman he loved hang."

"Stop," Fiona whispered. "Please stop." She put a hand to her mouth to keep the sobs within. There was nothing she could do about the tears, though.

Amelia's expression immediately shifted to concern. She stroked Fi's hair gently. "What is it, sweetheart? What made you leave London?"

"He does nae love me," she said through sobs. "He told me so. He said he did nae want to marry me. I lied to him. I ruined his good name. I betrayed him. How could I stay there and see him every day, knowing the damage I'd done? I'm not strong enough to endure a daily reminder of the love that I'd lost. I cannae bear to be left again."

Amelia pulled Fiona's head to her lap and let her cry. "Well, then. That is a pickle."

⁓

"Well, haven't you bollocksed it all up?"

Edward looked up from the glass of scotch that was sitting in the middle of his ledgers. He hadn't noticed the room darken around him, but only weak light came through the open windows.

Slowly, his eyes focused on the figure standing in his doorway—tall, with the typical Stirling family black hair and blue eyes. Not William, though. That realization still hurt even through the numbing layers of drink.

"Cousin. When did you get here?"

Graham Dunburton's expression was filled with pity. "I've been standing here for five minutes." He strode forward and dropped this morning's copy of *The Times* on the desk. The headline read DUCHESS OF DECEPTION.

Edward stared at it for a long moment before picking it up and tossing it into the basket under his desk. It had been almost a week since Fiona had appeared before the magistrate, and the gossip whirlwind was not yet running out of steam.

Soon, the press would get tired of printing only the facts and would supplement their stories with biting commentary "from sources close to the Wildeforde family." Simmons had already had an influx of unsolicited applicants for service roles, despite not advertising any vacancies. No doubt these people saw a chance to better their lives by selling out his.

"Here, join me for a drink," Edward said. He pushed his own glass toward Graham, then thought better of it and stood, balance slightly askew, and retrieved another glass from the shelf.

"You don't drink," Graham replied, looking at him with an arched brow.

"Correction. I *didn't* drink." He tipped the empty glass in his cousin's direction. "But now that I've got no reputation to protect, I figured I might as well start."

Graham took the glass, just as Edward's grip on it loosened, and he poured his own drink before taking a seat in the chair opposite. "Are you well?" he asked, concern filling his voice.

Edward chuckled. Was he well? No. His heart had been torn from his chest and ground into paste. His wife had left him, his family was torn, and the very fabric of his life—his name, his esteem, his moral code—had been rent apart. The only silver lining had been his mother's immediate departure from London.

"No. I am not well. But it's what I deserve."

Because he did deserve it. He'd written to his brother and General Hastings in an attempt to reverse the commission he'd purchased for William and bring him home.

His brother had returned his letter unopened, and Hastings had responded only to politely inform Edward that William had signed on for an enlistment of seven years and, by law, 1828 was the earliest he could be released from his duties.

Edward didn't know which despicable act was worse— forcing his brother into the military or forcing Fiona into marriage. William might be facing gunfire from enemy forces, but only for seven years. Fiona would be his duchess for the rest of her life, and Graham's presence was a reminder that it, too, could be deadly.

"Talk to me, cousin," Graham said. "One moment you were choosing a perfectly respectable bride from the latest crop of debutantes and the next you're married to a woman of working-class background who was traipsing around London in men's clothing. Surely, you can appreciate my confusion."

"You married a shopgirl."

"Ahh." Graham winced. "So, you *love* her? You'd better start at the beginning."

And so he did. Over the course of an hour and several more glasses of scotch, he told his cousin everything, from the moment he met Fiona five years ago to the message she'd passed on through Rollins when she left.

Graham's expression morphed from curiosity to shock to pity. "So, just to clarify, you forced Miss McTavish— a woman you've described as stubborn, self-reliant, and bloody-minded—to marry you."

Edward snorted. "Foolish, huh?"

Graham swirled the remaining few drops of his drink, studying them as though the answer to this debacle could be found in the patterns the liquid formed as it clung to the glass. "Under normal circumstances, yes. That would be idiotic. But I can't see any other option that would have *guaranteed* she be released from prison."

This had been the argument Edward had been having with himself for days now. An argument he couldn't win from either side.

"I could have found Tucker or her father and forced them to tell the magistrate that she had no part in it."

Graham shook his head, lips pursed. "How? Where? There's been no talk of their arrest in the paper. If the Home Office hasn't found them in a week, how were you going to find them in hours?"

"I could have paid the magistrate to release her regardless of what the evidence was."

Graham's headshaking grew more determined. "When her arrest was so public? He wouldn't have done it. Not even for you. His career and reputation would both have been ruined."

Patterson had known exactly what he was doing when he chose to arrest Fiona at a ball. Any chance Edward had had to make the situation go away quietly was scuppered by the sheer volume of witnesses.

"We could have gone to trial and I could have sworn under oath that she was with me at all times."

"And she would have been in prison for weeks before it came time for a verdict, and even then, it wouldn't be guaranteed."

Edward ran a hand through his hair. The very mention of Fiona in prison was enough to dredge up the same breath-sucking, stomach-clenching dread that had gripped him the night she'd been led away by officers.

"There must be something I could have done differently." Something that didn't result in the complete implosion of his life.

Graham raised his eyebrows, pinning Edward with a you-bloody-idiot stare. "Well, *yes*. You could have had a reasonable, rational conversation with her outlining all of the above points rather than telling her that you didn't actually *want* to marry her, but she would have to do it anyway."

And there was the crux of his problem. Once again, he'd simply acted, doing what he thought best without caring for anyone else's opinion on the matter. He'd done it five years ago when he'd chosen to leave Fiona instead of explaining to her the dangers of the *ton* and giving her the choice to face them or not, and he'd done it again when he bought William a commission against his will.

I am a foolish, arrogant bastard who didn't deserve the people I had in my life.

"The thing is," Graham continued, "you've already left her once. Five years ago, you had a choice between her and society and you chose society. How can she be sure you won't leave her again? How can she trust that you won't push her needs aside to appease the good opinions of others?"

She couldn't. Their entire relationship he'd been sure to point out all the ways she didn't fit society's mold. "Damn, I've made a mess of things."

His cousin nodded his assent. "You need to tell her how you feel. You need to apologize, profusely, and you need to show her that you value her more than you value what others think of you."

Edward rapped his fingers on his desk. "And I need to do all of that while still respecting her wishes for me to not contact her."

"Especially that."

Chapter 37

The lamplight in her working space guttered, the flames throwing leaping shadows across the walls of the office. Beyond the room, downstairs in the factory, the machines had gone silent and the general hubbub of voices had dissipated as the men had gone home for the evening.

No one was left working but her.

She crumpled the sheet of paper in her hand and tossed it into the wastepaper basket that was overflowing with discarded ideas.

Finding a distributor for her matches was a dream long gone. She had traveled direct from the courthouse to Viscount Chester's offices, and he had made it clear that while she may not be guilty of treason, she was certainly guilty of deception and she was no longer someone he was willing to bet on.

Other distributors, ones that had already rejected her, were unlikely to change their minds now that she'd alienated her entire client base, and her chances of finding a backer within the *ton*—the very people she'd lied to—was unthinkable.

She should have accepted Edward's offer of help when she had it. Had she met with Viscount Chester as Fiona, with Edward's introduction and recommendation, the contract would be signed, and they'd likely be heading into production by now.

Instead, she had spent the last two weeks looking for a new project, something that could make a difference in this world while simultaneously putting a roof she owned over her head.

She poured oil into a new lamp, lit a wick from the existing one, and gave the room some steady light for her to work in. Then she sat with a blank page in front of her and waited.

Nothing came. Eventually, she heard the *thunk, thunk, thunk* of heavy boots on a metal staircase. Not John, he was still in America. Not Ben, Amelia had gone into labor a mere hour ago. "Oliver? Is that you?" The foreman had formed a habit of checking in on her hourly. He was not a man of many words when it came to feelings, but he'd shown his concern with the excess of cakes he'd brought to her from the local bakery and the way he always had an excuse to stay back at work until she was ready to go home.

A month ago she would have chafed under such intense concern. The old Fiona would have pushed him out the door with the insistence that she would be fine on her own, that she'd been the last one to leave work a thousand times before this and she could be the last to leave tonight.

Now, she was simply grateful for his company on the way home, even if they most often walked in silence. Edward would have stayed to walk her home. Not because he was an overbearing jackass, but because he had cared and would have wanted to help.

"I'm ready to go," she called as she neatened the papers in front of her. "I'm not getting anything done here anyway."

"That be a shame, wee bairn."

She whipped around to face the door, her heart leaping. Her father stood there, leaning against the doorframe, his usual roguish smile on his face. Relief was what filled her as she realized that he was alive and well. Then rage.

She pushed back her chair and stood, arms akimbo. "You're alive then. Thank ye for letting me know, although ye could've sent word weeks ago."

"Och. You're a big lass. Ye dunnae need to be tied to th' apron strings."

He didn't care, not a whit, for the cloud of worry she'd been under. Hadn't thought it necessary to inform his daughter that he was neither dead nor arrested. She waited for the shooting pain such realizations always caused but it didn't come.

"Dare I hope it was Tucker who was shot?" she asked, starting to clear her worktable and pack up for the night. It was late. She would begin again in the morning.

"Tucker will be all right. Th' ball lodged in his shoulder but he knew a sawbones who could take it oot wi'oot informing th' authorities, th' mangled fannybaws."

"Bonny. I'm so glad." Tucker could go rot. It was a shame the ball hadn't done more damage. She dumped the dishes into the sink and then turned to face him, wiping her hands with a cloth that hung from the bench. "What do ye want? I've nae more ideas for ye to steal."

Alastair *tsk, tsk*ed. "Now, dinnae be lik' that. Ye'v got a smarter head on yer shoulders than yer auld da does, and a lifetime tae make yer fortune. Ye shuid have wanted tae help us oot."

She couldn't help the way her jaw dropped. How dare he try to turn the tables so that *she* felt guilty, after all he put her through. She shouldn't have been surprised, though. Her father had always been a master at playing the victim. Had they had this conversation a month ago, she'd likely have been the one apologizing in a desperate effort to keep a grasp on their perpetually slipping relationship.

She no longer felt compelled to do so.

"I support yer grievances, Da, but I do nae agree wi' yer methods. Folks die in these uprisings. Good people like Jeremy."

He shifted, turning his attention to the shelves that stored all the bibs and bobs that Ben and John had collected as they designed their steam engines. "Weel, on this we cannae see eye to eye."

And they never would. Her father was stubborn and immoveable. His opinions were cast in iron and there was no bending, no compromise. Not even for those he supposedly loved.

She swallowed hard as she looked at him—his wild curls more grey now than red, like a dying ember; his green eyes shuttered; his face a landscape of shadows and deep crevices. She was more like him than she'd care to admit, in personality as well as appearance, and she was currently staring into her future.

She turned back to the sink and dumped in lukewarm water and a cake of soap. "Ye didnae answer my question. What do ye want?"

Alastair turned, putting down a prototype gasket and crossing to her, then leaned his hip against the bench as she scrubbed the dishes furiously. "I wanted tae see ye, wee bairn."

She didn't meet his gaze. "Ye could've seen me at home."

"Ah, see that's th' thing," he said as he pulled her hands from the soapy water and held them in his. "I'm nae going home. 'Tis nae safe."

So he was leaving. Again, she waited for the hurt to come. Again, it was nowhere to be found. There was no numbness to replace it, no hole where the pain should have struck. In fact, it was the opposite—her heart was whole and healed. Her father could come and go as he pleased; her happiness was no longer tied to his whims.

"I'm glad ye said good-bye this time. Do I get to ken where you're going?"

He squeezed her hands tightly. "I dunnae think so, lass. I would nae have you lie tae yer husband."

Her chest constricted. "My husband does nae want aught to do with me. It's been weeks and he has yet to write." She had done to Edward exactly what her father had done to her—left without either an explanation or a good-bye. If he never forgave her for abandoning him, it would be exactly what she deserved.

Her father *tut-tut*ted. "That does nae mean he has nae been trying tae get yer attention, bairn. Have ye truly given up reading th' papers?"

"Pardon?"

Alastair smiled. "Give him me regards, when ye see him next. Tell him that if he treats ye ill, I'll cut off his baws myself." He leaned forward and kissed her on the forehead. "Until we meet again."

As he left, so did the future he embodied. She would not make his mistakes. There was still time to reverse the path she was on.

Edward. It was time to go home and beg his forgiveness. But what had her father meant when he mentioned the papers? She crossed to the box by the stove, where she and Benedict kept the flint and kindling and logs. On top of the scrap pile was this morning's copy of *The Times*.

She had been studiously avoiding the paper all fortnight,

sick of seeing her story told over and over, rife with false assumptions.

But, for once, the headline wasn't about her. It was about Edward... and another woman. She grabbed the newspaper. Edward had been caught kissing Lady Walderstone in the middle of a ballroom, much to the anger of Lord Walderstone, who had been dancing with her moments prior.

Huh? She read that first paragraph over again. It made no sense. Fiona was fairly certain she'd met Lady Walderstone, and the woman had to be close to seventy years old.

She reached into the box and grabbed yesterday's paper. Edward was on the front page again, this time for riding through Hyde Park in his nightclothes.

What the devil was going on? Either he had lost his mind, or...

No. No, it couldn't be. He would never. There was no way the perfect Duke of Wildeforde would willingly torch his own reputation. It was far more likely that he'd contracted some kind of madness.

She picked up a third paper. He'd been at the gaming tables, playing hand after hand, *losing* hand after hand, without even looking at the cards he was dealt. He was taking extraordinary measures to destroy the reputation he'd built— or at least what was left of it following Fiona's scandal.

Hope blossomed within her. What if he'd not come after her because she'd told him not to? What if he was simply showing her that he could respect her wishes? What if there was a chance that he could forgive the things she'd done? If that was the case, then the next steps were hers to make.

If the perfect Duke of Wildeforde was willing to ride through London in naught but his smalls to show her that he had changed, then what was she willing to do for him?

Chapter 38

Edward wasn't home.

In every version of the events that she had played out in her head—both the ones that went well and the ones that failed dismally—Edward had come home after a day in parliament.

He'd come home to her in a perfectly respectable dress, to a perfectly planned, twelve-course meal. In some scenarios, he'd gathered her into his arms and kissed her senseless before she even said hello. In others, he'd instructed her to leave.

In none of them did he simply not come home.

Fiona sat on the top step of the staircase, her skirts billowing out around her. She'd chosen the green, embroidered with lilac flowers on the hem and the sleeves, because he'd told her once that it was his favorite color. The carefully pressed fabric was beginning to crease where she'd twisted it up in her hands while she waited.

"Has he come home late often?" she asked Mrs. Phillips when the housekeeper brought her a pot of tea.

The housekeeper nodded. "His habits have been disordered in the past few weeks."

That information would have been useful at ten o'clock this morning when she'd arrived at Wildeforde House with a trunk, a carriage full of ingredients, and a menu she'd been slaving over for days.

"I'm sure he's simply delayed due to work. Perhaps there's been an emergency session." Or perhaps he was out causing another completely unnecessary scandal. She should have returned to London sooner. According to *The Times*, Edward had walked down Bond Street yesterday making lewd comments toward every gentleman he passed.

Mrs. Phillips looked around, as if to make sure no one was listening. "He's been drinking."

"Drinking? By himself?" Hell, maybe he hadn't been sending her a message. Maybe all these scandals were simply the result of him getting foxed after decades of sobriety.

Fiona swallowed, an uneasy feeling settling in her stomach. She could have misread this so easily. She'd been gone for almost a month. What if, while she'd been miserable and pining for him, he'd moved on with his life? A life unfettered by the restrictions of his position and reputation, because she'd destroyed all of that.

Now that Fiona had thoroughly ruined him, there was nothing holding him back from the life that many men of his ilk led. Hell, he could be wooing an actress.

Fi could feel the blood drain from her face, and she had to grip the edge of the stairs to keep from racing out of the house and back home to Abingdale. She drew in a shaky breath. After everything she had done, he had the right to come home and break her heart. Staying to give him the choice was the least she could do.

Mrs. Phillips patted Fiona comfortingly on the shoulder. "I'm sure he'll be home soon, Your Grace."

Your Grace. Fiona's hackles rose whenever she heard the ill-fitting words. No one in Abingdale had dared use it, but if she was going to show Edward that she was willing to try and be the duchess he needed—respectable, amiable, somewhat conventional—then responding to the honorific fell into the "bare minimum" category of things to be doing.

"How is Mrs. Price? Is she furious? All that work the kitchen staff put in today, with no notice…Will it keep another hour?"

"Don't you worry about Mrs. Price, Your Grace. It's not the first time an exceptional meal has been spoiled by an unpredictable lord or lady. The dowager duchess was notorious for it."

It was small consolation. Fiona's eyes stung with tears. "It was an exceptional dinner, wasn't it?" Her voice quivered.

The housekeeper gave her a kind smile. "Yes, Your Grace. You did a lovely job."

Fiona nodded and dabbed at her eyes, her gloves absorbing her tears. The only thing the silk was good for.

Planning a menu hadn't been fun. It certainly would never be the sole focus of her day, and, in truth, she'd likely allocate the responsibility to someone else. But she did want to show Edward that she would meet halfway if he could.

If he came home.

⁓

Hours later, Fiona woke, her head resting at an odd angle against the wall. She straightened, rolling her shoulders in circles and stretching her head from side to side as she tried to work out the kinks that had formed.

What was the time? How long had she slept? Where was Edward?

The foyer and staircase were dim, with only a handful of lamps lit to guide the way. She stood, reaching for the banister to steady herself. The muscles in her legs, frozen from the awkward angle she'd slept in, protested painfully.

"Fiona?"

Edward moved from shadows into the light. He was home. Behind him, Simmons was hanging his coat. That was why she'd woken. She must have heard the door close.

"Fi?"

Oh, God, she needed to say something.

"Are you well? What the devil is the matter?" Edward rushed up the stairs two at a time as she stumbled down them. They met halfway on the landing, Edward taking both her arms to steady her.

"I…" She looked up at him, all memory of her carefully rehearsed speech evaporating. She inhaled the scent of him, that ink and leather, and relief at his nearness soaked through every part of her.

She gripped his forearms tightly. "Edward, I…"

He pulled back. "I kissed Lady Walderstone," he blurted out. "In the middle of the dance floor. I swept her out of her husband's arms and kissed her."

He looked so serious, so worried. She pressed a hand to his cheek. "I heard. Is it serious between the two of ye?"

Her attempt at humor did not land. His brows furrowed in confusion until he shook his head and continued. "And I lost an obscene amount of money this afternoon betting on whether or not a horse outside would take a shit. It's documented in White's betting book. Forever."

"Well…" She pressed her lips together trying not to

laugh as he regarded her so earnestly. He had such a grave expression as he ran a hand through his hair.

"And I ran through Hyde Park naked this morning. Although, to be fair, it was very early when no one was around, so I'm not sure the gossip rags will ever know about that one."

Fiona's whole body began to shake, and she realized just how long she'd been so tense. She put her fingers to his lips before he could confess to another outrageous act.

"Your Grace," she whispered, "are ye *trying* to start a scandal?"

He cradled her face in both of his hands, his lips just inches from hers, his gaze fixed on her. "I would start a thousand of them, if that's what it took to show you that I don't care what they think. I don't care if I'm their perfect duke. I don't care if you're their perfect duchess, because you're perfect for me. As you are. As my wife. That's all that matters."

She swayed toward him, the relief making her giddy. "Even if I never throw a dinner party?"

He smiled and nodded, wiping a tear from her cheek. "Even if."

She put a hand to his chest and through all the layers of fabric, she could still feel the steady thrum of his heartbeat. "Even if I continue working?" she whispered.

He put a hand over hers, pressing it to him. "You wouldn't be happy if you stopped, and I want you to be happy."

She bit her lip, hesitating for an anxious second. "Even if my being incredibly unconventional and not a little bit scandalous impacts your siblings' prospects?"

Edward's smile dimmed; a brief flash of pain crossed his face. "I used to want Charlotte to make a good match," he said heavily, "with a well-esteemed gentleman who could provide for her every want. Now, I hope that she finds a love like I have. I don't believe a man who's worthy of that love could find fault with an intelligent, passionate, strong woman like you."

Fiona's throat went tight, so she nodded, unable to respond.

He took both her hands in his. "I didn't do this properly before, though I had every opportunity." Edward dropped onto one knee and Fi's heart rate quickened. "Fiona Agnes Stirling, formerly McTavish, will you let me love you with all of my heart, forever?"

"Yes," she whispered, the single word all she could manage.

Edward stood and gathered her in his arms, pressing his lips against hers in a kiss she felt to her toes. He wrapped his arms around her hips and lifted her off the ground as she held his face in her hands and kissed him back. Thoroughly. With every bit of relief, joy, and hope inside her.

When he finally let her go, once her feet were firmly on the ground, she took his hand. "I have something to show you."

She led him down the stairs and through the empty halls to the dining room, where she took a deep breath before pushing open the door. The meal, at least the first few courses, was laid out on the table. She gestured to it, somewhat halfheartedly given it was cold and there was only a single lamp lit in the room, so a third of the table was cast in shadow.

It was tempting to just say "Surprise!" and leave it there. But she wanted to tell him what had been haunting her for weeks.

"I am sorry. I am so sorry. I should have been honest. I should have come to you for help instead of deceiving you. I tried to do it all on my own because I dunnae ken how to trust people. But that isn't fair, because you've been there every time I've needed you. You earned my trust and yet

I still withheld it, and that was a stupid, stubborn, unkind thing to do."

He brushed a lock of hair from her eyes. "Fi—"

"Nae. You cannae say that it is all right, because it's not. You cannae say that it's forgiven because I haven't earned that. But I will. I will earn your forgiveness. I will be better."

He pressed his lips together. She could see how badly he wanted to smooth it all over with a few words but he didn't. She had asked him not to and he respected that by responding simply with, "Thank you."

She smiled, feeling lighter than she had in weeks. "I asked for help, you know. I let Amelia teach me everything she knows about food and floristry."

"You did?" He put his hands on her hips and guided her to the sideboard, where purple hyacinth and geraniums were arranged in a vase. "What does this mean, then? I don't think I've ever seen this combination of flowers before."

Fiona snorted. "This means *idiot*. Funnily enough, it was the first thing Amelia showed me. The hyacinths mean 'I'm sorry.'"

Edward laughed, a deep belly laugh that reverberated around the room and sent Fiona into an exhausted, delirious fit of giggles. They tried to compose themselves, but every time one of them managed to constrain their laughter, they'd take one look at the other and then start all over again.

"Oh," Fi said, holding her stomach. "It hurts."

Edward straightened, having bent over the sideboard in his hysteria. The moment their gazes met, he pressed his lips together and swallowed hard, shaking his head slightly. "I can't look at you." He turned away from her and she heard him draw in deep breaths. He crossed to the table. "Is this edible?" he asked in a strained voice.

"I planned it; I didnae *cook* it." She tried to ignore his snort and pulled out a chair for him. "Here. Sit. Let me." By the time she'd finished piling his plate with food, she managed to find her composure.

"Don't get too attached to this," she said as she set the plate in front of him. "I'll plan a meal when it matters, but most of my days will be spent working." She said the words lightly, but her breath caught in her chest as she waited for his response.

He grinned, reached up, and tugged her into his lap. "That's perfectly fine. In the morning, I'll show you the plans I've drawn up for your lab."

Chapter 39

London, 1822

I ken. I'm running late," Fiona said as she hurried into their bedchamber, dusting her hands on her breeches. It had been a good day in the lab. She was close, so close, to having a product worthy of a patent. But the heady thrill of success meant the day had escaped her.

Edward turned away from the full-length mirror he was using as he buttoned his cuff, his eyes going wide when he saw her. "Tell me you're not going dressed like that."

"Ha ha. Very amusing." She was already untying the neck of her shirt as she crossed to give him a quick kiss. He sank his fingers into her hair and the kiss lingered, the warmth of which made her wish they had more time.

She pulled away. She had to dress. As she took a step backward, she caught her reflection in the mirror and her own eyes went wide. She'd known about the soft grey ash that covered her from shoulder to hip. She'd forgotten that the earlier accident had covered her face with it also. Only where she had wiped it away from her eyes and her mouth was free from the powder.

"I am going to be really late."

Edward nodded. "You are," he said as he pulled the service cord. "But you can probably convince the French ambassador that powdered hair is coming back into fashion."

She pulled off her shirt and unlaced her breeches, conscious of Edward's sharp intake of air at the sight of her in her stays and drawers. He stepped toward her, his hands reaching for her hips. "Nae," she said as she moved away from his grasp. "You are ready to go. You dunnae want ash marring your clothes when you're looking so perfect."

And he was looking perfect. He'd chosen to wear all black—a midnight aesthetic accentuated with star-like diamonds that made the deep blue of his eyes flare to life. Thank God for formal dinners and men's evening wear. She would spend the next six hours half thinking about how beautiful he looked and half thinking about how much more beautiful he'd look the moment they retired.

A housemaid entered with a pitcher of hot water, and Fiona began to quickly wipe herself down.

"Do I want to know how you ended up looking like Great Aunt Gertrude's ghost?" he asked as he crossed to her wardrobe.

"Green one, please," she said, gesturing to the two dresses he held up, and then turning back to the chore of cleaning herself. "The cylinder was nae tightened properly. It burst open when I pulled the trigger." She'd spent months designing a device that would put out fires, using a combination of compressed air and pearl ash. Getting the right pressure in the copper cylinder was proving to be the tricky part.

She grabbed her chemise from where it hung over the back of her dressing table chair and slipped it on. Edward assisted her with the rest. "You should go down," she said as he started on her buttons. "Send Mrs. Phillips to help."

Edward shrugged. "Charlotte has it all in hand. She's charmed every diplomat in England. We could be two hours late and they probably wouldn't notice, they're so besotted with her."

Char had been a godsend this past year. When she finally decided to accept one of the many proposals that seemed to flow constantly, Fiona was going to miss her presence dearly.

Edward sat on the bed and watched as Fiona ran some kohl against her lashes and dusted some rouge across her cheeks and lips. "We really do need to discuss the king's treaty during dinner tonight," he said. "We got nowhere with it when the ambassador visited last week."

"Aye. I ken. But it is not my fault that the ambassador likes to tinker with things. He's very proud of his creations." Last week he'd given her a hand-carved jewelry box with a unique type of catch. It was an impressive effort for a man who typically worked with words and not hands.

Finally, she pulled her long red curls into a simple queue and adorned it with jeweled clips. It was far from the fashionable coiffures that most women of the *ton* sported, but it was easy and practical. She simply did not have time to spend sitting in front of a mirror while a maid did her hair.

Thankfully, society had come to accept the fact that the Duchess of Wildeforde did not do things quite the way others expected. She was no longer "singular" or "odd." Instead, *The Times* found words like *unique* and *unprecedented*. Fi did not care a whit what the gossips called her, but she was grateful that the scandal had subsided and Charlotte's prospects had come through unscathed.

She stood, keen to head downstairs and get to a different

kind of work. "Are you ready?" she asked, holding an arm out to her husband.

He took her arm and used it to pull her against him, her body flush against his, his hand on her arse. He captured her mouth in a deep kiss, exploring her with his tongue and setting every molecule of her on fire. Her hand gripped his shoulder, her fingers digging into his dress coat.

By the time he broke away, her head was spinning. "Now I'm ready."

Don't miss Charlotte's story in

How to Win a Wallflower

Coming Fall 2022

About the Author

Samara has been escaping into fictional worlds since she was a child. When she picked up her first historical romance book, she found a fantasy universe she never wanted to leave and the inspiration to write her own stories. She lives in Australia with her own hero and their many fur-babies in a house with an obscenely large garden, despite historically being unable to keep a cactus alive.

You can follow her writing, gardening, and life adventures on social media or by signing up for her newsletter at SamaraParish.com/newsletter

SamaraParish.com
Facebook.com/SamaraParish
Instagram @SamaraParish
Twitter @SamaraParish
Pinterest @SamaraParish

Get swept off your feet by charming dukes, sharp-witted ladies, and scandalous balls in Forever's historical romances!

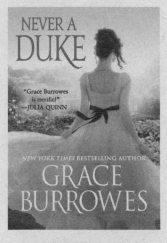

NEVER A DUKE
by Grace Burrowes

Ned Wentworth will be forever grateful to the family who plucked him from the streets and gave him a home, even though polite society still whispers years later about his questionable past. Precisely because of Ned's connections in low places, Lady Rosalind Kinwood approaches him to help her find a lady's maid who has disappeared. As the investigation becomes more dangerous, both Ned and Rosalind will have to risk everything—including their hearts—if they are to share the happily-ever-after that Mayfair's matchmakers have begrudged them both.

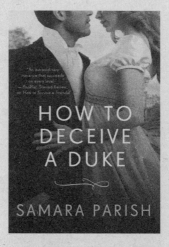

HOW TO DECEIVE A DUKE
by Samara Parish

Engineer Fiona McTavish has come to London under the guise of Finlay McTavish for one purpose—to find a distributor for her new invention. But when her plans go awry and she's arrested at a protest, the only person who can help is her ex-lover, Edward, Duke of Wildeforde. Only bailing "Finlay" out of jail comes at a cost: She must live under his roof. The sparks from their passionate affair many years before are quick to rekindle. But when Finlay becomes wanted for treason, will Edward protect her—or his heart?

SAY YOU'LL BE MY LADY
by Kate Pembrooke

Lady Serena Wynter doesn't mind flirting with a bit of scandal—she's determined to ignore Society's strictures and live life on her own terms. But there is one man who stirs Serena's deepest emotions, one who's irresistibly handsome, infuriatingly circumspect, and too honorable for his own good...Charles Townshend isn't immune to the attraction between them, but a shocking family secret prevents him from acting on his desires. Only it seems Lady Serena doesn't intend to let propriety stand in the way of a mutually satisfying dalliance.

THE REBEL AND THE RAKE
by Emily Sullivan

Though most women would be thrilled to catch the eye of a tall, dark, and dangerously handsome rake like Rafe Davies, Miss Sylvia Sparrow trusted the wrong man once and paid for it dearly. The fiery bluestocking is resolved to avoid Rafe, until a chance encounter reveals the man's unexpected depths—and an attraction impossible to ignore. But once Sylvia suspects she isn't the only one harboring secrets, she realizes that Rafe may pose a risk to far more than her heart...

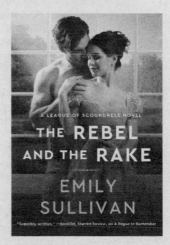

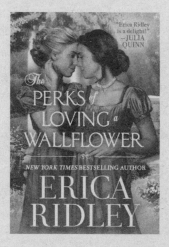

THE PERKS OF LOVING A WALLFLOWER
by Erica Ridley

As a master of disguise, Thomasina Wynchester can be a polite young lady—or a bawdy old man. Anything to solve the case—which this time requires masquerading as a charming baron. Her latest assignment unveils a top-secret military cipher covering up an enigma that goes back centuries. But Tommy's beautiful new client turns out to be the reserved, high-born bluestocking Miss Philippa York, with whom she's secretly smitten. As they decode clues and begin to fall for each other in the process, the mission—as well as their hearts—will be at stake...